PRAISE FOR ALYSSA RICHARDS

"I'd happily read anything Alyssa writes next." —Jeannie Zelos Book Reviews

"...undoubtedly Alyssa Richards has just become one of my new favourite authors for this year." —Living in Our Own Story Blog

"This is well written with complex characters who reveal more of themselves as the story progresses. It is a great mystery with paranormal elements that make it enthrallingly different and captivating."--Splashes into Books

"I felt like I was standing right in the middle of a Movie Set of something between Pierce Brosnan's "The Thomas Crown Affair" or Sean Connery's "Entrapment". I was sucked into the story from the beginning and I could not stop reading. It was such an interesting mix between the paranormal – romance and crime elements that kept me reading and wondering what might happen next."--Jeri's Book Attic, THE FINE ART OF DECEPTION SERIES

"An intriguing read that kept my interest until the last page. Very enjoyable and definitely recommended."--Archaeolibrarian, THE FINE ART OF DECEPTION SERIES

"This book was loaded with mystery and suspense. The plot was well executed and kept me on the edge of my seat. The sizzling passionate scenes between Addie and Blake were red hot." --Smut Book Junkie Book Reviews, THE FINE ART OF DECEPTION SERIES

"The plot is unique in a way that you will keep thinking of its awesomeness for a long time after finishing this book. There was so much positives in the book, that kept me awake with my Kindle at night, in spite of my recently sleep deprived life. This book has exceeded my expectations in every way. You should definitely read it, if romance, suspense or paranormal genre suits you."-- Books are Magic, THE FINE ART OF DECEPTION

"I was very drawn to the characters. Richards did an excellent job weaving you into their world whether it was the good guy or the bad guy you just wanted to know what they were thinking, doing and their next move. I definitely recommend."--The Reading Pile, THE FINE ART OF DECEPTION SERIES

THE HAUNTING OF ALCOTT MANOR is a fascinating tale of tragedy, ghosts, and soulmates. Mystery fans will enjoy this heroine's efforts to track down clues -- both tangible and ghostly -- while trying to find the truth about a woman's death. Romance fans will adore this match-up of a strong heroine and an enigmatic yet endearingly charming and earnest hero. —Fresh Fiction Review

This was a great read, great twists and turns. ...and the end...? WOW! What's really getting me right now though? Henry and Gemma at still with me....days after I've finished the book! I cried with them, I loved with them, and they touched me deeply! —Amazon Reviewer, THE HAUNTING OF ALCOTT MANOR

A MURDER AT ALCOTT MANOR is very definitely a thrill-a-minute tale of evil trying to keep a stranglehold on the living. This is a perfect book for readers who enjoy non-stop action and suspense with a dash of sexy. —Fresh Fiction Review

LOST IN TIME

BOOK 3 THE FINE ART OF DECEPTION SERIES

ALYSSA RICHARDS

Ebook ISBN-13: 978-0-9792265-8-8
Editing done by Book Alchemy, LLC
Proofreading by www.221bBakerSt.net

Sign up for Alyssa's newsletter at to receive special offers and news about her latest releases.

You can follow her on:
Instagram

Contact Alyssa at:
authoralyssarichards@protonmail.com

For Richard, with gratitude

1

———

Blake held on to the side of the windshield of John's Model T and braced himself, both for the next hard-hit bump and for the night that lay ahead.

Dust from the vacant dirt road kicked up and found its way into his nose and mouth. Tiny granules of grit crunched between his teeth and he spit out the open window.

He didn't have to turn his head to the left to see John's occasional stare bearing down on him—he could feel the hardness of it on the side of his face. John didn't want them to make this trip.

"Everyone in this meeting is armed. None of these guys know you so they'll assume that you're either a copper trying to take their operation down or a rival who wants to take their business away from them." John Montgomery, Addie's grandfather, white-knuckled his hands at ten and two on the thin black wheel. His car hit almost every hole on the rarely traveled road and jostled them like children on a cheap carnival scrambler.

John smoothed one side of his perfect white hair.

"They're always thinking about how to kill you. Remember that and don't turn your back on anyone. Even when you're inspecting the pieces. Got it?"

"Got it." Blake stared straight ahead. He'd spent the last hour of the drive trying to ignore the fear and the worry that had grown intertwining roots in his heart. Fear that no matter what he did, he might not find his mother. Worry that he couldn't do enough to protect Addie.

He swallowed hard against his throat, which had become as narrow and dry as the road. This was the last sign of nervousness he could allow himself for the next few hours.

The car slowed when they entered the grass-edged drive of the warehouse-type building. A round man in a brown pinstriped suit stood at the doorway and held his tommy gun at his side. Finger on the trigger.

Several men were ahead of the. They stepped from their cars, and searched the darkened lot. They looked around once again, then they went inside.

Blake seen that look before. It was a paranoid-guilty expression that settled scores too quickly.

There weren't any windows on the oversized, silver-tinned shack, but he knew what was going on inside. Even though this was only 1922, the black market for antiquities was already an ancient and dangerous tradition. And where there was art theft, Otto was bound to be nearby.

"Floyd," John said to the guard in the pinstriped suit.

"John." He nudged the end of his tommy gun into Blake's chest. "Who's 'dis?"

"Nephew of mine. I brought him into the business a couple of years ago." John moved the tip of the gun away from Blake's chest. "If you blow a hole in him my sister will never speak to me again."

"I wasn't expectin' no one else with you." Floyd returned his aim to Blake.

Blake's heart pounded hard in his chest.

"Floyd." John faced both palms outward in surrender. In slow-motion carefulness, he reached into his jacket pocket and retrieved a fat cigar, and handed it to the man with the gun. "I take responsibility for him—he's my blood."

Floyd accepted the cigar and nodded to the entrance. "It will be if anything goes wrong in there."

The windowless tin warehouse was empty except for the four men who stood around a few opened crates, three of the men held tommy guns.

The one man who didn't hold a gun extended a hand to John. His brown eyes, flat with unfeeling meanness, locked hard enough on Blake to leave a mark. "John. Who's this?"

The man's long dark hair was slicked obsessively neat across the top, excepting two pieces of hair that fell onto the shaved sides of his head. He attempted style and attitude with a tipped-up collar on his knee-length trench coat. He missed the mark with rumpled, high-waisted pants that were held up with a belt as well as suspenders. Blake recognized him immediately, even though he had only seen him in a photo a few years ago.

"My sister's son. I brought him into the gallery a while back. He has a thing for art. He's good."

Blake held still, his hands out and on his hips where everyone could see he didn't hold a gun.

He'd been shot by this man before.

Not in his current life, but in his past life when he was Jack. The fear that it could happen again remained like a memory in his soul. That trace sent a shot of adrenaline into his heart that felt remarkably like a bullet.

The man was Gary Walker. Otto's past-life incarnation.

If it wouldn't have ended his own life again, Blake would have killed Gary on the spot.

2

The rapping on the glass of the front door was unrelenting. Something was wrong because I'd closed the gallery hours ago. People didn't have art emergencies.

I dashed upstairs from the kitchen and into the main room that looked like an Italian villa. Emerald walls. Fortuny lampshades atop light sculptures of naked cherubs, and finial-topped couches and chairs. I prayed that when I got to the front door I wouldn't find a policeman asking me if I knew a dead man by the name of Blake Greenwood.

The man in the dark rounded hat waved and smiled from the other side of the glass.

I exhaled hard. "We're not open."

He showed me a thick navy blue book. "Just a few moments, please. Please?" A glint of watery desperation showed in his eyes and he raised the blue book again.

An artist. I sighed. I wasn't supposed to let anyone in while I was in the gallery alone. It was a rule my father had set since no one knew where Otto was. Even though we thought Carolena was with him, we had to assume my gifts would still be an attractive possession for him.

"An artist I met in Paris some time back suggested I contact you here for representation."

I had a hard time turning down artists, especially the hungry ones. Most were extremely talented and without enough financial support for their work.

I opened the door.

I would have let him in if he had said the drunk on the corner had referred him. Not that I could do much for him other than to offer encouragement. We moved very few significant pieces of art through the gallery since the shop hadn't been present in the original 1920s.

Dad and Grandad started the art gallery years ago as a way to make money. After they had more than enough, they kept it simply to have something to do every day. There was a risk of having it. Any business we did could disrupt the natural flow of things in the future—something my father and grandfather harped endlessly about. Blake, too. Who was terrified that we would have some kind of inappropriate interaction with Jack or Sarah and mess up our future together.

As much as possible, we lived by the Boy Scout attitude of "leave no trace". In fact, those were usually the last words one or all of the three men said to me when I walked out of the gallery each day. "Leave no trace, Addie-belle! Leave no trace!"

The artist removed his hat and coat and glanced around our gallery. My father had chosen the furnishings wisely for the gallery shortly after they'd arrived in the Belle Epoch era. The gilt wood console table between the front door and storefront window was from the eighteenth century and lovingly crafted. I didn't know what it was worth in the twenties. In our time it would easily fetch between $30,000 and $40,000 at auction.

Calculating the value of the furnishings, both here and among my grandfather's storage items, was how I often entertained myself. Kept in good condition, all their furnishings would bring in over a million dollars. I was fascinated to be in the past, and to know ahead of time which pieces would and wouldn't appreciate well.

The artist handed me his portfolio that featured pencil-drawn etchings: city scenes of Venice and battles from WWI. I pressed close to the small cards that captured Venetian life as clearly as a photograph or a video from a smartphone. There wasn't a speck of white to be found, and the transitions from light to shadow drew my eye across the page in a brilliant story.

The artist's name was Clifford Addams and with his trained touch, he had mastered the appearance of movement—the hallmark of all great artists. The waterway beneath the arched bridge appeared to roll and swell, a boat tipped and rocked, and people pushed and shoved their way along narrow walkways with arms full of nondescript items.

I hovered over the book of cards, most of them small enough to fit in my outstretched hand. My fingertips traced the very edge of the scene to read it more deeply. The sounds of early twentieth-century Venice drew me in. I forgot that I wasn't in the room by myself.

There were cards that were filled with battle scenes dark with explosions, smoke, and bodies. The mood changed considerably.

"Not these." He waved his hand and turned the page backward to the scenes of life in Venice.

"I think these would do very well in our gallery, Mr. Addams—"

A thick presence permeated the air and chills spread from my gut outward and down my arms. The artist shifted his weight.

I noticed the right half of a young man about the age of nineteen peering from behind him. A ghost. Nearly transparent and focused intently on the sketchbook. Dressed in his Royal Navy blues, white cap, and blue band around the bottom. His eyes were narrow and hardened. The word *Virginia* was written on the dark blue band of his hat.

"Our gallery is full at the moment."

Mr. Addams' shoulders drooped with the weight of rejection.

A pang of empathy rang through my heart. I struggled to remember where Clifford Addams' art had scattered in our current day. He was one of the most brilliant artists of his time, studying with Whistler in his early twenties, though his ultimate reputation as a fine artist became as fragile as his etchings in front of me.

"Let me see what I can do," I said.

The boy in the Royal Navy uniform circled me and stared. "Do better than try, why don't you?" His breath was stale and cigarette-scented. His rage caused me to catch my breath. He was the tenth ghostly war vet I'd seen today, most of them angry that their lives had been cut short. We were only four years on the outside of WWI and lost soldiers weren't hard to find.

The artist in front of me sighed with the relief that hope brought.

"I'll have to check with the owners." What I was going to do was see if someone remembered more about Addam's history and maybe I could encourage him in the direction he had originally taken.

"Thank you, Madam." He bowed slightly. "If you could, please."

I closed the book with care and ran my fingertips across the cover. "These battle scenes...you served in the war?"

"Yes ma'am, the Royal Navy."

I nodded. "You made it back home."

The boy behind him lit an etheric cigarette and inhaled the smoke with an audible gasp. He blew the smoke in my direction like an insult, across lips that curled into a sneer.

Clifford pushed his tongue across his dry lips, slow and deliberate, like he didn't want to answer. After a hard swallow, he said, "I did, yes. Though many others weren't so lucky." He slipped on his long black jacket. "I lost several friends. One who was like a brother."

I patted the dark blue cover. "These are quite moving."

"Thank you, though I can't—I don't want to sell the war scenes. Not yet." He gathered his book from the table.

"I understand." My voice was whisper-quiet. "I know it's hard. There are many things in this world we can't control."

His polite smile was burdened with problems he couldn't solve, scenes from the war he couldn't unsee, and guilt that followed him more closely than he realized.

"Oh, who referred you to us again? I didn't catch the name."

"I didn't know her name. I met her when I was in Paris for several weeks. She was in the Louvre on their late nights, mostly sketching different items from the former palaces. Lovely woman. Dark hair, blue eyes, beautiful French accent. She referred me here, and a few other galleries."

A shot of electricity jolted through my awareness.

"I may know who this is. Did she perhaps wear a gold jeweled bracelet?" I twisted my left wrist inside of my right thumb and middle finger. "It would have dangled."

"Mmmm. Not that I recall. I do remember that she wore the most stunning ruby and diamond ring, though. A cabochon. Quite raised, diamonds. Unusual piece."

A detailed image of Carolena's ring held front and center in my mind. It was the engagement ring Otto had given her long ago, when Blake was born. "Yes, I think that's her. That's my friend." My heart hammered with so much excitement I had to catch my breath. "Which of the former palaces? Napoleon's or Louis', Henri's?"

"Ah... First time I saw her was about a year ago in Anne of Austria's Summer Apartments. The next time was about a week later in Napoleon I's living quarters. Both have exhibits on the royal jewelry, quite fascinating."

"A year ago," I echoed.

"It's been a while. Are you looking for her?"

"I am, yes. We lost touch a couple of years ago."

"And here I am not much help at all. Although I did have the sense that she lived in Paris. Or in the area. I think she mentioned she was at the Louvre almost every week."

We agreed he ought to check back with me about his art. He tipped his hat with a gentleman's nod and left.

His ghost buddy latched his arm around his friend's back and they walked down the sidewalk. One of them, at least, completely unaware that their friendship continued.

The *aaoogha* sound of a Ford Model T's horn yelped from the traffic that dragged along Fifth Avenue. I closed the front door. The service door slammed at the rear of the gallery. Someone was on their way in.

3

Blake stood still.

Gary examined him from tip to toe, walking around him like a wolf inspecting his next meal. Blake had to will himself not to do the very things he wanted to. Like grab Gary by the throat. Slam him to the ground. Choke the life out of him.

"I'm not a fan of new people, John. Not last minute." His eyes held Blake tight with his paranoia.

"I've had him for two years. He's family. He's good."

The echo of animal claws scampering across the far side of the metal roof disturbed the man's concentration and the intensity of his stare relaxed.

"Egyptian?" Blake gave a brief point to the open boxes.

"Yeah. Know much about 'em?"

"Quite a bit. May I?"

The man gestured toward the crates in a be-my-guest sort of way.

Blake remembered John's advice about keeping his back clear, a piece of advice he'd first heard when he worked with the FBI. He circled to the side where no one would stand behind him. Everyone watched him lift a black vase from the straw with two hands. He brushed some dust from the surface and examined the figure of the Egyptian god Anpu painted on the side.

John leaned toward the man. "I'm looking for someone. Tall guy, gray hair, American. Goes by the name Otto Albrecht. Travels with an attractive, dark-haired woman who has a French accent."

Gary nodded his head up once. "Yeah, I've heard of him. Always asking about art, wants to know who's painting what."

Blake inspected a few other pieces. He pretended not to hear their conversation.

"Know where he is?"

"Eh. I might be able to find out. What's it worth to you?"

Blake replaced an Egyptian urn to the crate. "It's genuine," he said to John. He would have said they were authentic no matter what. But these were and probably stolen from a tomb.

"How about if we buy your Egyptian pottery and you tell us where Otto is?"

"Junior here thinks these are a good investment, ay?" Gary said.

Blake met the glare on Gary's face that was hungry for conflict, hungry for triumph. Gary hadn't done anything to him yet but he would. He would wreck his life a million times over, destroying him in every way possible. Lifetime after lifetime. Blake hated him, and in this moment, more than he wanted to breathe, he wished the man were dead.

John stepped between them. "He knows his stuff. If he says it's genuine, I believe him. Let us know where Otto Albrecht is and we'll take these crates off your hands."

A door slammed and Blake glanced to the back of the warehouse. It was a beautiful blonde. She wore a sleeveless, ankle-length navy-blue dress with silver sequined detail that cascaded from top to bottom like streamers from a party. She stood a good forty feet away from him. A living, breathing memory. Her very presence kicked a place in his heart so tender he almost fell to his knees.

"Wait outside, would ya? This is business," Gary said to her.

"Sorry, Gary."

She could have been a reincarnation of Addie, though this woman was the earlier version of her. She was nearly exact in appearance. Except for the voice. It wasn't quite right, not the same.

"Dames." Gary drew hard on his cigarette.

"I'm going to step outside for a cigarette," Blake said. He figured everyone knew he could have smoked inside. But he also thought everyone knew the deal would go better if he weren't involved.

John's eyes narrowed slightly in a quiet warning to Blake, then he slapped him on the back twice and combined it with a push in the direction of the door.

Blake checked over his shoulder several times since his back was unfortunately exposed.

"Martin, tell Floyd to go out to the main road and wave off the other seller. We're done here," Gary said.

BLAKE SAW Floyd walk up the dirt road, tommy gun in hand, to let the next seller know the stolen Egyptian goods had been sold.

Made it just in time.

Gary knew about Otto. This was not surprising to Blake. It made sense to him that the part of him from a present life would be attracted to the part of him from a past life. Assuming there were similarities. From what he understood from Addie's past-life flashbacks, not to mention what he'd just witnessed inside the warehouse, there were definite similarities between the two men.

Now Gary, who was past-life Otto, would sell out his present-day self and give them his location as soon as he had it. Blake would then rescue Carolena and send Otto to a humiliating end. Just as Otto had done to Blake, who was Jack in his 1920s life.

This was the first real progress they'd had in two years of searching for Otto and Carolena. Two long years. The last one was filled with more empty leads than the first, all of them adding up to too many failures that nearly sucked the soul from his body. It was appropriate that Otto should screw himself. And about time, too.

He couldn't tell Addie how he had gotten this lead. Or Philippe, either, for that matter. Philippe didn't keep secrets from Addie. At least not since they had arrived here. This was a little facet of Philippe's personality that made Blake want to lay him out. They were brothers. Half-brothers. Philippe's loyalty should have been to *him*.

So he had to keep this trip and all the others like it a secret. If Addie knew where he was and with whom he was meeting, she would insist upon being involved. He couldn't have that. He'd failed to protect her twice already, at least that he knew about.

The first time was in 1922. When he was Jack he promised her he'd take her away from Gary—past-life Otto, her abusive lover. But something went wrong in the plan and Gary killed Jack. Jack left her pregnant with his baby and to fend for herself in the face of Gary's rage over her infidelity.

In this life, he'd pulled her away from Otto once again, and promised her a life of wine and romance in Paris. But after his father kidnapped him, she was left to fend for herself and fight a dangerous path through time. He shook his head and kicked a rock across the dirt drive.

This time, it would be different. There would be no mistakes. He would rescue his mother and protect Addie. He wouldn't fail again.

He wasn't entirely sure what they would do with Otto. They would figure it out. He stared into the starry night and inhaled the cold air deep enough to make the bottom of his lungs ache. Their plan was coming together.

He sniffed again and caught the faint scent of cigarette smoke on the breeze. It was coming from the backside of the warehouse. That was the direction where he'd seen Sarah go.

His steps were light and soft, avoiding sticks, dried leaves, and any other noise that might cause someone to blast his head from his body.

Around the back side of the building, he saw her. She sat on the edge of a tree stump, staring into the blackness of the woods. So lost in her thoughts she was unaware he was nearby. She leaned on her knees, her heels lifted such that only the balls of her feet and her toes touched the ground. Her platinum hair was styled into waves, and her long dark eyelashes reached beyond her profile like she was a porcelain doll.

His heart ached with unexpected, crippling tenderness. In this environment, he should have been guarded, unemotional. Though seeing her was like greeting a stranger, only to be punched with the realization that you were in love with them. He had already lived this reality once before when he met Addie.

Here she was again, only for the first time in 1922. As Jack he would already be with her, planning their life together in a fated end neither could fathom at this stage. Perhaps she already carried their baby. *His* baby. His hand clenched into a fist, he fought the unreasonable need to carry her away from Gary and all that he threatened.

Protect her. He had to protect her.

Her cheeks hollowed with a long inhale through the polished black cigarette holder. Red embers at the tip of the cigarette glowed in the shadows of near-darkness that surrounded them. She rarely blinked, her stare into the woods focused on something deep within, something only she could see.

Walk away, Blake.

Without a discernible shift in her awareness, her laser-like focus turned in smooth precision until it trained on him.

Something shifted inside of him.

"What do *you* want?" She blew a stream of smoke that curled in his direction. He had expected her to be startled. Instead, she was unbothered by his presence. Her eyes narrowed in a tough girl I-dare-you-to-mess-with-me threat.

He chuckled, impressed with this side of her that he hadn't remembered. She was probably well-accustomed to random thieves and thugs.

Her lips parted a fraction of an inch, just in the center, like a cover model from the future. Her eyes and her presence mesmerized him like a magician charmed a child at their first magic show. He remembered kissing those lips, the softness of them against his own, their wet heaven dragging along his skin. There was the way they smiled at him and showed him how happy he made her. His heart melted—inappropriately so considering his surroundings—into a warm puddle. He couldn't make himself walk away.

Then, as subtle and as definite as a directional shift in the wind, he saw her irritation turn to curiosity.

"Do I know you?"

There it was again. The easy-to-hear difference between the two women: her voice. The distinct Yankee accent, the flat, more nasal intonation that didn't match Addie's Southern-around-the-edges style that flavored her words. He had to bite the *yes* in his mouth to keep it from coming out. Of course she knew him—as no one else did or could.

"No."

She studied him with an intensity that made his soul warm. Electricity crackled and popped between them like the brewing of a storm. Her eyes darted away and he knew that she felt it, too.

"You travel with a dangerous group." Blake nodded toward the warehouse.

She blew a long, thin stream of smoke toward the woods, then cut her gaze at him. "Who *are* you?" The edge to her words was as sharp as a blade.

"No one." He felt a grin tip the edge of his mouth.

She paused, their gaze held one another close in spite of the few feet between them.

"Gary has done a lot for me. And this is better than what I came from. He cares about me; he buys me things." A flicker of rage danced in her eyes, like a rising flame. He'd touched a nerve. "Did you used to see my show at Murray's? Is that where I know you from?"

"Murray's?" he asked.

"I used to dance there. Everybody goes there. It's where I met Gary."

"No. I must have missed it. And I think you'd be better off without Gary."

Her eyes squinted and she appeared to search her memory bank. "I know you from somewhere."

"Maybe from a past life."

She laughed one loud "ha" that sent an echo through the woods, and a familiar happiness flowed over his insides like hot chocolate. "Yeah, I'm sure I was Cleopatra and you were Marc Antony."

He chuckled at how she softened the t in Antony. He walked a few steps toward her. "Hopefully a couple with a less tragic ending." He knew he couldn't, though he wanted to hold her, to kiss her and to protect her.

"Careful." She glanced behind her and at the door. "Gary doesn't like it when men get too close."

"I'm not afraid of Gary."

"You oughta be. He'll kill you if he thinks you like me."

Blake nodded, sure and slow. He knew this to be true. He wanted to know what happened to her after he, as Jack, was killed. Did Gary take her back or did he kill her and the baby, too? There was no way to know, at least not at this point in time.

She pulled the spent cigarette from its holder and tossed it to the ground. "I think you should go now, Mister."

"Yeah. Probably," he admitted. "Right after two things."

"*What?*" Her one word carried a razor-sharp edge, and he hoped she used that tone with Gary.

"I'm looking for two people, and I'd like to know if you've seen them." He described Otto and Carolena in detail, right down to her eye color and her French accent.

"Yeah, I've seen 'em. Not for a while, though."

"When was the last time you saw them?"

"It's been a year or so, I guess. Seems like I heard the man say they were going abroad, to Paris. Lucky devils. You know 'em?"

"We go way back. Not quite as far as you and I, since you were Cleopatra, but we have history together."

Her smile was easy and relaxed, she giggled at his comment.

"And second?" She fiddled with the clasp on her gold cigarette case.

"Just this," he touched the outside of her arm and her gaze lifted to his with a slow blink. "Be careful."

Her case fell to the ground and popped open. A row of cigarettes held tight inside the case but a folded piece of paper fell out. Then the substantial metal warehouse door groaned when it opened.

Blake covered the note with his shoe.

Sarah rose as though she were leaving.

"What the hell are you doin' back here?" Gary's tone was an undisguised threat.

Blake fought his protective instinct to attack and flip him flat to the ground, the way they'd trained him in the FBI defense courses.

"Thank you, baby." Sarah ran her hand along the side of his face and she stepped inside the open door.

The hard rage on Gary's face calmed a fraction at her touch, though his eyes never left Blake. "Leave."

For the sake of Addie and all that she used to be, Blake shoved his hands into his pockets and kept his actions to a single nod. When the door slammed shut behind Gary and Sarah, Blake picked up the note and the cigarette case and put them into his coat pocket.

He turned the corner, walked toward the car, and saw

Gary's men load one of the smaller crates into the back seat. John supervised. Gary and Sarah were nowhere to be found.

"Where have you been?" John asked.

"I walked around back."

John didn't ask him for what reason, the expression on his face said that he already knew. "You'd better stay away from her—you're going to get yourself killed."

Gary's men slammed the car door and John and Blake climbed into the front seat. "There's nothing you can do for her." John started the engine, the beam from the headlights only showing a few feet in front of them. "This has already happened. You could really mess things up."

Blake held on. The car chugged uphill to the main road, bouncing over rocks and in and out of holes. "I want to shove my gun down his throat. If I taught Gary a lesson in this life, maybe Otto would be less likely to mess with me in the present day. He'd weaken."

"You don't know that. It could get worse." John adjusted his fedora for a lower, more snug fit as if to emphasize his seriousness. He pressed the accelerator to the floor.

"It would get better. Easier. He would respect me the next time we met. He would inherently know not to mess with me or anyone I care about."

"Didn't *he* kill *you* in the last life? *You're* still going after him. No one can say for sure what would happen. The point is, if you change something, you could end up with a life far worse than what you've got."

"I can't imagine having anything worse than Otto as a father."

"Don't tempt that. They can also just be different, and enough difference could change your life forever. When you were just a boy, he would have done anything for you then. You and Carolena were his entire world."

"Didn't last."

"Those interactions helped make you who you are today. He taught you about art and started that hunger inside of you. If you change this—" he thumbed toward the direction they'd just come from "—then you change that, and who knows what *that* will become. You'll be different. One little change in this domino line of experiences affects everything that comes after it."

Blake thought to the many childhood conversations Otto had with him about art and their histories, how they fascinated him and show that somehow stoked an early hunger inside of him. His memories tempered his anger to a less vicious level. Though his hatred of the man still made Blake want to see him dead.

"Sarah said Otto and Carolena went to Paris. Or so they said last time she saw them." A pang of guilt hit his nervous system like a gong for leaving her behind.

John glanced at Blake. "So, Gary lied."

"Maybe not technically. We don't know if they're still there. He may not know either. Or maybe he wants to get to Otto first for something. Do you really think he'll look into it?"

"Hard to say with him. He was pretty pissed off after he brought Sarah back into the warehouse. Did you say something?"

"No," Blake said.

"Well, you *did* something." John nodded to the top of the hill where Gary stood with two of his men, one on either side of him. They formed the 1920s version of a triumvirate in the middle of the road, complete with tommy guns that flanked their leader.

John slowed the car to a stop.

"I've got this," Blake said.

"Oh, no you don't." John grabbed Blake's arm and held on. "We'll just let them have the pottery and we'll be on our way."

"He doesn't want the pottery. He wants me." Blake broke free from John's grasp and lunged out of the car.

4

I grabbed the ring of brass skeleton keys that jingled against one another like small bells. With each turn of the front door lock, they sounded the beginnings and endings of my workday.

"Hello, love. Were you going somewhere without me?" Philippe entered from the service door, handsome and dapper in his light tan suit, brown bowtie, and color-coordinated fedora. The left side of his mouth tipped up in a grin fit for the big screen. His newly developed muscles showed off in the lines of his suit jacket.

We'd known each other since we were children. His father, Otto, and my grandfather, John, were business partners in an art appraisal and restoration firm. Alexa and I and Philippe, and his brother Nicholas, all grew up alongside one another until Otto and my grandfather had a falling out. It was, in part, a disagreement over thirteen masterpieces they'd stolen from the Isabella Stewart Gardner museum. Then Otto banished my grandfather and father to the past.

Philippe and I remained quite close as teenagers, and at

the time neither one of us knew what his father had done. We drifted apart. Until he helped me escape when his father kept me hostage. Afterward we rekindled our friendship, thanks in large part to the time we shared in the 1920s.

"Just locking up. Did you lift again today? That's two days in a row. Must have a hot date tonight."

His grin shifted into a heart-stopping smirk and he chuckled. "No date tonight. You?"

"Mm-mm."

"Dinner?" He searched the floor around us as though he'd dropped something.

"Sure, what are you looking for?"

"The yellow feathers. You have that cat-that-ate-the-canary look about you. What's going on?"

"Oh," I chuckled. "That man—"

Philippe scanned the room and quickly glanced at the people traffic on the sidewalk. "Someone was here?"

"Just an artist looking to sell some etchings. But—"

"Addie—"

"It would have been rude to say no." I slipped into my cream-colored velour topcoat and pretended to pick something off of one of the kimono sleeves.

"You're not supposed to—"

"I know. I'm not supposed to let anyone in when I'm here alone. But Blake is gone again and I thought it might have been—" I rubbed my face with my index finger, just below my eye. "Anyway, turns out it was Clifford Isaac Addams. Do you remember his work? I gave him a little encouragement is all, and no harm was done."

He pressed his lips together for a long moment, like he held back a scolding he knew I deserved.

I had been careful not to change the future.

Whenever someone changed the past they left a trace of

themselves and their efforts on that moment in time. As a result, we would occasionally catch a brief glimpse of Otto or my grandfather from years ago when they first visited this era. Just a momentary appearance, and then they would turn a corner or walk into a store and they were gone.

Like when my grandfather and Otto recovered several pieces of art that had been lost in our present time. They came across it by accident and returned it to the present when they crossed through the painting. We saw them skulking out of someone's house and walking to where Wentworth's atelier had been at that time.

"And?" Philippe asked.

"Clifford said he'd met this woman in Paris who had referred him to our gallery. They met in the Louvre. She had dark hair and a French accent."

"There are a lot of women in Paris with dark hair and French accents."

"And...a ruby cabochon ring with diamonds. Which is pretty hard to ignore considering she referred him to our gallery."

"He met her recently?"

"About a year ago. Roughly."

Philippe's concern appeared to fade more into curiosity. He adored Carolena, who had been like a second mother to him when he was growing up. When she and Otto were together years ago, she had taken a liking to Philippe. They shared a special bond. I knew he'd do anything he could to help find her.

After a moment's thought, he said, "I guess that is hard to ignore."

"They met in The Louvre, which is not a small place, I realize. But I think we should check it out. It sounded like she made weekly visits. So, if we spent enough time there, we might see her."

"If it was her, a year is a long time. They could have moved on."

"We won't know unless we follow up on it. This tip could be a real turning point for us."

"Let us hope." Philippe swept me into a waltz and hummed traditional French music.

WE WALKED ALONG FIFTH AVENUE, our steps matched in tempo and stride for our almost-usual evening sojourn to Camille's for dinner and wine. It was a favorite in my day. With Blake gone much of the time, I appreciated Philippe's friendship—mostly how it mimicked what we had shared when we were younger.

"If we go we would have to take an ocean liner, I've not been on one from this time. Have you?"

Philippe nodded with a closed-lipped smile full of memories. "Once with Otto and Carolena when I was younger. It was, hands down, the most elegant form of transportation I've ever seen. The interior was just like the beauty you've seen from old pictures of the Titanic, only without the iceberg."

"Philippe." I elbowed him.

"It was called the RMS Majestic, I think. Gosh, that was a long time ago."

An unmistakable tingling sensation crawled along the upper part of my back, slow at first, then it escalated into a shiver. That trace of energy on my skin was my one surefire sign that I had someone's attention.

I stopped cold and searched the crowded sidewalk

behind us. "Someone is watching me."

Philippe's head jerked upright. He searched the area.

We had been on the hunt for Otto and Carolena for two years now. They were here, somewhere in this era. We knew Otto would turn up when we least expected it. Which was fine, but we wanted to be the finders, not the findees.

We rushed off the main sidewalk and leaned against the cold brick side of a storefront building. Throngs of pedestrians passed by, none of them familiar.

The spring wind rushed toward us with too much memory of winter on its current and my body shivered. Philippe wrapped his arm around my shoulders and tucked me close to him. It might have been because of the wind, or maybe more so because of who we thought could be nearby. He had become very protective of me in Blake's absence.

We waited until the sensation across my upper back faded, until we were certain, at least, that we were safe. "Maybe it was nothing," My voice was as soft as my confidence at the moment. The thought of Otto being nearby made me think he had the upper hand in some way. He had proven himself unbeatable too many times before.

"I don't see anyone." Philippe glanced in each available direction then returned us to our place among the steady flow of sidewalk strangers. "Let's keep moving."

I inhaled the cool breeze, the oxygen almost reached the fuzzy places of my brain that the espresso hadn't touched throughout the day.

"I didn't see Blake at the gallery today." He looked over his shoulder.

I held my breath for a couple of beats to get through the anger that tightened my chest. "He wasn't there."

"Traveling still?"

"I guess. I don't know where he is." I said it more quickly

than I meant to. "Last I heard he was chasing some lead on Otto. Or maybe it was a tip on Carolena's whereabouts, or…I don't even know anymore."

The telltale prickles tiptoed across my upper back and I spun around quick and lithe as though someone had tapped my shoulder. The majority of the sidewalk traffic was made up of men in dark suits and black hats—they all dressed relatively the same. They dodged my still body, which was parked in the middle of their thoroughfare.

"Come on." Philippe's eyes scanned the area and he pulled me farther along with the crowd. "Let's get to Camille's."

After one last view of the crowd, I agreed. Although I *had* sensed someone watching me, it could have been anyone. Whoever it was must have moved on.

"Did you get any sleep last night?"

"Why, do I look tired?"

"You look amazing, as always. I can just tell when something is bothering you."

"I got a little sleep. Not much."

Philippe didn't ask me what was wrong, but he held his stare on me for a long moment—ten or twelve steps, at least. It was long enough that I felt I had to confess.

"Okay. I'm having the nightmare again. That one where I'm standing in my grandmother's backyard in Savannah."

"Tell me about it." He squeezed my shoulder, encouraged me.

"I already have." I made a smile and sighed.

"Tell me again."

"No."

I felt his determination shift into high gear and I knew I wasn't getting away with that answer.

"The more you talk about these things, the less power

they have over you. Especially where you-know-who is concerned." He pulled me closer. I leaned my head on his shoulder for a brief moment, a silent thank-you spoken between the closest of friends.

"Fine." I exhaled. The retelling of certain nightmares carried a kind of vulnerability, and I glanced around to make sure no one was listening. I lowered my voice. "I can't see them but I know my family is inside the house. All of them. Safe and sound, laughing, eating, carrying on with life as usual."

"So, you're a child in this dream."

"Yes, I must be. Because it's an easy time, you know. No responsibility, no worries or stress. I'm looking to the south-west end of our property, where the water meets the grass, and I'm sort of distracted and feeling optimistic about my life. You know it's that innocent time when you only dream about what's possible. It doesn't occur to you that things could go wrong."

Philippe steadied his light tan fedora against the wind with his index finger and thumb and nodded. His lips curved naturally into a carefree smile that told me he did remember that time.

"Then Otto walks up. He laughs and points. At what I'm not sure, initially. Then I figure out he's laughing at everything that's important to me—my dreams of the future, our family, and our home. Everything we have. Even the fact that I felt safe." We walked a few quiet steps together before I tipped my head toward him. "What do you think it means, this recurrent dream?"

Philippe tugged me closer. "It's as if he's saying you can't go home again. To everything you've wanted, to everything you've cared about." He looked at me with a side glance, then pressed his lips to my cheek for a solid two seconds. "Leave it to my father to ruin a good dream."

We walked into Camille's, and the maitre' d escorted us to our favorite booth. Heads turned toward us and we settled into our well-practiced, mild-mannered response. Our goal was to be as *unnoticed* as possible.

It was the twenties. There weren't any smartphones, tablets, or computers, and people were more in the moment, more present. They noticed one another, so we had to be careful. We did not want to be or do anything too memorable.

Being in the twenties was like living in a moving, breathing museum. True to the analogy, you could explore but you couldn't touch or change anything. There could be a steep price to pay for that. Though I wished we were here for a reason other than to rescue Carolena, I loved everything about the era—the fashion, the post-war enthusiasm about the promise of better times and economic growth, the artists and their art, the jazz age, and so on.

Our usual table was covered with a thick, white table-cloth, more durable than what we'd find in our present day, and softer, as well. Two tiny candle lamps with deep red shades and white porcelain ware with a burgundy band around the near rim of each piece sat in their standard places. Everything felt sturdy, well-crafted, and made with care.

As visitors here we had very little uncertainty. Of course, between the five of us and the support we had from family back home, we knew what was about to happen. Though I doubted I would have the same enthusiasm in any other decade, everything about the twenties made me smile from the inside out.

Philippe took my hands in his, our fingers glided together. "Ultimately, though, you can't let him."

"I can't let him what?"

"Ruin a good dream."

I nodded and appreciated the advice and the comfort. My relationship with Philippe had turned out to be just a turning of the page from the friendship we'd shared as young people. The playful easiness was still there. Now that he had been away from Otto for a few years, he'd become his own man—handsome and brave, strong and caring. It never ceased to amaze me how he and Blake turned out so well considering that Otto was their father. Any amount of good parenting was a tribute to their mothers, I guessed.

"What do *you* think your dream means?" He opened his menu and watched me over the top of it, his brown eyes full of cautious mischief.

I tucked my upper lip between my teeth and bit it hard for a moment. "I think all dreams are messengers in some way. Delivering pieces of wisdom we wouldn't otherwise pay attention to. So, somehow that I can't go home again. Though *how* I can't go home again, I'm not sure. Do you think it means home to our current day? Or that my family will never be together again? Or that none of us have a happy future for as long as Otto is free?" None of the options were good ones.

"Could be any of them, I suppose."

"I want my family together again. They deserve that. We all need that." I didn't talk about that too much because I figured everyone knew that's what I wanted. I had wanted my family reunited since Otto had torn us apart.

The dark-haired waitress had short frizzed curls that framed her face and she placed red wine, fresh bread, and butter in front of us. She smiled at Philippe and bounced in a short almost-curtsy before she left. It was a humble, girlish move that typically meant that she didn't speak much English.

"She seems very happy to be here," I said of the waitress. "Life can't be all that easy for her, and yet she's almost gleeful. There's just something about this decade."

"She has something to look forward to. It's an exciting time, this place in—" I knew he almost said *history*. But that just felt odd and surreal. "Well, this place. Take the first option you suggested—how would you feel about not going home again?" he whispered in a low tone.

"Honestly?" I sighed. "I've thought about the possibility. Considering my father and grandfather's experience, that's a very real option. I have mixed feelings, I guess. I mean, it wouldn't be the worst thing. I like the twenties. I know what's going to happen next and when. As long as we find Carolena and take care of Otto, I could be happy here. There are lots of interesting people in this era I'd still love to meet."

"Your feelings don't sound all that mixed to me. And I'd recommend you be careful about meeting interesting people. You could really disrupt the present."

"No, I know. I wouldn't upset anything. I'm careful."

The feelings of safety from the early part of the dream came back to me and I savored them like a creamy chocolate dessert. Rolling the visual snippets over and over in my mind—the tips of the soft emerald grass that were tall enough to bend with the ocean breeze, my grandfather's boat rocking on gentle waves, and the seasoned tang of pine from the far edge of our property filled the air. My entire world was comprised of a few acres and I was deliciously happy with that containment. I stopped the dream before Otto appeared and hit replay again. And again.

"Addie?"

"Yes?"

"You miss home?"

"I miss...what it used to be. In all the best ways of that dream. The simplicity of life, my family being together. I can't stop thinking about it—the innocence of it all."

He sipped the last of the wine from his glass. "And?"

"And I've decided I'm not content to reflect on it as just a once-beautiful chapter in my life. I have to have it again. That goodness, the happiness, and contentment. The simplicity. The love."

"I know." His gaze settled on me and agreement passed between us as easily as it did with childhood friends. "It's one of the reasons why I'm here." He bit into the last third of his piece of bread and stared at it. "Everything is better here. Not perfect. But far better."

"In a way, I think being here is the closest to that time. Sans Otto, of course."

"I'll never go back." His voice was resolute. Decided. Though I had known he felt this way, I understood his position now in a deeper sense.

"What about Blake? What does he think?"

"He wants to find Carolena, have Otto rot away in a jail somewhere." I pushed a few green beans around on my plate.

"Everything okay with you two?"

I inhaled a deep breath, but then only said, "Yeah." My voice sounded thin and I knew I wasn't convincing.

Thankfully Philippe didn't press. He just nodded. "Good," he said.

I glanced up and found him staring, though.

"How long has he been gone this time?"

I put my fork on my plate. My appetite disappeared with the arrival of this topic. "Several days. Grandpa had a lead."

I opened my mouth to say something else but then I closed it. The man was trying to help his mother and I sounded selfish. "Everything is fine. It's just that—when we met, Carolena was safely hidden away. He thought he was going to put Otto in jail forever by moving through legal channels. That didn't work and now that Otto has his mother, Blake's in an unfamiliar time and without the support of the FBI—he doesn't have any credentials or power here.

"We've not been able to find Carolena. He's worried. He's stressed. He has to do whatever he can to find her. We all do. We all have." My voice pitched high. "I guess that all of that has taken its toll on our relationship."

"Throughout all of this, he's put you last."

Philippe always did aim for the core issue of any problem. Anger and fear mixed together in a hot liquid and stewed in my heart. I chose not to address his statement. "Carolena needs his help. I can't blame him for his obsession to find her."

"I know that, but this is not an easy time. It would go more smoothly if he didn't shut you out."

My sigh carried a heavy load of frustration. "I can't ask him to stop what he's doing." I said more harshly than I had intended.

He didn't say a word, but his brows lowered and I felt his energy home in on me like a lens coming into focus.

"Okay." I quickly decided to drop the defense. Philippe would make me shoot it straight, anyway. "I guess this has been going on for a while, and I'm worried." I rested my forehead against my fingertips, exhausted. "I just had it in my mind that we'd work together as a team while we were here. But I don't know where he is half the time, much less what he's working on."

"He's focused." He smiled tenderly. It was the kind of smile he reserved for me, soft and understanding, the one that said "I'm on your side". I wanted to curl into his arms.

For the past two years, Philippe had been there for me whenever Blake wasn't around. He understood how difficult it was to spend so much time alone and not be allowed to build relationships with others in the area.

"He's *too* focused. No room for anyone else."

"He's his mother's protector. He's probably felt that way since he was a boy. When he showed up in my life he was my protector and rescuer, too," I said.

"You're making excuses for him."

The expression on my face obviously clear, he put both hands in the air as if I'd pointed a gun at his chest.

"I didn't say he was handling this well. I'm just saying I understand why he's doing it."

"Look. I'm not telling you how to handle this. But I know you. You can't go on like this. Maybe you should talk to him."

"I—"

"I'm sure you have talked to him. But, try again."

I smiled, lips together and making no promises. I could bring this up with Blake again, but there was no talking him out of something he wanted to do.

WE LEFT Camille's and made our way toward the gallery. We kept our eyes peeled for anyone familiar and Philippe shared where he'd searched for Carolena that day. He often worked in the gallery with me, but he had also made a number of inroads with other gallery owners and museum directors and employees. My job was to run the gallery and try to find any news that might relate to Otto.

I had relationships with most of the artists in New York and kept my ear to the ground for any rumors of big or unusual purchases. Blake worked the cop precincts and the underworld.

My father and grandfather worked everyone they knew in the art community, including their special connections at the Metropolitan Museum of Art and less-than legal connections like Gary Walker.

Grandpa met him several years ago while doing a little sports betting. I had seen a photo on Grandmother Grace's bedroom wall of the two of them together. From my own visions, I recognized Gary immediately. He was the past-life incarnation of Otto Albrecht.

Philippe tipped his head toward the street on our left. "I have to pick up a frame for your grandfather. Come with me."

I gestured in the direction we'd been heading. "I think I'm just going to go on back. The gallery isn't that far."

He held his hand out and waved in the universal come-on-come-with-me sign.

"I'll be fine. I'll meet you there." I lengthened the word fine into a groan that lasted two beats and widened my eyes in mock frustration.

He moved his hand to his hip and scolded me with an arched eyebrow for a second. "Be. Careful." He kissed me on the cheek. After a few steps down the side street, he turned and waved. He'd known I hadn't yet moved. I didn't know what I would have done without his friendship these past two years. I waved in return.

The wind blew the longish white strands of fur from my

collar to my red lipstick-covered mouth and I blew it away. I waited, but Philippe turned the corner and didn't look back again.

I'd lost the brisk pace I'd shared with Philippe and slowed into more of a stroll that was weighted with thought. I understood Blake's tireless need to help his mother. Though I wondered if his efforts seemed like more of an obsession to remove Otto from the planet. One helped the other, I guess. He and I had talked endlessly about how we needed to function as a group, a team. But he preferred self-reliance. Which left me shut out and alone most of the time.

I wouldn't admit it aloud, but Philippe had been right. Blake did put me last. At least since we had arrived in this era. Or shortly thereafter.

At the next street and a block down, a vendor rolled up his red and white striped awning on all three sides to close up for the day. Street vendors weren't much different here than they were in the present, though there were a lot fewer of them now. They tended to smile more. With another half hour or so to kill before our entire crew would gather at the gallery, I took my sweet tooth one block out of the way for a treat.

His store was stationary against the windowless wall of a tall gray building. I admired several nearby movie posters that advertised the latest silent film, *Ashamed Parents*. I adored silent film and made a mental note to see this one. The vendor scooped several varieties of loose candy into a brown paper bag. I handed him my coins and they clinked together in his hand.

Chocolate had become my usual evening fare. Good medicine that helped sedate my frustrations, moderately anyway. I popped three round balls of chocolate into my mouth and crunched. It wasn't my imagination and Philippe was right. Everything was better here. Even the chocolate. Lack of preservatives and pesticides, I decided. I headed toward the direction I'd come from. Prickles crawled along the back of my neck again and I slowed my pace, scanning the area.

Slowly, I turned to see who my perpetrator-at-a-distance was when a man slid behind me from the other side and gripped my arms tight. He nearly lifted me off of my feet and ushered me into the nearby alleyway. The familiarity of his spiced citrus cologne sent me into a dizzying falling-through-time feeling. "Wait—"

My thoughts whirled through my brain in a nonsensical circular motion. This was someone I knew.

He spun me quickly, pressed my back against the cold roughness of a brick wall and he kissed me. The small paper bag tipped from my hand and candy coated gum balls bounced on the bricked street like happy children set free for summer vacation. I tried to see his face but his features were too close.

It was a secret kiss, a stolen kiss, a private kiss. He had spirited me out of sight with sure strength and determination. His lips against mine were passionate, as though he knew how to kiss me, as though we had done this before.

My lips responded in kind, shockingly so. This wasn't Blake, what I was doing was wrong. Yet the familiarity and the passionate attention awoke something deep within my heart.

His lips trailed to my ear. "Since when do you eat chocolate?"

Unexpected joy burst in my heart at the whispered richness of his voice. This had to be a mistake. I pushed my palms against his chest to create distance, but he pressed closer.

"Sassy—"

Only one person used this nickname with me.

"Jack." I breathed his name in a whisper. For the first time in who knew how many lifetimes, I was in Jack's arms again.

Not in a dream or a memory, but here.

With him.

5

———

"Even after the past two years together, I often wonder." Otto ran his long and well-manicured thumb over Carolena's hand. "I open my eyes each morning, and I wonder if you'll be there. Next to me." The words were tender, and his voice was soft, but she saw the paranoia flash in his eyes. Just for a moment, like the quick wink from a faraway star.

If she hadn't known him, she wouldn't have even seen it. The meanness—it was there. The sweetness was an act, the masquerade of a sentimental moment, and beneath the words was his unsaid warning.

"And where would I go, *mon amour*?" Her tone steered just shy of condescending. She selected a pink macaroon—pink intentionally—from the towered dessert tray and put half of it into Otto's mouth. She ate the other half herself.

"Home?" he said with his slightly full mouth.

"I am home if I am with you and that is the way I want it. So, you need to stop with such concerns." She waved her hand three times as if she shooed a fly away from their afternoon tea. "If I was going to leave, I would have. *Oui*? But I choose to be with you. Here. In this gorgeous era where we have always been our happiest." She ran her thumb along his chin and brushed a few pink crumbs away. She hoped the mothering touch would settle him.

A waiter hurried by one of the many tall palms lining the hotel restaurant area and Carolena waved at him.

"*Oui, madame.*" The short, thin waiter with dark hair half-bowed to her.

"We need a fresh pot of tea and more lemon."

His round glasses slid toward the end of his nose and he quickly pushed them up again with his middle finger. "*Oui, madame.*" He removed the empty porcelain teapot from the table and left the dining area.

"You were the one who was out very late last night. Where did you have to be that kept me waiting for you for so long?"

"There was a shipment from the Middle East, a number of Egyptian items. I was going to check them out."

"Egyptian... And what did they find?"

"Well, I had hoped these items were from King Tut's tomb. I would gladly change history to have a few of those items for myself. I soon remembered that Howard Carter isn't due to discover that until later this year. November, I think." Otto's voice sounded different when he discussed stolen art, or even the potential of obtaining stolen art. It took on a power, a strength that came from being unbeaten, and it gave Carolena an uncomfortable chill.

"Then what were the items?"

The waiter returned with a fresh pot of tea and poured them each a cup.

"I don't know. Odds and ends brought in from grave robbers I would expect. Nothing big enough to interest me. I was waved off anyway. Some other buyer beat us to it."

"Who?"

"I don't know for certain, though I have a pretty good idea. An older guy and a fairly young guy, I heard. Of course, knowing Gary, he probably took their money and knocked them off." He raised his teacup to her. "Let's finish up. I want to get home with these." He patted several large rectangular packages wrapped in plain brown paper.

"I still don't know why you didn't leave those in the hotel room." She clinked her delicate cup against his in a toast and forced a smile. A sick feeling reached to her psychically.

"Too dangerous. What's the matter, darling?"

"Mm—" She scrunched her expression as if the tea held rotten eggs. "It's the tea. It isn't good." She set her cup into her saucer more loudly than she meant to.

Blake. This was his vibe that she sensed. As soon as Otto mentioned the young man, she knew this was her son. *Our son.*

"You look a little pale—"

"I think I just need some fresh air." She pushed her chair away from the table.

"Don't be long, love. We have a ship to catch."

Once outside, she lit a cigarette and inhaled the smoke deep into her lungs. "Time to tune in." She blew the smoke into the cool air that whipped past her. She leaned against the outer wall of the restaurant and closed her eyes. To any random passerby, she was just resting her eyes or enjoying the sunshine on a cool spring morning.

She'd done this millions of times before. The connection between them was strong and it only took her one quiet moment for her to find his energy.

6

His forceful hand pressed inside my open coat. "I didn't know you were going to be on this side of town today. Who was that you were with?"

Chills of emotion fled over my body and I struggled to find my focus. He thought I was Sarah and I had to be careful. I needed to extricate myself from this situation subtly and without creating any new futures for either one of us.

"This is dangerous, Jack. We shouldn't—"

"I know. Gary might be around here today. But when I saw you, I just had to have you. If only for a moment."

Neither of us spoke for a while. His kisses were the very physical demonstration that I had been reunited with a love I thought I'd never see again. I ran my hand along the side of him. He was large and solid, not at all the ephemeral memory of him that had moved through my dreams.

A man yelled in the distance and I pulled away. It wasn't impossible that Blake might happen upon us. I placed my hand on his chest to create distance. "I have to go."

He pulled me close. His all-too-present love for me took

over the space within that Blake's perpetual distance created.

"Not yet," he said between kisses.

I ran my thumb between the corner of his lips and my own. His were different from Blake's. Slightly less full on the top. And his kisses were different, softer in a way. Not like Blake's. Though this *was* Blake. Our timeless love, as restless and feverish as it had always been. Our connection drew me closer to him along this inevitable path of true love. Forever love. I remembered how much I wanted this kind of connection in my life and how much I needed it.

Memories of past and present collided and tossed my heart into the air. I landed in a strange place where both lifetimes were real at the same time, as well as the reasonable and illicit nature of our together.

"I have to change our plans," he said against my neck. "You need to meet me at my house at seven instead of six. Gary is going to stop by that day and I don't want you to run into him. There will be a party to cover for our comings and goings. Bring a small package to the gathering that night so that it looks like you're just making a usual delivery to me from Gary. Something legitimate. Just in case you're caught."

I quickly realized that Sarah couldn't possibly know about this change in plans. "No—no. Jack, stop. I'm not who you think I am."

His eyes scanned my hair, the features of my face and my clothing. They narrowed in suspicion and he stepped away fully. "What are you playing at?"

I closed my jacket and straightened my dress. The heat between us lingered among his confusion.

"I don't understand this. Sarah?"

I shook my head. Memories of the past-life portrait of

me, past-life me—Sarah, came to mind. Except for a few dissimilar features, I did look much the same from this past lifetime to the present day. It was reasonable that he confused the two incarnations of me. For now, I just needed to get out of here without creating any new wrinkles in time.

"I'm not Sarah." I turned away.

He caught my arm and held it firm. His crystal blue eyes, the windows that had always revealed him to be fearless, now showed worry. My identity was a puzzle he couldn't solve.

I thought of the time and the year, spring, 1922. This party at his home, this must be when he died, it had been warm weather. Late spring, it must have been. I, as Sarah, must already be pregnant with his baby.

I wondered if Gary—Otto's past-life incarnation—killed the baby and me. Or did he take us back and claim the baby as his own? I fought the urge to protect Jack from everything he was about to face.

"Sarah?" The concern in his voice and the whisper-soft touch of his fingertips on my face made me want to fall into his arms again. Maybe it was Blake's ongoing emotional distance or his continual physical absence. Or maybe it was seeing Jack again in person, alive and well and feeling his love for me again. Like the flip of a switch, I realized how starved I was for the connection I hadn't had with Blake for some time now.

I traced the structured outline of his jaw, and my index finger glided around his top lip, then pressed just inside his lower lip. His exhale drifted across my finger. I melted into his arms. The honeyed taste of him uncovered memories within me that I'd not remembered before.

The simple joy of our laughter at a picnic near a stream,

my flowered dress trailing behind me on a swing, long hours together near a fire—it was the night he'd placed the sapphire ring on my finger. The heat between us was too intense, and I nearly lost myself in the knowing that I never wanted to be with anyone else, that I'd found true love.

He broke our kiss with an abruptness that made my head spin. "Sarah?"

I wondered if my kisses were slightly different now as well. Whatever it was that tipped him off, something made him finally believe me. I wasn't Sarah. At least not anymore.

I held the side of his face in my hand. "Be careful, Jack. Take care of yourself." I kissed him one last time. Soft and gentle. It was the sort of good-bye kiss where you tried to seal all the sensory details into your memory, so you could experience it again later.

I gathered the wide, fleecy collar of my coat together at my chest and turned away.

"Sarah—"

The question and the urgency in his voice made my heart clench. I broke into a light run and didn't stop until I was several blocks down Fifth Avenue and well into the thick crowd where I knew he wouldn't chase me. With the potential of Gary in the area, Jack wouldn't risk a public scene.

I searched behind me. Several women in cloche hats and silky slip dresses giggled and dodged my sudden halt. I searched for him with one long look but he wasn't there. The tingling sensation along the upper part of my back was also gone. Jack was the one following Philippe and me when we were on our way to Camille's. I took a few more steps forward and stopped again. This time, I thought about everything I had just said and done. God help me, I hope I hadn't changed anything. I examined everything—the kisses, the brief discussion. He would think it odd that I looked so much like Sarah. But it wouldn't go beyond that.

My fingertips trailed the sensation of Jack's illicit kisses on my lips and an unexpected smile met my hand. I couldn't deny how satisfying it was to finally connect again with Blake.

7

———

"Argh." Blake winced from the pain in his ribs.

"This should help." John wrapped bandages around Blake's rib cage. "Nothing you can do but stabilize them, even if they're cracked," he said. "Of course, you could get them x-rayed. That's a heavy dose of radiation in this day and time. Up to you. I'll drive you to the hospital if you want." He pulled the bandages tighter in another wrap around his midsection and secured the end.

"No. I'll take some ice, though. Aspirin if you have it."

"I'm off to get you some ice from the kitchen at The Plaza across the street." John gestured with his head to his left. "I'll get some aspirin while I'm out."

Blake felt the lump on the back of his head. "Two bags of ice."

John nodded in agreement.

Heels descended the wooden steps that led to the small kitchen. The rhythmic *click-click-click* was slower than anyone else's step in the firm and Blake knew these footsteps were Addie's. Since she'd fallen down those same steps when she arrived two years ago, she respected that steep incline by showing it a careful pace.

He also knew she would be mad when she saw him like this. Actually, scared, worried, *then* mad. Scared because he was hurt. Worried until she knew what happened and if he'd be okay. Then mad because he hadn't let her know where he was going or when he'd be back.

He dreaded all three stages.

If they were living in their own present day he would have sent her a text to let her know he'd be gone for a few nights. That he was okay. Here, that was impossible. And he couldn't tell her *where* he was going because she was stubborn enough to show up and try to help. He couldn't put her in that kind of danger.

"Oh, my." Addie put her hand to her chest when she saw them.

"I'm fine." He reached out for her and ached to feel her in his arms. They'd been apart too long this time.

"Just some bruised ribs, we think." John added tape to the bandages on Blake's right side.

"You think?" Addie's sarcasm snapped at the both of them. The scared stage was in full swing. "And what about this?" She made a circular motion toward Blake's left eye. He knew that was going to turn black and blue soon enough.

"I'll go get that ice." John patted Blake twice on the shoulder. Blake thought that pattern might be a physical translation of the words: good luck. "He's okay," he said to Addie and patted her three times when he passed by her. Everyone in the room knew that meant "I love you." He shut the door behind him and the sound of his steps disappeared far more quickly than Addie's had arrived. He was a man in excellent shape for his age. Or almost any other age for that matter.

"I'm fine." Blake braced himself for her next reaction and mentally checked *scared* off the list. "Now that they're wrapped, they don't even hurt."

She breathed deeply and ran her fingertips along his bare chest, one of the few parts of him that didn't hurt. A hit of adrenaline shot through his veins and his chest rose under her touch.

"You're bandaged." She opened her mouth and her soft kiss grazed against his lips. He tasted red wine.

The worried stage wasn't going too badly.

"What happened?" She scooted a chair in front of him. She rested her hand on his knee.

"I miscalculated the amount of security they had."

"Where?"

He shrugged. "A meeting."

"What does the other guy look like?"

"Confused, mostly. I pushed my way out of it. One of them got a few punches in first."

"One of them?" She lowered her gaze and shook her head. "You can't just disappear like that for days at a time. You have to tell me where you're going. No one knew where to look for you."

He nodded in understanding, but not in agreement. The men he dealt with were murderers. He wouldn't bring her into that.

She sighed loudly enough to overcome the stillness in the room. He knew she was moving to the next stage and he wondered if they could skip the anger phase altogether. He tried a distraction.

"Did you have any luck today?" He'd asked that same question so many times over the last two years that even he was tired of hearing himself ask it. He was even more tired of hearing the negative responses.

"I think so." Her touch was warm. She had that I'm-so-glad-you're-here-touch that sometimes accompanied their many reunions as of late. He figured there was anger beneath her caress, waiting to punish him for staying away too long and without communication as to where he was. He couldn't blame her.

For him, her touch had a specific effect on him. It was an infallible law, like gravity. Even with the lack of sleep from the night before and the pain from his head and ribs, the feel of her skin against his, warmed his heart. He'd have to wait for her anger to pass, until she was willing to welcome him back.

"What do you mean?" He waited for a story of little to no progress and proactively tamped his frustration.

"Well, I spent the day in the gallery. I did meet an interesting artist—I'll get to that in a minute. Philippe and I had dinner at Camille's. Then... I saw Jack on the way home." She leaned away, like a cat who had just batted a ball of yarn and wanted to see what it would do next.

He didn't want to know about her dinner with Philippe. He didn't like the connection they had developed with one another and he'd told her as much. "Jack who?"

"Jack you." She stared at him with a get-it-now? raised eyebrow. Though he didn't. "Jack. Who you used to be in this 1920s life—Jack."

Blake realized his mouth was open and he closed it. "Did he see you?"

"He saw me. He pulled me aside, thinking I was Sarah."

He swallowed involuntarily. "We're not supposed to have anything to do with our past-life selves." She glanced at the floor and he knew he was a hypocrite for scolding her. He had just met with Sarah and had been completely taken with her. "What did he say?"

"Nothing at first." She laughed and shook her head. Not in a disappointed way, but more in an overly flattered way. "He snuck up behind me, scooted us into this alleyway, pressed me against the wall of this building, and...he started kissing me." She should have been upset about what happened. But she appeared distracted and dreamy, like the football quarterback had just asked her to the prom.

She exhaled, slow and thoughtful. "He thought I was Sarah. So he followed me until I was alone and then I think he was excited to have a few stolen moments with her. I couldn't do anything for a few minutes—"

"A few *minutes*?" Jealousy burned in his gut. Blake mentally kicked himself for not being around to protect her. Jack would never have approached her if he had been with her.

"He moved so fast, I didn't know who he was. Then after I figured that out I had to decide how to handle it. I had to be careful. So, it took me a minute."

"So you kissed him back." His hands curled into tight fists.

She laughed a little and his teeth clenched, too.

"Are you jealous of your former self?"

Now he was the one who shook his head. "What? No, I'm not upset, I'm just trying to figure out what happened."

One of her eyebrows raised in that I-know-better expression of hers. "Yes. I kissed him back. What else was I going to do? Sarah would have, right?"

To calm down he reminded himself that nothing could part him and Addie, not even death. Though he still hated the idea of her kissing another man. Even if it was him. Sort of. "Right. How did you get away from him?"

"I wasn't going to tell him that I wasn't Sarah. I was just going to slip away. Then he started talking about a change in some plans they had made. So I had to tell him." She inhaled a deep breath and the faraway look in her eye annoyed him. First chance he had he would kiss her until she couldn't remember the name Jack. "He didn't really believe me at first. In the end, I guess there must be just enough differences between the two of us that made him believe me. Finally, anyway."

Rage filled his chest. He had an undeniable urge to find his past-life self and knock him flat. "You think everything is okay?"

"Yeah, fine." She waved off his concern. "I was careful and got out of there as soon as I could." She smiled with an odd contentment that made him search the room for something to hit. He should be the only one who could put that smile on her face.

"You were gone for a long time on this trip." She stood and he wondered if she was going to start the anger phase by leaving the room. This stage usually took a couple of forms—a heated argument or an ice-cold silent treatment.

Sometimes it was possible to head off her well-deserved temper with an apology. Or even several apologies. "Addie— please. I know you're angry and I'm sorry." He braced himself for the second time since she entered the room. "Let's just—I'd rather not—"

She pulled her chair next to his. Then she sat down, leaned in and wrapped her arms around him.

This was the fourth or fifth time she'd surprised him in just the past few minutes. He wasn't complaining. He felt a smile pull at the corners of his mouth.

He followed her lead and welcomed her close to him. What did I do to deserve this?"

"Nothing," she said without a doubt."But you were good in a past life."

"I must have been awfully good," he whispered against her lips and felt his resentment of Jack that sat solid in his chest. Paranoia slithered through his brain and he wondered just how much of an ace his past-life self was.

He mentally kicked himself for leaving her alone too long and too often. He knew he wasn't available enough to her, not even when he was physically there. Not like she wanted. Had he been able to move without hurting he would have taken her in his arms more completely. She was his. No matter the lifetime, they were meant to be together.

She unbuttoned his shirt, her fingers stroked against his chest. Her touch removed obstacles between them, brought him back to the forever they shared. She was more beautiful than any masterpiece he'd ever seen.

She kissed him again. "I've missed you. So much."

The scent of her breath was sweet and he hated the idea that someone else had been close enough to know it as he did. Even if that someone else was him when he was Jack.

"I missed you, too." She was an endless craving for him. Even together, like this, he wanted more of her. She was his life-long fantasy come true.

"Promise me you'll always be careful, Sassy." He removed the pins that held her hair off her neck and he gathered her long silky hair in his hand. "I don't want anyone else getting close to you. I don't know what I'd do if I lost you."

Car engines roared nearby and rattled the small window that had been painted dark green. Traces of engine exhaust seeped through the slightly parted edges and mixed with the citrusy-floral scent of her perfumed skin. Everything outside of this room was loud and restless and chaotic and hurtling toward some tragic end—like Jack and Sarah, and

Carolena and Otto. Even this decade would end in a crash that would be felt around the world.

Addie was his only haven. She sheltered him from his own fears in ways she probably didn't even know. In a way, he didn't think he could put it into words, other than to say that her steady love anchored him and kept him sane. Without her, he didn't know who he would become.

For now, he was her everything, though he knew that soon she would still want the more he couldn't give. And he would hate himself for that. He was caught in an unbearable conflict—between the connection she needed with him, and the things he had to fix and the price he had to pay for that.

He could have stopped her before this started and talked this out. But he needed to feel close to her, to feel the love and the passion that he knew she still had for him. He had to know his search wasn't for naught.

He held her full weight against him. They were together and timeless.

He thought she held him tighter than she usually did when he returned from the trips he wouldn't tell her about. From the outside, it might have looked like she was holding on. But to him, today and strangely, he felt she was slipping away.

She was the reason he'd left and she was his motivation to return. Although their reconnecting was different this time. He concentrated on the intangible place where their hearts connected and intertwined, the sacred space where he could always feel the love they shared.

It was offbeat, changed.

Like he'd come home to a slightly different person.

8

———

My grandfather popped the cork on a bottle of wine he'd had hidden beneath the sink, behind bottles of various cleaners. "I think we all need a little of the demon drink."

The 18th Amendment ushered in the era of Prohibition just three months earlier, but that didn't mean anything to us.

Knowing that Prohibition was coming, my grandfather bought a nearby warehouse and stockpiled French wine in the years before it took effect. We were never without.

My father placed wine glasses on the tall wooden table that had become the centerpiece of our evenings. The table was made from raw, mostly unfinished wood with long, uniformly carved legs and it was just the right height for the plain wooden stools that surrounded it. The arrangement was a more appropriate aesthetic fit for the galley of a naval ship than the kitchen of an elegant art and antique appraisal firm. Though that's the way my father and grandfather kept the nonpublic side of their business. Simple. Functional. It was where we met every night to discuss the progress we'd made during the day and to make our plans for the following day.

The decor lent a sort of suitability and definition to our task at hand. Our efforts to locate Carolena and Otto were without flourish or excess.

The wine gurgled when he poured generous servings into the perfectly round silhouettes. Piquant flavors of black cherries, licorice, clove, and spring flowers floated into the air and ignored our somber moods.

Above the waistband of Blake's pants were the white bandages that kept his ribs from moving too much. The muscular outline beneath his bare skin bulged like armor. Blake's shirt, jacket, and vest were across the room, along with a bottle of Bayer aspirin and two bags of melted ice. The twenties didn't offer much in terms of pain relief, but we were glad to have at least a few items that helped.

"You okay, Blake?" Philippe gestured to his ribs and bruised face.

"Fine." The energy behind Blake's glare might have knocked anyone else off his stool. Blake had suggested to me on more than one occasion that he thought Philippe's feelings for me extended beyond friendship. So, Blake often worked to make certain boundaries clear. I had suggested he might not feel this way if he hadn't been gone so much.

To his credit, Philippe held his own and returned the look. Years of practice with Otto, I supposed. The pressure from each of them was too much, like I was in the middle of some medieval duel. I was pretty sure they had both forgotten that I was even there, so I slipped out from between the two of them to stand across the room near my grandfather.

"Sibling rivalry?" my grandfather whispered.

I shrugged. Drank my wine. The historical lack of

progress with our search often birthed the addition of dark moods to Blake's personality. I had frequently found him late at night, sitting in our library alone, without light, staring out the window. "I'm fine," he would say. I wondered if this was a shade of that.

Blake focused on his substantial black notebook with the spiral clasp and lined paper. With a bright yellow pencil, he scribbled notes and dates and plans. It was a complete documentation of every effort we had expended to date in search of his parents, and what he intended for us to do next.

"We'll find them, Blake." My grandfather's tone was confident and inspiring. Though he'd been consigned to the past for twenty years with no escape, he didn't project any of his disappointment onto our search for Carolena. "This will work out."

"Of course it will." My father tossed his black fedora on the counter. Even though the sun had set, traffic still rumbled by. The noise was louder than engines in our present day.

"I did find one lead." Blake's voice growled with fatigue and frustration I'd not seen when he first arrived home. "I can't attest to how reliable it is, and it's about a year old."

Philippe and I exchanged a glance. I hadn't yet had a chance to tell Blake what I'd learned from our visitor earlier in the evening. I was surprised to hear that he, too, had an old clue to a relative's whereabouts.

"Someone who knew Otto and Carolina in passing said they were heading to Paris about a year or so ago. They didn't know if they went or not. Just that they were talking about it."

"I think they went," I said.

Blake's stare landed on me without any of the emotional

softness I'd felt from him less than an hour ago. My heart steeled itself.

He was focused on his obsession now. "How so?"

"I mentioned it earlier, we had a visitor late this evening, just before Philippe and I went out for dinner." I sat across from Blake at the table and leaned forward on crossed arms. "He was an artist and said he was referred here by a woman he met in The Louvre about a year ago. She matched Carolena's description perfectly."

Blake opened his mouth. I knew he was prepared to object to the fact that the details were too general.

"And she wore a ruby and diamond ring. A cabochon ruby."

He leaned away from the table. "Really?"

"Yes. I didn't have a chance to tell you."

"Good work, Addie." My dad nodded to Blake. "Good job. Sounds like we have our first real lead."

"Too coincidental not to be true." Philippe ran his hand through the long section of hair on top of his head. "We ought to check it out."

"I'd say so." My grandfather raised his glass over the center of the table. "To our success."

Philippe, my dad, and I joined in. Blake was the last to follow.

The five of us clinked our glasses together.

Blake sipped from his glass to complete the toast. He never withheld from such traditions—to do so would have been unlucky. Maybe it was how long he'd been away, not knowing when he would leave again. I didn't know, but watching his compliance with this meaningless societal rule, I felt distant from him, like a thick, invisible space had wedged itself between us. I shot the last two gulps of my wine in one swallow and asked for more.

It had been a tough search with no leads until today. Our biggest problem in trying to find Otto and Carolena was that we didn't have any pictures of the couple we could show around, so we were relegated to describing their appearance when we asked about them. Not terribly effective considering that Otto didn't have too many distinguishing physical characteristics—we could have been describing any number of men. We thought the fact that Carolena was French and always elegantly dressed might make her recognizable, but it hadn't. Instead, we'd been led to every reasonable facsimile on the island of Manhattan. I assumed we'd have the same struggle in Paris.

Blake stepped across the room and reached into his gray woolen vest pocket that was slung over the arm of a straight back chair. "On the way home I made a list of places we need to check once we're there. Obviously, we'll move The Louvre to the top." He laid the unevenly torn scrap of paper on the table. It was one of those little moments that jerked me into the astonishing realization of where we were. Like Blake's antique fashion, the rattling pass of a Model T, or seeing a magazine that touted some new performance by Charlie Chaplin. We weren't home. We were trying to find Carolena in 1922.

"It's possible that we may not locate her in The Louvre right away. While we try that, we can assume that Otto is never without an agenda, one that usually involves expensive art, so I think we need to connect with the artists who he'd be interested in. Picasso, Mogdilani, and so forth. It would be very much like him to try to claim one or more of their masterpieces before they were sold or placed in museums. Much easier to get ahold of it that way, and—" Blake gestured toward my grandfather and father. "If you all have any other private art contacts over there, we should visit them as well."

"Did Mr. Addams say if Carolena was alone when he met her?" Philippe asked me.

"He didn't say that anyone was with her. Only that she usually showed up on the two nights when The Louvre was open late. He said she was sketching and was partial to the former palaces."

"Would Otto let Carolena visit a gallery on her own?" Philippe asked.

"Not likely. He was always possessive of her. I doubt that's faded with time." My father tipped his stool onto two legs. I had to bite my tongue so I wouldn't tell him to put "all four on the floor" as Grace had often admonished Alexa and me to do. It seemed a lifetime of worrying about him and my grandfather's safety wasn't going to disappear anytime soon.

"I agree. He's probably already calculated that John and Campbell are here. He has to consider the fact that Blake might have lived. I doubt he'd risk the chance that one of them might see her if she were alone," Philippe said. "He's probably paranoid about losing her."

"Probably," I said. "Do you think he would take her out of the 1920s?"

Philippe shrugged. "Anything is possible with Otto."

My grandfather crossed his arm in front of him and ran the side of his index finger back and forth beneath his lower lip. I'd seen him do this on numerous occasions when I was younger. It usually meant he was trying to figure how to untie some series of problematic knots in his life.

Blake wrote our Parisian plan into his notebook in evenly spaced black print. Trained by the FBI before he became an informant, he was nothing if not overly organized in his approach. I was more of a go-with-your-gut kind of gal.

I ran my hand across the back of my hair and felt the pins I'd replaced to hold my faux bob intact. Long hair was not en vogue and I didn't think it wise to cut my hair into a bob just yet. That was still too fashion-forward for the day, a symbol of strength that women were equal to men, and I needed to stay unnoticed. I wanted a helpful response from those I spoke with; not resistance. Old-fashioned worked best to that end with most, though I couldn't wait to let my hair fall for the evening.

"Is everything okay, Grandpa?"

"Yes, it's fine." His gave me his most reassuring smile, the one that made me feel that all was right in the world. It left his face more quickly than usual. "Alfred's late," he said to my father in a low voice.

My father returned all four of the stool legs to the floor, checked his gold watch, and met my grandfather's quiet stare.

"Alfred, who's watching Wentworth's atelier?" Philippe asked.

"Maybe Lowell is just running late to replace him," my father said.

My grandfather stared at the far wall, and the length of his index finger glided in slow motion below his lip. "I'll give him until the bottom of my wine glass, and if he doesn't show up by then we'll have to check it out."

"I think we should leave now." Blake was already buttoning his shirt.

"The fewer trips we make to Wentworth's, the less we run the chance he could become suspicious. We don't want him moving his art again."

Blake nodded once to my grandfather but reached for his vest.

THE STREETS WERE empty on this side of New York at this time of night. My grandfather walked next to my father. They said things to one another I couldn't hear since they each jingled change, keys, and other odds and ends inside their pockets.

Blake and Philippe and I followed close on the short walk. Blake's and my clasped hands were tucked warmly inside of his coat pocket since spring had not yet sprung. Once the sun went down it was cold enough for coats. The stars shone bright. The lack of planes in the sky let the silence ring clear.

"I'm sorry," Blake whispered softly just behind my ear. "I know it's hard for you when I'm gone for so long. Especially here, where you're so isolated." He unhooked his hand from mine and hugged me close.

"You need to let me in more on these trips and things," I said. "I want to be a part of the plan. Not just the debriefing session."

He nodded and pulled me in tight again, this time with a kiss on my head. "I feel very strongly about keeping you safe."

One lone figure turned the corner and approached us on the otherwise empty sidewalk. His broad frame and newsboy cap lumbered forward.

"Alfred," my father called.

The man stopped abruptly, then moved toward us more quickly.

"What's going on?" my grandfather asked when Alfred's red cheeks and plaid jacket came into view.

"E's gone, sir. We looked everywhere, even crawled through a window, and nothin's outta place. 'e didn't come back from his late lunch. I do'n think 'e saw us watchin' him. Maybe, I guess."

"Who's gone?" Blake asked.

"Wentworth, sir. 'e's jus' gone."

9

A black iron, blunt-tipped fence surrounded Wentworth's atelier, but its gate that led to the sidewalk was ajar.

"I stood my shift o'er there, outta sight, just like always." He looked at the brown, cream-colored face of his watch. "'e leaves at noon or a little after for lunch. Sometimes that woman who works with 'im brings it in for 'im. But today 'e didn't leave until 2:30 and 'e hasn't been back."

We all looked at the building like it was going to replay the day's events for us.

"Could be sick," my father suggested.

"Was he carrying anything? Or did you see others carrying things for him?" my grandfather asked.

"No sir. Nothin'." Alfred crossed his arms against the cold. "'e jus' wore that black coat and the scarf around his neck."

"Cravat," Philippe said.

Alfred glared at Philippe. Apparently, he wasn't over the altercation they'd had when we first arrived.

"We need to check," Blake said. "Are the doors locked?"

"Yessir. I went in through a window on the other side," Alfred said.

We made our way around the back of the three-story building and my father retrieved a thin silver instrument with an iron-gray handle from his wallet. He held his hand steady in front of the keyhole on the backdoor and didn't move. "I can't break this lock because if the paintings are still in there, we need to keep them safe. Wentworth might just be on a brief sojourn."

He stepped away from the door and Alfred pointed toward the second-story window he'd climbed through.

"Up the trellis?" I asked.

"Yes, ma'am."

I shook the vine-covered latticework that didn't look like it would hold me, much less him. Blake stood behind me, hand on my back, while I slipped my gold, low-heeled shoe into the square opening. Step by step, I made my way to the back porch roof. It was slanted more than I realized, and slightly damp, so I stayed on all fours until I reached the window.

I raised myself to my knees and lifted the window that was unlocked, as Alfred said it would be. Though as I climbed through the window my knee slipped on the damp roof surface and I tumbled into the room.

I stood, adjusted my dress and waved outside to the small crowd of loved ones below. Excepting Alfred, there was a collective sigh of relief.

The room was full of supplies: brushes, paints, canvases. I thought of how these simple materials combined with Wentworth's gift to create the portal we had traveled through. It was, by any account, one of the most miraculous creations ever.

There were two staircases to the ground floor, a spiral

one that led to the main room, and a more standard, straightforward design that poured toward the front door. Though I wanted the spiral one, I couldn't remember the last time I'd been on a spiral staircase, so I chose the latter. The bottoms of my gold shoes were slick and wet and I didn't want to know what it felt like to hit my head on an iron step like that.

Once everyone was inside we found our way to Wentworth's main room, the same one Philippe, Blake and I fell into, at different times when we'd first arrived in the twenties. It felt much the same as I remembered it, aside from the new and distinct air of vacancy. I no longer agreed with my father's suggestion that Wentworth might just be on a short trip. He felt quite gone to me.

I touched a few different objects to get a sense of his most recent intent: a paintbrush, an empty frame, a small cart littered with paint drips. His passion for his art spoke first but only for the purpose of getting his emotions onto the canvas. He literally poured the grief from the loss of his wife and family into the painting. His energy was fitful. He was desperate for the grief leave his body.

Most curiously, though, were Wentworth's paintings. These studies for the anticipated mural were spread across the room, in order, as he had originally intended them to appear. They were still on the wall where I'd last seen them.

"Why, if he's gone, did he leave these?" I asked.

My grandfather searched behind us, I supposed to make sure that Alfred had stayed outside as had been requested. "Addie." My grandfather nodded to the paintings. "Do your thing."

I exhaled hard and readied myself to be sucked into Wentworth's world again. Though I dreaded the potential confusion of Wentworth's grief-stricken world, I welcomed the reassurance this connection would bring. Everyone needed to know they had a way home, a way to safety. My test drive here was like starting the getaway car to make sure it still ran.

My left ring finger traveled across the cool canvas of the Wentworth painting that was farthest on the left. My bottom lip flattened between my teeth and I waited for the magic to happen. Any second now, the colors would crawl up my hand, and the painting would pull me possessively into the world Wentworth had unknowingly created.

The paint didn't respond to my touch.

I wiped my hand against my dress and began again. With a different finger this time, though with the same left hand. It occurred to me that someone, as Carolena had, could have placed a sealant on it. With that in mind, I pressed the surface of the landscape repeatedly to see if a spongey protective layer had been put there for protection.

There wasn't one there. I scowled at the art.

Out of habit, I scanned the upper corners of Wentworth's atelier for cameras, a practice I had developed over the years whenever I touched art that wasn't my own. I shook my head. *No security cameras in 1922.*

"Nothing?" Blake placed his hand on my back. The usual calming influence traveled through his palm and caused me to take a deep breath. It was followed by a fierce protectiveness that nearly strangled me and caught my breath before the exhale.

I thought about how Otto's safeguarding of Carolena became something paranoid and obsessive. And I remembered Carolena's concerns that Blake was becoming more like his father. I stepped away.

One by one I went down the line of paintings and tried each one. None of them worked. None of them had sealants on them. "These aren't Wentworths. At least not the ones we traveled through. When did they first notice that Wentworth didn't leave the building at his normal lunchtime?" I asked.

My grandfather cleared his throat. "Just yesterday."

I looked at my ring watch—a new time checking habit I cultivated in the absence of my cell phone. "That's less than twenty-four hours. Who else knew about the art?"

"All of us. Otto." My father's eyes were wide and his pupils were constricted beneath his raised eyebrows. "Carolena. Those at home, Ellen, Grace, your mother. Alexa."

"Jack," I said.

Everyone turned toward me.

"Well. On our trip over, before Philippe and I exited the painting, I saw him. Wentworth was showing him the painting."

"Did he tell Jack what it could do?"

"I don't think so. Not that I could hear, anyway. But when we arrived, he was already looking at it. So, I don't know what could have been said before then."

"For years he's been moving the art to keep people from finding out his secret about what the art could do. He's not going to share that information with someone," my grandfather said.

"Maybe he had too much whiskey one night and let something slip to a friend."

"Yes, but Grace gave me a copy of Arthur Wentworth's memoir. Everything was in there—how he finished these paintings when his wife and children died, how his emotional longing for them and his intent to have them back opened a portal for him in the painting, how he went through the paintings to one year previously and prevented their deaths."

"He told everyone back then, and he circulated that

memoir to who knows how many people, though Monet was the only one to believe him. What if someone finally bought his story and decided to take the paintings for themselves?"

"Maybe," Blake said. "That doesn't explain where Wentworth is."

"He could just be vacationing. He hasn't been gone that long." My grandfather's index finger slid beneath his bottom lip. "My bigger concern is that the paintings are gone. So, either Wentworth took them with him. Which is possible, maybe he had a concern about security. Or someone else took them away from him. For what reason, we could guess."

"Were they painted by Wentworth?" Blake asked.

"I didn't look for that. I was just trying to get in." I stood in front of the middle painting and inhaled deeply to center myself. Then I placed the pads of my fingertips against a place on the canvas I'd not yet touched before. I hoped I'd see bits of Wentworth's life, or maybe I would sense a canvas on top of a canvas. Perhaps he put a mock of his original pieces on top of the authentic ones as a kind of security while he vacationed at the coast.

I found pieces of the artist's life, as well as his intent while he painted the scenes. In fact I found more than enough to know exactly who the artist was. Figuring out why he did this wasn't hard, either.

His energy wound through me like a cheap wine, nauseating me with every turn through my system. I faced the group of men and I knew they didn't want to hear what I was about to say.

"It's Otto. These forgeries are his."

10

———

Grace Montgomery put her purse on Addie's kitchen island. The tiny gold feet on the bottom of the structured bag clicked against the wood surface. This was her almost-weekly jaunt to John's condo in New York to pick up any messages her family might have sent.

She lifted the library window to let in fresh air. The dull roar and distant honks of city traffic rolled in as well. She hated the city. But this is what she had to do to get correspondence from her family.

The front door slammed.

"Limo driver was something of an ass." Fowler Grant's deep voice boomed through the foyer.

"Welcome to New York." Grace swiped a finger across the edge of the bookshelf and examined a thin layer of silvery dust on her finger. "We need to get a cleaning crew in here before we leave."

Fowler turned the kitchen faucet on. "We need more soap in here."

"Make a list. We'll have it delivered." Grace focused on

the fragile F. Scott Fitzgerald book she'd opened. There were four aged envelopes inside, each as delicate as though they were a hundred years old. Her name was written on the outside of each—two in perfect script, the next one printed, and the third one printed in all caps. Without looking inside, she knew who each of the letters was from.

The two scripted ones were from Addie, the earliest dated from late last week. She wrote to Grace as though she were away on her first trip abroad, detailing never-before-seen sights and scenes. She always included a picture or two and Grace was especially grateful for those. Addie knew how much Grace loved photos.

Thought of you today when we visited Central Park. Here's a photo of sheep grazing in—where else? The Sheep Meadow in Central Park! Hard to believe that the city was once so bucolic. Of course, that's Philippe acting silly next to the sheep there in the middle. That one actually gave him a dirty look when we left.

The next one is the two of us at the Central Park Zoo. We found someone who was willing to take our picture (after a quick camera lesson) and we didn't have to worry that they would run off with our camera. I had hoped to see the bison who was featured on the U.S. buffalo nickel. He lived here. Turns out he died some time ago.

Blake's been away for a while. Again. He still won't answer questions about where he goes. We potentially have one lead to his mother.

I appreciate your earlier advice not to worry. Though I do. Blake is obsessed with the search, which I understand. I've been there. Searching blindly for a loved one and worrying for their safety takes its toll. I don't know how he'll handle it if we aren't successful. I fear he'll be forever changed.

"Who wrote?" Fowler placed two chilled bottles of water on the coffee table.

"I got the trifecta today: Addie, John, and Campbell. Photos, too. Here. This is Central Park." Grace kept her smile more youthful than most grandmothers. She maintained white teeth and did beauty treatments to eliminate those tiny lines around her lips. But when she talked of children and grandchildren, she knew her smile beamed with the same pride and pleasure that all mothers and grandmothers had. It was just pure love.

"Look at all those sheep." Fowler clicked his tongue against the roof of his mouth and adjusted his round glasses. "Perfectly pastoral." A car horn honked just beyond the townhouse. "Not like our time." He nodded toward the letter. "What does she say?"

"She's worried about Blake, who is isolating himself in this search." Grace read Blake psychically, her eyes squinted, her vision softened. "He's put the whole world on his shoulders, insistent to solve these problems himself. That never works out well."

He took a long sip of water. "That's controlling. Not helpful."

"His father used to do the same thing. Before the theft, before he changed into who he is today. He was a wonderful protector to Carolena and Blake. Even to his first family, it was admirable how he took care of everyone."

Fowler patted the empty seat next to him and handed Grace her water.

"What's wrong with that picture frame?" Grace lifted one of the many photos of family she had framed and placed on the library shelves. She'd brought the photos from Savannah, so she would feel at home. Some of the frames she had found in the townhouse, a few others she picked up at a local gift shop.

One of her favorite photos was the one she had taken

when Lexie, Addie, and Blake first arrived in Savannah. Grace snapped their photo on the front porch and sent a copy to John and Campbell. It turned out so well, she framed one for herself.

"It's fogged." She rubbed the glass with the front hem of her shirt but the smoky glass remained. "Cheap frame. I'll get a new one."

She angled the frame and examined Blake's face. "Anyway, Otto changed. All that positive protecting became something else. There is a shadow side to every personality, and Otto's darker side is quite black."

"You think Blake is following in his father's footsteps?"

She replaced the frame and the metal clinked against the wood. "He already does. The question is how far he will he take it."

"As men, most of us are genetically predisposed to protecting and providing for those we love."

"Control is highly overrated."

"Hardest lesson for a man to learn."

"He'll lose Addie if he doesn't. Same as Otto lost Carolena."

11

Blake threw something across the room.

Philippe paced and muttered something I couldn't hear. My dad and grandad argued with one another.

I went back to work.

Otto couldn't have taken Arthur Wentworth's mural studies just to keep us here. He *was* the king of revenge and chief tie-er of loose ends, I'd give him that. Even so, if he had a Wentworth or three in his possession, that had to mean that he was going to do something with them. Not just leave us stranded.

I let my four left fingers travel over the hills of painted shapes. My senses were focused and perked to listen for messages inadvertently left on the canvas by the artist. Or rather by the forger.

I moved my fingers in the direction of his brush strokes, some of them swirling down and to the left, others circling to the right. All the movements were filled with dreams of a happy life that he and Carolena would share.

Sometimes they relaxed on a beach, Carolena's black

bathing suit stretched low over her thighs, matching the turban wrapped around her hair. Other times they danced the mambo that was accented by her below-the-knee red dress.

Memories of Otto and Carolena and Blake together when he was just a young boy. Otto threw an underhanded toss to the sweet child who swung with his oversized bat, his eyes and mouth flew open with surprised joy when he made contact. Carolena jumped up and down, clapped and screamed for him to run the bases.

"Are you sure you read that correctly? What about the other paintings? You haven't even looked at those, yet," Blake said.

His voice didn't fit with the scene I read and my senses tugged me into two different directions. When I read an object or a painting, I was completely open to whatever came through—scenes, voices, scents, anything and every-thing. Something within me knew, however, that this voice didn't fit with what I touched. I was tugged from my place in this proverbial theater and thoroughly annoyed at the inter-ruption.

"Addie, you ought to check it again," Blake said.

I opened my eyes and found Blake standing unreason-ably close, such that his face was almost out of focus to me. "What are you doing?"

"Just read it again for me. I want to make sure these are Otto's forgeries." His eyes were focused in that mastermind control mode I'd seen too many times over the past couple of years.

"Are you *kidding*?"

He had always trusted my readings implicitly. Lately, though, he didn't trust anyone's information where this search was concerned. Therefore, he had apparently become an expert in matters he knew nothing about.

"Then do *you* want to do this?"

He rubbed his nose with his index finger and thumb. His lips pressed so tightly together I knew his teeth had to be ground against one another.

"If you want me to do this, then you need to let me do it. I need some space." I put my hand on his chest and pushed him back a step, gently but firmly. "And don't interrupt me when I'm in the middle of a reading. It breaks my concentration and its hard for me to get back into it."

"I'm just trying to help." His voice was low in what was now an otherwise quiet room. His energy was steeled with that no-one-can-do-it-better-than-I-can demeanor, which left no room for me.

"No, you're trying to control the process, and that's the opposite of helping. If you want me to do this, then you need to let me do this." I'd lowered my voice to an angry whisper. But when I glanced over my shoulder it was obvious that our conversation wasn't private. My father and grandfather had walked to the other side of the room and looked out the front window. Philippe leaned against the edge of a tall bookcase with his arms crossed. He looked away when our eyes met, but his awkward turn made it clear he had heard us.

"Would you just check again?"

"Blake. Before you interrupted, I was watching a home movie that the artist of this painting was remembering while he painted. You were about three or four, wearing a white baseball cap with blue pinstripes and a navy-blue bill. Your plastic bat had an oversized barrel to increase your chances of hitting the ball. Otto pitched to you, Carolena cheered like a madwoman when you hit the ball. You pounded each base with a double-footed jump. Where y'all were playing, I don't know because you—"

"Central Park. It was Central Park every Sunday for baseball and ice cream." His energy remained solid and characteristically unyielding, although I sensed a distant sadness I well understood. It was the mark left from the childhood loss of a loved one. "He told his other family he was at the office on Sundays." Blake gave Philippe a fleeting look. "So he could spend it with us. It was our one full day together."

Otto would have left within a couple of years of that memory. A remembrance that was beloved by more than just one person. The rest of Blake's childhood was spent without his father, and to date he lived his life trying to protect his family from him.

I took a deep breath, the word *sorry* not quite the word I was looking for. If I had used that word, I wasn't sure who deserved it more. Philippe for having to endure a childhood with Otto as his father, or Blake for growing up without one.

"My point is just that I don't think Wentworth would have that information about you and your...parents. I will look at the other two paintings, though I doubt they will be any different than this one. My experience with Otto is that he isn't someone who typically walks away from money. If he took one painting, he probably took them all."

I glimpsed the other two paintings out of the corner of my eye and exhaled hard. It would take a while before I was calm and centered enough to read the rest of them.

SOME TIME later we embarked on a silent and somber walk to the gallery. We decided that Otto must have pushed Wentworth to leave his atelier for a while. No one could be sure for how long. We assumed he would return at some point.

Once we arrived we sat on the couches and cushioned chairs in the gallery and drank red wine to soak and soothe our heavy disappointment.

At one time we had been visitors. Now we were captives.

Our delicately balanced lives had just shifted beyond our control.

John and Campbell were the least surprised, and though disappointed, not too dramatically upset. They'd been stranded a long time ago.

Blake was the most distraught. Otto had beat him to the punch. They were competing for the same prize once again. Last time, it was me. This time, it was Carolena. Blake was well aware he'd lost this round.

Memories that I'd seen in forgeries continued to dance in my mind. Something was off. Some little thing nagged at me for my attention.

"Cookie?" Philippe offered a plate of oatmeal cookies in my direction. His dimples creased when his smile appeared. He reminded me of a young Marlon Brando, when he was young and handsome and could do no wrong. "Mary made them earlier today."

"Oh my gosh. That's it."

"What's it?" He stood upright with the plate still in his hand.

"The painting. It didn't just hold Otto's memories."

Blake drank a long sip of wine. "What do you mean?"

"Well, there were his memories of when you were a boy. But then there were these other scenes with Carolena and him. Something struck me odd about it when I read it—anyway, I just figured it out. Those scenes—one where she's on the beach, another where they were dancing. Her clothes, they weren't a 1920s style or even a current day style. The bathing suit was more of a 1930s fit. And the dance scene, her dress, 1940s, I think."

"I don't understand," Philippe said.

"Those aren't memories. He's planning for the future."

"He's going to take her through time." Blake stared at the floor and I could almost hear the sick thud of his hopes hitting the ground.

The service door opened and I sat stick straight. Who could be walking in—Jack, Otto?

"Ruth, honey. Come in." My grandfather rose from his roost on the Louis XV style armchair.

A young woman with long, brown hair combed far to the side and held together in a loose braid, stood at the back of the gallery. "I'm sorry to intrude." Her voice was soft and feminine, almost delicate. A boy with brown hair and blue eyes held her hand at her side.

"Ruth?" My father placed his wine glass on the coffee table. "Is everything okay?"

She waited until he was close and her whisper softened even further. "He's warm. I want a doctor to look at him."

"I'll go with you." My father grabbed his coat.

She stared at the rest of us with wide-set, doll-like eyes that were so perfect they appeared unreal.

"Is everything okay?" I walked toward them.

"I'll see everyone tomorrow." He ushered Ruth and the boy out the door.

12

Blake and I sat next to one another in the library of the condo. Side by side, and only inches apart, but I could barely sense him next to me. He studied his notebook. His attention and energy were so completely focused on something else—like he was someone else—and it was as if he wasn't even in the room with me.

I'd had one too many glasses of red wine before we left the gallery. I was now tired and my world spun a little. Our way home was gone, right out from under our noses. I might have also felt nervous about Blake walking me home. It was hard to know if he would be the Blake I fell in love with...or the man he had become.

Otto figured out how to strand us here. Even more concerning was the fact that I'd seen how he wanted to take Carolena through time. Once he left this era with her, we would never find them or any of the Wentworths he took, either. There was no telling where he would have hidden them.

Ruth. Who was Ruth? My grandfather said it was a neighbor lady, a single mother who my father helped to watch out for. I wasn't sure that was the full story. I thought I picked up on a softer, more romantic connection between her and my dad.

I reached for Blake. Tried to connect with him the way we always had. The way we *always had*. My mind flooded with the citrusy scent of Jack's skin, his possessive touch, the understated, velvety wave in his voice.

I knew what Blake seemed unwilling to entertain—that we may never find Carolena. It was possible that she didn't want to be found. This wouldn't be the first case of a woman, a mother, making a decision to protect her child. If she didn't want us to find her, I doubted that we would.

I pushed my fingers over his chest and through the curl of his hair. My hand skimmed over tightly wound bandages.

Prior to our few homecoming moments at the office today, we hadn't spent much time together. I missed him. I missed what we had.

He's put you last. Philippe's voice echoed through my mind.

I shook my head and stifled the stabbing sensation in my chest.

It wasn't just that he'd put me last. He had pushed me to the outside. We were here as a team. We'd agreed to stay here and work together to find his mother, and then to get my family home. But he had gone rogue with the agreement.

Now there was this palpable distance between us. I reached for him, trying to rekindle what we had. What I believed was still there. Somewhere.

Blake didn't respond.

Moonlight streamed in the dark night and just beyond the window. The city was quiet at this time of night, at least around our area. The warm honeyed scent of Blake's skin surrounded him like an aura. He continued to stare at his notebook.

"Are your ribs okay?"

In the luminescent glow of our night, his chest rose and fell with a deep breath.

"Manageable." His words were thick and heavy with fatigue. "How about yours?" Distractedly he kissed the top of my head.

I smiled and rolled into the carefree feeling of what it had often been like between us, into the connection we'd always shared. I could feel the ends of the threads of us there, detached and wiggling in a wind of uncertainty. If only I could find a way for us to weave it forward again.

"Are you tired?"

"No." He stayed focused on his notebook, and trailed his fingers along my cheek.

Then, he kissed me and tangled his fingers in my hair.

He loved me.

He went back to his notebook.

There was also that something else. It might not have been a missing part, though it was definitely a—something else. Something heavy and dense between us—a wall, a block. A dead end. My heart sank and I turned away from him.

"Come to me, Sassy." Blake put his notebook down and pulled me closer. "You're thinking too much."

He teased and sucked at my neck, leaving what I knew would be a small red brand in his wake.

The fear of us ending seemed silly now, with the feel of his love all around me. Our connection was as it had always been—strong enough to shut out the rest of the world, powerful enough to nearly consume me.

I knew our connection tonight would cross over into the sunlit days and close the gap between us.

But my mind was surprisingly giddy with thoughts of Jack, how he was Blake and how I'd finally recaptured the essence of our love for one another again.

~

In the 1920s, I slept. Hard. Once my eyes closed for the evening I didn't move until morning.

A little girl I'd never seen before had danced through my dreams. We sat together on a red plaid picnic blanket spread on the grassy banks of Grace's oceanfront property. We drank lemonade and played go fish and when I kissed her blond head she smelled of sweet cherry muffins and butter-cream icing. I missed her. Strangely so.

My alarm clock rang like a fire alarm and scared the wits out of me.

The dream disappeared.

I did miss those subtle chimes I could play through my phone as an alarm.

I stared out the dimly lit bedroom window that I'd woken up to so many times before in the current day. Only now I saw it as it was 100 years earlier. Grandpa and Dad agreed that Blake and I ought to share the condo. It was paid for and it was the easiest solution for the two of us. Plus, family needed to be here to protect the Fitzgerald book that transported messages from home.

I thought of Blake, how he was in the guest room now and how our last twenty-four hours had gone. I'd almost felt that full reconnect with him last night. Maybe it had been there. Though I couldn't be certain that it wasn't a wish or a memory. I'd had just a little too much wine before we came home, and when I reached for him I wasn't completely sober. Not drunk, just not perfectly in tune with my finest senses. At that moment, Jack was there. Though it was the feel of Blake's energy and his love that coursed through me.

I fortified myself before I faced Blake. If the distance was still there, my mind would race with more worries as to what this meant. I didn't want to face any potential realities of that right now. Not before coffee. Not ever.

From the moment I'd met Blake he'd been responsive, protective, and kind. Loving, in a way I'd not experienced before. In this life, anyway. I'd have to say that I'd grown accustomed to that quality. Being first in his life, sharing the love-of-my-life connection we'd always had. I could say it spoiled me. Though it was really more accurate to say that it strengthened me. Being loved like that, so completely, it changed me. A love that profound heals wounds and unfulfilled needs that I didn't even know I had. Neither is it something I could go back from. That kind of love was my standard.

Now, being on the outside of his bullseye focus wasn't something I'd ever get used to. He'd have to let me in. We had to find a way forward as a team.

My heart banged in my chest at that annoying feeling that he might have pulled the rug out from under me. If he'd left again and without letting me know where he was going, I would strangle him.

I cursed into the first two empty rooms I visited, and also at the cold meal remnants on his breakfast plate, which I found on the kitchen counter. There was a noise, like paper shuffling, and I walked into the library. He sat in pajama pants and bandages with coffee and a dozen index cards in front of him. Streams of early sunlight cast across the room and highlighted his work. I exhaled strong enough that I thought I might blow the curtains on the other side of the room.

"What are you doing?" I gestured to the lines of index cards in front of us.

"Organizing our next steps." He patted the cards with his left hand, while his right hand glided up the back of my leg. "Everything all right?"

"Yeah, I was just worried that you were gone again."

His blue eyes were clear and cool and never wavered. "I'm sorry about that. I'd tell you where I was if I could."

I lowered myself to the place next to him on the couch. It was an apology and I knew what he said was true, he didn't want to worry me. Nonetheless, I could see that he would do this again. He would just take off, maybe in the middle of the night, and I wouldn't know when I would hear from him again.

"It does worry me not to know where you are or when you'll be back, if you're hurt or if you need help. I don't think you could handle it if I did this to you." I grabbed the crocheted blanket from the back of the couch and wrapped it around me.

He tucked a lock of hair behind my ear. "No. I probably couldn't."

"So, you need to let me in on your plans."

His smile was loving and slightly amused, and the backs of his fingers caressed the outline of my jaw. I noticed he didn't offer any agreement. "Blake."

"I can't, Sassy. I never know what's going to happen when I'm with these people and I won't put you in a position where you might get hurt."

There were no traffic noises from the other side of the slightly open library window, just a menagerie of songs from small birds who celebrated the arrival of the morning. Then I noticed something else—the quick pace of my breath. I heard it before I felt it. Blake was here in body, but energetically he was gone again. Mentally, emotionally, he was somewhere else.

He's put you last.

"I hope you understand that. I'm just protecting you."

You can't go on like this.

"Look. I don't necessarily need to be in the middle of a fist fight." I pointed to his ribs. "But I do feel very much like I'm on the outside of the plan and the approach. We're in this together, you know."

"You're right. Let's talk about what I'm thinking here." He squared his body with the cards. I knew as soon as he had them organized the way he wanted them, he'd paste them into his black notebook. Then he'd be relentless about following his plan.

He pointed to the individual rows of cards. "Here. I've done some research on ocean liners, places to investigate in Paris, as well as some things you all can do here while I'm gone."

I shot up like a jack-in-the-box, motivated by enough anger to make my head swoon. "You are not serious."

He looked at the cards and then to me again. "About what?"

I shook my head with a small laugh and went for my robe, and a cup of coffee. My lips stayed sealed just tightly enough to hold back the tirade I wanted to unleash. They opened long enough to take a few sips of coffee, then I pressed them tightly together again.

My plan was not to have this discussion with him until I was fully caffeinated. Blake wasn't a man easily convinced to change his mind.

He stepped into the kitchen, lowered his coffee cup and it rattled against the narrow, porcelain counter.

We stared at one another and I decided I would give him another thirty seconds to tell me he'd changed his plans before I began.

"Addie, it's safer if you stay here. If we know or at least think that Otto is in Paris, then I'd feel a whole lot better if you were as far away from him as possible."

Of course, he didn't move in that direction. "You don't know that I'm safer here. And you wouldn't even have all the details for this lead without me."

"Any amount of distance from Otto is the safer option."

"Blake. You're— You can't—" I waved my arm as if it could make my point, then I gave up and growled in frustration. "You're not reading the situation objectively to determine what the right next steps are. You're just pushing me into a proverbial ivory tower while you take off to save the day."

"This is common sense."

"No. Actually, it's arrogance. And...frankly, a little stupidity."

Blake ran his hand through his hair for the tenth time this morning. "That's a fine thank-you."

"A thank-you for what, exactly?"

Maybe it was because the Wentworths were gone, but our existence here had taken on a feeling of stale, sticky permanence. Before they disappeared, we were tourists, visitors in a land not quite our own. We had the freedom to come and go if we chose to do so. Now we were stuck.

That endless feeling of forever was gone now that he was home from his most recent trip. Our relationship seemed to have morphed into something tight and more restrictive. Ill-fitting.

He pointed his finger in my direction. "You're not going to Paris." His eyes were so focused and fierce I half expected flames to shoot out and hit me in the face.

He waved his hand in a that's-it motion. "You're not going." He left the room and shut the bathroom door behind him.

13

Blake leaned against the sink and gripped the cold porcelain with both hands. Anger pumped so hot and furious through his veins he thought his chest would explode. He needed to calm down. He also knew he didn't have a shot of getting anywhere near calm.

Addie was going to push him on this. Had this been two years ago and if they'd been home, she would have responded differently. He would have said, "I have to take care of Otto," and she would have said, "Be careful. Carry a gun." That would have been it. She wouldn't have wanted any part of him. She would have been too afraid of Otto to get involved.

But here? She was different here. The only way he could keep her out of the fray was to keep everything from her—where he was, who he was with, what the leads were. It ticked her off, he knew. There wasn't any other way.

He glanced in the mirror. His features were drawn and tight. He hardly recognized himself. He could *feel* the difference, too. Something had shifted inside of him. Something was missing. He felt strangely alone and angry. Not the kind of angry that would fade after a while. It was more like a fast-growing vine that wound itself around its host and eventually strangled the life out of it. None of it made sense to him.

Sarah's image popped in his mind, sitting there behind the warehouse as he had seen her, blowing smoke into the night. He watched her turn toward him in his mind's eye, as she had done only hours ago, and his heart leaped and skipped a beat mid-air.

Then Gary walked into the scene like a direct hit and his heart raged like a bear who stalked its hunter. "That's what this is," he said to his reflection. *Leftover past-life feelings.* Being so close to the life that was about to be so easily snuffed out by that—, it was bringing things up for him. Control issues, yes, that was a real thing. Carolena had long warned him about them. *They're not a strength* she'd said. "Yeah, but they could be effective," he said aloud.

He splashed cold water on his face, then leaned on the sink again and stared at himself. That's what this was from. Seeing Sarah. Some part of his soul remembered what it was like to lose her and to have a brilliant future with her ripped right out of his heart.

He needed to get a grip on himself. He couldn't take that out on Addie. It wasn't her fault. No, she wasn't going to Paris with him. But from now on...he leaned in close to his reflection. *You need to be the person she fell in love with.*

Beads of sweat had bloomed on his upper lip and he wiped it with the back of his thumb.

The bathroom door swung open so fast and hard that it hit the tile on the opposite wall. "I know you weren't talking to me when you said I wasn't going to Paris."

He exhaled hard. He could barely see her reflection in the fog-covered mirror. "I meant what I said. You can't go."

"I *can't* go. Seriously?"

"Seriously." Blake met her eye to eye. "Do not push me on this."

"Just so you know? I'm going to push you on this. Who do you think you are trying to handle this all on your own? Or is this men's work, Blake? Are you only taking the men? Leaving the womenfolk at home?" She said it sweetly, warmly, and that made Blake nervous. Calm tone and sarcastic words were never good indicators when they traveled together.

"That's not necessary."

Her nostrils flared just slightly and he knew her anger just ratcheted up a notch.

"You don't make decisions for me. *I* make decisions for me. And *I* say that I'm going. My family's future depends on finding Otto and those paintings. Besides, you need me with you. We're better as a team."

He took a deliberate moment to make sure his voice was calm so that she wouldn't resist him. He needed her to be safe. "What I need is for you to stay here and out of harm's way."

"Out of harm's way." She said each word distinctly though her chest was heaving. "Since when did you become my caretaker?"

"Since when did caring for your safety become a problem?" Blake shook his head. He dropped his boxers to the floor and stepped into the running shower.

"Since it gave you a reason to shut me out."

"Shut you out? You are one of the two most important reasons I do any of this. How do I shut you out?" He knew the answer to that question before he asked it. He did shut her out.

She half-sighed as if some of the wind had left her sails

and he thought he might be winning this argument. Having Addie stay home and far away from Otto would give him one less thing to worry about while he was in Paris.

With her around, all of his usual worries for her were a distraction. Was she safe, was she happy, was some energetic influence too psychically overwhelming for her? His list of concerns for her was endless, but the first two categories covered nearly all of them.

She pressed the tip of her index finger to make her first point and he realized he wasn't winning at all.

"One, you shut me out energetically. You do everything in your power to keep me from reading you. Just when I get close enough to sense the tiniest bit about you, you have some weird ability to turn yourself into a cement block and I can't read a thing.

"Two," she lifted her next finger. "You shut me out emotionally. The only time you let me in—really let me in to be close to you, is when you hold me. Even then there's no guarantee.

"Three, you take off without letting me know where you're going or when you'll be back.

"Four—"

"All right!" His voice was loud and razor-sharp and the short echo in the nearly all-tile room made her jump.

It was the first time he had ever raised his voice to her and something in his chest cracked. *Way to go. You've already broken the promise you made to yourself not two minutes ago.*

"I'm sorry." He reached to her to soothe whatever part of her he'd bruised. Her eyes turned hard, her jaw was set to firm and he pulled away.

He ran a strong hand over his face, water dripped from his every angle. "All right." His voice was a bare whisper now.

They faced one another in the watery silence. Neither one of them moved, their eyes locked hard enough on the other that he could feel her against him.

Blake extended his hand again.

She shook her head. From the expression on her face it appeared as though something had just left her, fallen right out from the center of her.

"Come here." His upward nod was slight. "I'm sorry."

She held steady where she was and resisted. Out of frustration he wound himself up to push, as was his habit when someone didn't do something important the way he wanted them to. He powered up his intent and was ready to dive in, to bend her will and make her come to him. He stopped just shy of following through.

He'd promised her long ago that he'd never push her. Besides, he wanted her to come to him because *she* wanted to. Not because he could make her do it.

"I'm not shutting you out now, Sassy." He offered his hand once again.

She closed her eyes briefly and shook her head just slowly enough that it said she knew better.

His heart pounded in a savage panic. They faced one another, silent. The shower water splashed into the puddle that was gathering in the bottom of the tub.

He ached with enough tenderness from wanting her that he knew her touch would probably slice him open. "Please?"

"No." She left the room and his heart thudded in his chest more slowly now, wrenching itself into what he thought might be a near stop.

~

THEY SAT in the library and on opposite ends of the small couch. Addie's arms were securely crossed in front of her. Blake was freshly showered and hoping to try again. She was understandably hardened and highly suspicious of him. He pressed his thumb up the arch of her foot, a movement that usually elicited a smile from her.

She pulled her foot away and tucked it beneath her. The anger had left her eyes but was replaced now with something far more deadly, in his opinion.

"What's going on with you?" Her lips were slightly pursed and pressed together in a hard-edged disapproval he'd never felt from her.

"I know—" He crossed his arms in front of him. He was going to tell her about seeing Sarah and Gary and how that affected him. But all that came out was, *I know*. He sighed with frustration at himself. He'd try a different approach.

"What do you need?" As soon as the words left his lips he regretted it. He meant to sound gracious, as in, he'd give her whatever she needed, whatever she wanted from him. Instead, it sounded discounting. Like a *what do you need to get over this so we can move on?* sort of thing. This wasn't her fault, but he was doing a good job of making her feel that it was.

A tiny breath of frustration blew across her lips. Her disapproval sank now into a glare of sincere disappointment that clenched his stomach.

"What do I *need*?"

"That's not what I meant." He closed his eyes and wished he could pick up the needle and move it back to the beginning of this morning. He'd handle it all differently.

"I never thought I'd hear that from you."

"It's not what I meant." His voice was low and soft. He searched her eyes for a place to connect with her, but all he found was an icy landing. "I'm sorry—" He reached out to her but she popped off the couch.

"Here's what I need from you."

He sighed hard, any hopes of her doing what he wanted, left.

"I need you to be honest with me. I need you to trust me and let me in. Because my entire world is built around you right now. Nearly every decision I've made for my life in the past few years has been based on the idea that you and I had a future together." He could sense the part of her that was breaking, and it threatened to break something within him, too.

"I'm alone here. I've risked everything for you and you're nowhere to be found."

"I'm here." He reached for her again, only to see her take a step away.

"You know what I mean. Physically you're here. Sometimes. But mentally and emotionally? You're absent. There's no real connection between us. Please tell me what a relationship is without an emotional connection. Not an occasional connection. But a day-in-day-out-deliberately-open-with-the-one-you-love kind of emotional connection that makes life worth living. Where is a relationship without that? It's nowhere." Her voice had become a third person in the room, saying all the things that hadn't been said before, all the things she probably hoped she wouldn't have to say.

"Okay. I know what you mean. And, again, I'm sorry. I've messed up. I know it. I've been away too much and for too long. I've been absent in other ways. It's just this search, it's owned me. We've not had any success with it. Except for this one lead and it's a year-old stale lead. I've been worrying about everything and everyone. Carolena, what she's given up, what she's putting herself through. What the rest of her life is going to look like if I don't find her."

Her gaze drifted outside the window. "The search. It's always the search. The reason for everything these days. It's been two years, Blake. I don't want to see her with Otto any more than you do. The bottom line is that she's a grown woman. She's old enough to make her own choices in life."

"This wasn't really a choice for her."

"It *was* her choice. That's my point. Without her choice, Philippe and I would probably be dead." She took a calming breath. "I'm sorry that she's with Otto, I am. I'm sorry that she's not back in her own time, living a life of freedom and leisure. But this was her choice, and honestly, if she doesn't want us to find her? We won't," she said reluctantly.

His heart sagged with weighted guilt that his worst nightmare might come true. "It's my fault. I should have known something was up at that hotel. If I'd been a second quicker to shoot, I could have gotten him."

"Seems like I remember you telling me that Otto was the one to blame for all of this. Not anyone else." She redirected her gaze back to him, and her eyes were soft now. The love he'd always known from her was back in the room.

"Yeah, well. He has a way of making everyone feel like a moron, I guess."

She lowered her head and laughed, just as she did once he convinced her to have lunch with him on that first time they'd met at the firm. It was the same genuine laugh she couldn't hold back that day and he'd known right away he had a special way with her.

But this time the laughter just wouldn't stop. Stress, he supposed. It was all spilling over in an unstoppable burst of silliness.

When she inhaled she accidentally snort-laughed and

now the silliness was game-on contagious. It got to the point where he red-faced howled with her, and though he didn't expect it, the weight of his guilt fell from his chest. He breathed with an ease he hadn't felt in years.

They both fell to the floor. She kicked her legs in the air and rolled to the side, her body shook in spasms of quiet laughter. He laid on his back, not even trying to stop the laughs. Not that he could have, anyway. He let it run its own course until he realized the room had gone quiet.

With a few more chuckles he rolled her toward him, her body still shaking with silent giggles. Her hands covered her face and she leaned into his chest. He rubbed his thumb along her back. Her breathing pattern was off.

"Addie?" He angled his head and pulled her hands away from her face. Her laughter had turned to tears.

"What's wrong?"

"I thought you were gone," she cried.

"When?" He wasn't sure if he ought to sit up to see her face-to face or lie still and hold her. He tried to sit up but she didn't move with him, so he just held her close.

"Today. Yesterday. Every time you leave, and every knock on the door. I just know it's a policeman coming to show me a picture of your dead body and to ask me if I knew you."

His heart was heavy and thumping and chastising him privately for putting her through this. "I'm sorry." He felt her body lose strength. She didn't relax—it was more of a letting go, like a collapse. "I'm so sorry."

"I just knew we were over. I couldn't feel that you loved me anymore. I'd forgotten what it was even like to feel that from you until Jack kissed me. I can feel the affection everyone else has for me. Except yours."

Jack kissed me.

A sharp pang of jealousy twisted in his chest when she said it. It was followed by a deep ache that he'd hurt her.

"I'm going to work really hard to make sure this doesn't happen again. Okay? I always want you to know how much I love you." He held her close to him and did the one thing he knew she needed most.

It wasn't a push, exactly, though it did force a connection of sorts. It was more of a gift, a genuine one, from his heart to hers. He closed his eyes and simply loved her with all that he had.

Her breathing calmed. She inhaled slow and deep as if she were drawing his love into her. She rolled toward him, her reddened eyes met his. "Like that." She smiled like she'd just inhaled a drug. "Please. Always. Like that."

For her, he knew, that experience of feeling how much he loved her was far better than just hearing him say it.

They held one another on the floor of the library, her head nuzzled against his bare chest, her thigh slung over his. He kept his heart open to her, to give her what she needed.

He still compartmentalized. It came naturally with his ability to push. He simply hid any thoughts and feelings from view that didn't match his intent. That's how he managed to hide his concerns and why she often couldn't read him.

In that private place of his mind that only he could see, he visited the concerns and worries that were layered on top of one another. Addie's stubbornness about accompanying him to Paris, the change in their relationship with one another, the anger that threatened to consume him. There was also the fact that their only path home was gone. Stolen. And Otto was planning to take Carolena to some other place in time.

Belle Epoch, maybe. Jumping backward offered more glamorous options. If they jumped forward he would have to avoid World War II and the The Great Depression. Beyond that, Blake wasn't sure where they would go. It was all part of the reason he didn't want Addie to go to Paris.

If Otto caught them, he would be only too happy to take her away from him. And this time, Addie would be lost to him forever.

14

They were half-way through their first bottle of wine. It was the first lazy Saturday they had shared in some months, and Blake knew they needed it.

She leaned against him, and he put his arm around her. "So, you're going. To Paris."

She looked up at him. "Yes." She studied his face. For a reaction, most likely. "I think you've spent enough time trying to do things on your own. We need to deal with this together."

He sipped his wine and chose not to tell her that he preferred handling things like this on his own. She liked the team approach. At any family meeting, her confidence in everyone was evident on her face. While Blake saw them as the backup team. It was quicker for him to function alone, more efficient.

"We'll have to talk with everyone else to see who wants to go."

He nearly choked on his wine. "Addie. As soon as Otto knows we're in Paris—assuming he's still there—he'll leave.

He'll move her, and then it might be another two years before we get a lead. If ever. We can't have the entire group wandering around the city."

"I don't know why you want to shut out their support—they want to help you. They know this era, they know the art community."

"I'm not much of a decision-by-committee type of person."

Her shoulders drooped slightly.

"It's a lot to coordinate. I think more strategically when I only have to plan for myself. It's nothing against your family."

"I didn't take it that way."

Though he thought she might have.

"What about all those years that you planned for Carolena, your sister, and her son?"

"They didn't ask for any starring roles in the play. They were happy to be hidden away, or at least to be anonymous."

"I see." She chilled slightly.

"I'm not saying you shouldn't go, but tell me why it's important to you to go."

"Because I have a lot at stake here, too. Because I love you. Because we're supposed to be a team. Not an order-giver and an order-taker." She dragged her tongue across her lips. "You know, sometimes it seems as though...you think you're smarter than everyone around you."

Blake sipped his wine because he found he couldn't look her in the eye. He'd been accused of this trait before. Arrogance, his mother and sister had called it. Come to think of it, Addie called him that earlier in the day.

"Sometimes, I am the one in the room who thinks more strategically, who has a better idea. Not always, but some-times." He was careful how he lobbed that out there. His mother and sister had worked hard to rid him of that better-than quality, though not entirely successfully. As the only male in the house, he had stepped into that protector role early in life and he took the job seriously.

He preferred to think of this trait as self-confidence or even a type of intelligence. "So you're saying that's why I don't like to work in teams?"

"I'm saying that's why you like to be the one in charge."

"I'm always open to a better idea."

"Mmm. Well. I just think you might find a better solution or overall answer to the problem if you were more willing to involve other people and their ideas in the process."

"I haven't been doing this search alone."

"Fairly alone. And pretty secretively. I think we've been through that." Her left eyebrow raised and her lips pursed in a please-test-me-on-that kind of expression.

Blake chose, wisely he thought, not to meet her challenge on that point. "So, how would you recommend we approach this lead? Notice I said *we*." He ran a finger along her jawline.

"Yes, I noticed." Her side glance and half-smile combination told him he wasn't getting away with anything today.

"I think you need to talk with my entire family and Philippe about their ideas on this lead and how best to find Otto. When you put us all in one room together, that's several lifetimes' worth of experience with regard to Otto."

He couldn't argue with that. Strangely. "Okay. I'll go with that." He had to admit that there were elements of this new Addie he liked—the spunk, the determination. It had all been there before, certainly. Just a bit unproven. Beaten down.

In the twenties, these qualities had found new life and

he found it attractive. He also found it slightly dangerous and scary when she pushed her into areas where he couldn't protect her. But he had to admit it. He liked this new strength.

"You're going to have to let Philippe decide for himself if he wants to go to Paris," she said.

His smile fell. "No."

"Because Otto is his father, too."

"I've agreed to take you, but I'm not taking him."

"You can't make that decision for him."

"I just did."

She didn't roll her eyes but she sighed loud enough that her frustration was evident. "No more than he could make this decision for you. I'm just saying that whatever it is, he's going to have his own opinion on this and you'll have to be open to it."

He rested his hands on his hips. "This is not a democracy. I'm here to do what I have to do to protect you and find my mother. I'll listen to his ideas, but if I don't agree with them, he's not tagging along." He brushed his fingertips along the side of her arm, an easy touch, but timed so that he reminded God and everyone that she was his. Something he felt compelled to do whenever the topic of Philippe came up.

Her lips parted and closed. She tilted her head one way and then the other, as though she were having a private argument with herself. "Y'all can work it out."

He led her into the kitchen. He didn't want to discuss anything relating to Philippe anymore. "Anything else we have to be serious about?" He lit the fire beneath the tea kettle.

"Yes. One very important thing. We need to come to

some sort of consensus about what to do with Otto when we find him."

"Right." Blake leaned on the counter. A sick feeling churned through his stomach. He'd thought through this question since he'd arrived in the twenties and he hadn't yet landed on a confident answer. "We can't leave him here, or he'll find a way to mess up our lives in the present day if we do."

"Agreed." She picked at a tiny fleck of something on the kitchen counter. "I think a French prison is a viable option. No one escapes from those places and the French are happy to imprison anybody for anything."

"Assuming we could get him into any prison, there is the potential he could escape or bribe someone for his release or they could let him out for no good reason." He'd been over this problem a million and ten times. He could easily define every angle of the challenge.

"I think we have to transport him home and get him to the FBI."

"Too many things could go wrong in a Wentworth painting. If Otto got loose in the space between here and the present, he would be forever lost in time, wreaking havoc wherever he landed. Plus, they don't have any proof to hold him back home."

"We can't leave him in the past."

The kettle whistled and Blake lifted it off the eye. "We're both thinking the same thing. Otto has to die." He knew that both he and Addie had wanted to kill Otto several times over the last few years. But every time he arrived at that answer as a solution to the current problem, it made his heart thump hard against his chest. "It's the price that has to be paid for our freedom."

She paused, her expression troubled. Her fingers loosely

covered her lips. "You can't kill your own father," she finally said.

"If it's what I have to do to help you and Carolena, then I'll do it."

She bit her lip."I don't know if anyone ever really recovers from killing their own parent. I have to wonder if this is what Carolena has tried to protect you from."

"Maybe. There isn't another option, though." He poured the hot water over two strainers of loose tea and thought it chilling that they discussed murder over tea. He placed her cup and saucer in front of her, and she whispered a quiet thank-you from behind the hand that covered her lips.

She dragged the saucer closer with her index finger and thumb. She turned the cup until the handle was perfectly pointing toward her right side. "Resigned to this solution, or not, I think, that if you do this, it will leave a life-long mark on your soul you'll never fully escape."

Blake sighed long and loud. Discussing this made him feel as though his protective layer of skin had been stripped away. He felt vulnerable, young.

"He's an evil man. He'll never change and the world is better off without him." He couldn't count the number of times he'd rehearsed those reasons in an effort to convince himself that they were justification enough. "I agree with you that it's probably some hard to erase karma if you kill your own father. I'd sleep better at night if he were rotting away in a medieval prison somewhere, than if I had to kill him. I'll give you that."

She stared at him with wide blue eyes that saw too much. "But we're planning it ahead of time. That's not just doing what you have to do in the moment to protect your family. This is premeditated homicide. Patricide."

And the grandfather of any children Blake would father

—he'd thought of this, too. He ran his hand through his hair and gripped it tight. That would make for a grand Christmas morning, wouldn't it? *Why don't we have two grandfathers who visit on Christmas like other families, Daddy? Oh, that's because I killed my father, sweetheart. Yes, I planned it all out ahead of time.*

"For your sake, I think we need to find another way."

"For the sake of everyone I care about, there isn't another way."

Something left her when he said it. Hope, he thought. "There are no easy answers to this, Addie."

"You don't want to kill him. I can feel that in you."

He licked his dry lips. "In spite of everything he's done, I don't *want* to kill him. That's largely why I agreed to work all those years with William and the FBI Art Crime Team. I just wanted him locked away someplace where he couldn't hurt us anymore. But that didn't work, and I don't think I'm left with any other choices. I live every day with the fear that somehow I won't have done enough to protect you and Carolena and that I'll lose you both."

"This can't all ride on your shoulders. I'll go out on a limb to speak for Carolena and say I think she's doing everything in her power to keep you from bearing the brunt of this responsibility. Because, who do you become after you kill him? What price do you pay?"

"What price do I pay if I don't kill him, and something happens to you or her?"

15

———————

Blake changed clothes and prepared to leave for a walk. He took my face in his hands, pressed his lips to mine in a long kiss and swore that nothing was wrong. That he just wanted some fresh air to clear his head.

"Are you sure you're okay?"

"I need time to think. I'll meet you at the gallery in a couple of hours for the evening meeting." He turned toward the door with a closed-lipped smile too tainted in sadness to be real.

"Blake—"

He crossed the room and took my hands in his. "I'm not leaving you. I'm not going to disappear on you. You were right. I've been away too much. We're in this together." He kissed my knuckles. "From now on you come first. No matter what. I promise."

I stared at our joined hands for a long moment. "Your being gone so much and without any word—"

"The trust has to be rebuilt. I'm up to that job. This is just a walk, I'll meet you at the gallery.

Blake rubbed his upper lip with the back of his thumb, then waved once and left through the front door.

Afterward, I was left with a strange sick feeling that lingered somewhere between my heart and stomach.

I missed Alexa. Though our relationship had had its challenges over the years, she was my go-to for any major problem. Over the past two years, we had written quite a bit, though that wasn't enough. I wanted to hear her voice.

Today I selected a page of crisp white stationery from the gold-trimmed mahogany secretary Dad placed in the corner of the library. I penned a quick letter to Lex telling her the high points about the past couple of days. I wrote how we had our first real lead, that Otto had taken the Wentworths, that I had insisted on going with Blake to Paris to help find the paintings and Carolena, how he resisted, and so forth. Then I wrote:

Something has developed between us since he returned from this last trip—a distance. I guess I shouldn't expect otherwise with so much on his mind. It's not that I do. It's just that there's this unfamiliarity there. An anger. I can't quite put my finger on what it is, but it concerns me. It's real.

With regard to Otto, I am trying to convince Blake that we need to find a way to stop him that doesn't involve killing him. I think if Blake does kill him—because he feels he has to—for me, then he'll resent me. Secondly, I wonder if he goes ahead with it, that he'll be so forever changed that we'll just fall apart.

There's a third consideration, which is that we never find Otto or Carolena and Blake is never able to overcome that, either. He really has piled the world on his shoulders. My very own Atlas. I have reminded him that Atlas didn't actually enjoy carrying the heavens around like that, and no one benefitted from that. It was actually a punishment from Zeus.

Blake said he rather liked being compared to Atlas.

Not sure when we leave. We'll probably discuss it at tonight's meeting. I'll keep you posted.

Enclosed please find and enjoy a small gift. Hope you love them. And I hope these don't disappear from someone's jewelry box because I'm doing this.

When Grandpa does something like this, he likes to think he's giving a piece new life. "It probably just got lost somewhere along the way and you're rescuing it."

One would like to think, anyway.

Oh, by the way...I met someone named Ruth. She popped into the gallery the other night. She had a little boy with her (maybe 10 or 12?) and they were on their way to the doctor. Dad hot-footed it across the room when they came in to the gallery. Grandpa said it's a neighbor lady that Dad watches over. Maybe. I wonder if there is more to their relationship than just friendship.

Wish us luck.

Thinking of you always.

With much love,

Addie

I WRAPPED a pair of silver three-inch drop jade and diamond earrings into the letter, tri-folded the paper around them, and sealed the envelope. I took my time to write her name in a large decorative script on the outside of the envelope. No one could say they mistakenly thought the envelope was theirs.

I held the envelope at arm's length and admired the way her name looked. I loved the loose coil that aspired to the highest point of the capital A, and the tail of the x that extended below the ending A. I did love writing letters and in longhand. I didn't miss email or texting.

I wrote another letter, this time to Grace and Isabella.

Though I thought my father or grandfather might have already let them know about the lead in Paris, I didn't want to be remiss. Actually, I didn't want to endure any of Grace's "it's a good thing" comments. As in, "It's a good thing your father told me you were going to Paris, because I certainly didn't hear it from you." Just the thought of her potential comment tweaked a sharp pinch deep in my heart where only Grace could reach.

I asked about the third F. Scott Fitzgerald novel that was in Paris somewhere. A few years ago she'd told Blake and me about three of his novels that transported information across time. One in Savannah and the other right here in my living room in New York. The third was in Paris somewhere, but I didn't know exactly where. Grandpa and Dad probably knew. But Grace would appreciate that I asked *her* about it.

We might need to access the book, which would require someone on Grace's end to be at that Paris location to receive and respond. I didn't think she or anyone over there who shared my last name would mind traveling to Paris for that purpose. Or for any other purpose, for that matter.

I slipped in a pair of diamond and ruby hair combs for Isabella and a chrysoprase and diamond necklace for Grace. When I opened the book I found a letter from her. Nothing important. She was in New York with Fowler to collect our "mail" from the book. She was going to get a new picture frame tomorrow. She told us to be careful and included a picture of Lexie and her dog.

A strange sensation soared through me for feeling reluctant to return home. Guilt? No. More of a realization that we might not get home. And a reluctance to discuss that with Grace. I knew how heavily it would weigh on her, Isabella, and Lex if I never made it home again.

I sent the letters. Then I showered and dressed and went to the gallery for the evening meeting with everyone else.

THE EVENING MEETINGS weren't formal, necessarily. The men didn't wear tuxes, I didn't wear a tiara. But we dressed. Usually, we went out for dinner and drinks after the most private part of our meetings. It was an easy way to continue the typically long discussions without starving everyone to death.

The men wore suits with vests, their hats always nearby. Tonight I wore a long blue velvet dress with gold-embroidered half moons,. Beneath I wore a pale blue silk chiffon and cotton lace teddy that was nearly fancy enough to be worn on its own. Nearly, anyway.

I took a cab to the gallery and arrived just before Grandpa locked the front door. "There's my girl." He'd said those words to me for as long as I could remember, it always affected me like a blessing. He kissed my cheek and guided me inside.

With each genuine touch or kind word, a thread from my past was sewn into the pattern of my present. It covered the heartache that had spanned two decades of my life and turned that pain from their once mysterious absence into a less noticeable piece in a larger, happier pattern.

"I'm well." I kissed and hugged him in return.

A male singer crooned "April Showers" through the radio. My father and Philippe stood near the drink trolley enjoying martinis with double olives. I scanned the area for Blake and expected a flood of relief at seeing him. Though he was nowhere to be found.

"Hello, love." Philippe smiled with the warmth of

welcome and friendship. As was typical, he offered me a soft place to land and for some reason, I was happier than I usually was to see him. "Wine? Or join us in a martini?" He winked. "In light of the Wentworth debacle, we're hitting the harder stuff tonight."

"I'd like to take a swim in a martini about right now."

"Long day?" My father hugged me and sealed it with his signature three squeezes, just one of the ways he said, "I love you."

"Ah, kind of. Wine, please. Red." I glanced toward the back of the room, hoping Blake might dash up the stairs.

Philippe popped the cork on a fresh bottle of wine and poured a glass for me.

"Is Blake on his way?" my father asked.

"I think so. He went for a walk earlier."

"Let's give him a few more minutes." My grandfather peeked out the curtain-covered window.

"Everything okay with you two?" my father whispered.

I nodded without saying anything. Philippe placed my glass of wine on the trolley and extended his arms in the offer of a dance.

"How are you?" Philippe asked. We swayed to the big band song from the radio.

"Good. We talked. As you suggested. It didn't go badly. We made progress, though I'm not sure what we resolved. It's complicated, I guess, with everything else going on."

"Life usually is." He sighed with empathy kindly given and for a moment it took away the full weight of my concerns. It was a comfort to be in Philippe's always-strong arms. His care for me was never held back or conflicted. It was just there, offered freely.

"What's this?" I brushed a few tiny crumbs from the corner of his face. "Snacking before dinner?"

"Yes, usually. Mary brought in a few appetizers." He nodded to the coffee table spread of cheese wedges, crackers, and a few grapes arranged on a doily-laden silver platter. Mary had been my grandfather's significant friend since before we'd arrived. She was so different from Grace and Ellen, I had mistakenly considered her a flavor of the month when we'd first met. But two years later she stood strong in his life.

As though he were without a care, Philippe sang along and twirled me into an unexpected dip that made me squeal.

"Looks like I'm missing all the fun," Blake said without a trace of humor. He appeared in the back of the room without the advance notice of any door slam, which was my usual alert.

"Well, there's the man of the hour," my father said. "Come in, come in. Let me make you a drink."

Blake left his stare on Philippe while he shed his jacket and pushed an energetic message that was probably loud enough for everyone to hear: *hands off*.

Philippe dragged his hand from my waist in reluctant compliance to what he'd been told to do. He handed me my wine and I reclined onto the green antique couch that wasn't yet antique.

"Addie?" Mary called from the top of the basement stairs. "Would you help me please, dear?"

"Sure." I smoothed my up-do, happy for the temporary escape. The steep stairwell still cautioned me to step slowly, and once downstairs I helped Mary assemble two more trays of appetizers. My job was to arrange small irresistible and iced pastries on a silver tray.

Mary was about my age, I guessed. Maybe eight years or

so older. Her platinum hair and smooth skin and flawless makeup made it hard to pinpoint.

We often walked and talked with one another in the evenings, either on the way to dinner or on the way home. She would thread my arm through hers and she held on tight with her other hand. I thought perhaps she was afraid of getting too close to the traffic, even though we didn't walk that close to the curbed edge. While she talked she would squeeze and pat my hand and I decided she was just affectionate. A trait I appreciated. Though I thought her mothering touch a complete mismatch to her sexy and fashionable presentation.

"Color me a bright shade of crazy," she often said on our evening stroll. Then she would inhale long and deep through her nose. "But I just love the scent of the city. Just something about the fume and the busy that makes me excited about the future." Her shoulders would push toward her ears and her bright red lips would part and stretch in the most welcoming smile. My mouth couldn't help but mimic hers. Her enthusiasm for life was infectious.

"Thank you for helping me." Mary's slim-fitting sweater dress was lined along the bottom with a row of fur. The full flounce along the hem twirled outward when she moved quickly and I knew that Alexa would have wanted that dress.

"Don't be silly. By the way, I love this new shade of red you're wearing." I waved two fingers at my lips. "It's such a true red, really the perfect tone for your skin." I thought about how neither Ellen, one of my grandfather's long-term loves, nor Grace would be caught dead wearing bright-colored lipstick. Grandpa had managed to select three entirely different women as partners in his life. I knew Grace wouldn't mind if she knew about Mary. She wouldn't flinch. Though I felt badly for Ellen, who I thought still loved and missed him.

"This is my favorite lipstick." She pressed three of her fingertips onto the top of my hand. "I have an extra tube at home. I'll share it with you."

"Thank you." My heart leaned into her in a sisterly sort of way.

On our walks, I'd learned that she worked at a fledgling company called Bloomingdale's Great East Side Bazaar on East 56th during the day and often spent the evenings with my grandfather. In fact, that's where they had met. Bloomingdale's. He was buying perfume for someone else and she stole his heart. So he often said.

"You and Philippe dance beautifully together." She took two more pastries from the white box and transferred them to the silver tray.

"I guess it's easy to relax with friends."

"Yes. Friends are the best treasure. Your grandfather and I were friends for a while. Did I ever tell you I was married once before?"

"No. I didn't know that."

"Mmmm-hmmm. My first husband died in the war."

"I'm so sorry."

"Well. We married just before he went overseas. We were very young. He never came home." She winced as though the memory hurt her heart. "When I met John, he understood. He's something of an amazing man, your grandfather."

"I'm sorry. He understood what?"

"Come on. Let's take these upstairs. Then I'm going to dash out for a minute while you all meet." Her hips swished from left to right when she climbed the stairs.

I'd written her off as a ditz when I first met her. Now I

thought much of that was an act. Still, I didn't always catch her wisdom.

"I heard from Grace today," I said when Mary left the room. "She's in New York to pick up the mail."

Blake laid a possessive kiss on my cheek and accepted his martini from my father.

"Any news?" my grandfather adjusted the navy silk scarf he'd tied at his neck.

"Nothing significant. Lex and Isabella are in Atlanta to look at some more galleries. Lexie's not too impressed with her options there. She prefers New York galleries, but those still aren't an option. I think Grace was just dropping in to let me know she was there."

"I would guess she's there with Fowler. Should have kept my eye on that man." He clicked his tongue against the roof of his mouth and stared into the distance as though he were revisiting a plan gone wrong.

I raised an eyebrow at him over the rim of my wine glass. Men were so territorial. "Seriously?" I didn't bring up the fact that he'd had a long affair, and a child no less, with Ellen. I wasn't sure how he could have any concern over Grace's affection for Fowler.

"He always had an eye for her." He patted Blake on the back when he passed by. "Good thing to watch out for." He pulled the cork on the wine bottle and poured a glass of wine for himself.

Blake glanced at me and then at Philippe.

"Oh, she did ask what she's supposed to do with all the Egyptian pottery she found hidden in the attic. What pottery is she talking about?"

"It's in the attic of my—well, your, or I guess, *our*, townhouse. Don't move it or she won't have it. Tell her to enjoy it. I just made her a wealthier woman." His voice held a strong note of satisfaction and he leaned against the back of a green silk-upholstered chair. "Since we're all finally here, let's get started. We have our first real lead, so let's decide what to do with it."

I noted his use of the word "we" and I glanced at Blake. I felt certain he still wasn't thinking in terms of *we*.

"I think you have to assume that Otto is planning something spectacular—he's armed as he's never been before. He has the Wentworths," my grandfather said.

"He doesn't have all of them. There's a chance we could find the others," Blake said.

My grandfather nodded with doubt. "We've been searching for them for over twenty years. So, yes, a chance. But maybe not much of one."

"He has the great love of his life," Philippe said. "That has to be empowering him toward some sort of fantastic goal."

"I wouldn't call that love." Blake's voice was low, and although it wasn't too obvious, I could hear the threat in his tone. It seemed all men in the room were interested in making their boundaries clear tonight.

"Be that as it may, she's his dream come true. I would imagine he feels pretty invincible." Philippe held the bottle of wine over my empty glass. "More wine?"

"Thank you." I held my glass for him while he filled it, then he filled his own.

Blake watched our every move.

There was one thing of which I was reasonably sure. These two men had entered into a competitive relationship that extended beyond the role of siblings, and I felt like the prize.

"If he is in Paris right now, he's surrounded by some of the greatest artists of our time. That's not only a temptation, it has to be part of his plan." My father gestured with his martini glass.

"He could take a Picasso, a Modigliani, a Chagall." My grandfather peeked out of the front curtains that were closed against the front window. "If he took those home that would add millions to his wealth, and it would make him a very important collector."

"He might leave the twenties entirely with Carolena. Since he has the Wentworths and her, I doubt he sees any reason to return home. Or to be anywhere close to where we are." The finality with which Blake spoke made it clear this was his biggest concern.

My father sank onto the green tapestried armchair and put his martini on the side table. "We can also be certain that he has the Gardner art. He took that art in the present so it has to stay hidden. Though it's a feather in his cap and probably a clue to his plans."

My grandfather shifted in his chair.

"That's what I think," I said. "Whatever pieces of art he gets now, he's probably buying it outright. So, wherever he goes in the future, he can proudly display that art. Then if or when he goes back to the present, he'll have the world's biggest private art collection. Think about the kind of unlimited wealth, power, and influence that would afford him."

"He will have stolen the world's most important pieces of art," my grandfather said.

"Making him one of the world's most important *men*," Philippe said. "That's what he's always wanted."

"Isabella Gardner has already acquired the Vermeer and the Rembrandt and most of the other pieces from the theft by now. If he wants to own those pieces outright all he has to do now is go back to the 1890s and purchase them before Isabella does," Blake said.

"Would Carolena take him there to do that?" I asked.

"She's always underestimated him. I would bet she's humoring him as if he were a child. She probably thinks he'll pick up a few pieces here and there and that will be enough for him. An enviable private art collection. But nothing is ever enough for him." Blake muttered his last sentence and I wondered who he was more frustrated with —Otto or Carolena.

Philippe cleared his throat. "We need to go to Paris to at least try to find and stop him. If they aren't there anymore, that's still where the next lead will be."

"Agreed," my grandfather said.

"Here as well," my father echoed.

Blake placed his empty martini glass on the coffee table and popped a square of cheese into his mouth. "I already have *our* tickets."

"Whose tickets?" I asked.

"Yours and mine. Picked them up on my way over." He smiled his gambler's smile, the slightly tipped corner of his closed mouth showed he'd figured out how to get the winning hand. He would listen to what everyone else had to say about this problem, he just wasn't going to let it dictate how he wanted to approach it.

"When do we leave?"

"Day after tomorrow. More wine?" He poised himself as if he were about to get off the couch and get it for me.

"I'm fine. Thanks." He'd followed through on what I wanted. Which could serve as a temporary placation before that thing between us became an issue again. In which case, I was going to have to stop calling it "the thing" and call it by another name, such as "need for control", or "building resentment", or maybe "Joe." Or, he was back on board with us. The us I'd bought into when I fell in love with him. All of that was secondary now, though.

"Let's talk about what we ought to do once we arrive in Paris. Five heads are better than one. Right, sweetheart?" Blake took his small black notebook and a pencil from his jacket pocket. He opened to a blank page and tapped the pencil twice.

"So, Addie is going with you..." Grandpa crossed his legs and rubbed the side of his index finger beneath his bottom lip.

"Yes. We've already decided." My tone dipped low and serious to close the door on that discussion.

He glanced at my father.

"Are you sure you want to do this?" my father asked me.

"I can't help by staying here."

"It's just that—" My father sighed. The room went painfully quiet. "I'd rather you not go. It might complicate things."

I pushed my tongue over my cabernet-flavored lips and stared at the small areas of teal that were woven into the rug under our feet. I knew what he meant. When Otto thought he'd lost Carolena forever, he came for me. "We don't know what he's up to. Whatever his next move, it could involve Carolena's gifts or, if he knows that I'm nearby he might want access to my gifts again."

I lifted my gaze and the worry in his expression transported me back in time to when I was six years old. I expected to look at my feet and to see them dangling off the edge of the couch, not quite able to reach the floor. I inhaled a deep breath of courage. "However, I'm not going to spend my life hiding from Otto. I appreciate your concern, but this is not your decision to make."

His lips thinned and tightened in that classic parental expression that showed his internal battle over what and what not to say. The loud of the quiet in the room intensified.

"All right, then," he finally said, like he knew nothing he could say would make a difference. "Then you'll want to stay at the Hotel Ritz."

"I'll make the reservation for you in the morning. This is late notice, and prime travel season for Paris, but I know some people there. I can make something happen for you." My grandfather pointed at me while he spoke. He meant business.

"Why The Ritz?" I glanced at my father, who made a second martini for himself at the drink trolley.

"The third Fitzgerald novel is there," my grandfather said.

"Ah." My head tipped back in a long nod. "I just asked Grace where it was."

"Well, don't tell her I told you first. It's in their library. You'll find a Monsieur Bernard, who manages that room for the hotel."

"Does he know about the book?"

"Not specifically. Not in terms of what it can do. But the library has many first editions in it and he is protective of all of them. It is his job to make certain that no one removes any of the priceless books—they've been there since the hotel opened in 1898. You'll have to get around him each time you go in there to send a note."

My father cleared his throat. "He's, um. More than protective, I would say. Monsieur Bernard was shot in the war, in the upper back." My father pointed to an area on the upper left side of his back. "He trusts no one. He's extremely paranoid. Rumor is that he even wears a bullet-proof vest under his suit and he keeps a handgun in his desk drawer."

"There are bullet-proof vests in the twenties?"

Grandpa nodded. "First edition. Like the library."

Philippe dropped several slices of cheese and crackers on his small round plate. "Why would the Ritz have a library of first editions that's open to the public?"

"Cesar Ritz started his hotel career as a waiter. When he finally opened the Hotel Ritz, he was entertaining much of Europe's elite. Having a library full of first editions was his way of showing them that they could feel at home in his hotel. Sort of like displaying fine art in the lobby. He said that the Ritz was where one could find 'all the refinement a prince could desire in his own home.' " My father's eyes were wider than normal, and his mouth sounded a little dry.

"And, of course, so many celebrities and royalty have called the hotel home since it opened," Philippe said. "Knowing Otto, I doubt he could have resisted at least a visit."

"You should write to Grace so she or someone can be in Paris to receive your mail and to help however they can. Mary will want to come with me, but she'll spend all her time taking in the Parisian fashion. She'll be out of the way while we stroll the museums and galleries and search for leads. Philippe?" My grandfather motioned to him with his half-full wine glass.

"I'll go by the ticket office in the morning to see what's left for immediate departure."

"Which liner are y'all traveling on, Blake?" my grandfather asked.

"Majestic."

"I know it well." Philippe raised his glass to him.

"Get a stateroom for me. I'll give you money tonight for the fare," my grandfather said.

"Me as well." My father's voice was a tad thin as if he weren't happy with this option.

"What do we do with Otto once we find him?" Philippe asked.

Blake turned to me.

"I never discussed it with him." My voice was as low and secretive as a whisper, my shoulders shrugged half way to my ears. I waited to see how Blake would answer the question. Even though there was no love lost between Philippe and Otto, he was still Philippe's father. There were also two fathers in the room.

"I've given a lot of thought to the very few options available to us when we do find him. Taking him back to the present is too much of a risk. If he breaks free and escapes into time, that could be disastrous. Jail isn't really an option because of the escape risk.

"Ultimately, I think he may have put us in such a situation that we have no choice but to kill him." I felt the adrenaline jump through his chest when he said it.

The somber stares from each man said they understood this unenviable position.

"I'm open to whatever effectively works. But in the end, I'll have to do whatever I need to do to protect the people I care about."

"Make the best decision you can. One you can live with for the rest of your life," my father said.

"You'll make the right choice, Blake," my grandfather said.

"Thanks, John." Blake's exterior was polished steel. On the inside, however, the conflict was strong. I just hoped that we could find a way to resolve this that didn't leave a mark on his soul. My grandfather and Blake continued a conversation about the Ritz.

Philippe said nothing and his lack of participation in the conversation was noticeable. Knowing him as I did, though, I suspected he hadn't yet decided how he felt about this. If he had just been told that Blake had killed Otto to protect me, he probably knew how to process that. But discussing Otto's murder ahead of time? That was something else entirely.

"Addie." My father startled me from my thoughts. "Just to be clear. I wasn't suggesting you stay here for any reason except that I think you could still be an attractive possession for Otto. Especially if Carolena is taken from his side." His need to protect me burst through my chest like a fiery bullet.

"Okay." My throat promptly turned dry.

Blake and my grandfather turned in my direction. All eyes were on me.

My grandfather leaned forward. "I don't know what Otto has planned, but you realize he has the Wentworths. If he takes you from us, you could be gone forever."

16

Though I'd never seen the Titanic first hand, I had watched movies and toured several exhibits that boasted recreated rooms. Every turn through the Majestic had me thinking about how it resembled the Titanic's opulent decor. From the carved pillars at every doorway to the marble flooring, to the double story rooms with al frescoes on the ceilings. It was more elegant than the first-class hotels I had visited.

We spent most of our travel week on the ocean planning for how we would approach our search in Paris. Blake took extensive notes in that notebook of his. He wrote out detailed tasks and assigned names and dates to each line item.

As much as I appreciated his organized approach it wasn't my style. For me, I just needed to get my feet on solid land first. Maybe get to the hotel and get a shower, then let my intuition guide me.

I agreed with Philippe in that it probably would have been difficult for Otto to deny himself a visit to the Ritz. Our next lead had to be found around there somewhere.

The idea of running into Otto and being on his most wanted list again sent my adrenaline a little too fast through the corners of my heart. Especially considering the new weapons he had at his disposal.

As a frequent migraine sufferer, I was more susceptible to motion sickness than anyone else in the group. Consequently, I had to take frequent walks on the outdoor decks for fresh air to calm my stomach. Fresh air helped some. Though not as much as modern medicine. Unfortunately, I didn't have access to that.

"You're looking a bit green around the gills again, Addiebelle. Let's get you up on deck." My grandfather said this once every hour or two and he was always right. I tried not to bring up how I felt. But apparently, when it got to be too much for me, it also showed on my face. In a lovely shade of green.

Blake was fairly oblivious to my battle with motion. The closer we got to Paris, the more intensely he focused on the plans he'd written in his notebook. Currently, he made lists on every major artist in Paris at the time and as many of their works as he could remember.

Philippe often walked with me on deck for fresh air. Occasionally, Grandpa would have the porter find Mary and she'd take over. Sometimes my grandfather walked with us. He was a distinguished gentleman with a woman on each arm. It was probably every man's dream. Except that one of the women was trying desperately to suck as much of the salty ocean air into her ballooned lungs as possible. Today Mary and I walked alone.

"So, you were away from your grandfather for long time, weren't you?" This was the first time she'd asked me this question. I had the feeling it had taken her some time to find the courage to ask. I thought maybe she didn't want to hear about his wife, my grandmother. Perhaps for fear that there was still a great love that threatened what she and my grandfather shared.

"He and my father moved away when I was young," I answered tactfully. "It took me a while to find them again." A tireless ocean breeze dipped and twirled across the deck like Degas' ballet dancers. Its crisp coolness on my skin calmed my stomach that followed the waves too closely.

"Oh," she mouthed. "Must have been sudden, I guess." Her thin babydoll voice sounded inauthentic and though I had long expected it to get on my nerves, it never did.

"It was unexpected and I'm just glad to have reconnected with them again. What are your plans for Paris?"

"I know that you and John and everyone are going to Paris on business. I'm going to shop." She ran a hand under her wide fur collar and pushed it toward her cheek bone. "The French are so far ahead of us in fashion."

We often had long conversations in the 1920s New York I had taken to referring to as home, and Mary always brought some sort of punch to them. Even though she was sometimes cryptic, I waited for it. We turned the corner at the ship's bow and I felt a little worse for wear for walking in the opposite direction that the boat was traveling.

"Now tell me about Philippe and Blake and how this works for you," she said.

The ship lifted subtly and my head and stomach swam. "I'm not sure what you mean."

"Well, when Blake's away you're with Philippe. When Blake is home you're with him. Right?"

I did my best to focus on her face in the event this was sarcasm or worse, female rivalry. Her blue eyes were wide and round and when I read her I found her emotions were just clean curiosity.

"No, I'm only with Blake. Philippe is just a friend. We grew up together. His dad was my grandfather's business partner."

Her Clara Bow cupid lips pressed into a tight smile that said she didn't believe me.

"It's true. We're just friends." My voice pitched high.

"I may not know much. But I know men." She pointed a slender finger at me. Her nails were long and painted in a moon manicure—where only the middle, pinkish part of the nail was painted, in her case red, to match the lips. The crescent tip and white base were left white.

"He's in love with you, sweetheart." She raised one of her perfectly arched eyebrows at me. Her lips pursed in a supporting act and she tapped her finger on my shoulder three times as if to say, "mark my words."

A too-heavy weight tightened in my chest and lumped downward to my midsection. "I don't think so, I— We're friends. He saved my life once. We're close, and we're each other's support system in a way, while we're here. Visiting. Especially when Blake is away." I was stammering. Her comment was intrusive. Assumptive. My friendship with Philippe had become very precious to me and I didn't want anyone messing with it. Especially by spreading rumors or just assuming that it was something that it wasn't.

"*Especially* when Blake is away," she repeated, and looked to the water.

"He's a good friend." I could feel how the words bounced off of her.

"Yes, I can see that. How do you feel about him?" She grinned with a let-me-show-you-something expression and I wanted to walk away.

I paused. "He's a lovely person, a friend from my younger years. I suppose I feel a certain closeness to him."

"Mmm. Yes, I can see that."

We turned the corner at the bow and headed in the opposite direction.

"You know when John and I went on our first date, I told him that I still loved my first husband, even though I'd never see him again. John just understood. He didn't ask me to give up that love. He didn't ask me to choose."

"He's a good man." I nodded with a sweet smile, though I'd decided she'd had too much champagne with lunch. We sat on a nearby bench. A couple at the forward end of the ship shared a romantic embrace.

"Nothing better than true love," Mary said.

"Mmm," I said.

She turned toward me and her happy expression fell for just a moment. Yes, we'd reached the end of the line with this conversation. She quickly restored her comforting smile. "It's a bit chilly. Shall we go in?"

"You go ahead. I'm going to sit out here for a while. The cool air does me good."

"All right, hon." Mary pressed her cheek to mine and kissed the air to the side of my face.

After she left I thought about what she had said. And had not said. Philippe's friendship *had* become extremely important to me. Maybe too much so with Blake's absence.

Philippe had been right. Blake had put me last. He'd taken me for granted. But to Blake's credit, he had heard me when I told him how his long absences had affected me. He apologized and promised not to do it again. For as many problems as Blake and I had had over the last couple of years, I did believe we could turn our life in a positive direction.

From here on out, I would have to make sure that I wasn't communicating otherwise.

SEVERAL HOURS later we gathered as a group in the two-story first-class dining room. It was the twenties and elegance could not have been more overstated. Every tuxedo played a supporting role to some evening gown that was actually more of a costume. My dress was no exception—a cap sleeved, gold brocaded satin, ankle-length gown that turned heads easily enough. Though the long feathered purse Mary loaned me really was my favorite piece of the outfit.

Blake looked the epitome of Jazz Age gentility in a classic black 1920s tuxedo—high waist, tight fitted jacket and straight pants. His poster perfect style was topped off with his slicked dark hair combed into a side part. It was a stunning enough combination that I often found myself staring at him, his faultless appearance still something of a marvel to me.

He held my hand occasionally, his white teeth framed his loud and hearty laugh and our entire evening floated along in glittered perfection.

The dining room was spacious enough, lined with statuary and lit with gold chandeliers. Though the arched windows that flanked the upper level remained closed and the air was stilted. I sipped on cool seltzer water to combat the motion sickness, though I longed for the fresh air outside.

The overabundance of waiters kept my champagne glass full. I ate what I could and leaned heavy on the comfort foods—breads and sweets. All of which worked until they didn't, and then fresh air was the only cure.

"Excuse me, gentlemen. Mary." With my champagne glass in hand, I offered a polite nod and felt what must have been a sickly green pallor cover my cheeks.

Everyone stood in gentlemanly consideration. Mary placed her napkin in her chair and rose to accompany me.

"No, Mary. Finish your dinner. I'm fine. I'm not going to walk. I'm just going to sit on that first bench outside." I pointed upward and to the right toward the general direction we'd been earlier. "Someone should enjoy this lovely dinner. It's our last on this ship."

Blake's body language told me his preference. Every part of him hovered and angled toward the map of Paris, and his bloody black notebook that laid between him and my father and grandfather.

Blake looked up at me. "We're almost through here, I'll see you when you get back?"

A faked smile was all I could conjure to offer assurance. After the endless amount of time they'd already spent planning today, I didn't understand what could possibly be left.

"Blake. May I see you for a moment?"

We stood off to the side of the dining room.

"How much more planning can you possibly do?"

"There's a lot to organize for this next step."

My patience was gone.

I took the stairs to the upper deck and sat on the first park-like bench they'd anchored to the floor. The ship's movement was more noticeable on the upper levels but the cool air negated any ill effects. For the most part the cool breezes made the nausea retreat, while warm, still environments had the opposite effect.

The temperature of the night air had probably dropped into the high forties. As quickly as the Majestic moved, the wind chill must have been in the lower forties. I'd left my shawl in the dining room, but with all the stairs between where I sat and where I'd come from, I wasn't going to venture back. Besides, I wasn't in the mood to see Blake just yet.

I'd bear the cooler temperatures for as long as I could. There were elevators available to me, however, I felt superstitious about those tiny cages with so much ocean beneath me. Trapped was not my favorite feeling.

The ocean lapped at the sides of the ship like a tide that constantly rushed in, never retreating. I sipped the rest of my champagne, which lulled me into a state of tipsy I rather enjoyed. The fresh air and alcohol helped me to roll with the ship's inertia, rather than to resist it. Although here, on the uppermost deck, there was just the feeling of speeding forward and very little, if any, back and forth.

A few feet away a young woman swirled her fringed shawl around her, and stared over the edge of the railing. There was nothing to see in the thick night other than a few waves lit by the ship's lights. But a dead soldier stood behind her, his head bowed.

I could hear him talking to her in a low murmur, telling her how much he loved and missed her, reminding her of the life they once shared, and the dreams they held together for a bright future. I knew the woman revisited old memories that wouldn't die for as long as he lingered nearby.

I identified with both of them. I related to her loneliness and his need to restore what once was. He turned toward me, most of the right side of his face was bloodied, the outside of it missing. "Can you help me?" He started in my direction.

I shook my head *no* and meant it.

The same couple I'd seen earlier toward the bow of the boat shared a romantic embrace near the railing and I gritted my teeth through a pang of jealousy. I missed Blake's partnership. Despite our conversation the day before yesterday he drifted easily into old ways.

He needed to be in control of this search. For as much as I understood that, we were not the couple we used to be. I resented that.

"There you are."

Philippe carried my shawl over his arm in his black worsted, double-breasted tux, proudly fashion-forward for the time. "I thought you might want this with you." He draped the wrap around my shoulders.

"Bless you. That chill was just about to do me in." I adjusted and widened the fabric until it covered all of my bare arms.

He sat next to me and wrapped his arm around my shoulders. "Do you want my jacket?" He paused before snuggling in any further.

"This is fine. Besides, you're blocking the wind." I chuckled.

"Always good to be useful." He tugged me closer to him. The ocean air whipped over the decks and twirled around us in damp, salty currents.

"You must be missing out on the men's evening cigar to have brought me this. I'm fine if you want to go back."

"Why would I want a cigar when I could sit with you? Besides, if I have any more cigars on this trip I'm going to be as green as you are." He tilted his head for a better view of my complexion. "Or were. You're looking much better now. Fresh air doing its job?"

"That and the champagne."

He gave me a small side-squeeze-hug and a sprint of his happiness galloped through me like a herd of gazelles. Leaping, playful, happy.

He's in love with you.

My sigh drew in and out in an even, heavy stroke. It was obvious to me now how he felt. I'd somehow overlooked his feelings in light of how important our friendship had become to me. I'd grown dependent on the love and the care that he gave so freely. We had a special connection, a steady one we both enjoyed, one I could fall into whenever I needed to, one that I'd been starved for. One that Blake had been too distracted to give.

Philippe and I were consistently on equal footing with one another. That's the way it had always been between the two of us, an even give and take. That kind of relationship offered a safe space where we grew close. With all the time we shared at the gallery, we just explored life forward together.

With Blake, our life together had become more tightly controlled. As in, he was in control and I was expected to flow with it. Which I didn't. We'd lost the easy-going trust we used to have with one another. I still had hope it could right itself.

I twisted my body so I could see his face.

"Are you warm enough?" he asked.

"Yes, thank you." I stared into his soft brown eyes.

His classic old Hollywood good looks and signature smirk belonged on a 1940s black-and-white film screen where, as the dashing hero, he would make women swoon.

He brushed my cheek with his knuckle. "You're staring."

"Can't help it. I'm just wondering how it is that you're still single."

His features fell slightly and his gaze shifted to the dark in the distance. He shook his head. "Busy. I guess." The three words were said slowly and I could feel him adding protective internal layers.

"It's none of *my* business, of course. Though I suspect I

haven't allowed you time to really develop a relationship with someone. I think I've been very selfish with you." I faced him now, and I tried to read him. I found our feelings for one another too jumbled together to see them clearly.

"You haven't been selfish. I enjoy our friendship."

I ran my fingertips over his jade and onyx gold cufflinks. Searching. Wondering if there was more information that could be had on this topic.

He lifted my hand away from them. "My word is good enough here."

Busted. "What about in our present day? Was there anyone?"

He chuckled. "A few. No one serious. Otto was always in the background of my life, dragging me into his schemes. I couldn't very well expose anyone to that."

"Well, as long as I'm not keeping you from living your life."

"No, not that."

"You've been such a good friend to me, I wouldn't want to take advantage of that in any way."

"You're not that kind of person." His gaze rested on his hand in his lap. "I'm capable of making my own decisions. So I think you're safe. Plus, you've been a good friend to me as well." His index finger brushed the top of my hand, just lightly. "So, thank you."

"We have shared a lot over these past couple of years, haven't we?"

"That we have." He kissed the back of my hand.

He must have kissed me a hundred or more times since we'd landed in the twenties—on the cheek, my hand, even once on the lips when we first arrived. I'd never thought much about it until today.

"Do you remember our first kiss?" he asked.

I felt my cheeks flush warm. Strangely. "Yes. I was fifteen and traveling through New York with Isabella. I'm surprised you remembered that."

"No one forgets their first kiss." His smirk was James Dean-perfect—bad boy-perfect.

"I didn't know I was your first kiss."

"Well, I'm glad you couldn't tell."

"You were my first kiss, too."

Philippe beamed. "I should have called."

"Countless girls are grateful, I would guess." I did remember the emptiness I felt when I never heard from him. I was careful not to bring it up.

He shook his head. "You know Otto was pretty mad when he caught us kissing that night. He said I couldn't have anything to do with you."

I nodded one long aha acknowledgment. "I guess that makes sense now. Knowing what he had done to my father and grandfather by then. Knowing what he knew about my gifts. He didn't want me to figure any of that out."

"You probably thought I didn't care about you anymore. But truth be known, I was heartsick in love with you. I barely left my room for weeks after that. Never really got over it." He ran his thumb over my hand. "My life would have been completely different if he hadn't kept us apart. Both of our lives, I would like to think."

He was right—our lives would have been very different. "I cried for weeks when you didn't call. I—"

"Addie." Blake walked up behind us and I quickly pulled my hand away from Philippe's grasp.

"You weren't in your room." His fiery glance shifted from Philippe to me.

"Enjoying the fresh air, that's all. Philippe was kind enough to bring me my wrap."

Blake nodded but his extended hand said he wanted me out of there. "I think I've worked out a way to get fresh air into your room at night."

I pulled my wrap around me, placed my hand in his, and a shiver went up my spine.

"Are you coming in, Philippe?" Blake asked.

He crossed his legs and extended his arm along the back of the bench. "In a bit."

ADDIE REFUSED to take the elevators, so they set about the long red-carpeted hallways and several flights of stairs to get to their stateroom. "Seems like I walked in on an intense moment between the two of you." Blake closed his mouth after he asked the question and his teeth clenched.

She shrugged. "We were just talking."

"Has he ever tried to kiss you?"

She rolled her eyes and shook her head. "Romantically? Yes. Once about fifteen some odd years ago when we were teenagers."

He wondered if their history, whatever it was, was part of what made him uneasy about the two of them.

"It was a long time ago and we were kids."

Their steps made hardly a sound, the occasional swish of her gold dress was the only noise in the otherwise quiet hallway.

She is mine. All mine. Nothing left for sharing.

"You finally wrapped up your planning for the day, I guess?" Her words were cut with sharp edges that snapped and bit.

"Mostly. Do you ever get the impression that he wants more from you than just friendship?" He was careful as to how he posed the question. She cared about Philippe and was likely to write off his concerns as conspiracy theories or annoying jealousy.

"We've been over this. He knows I'm with you."

"That doesn't mean anything to most people."

"I'm well aware of how self-important people can be. Philippe isn't like that." Her steps were quick and he took longer strides to catch up.

"Even so, do you think it's wise to spend so much time alone with him?"

"You'd rather I simply spend time alone?" She stopped at the top of the stairway, the fire in her eyes told him he'd stepped on a live wire. He *had* spent most of this time on the Majestic in ongoing conversation and developing a search plan with John and Campbell. Before that he had promised her that she would come first.

"Philippe is a friend. He brought my shawl because he was concerned that I might be cold. That's it. If you don't want him to do that, then maybe *you* need to be the one who thinks to bring me my shawl." She continued down the stairway without him.

Her needle-pointed remark stayed behind and threaded the shame that writhed inside of him. That familiar self-loathing taunted him, told him that he would never be able to do enough to protect her.

Even though he'd dedicated the last two years of his life to running down every possible lead, not all of them in New York. Which meant he was gone sometimes for days at a time, it wasn't enough.

"Paris is a big city, there are a lot of places Otto could be. I wanted to make sure that we had an organized approach, everything that's important to me is at stake here." His hands curled into fists. As soon as the words fell from him mouth he regretted it. She had just called attention to the fact that he had put the search ahead of her again and he defended his actions.

"Everything that's important?" She took several steps in his direction and glared at him with a polished hardness that hid the hurt, though he knew it was there. "Just a heads up, Blake. All the planning in the world doesn't guarantee a win. I think Otto has shown you that."

He stood paralyzed on the red-carpeted hallway and watched her descend the steps. Her words exploded like roman candles in his head.

Everything he had done to protect her and Carolena had backfired on him. She and Philippe had grown too close and it was his own fault. He should have worked it differently.

He tried to remember that they were soul mates—together in the last life, and together in this one. They were paired by forces beyond this earth and nothing would part them.

But a flash of anger burned through him like a lit match. It was back again, that rage he didn't recognize. He felt alone, as though he'd lost her, as though she'd left him.

A dewy sweat of panic and nerves coated his skin and he wiped his upper lip with the back of his thumb. The first and the last time he'd felt this way was right after he'd seen Sarah. Jack would be dead soon, if he weren't already and her life would be drastically different. He tried to rationalize that this reaction was still a part of that. A past-life hangover, that was all.

He glanced around and realized Addie was gone. His heart slammed against his chest and he ran down the steps after her. He couldn't lose her again—not to fate or Philippe or his own stupidity.

17

Blake stopped at the door to catch his breath and to figure out what he would say. "I'm sorry" didn't seem to cover it. But he couldn't think of anything else. He *was* sorry. Sorry that he had made her mad, sorry that he had hurt her, and sorry that his obsession had come between them.

He couldn't put his finger on it, but he felt like he was losing her. He didn't think she would cheat on him, he didn't think Philippe could convince her to run away with him, and he didn't think she would just take off in this era. Still, the feeling was there, like a pot full of fear and rage, ready to boil over.

He opened the door quietly. Addie stood on the promenade with her champagne glass in hand, looking onto the dark ocean waves. The ship's engines rumbled like distant thunder.

She didn't look up when he opened the door to the balcony, neither did she turn around. His heart clenched in a sick panic that made him close his eyes for a minute.

He stood close behind her. "I'm sorry," he whispered.

For a while she didn't move, she just stared straight ahead as if he wasn't even there. Then she shook her head. "I just don't understand it. I mean—I really don't. After all the time we had to spend apart from one another in this life, after all we've been through together, how could you possibly think that any sort of distance would be the right choice?"

"I love you and—"

"Then why do you treat me as though I'm some sort of a threat to your happiness?" Her mouth was slightly open and ready to pose more questions that didn't have answers. Her head shaking back and forth, she searched his face as though she didn't know him, as though she must have missed something all those times she'd seen him before.

"What? I don't—"

"You do, Blake. You try to shove me into a proverbial ivory tower so you won't have to worry about me. The one thing we've always shared is a deep connection. But since we arrived in 1920 all you've done is back away from that."

"All I do is worry about you! All I've done since we got here is tried to protect you and what we have—"

"You don't protect a living thing by shoving it away someplace." Her voice was strong, loud and accusatory. Tears filled in her eyes. The hurt she'd hidden was breaking through. "That's what a relationship is—it's, it's a living, breathing thing with a heartbeat. It has needs—viable needs—like kindness and togetherness and nurturing and... connection, for crying out loud! And just like any other living thing, when it doesn't get what it needs for survival, it dies."

She poked him in his chest before she made her way to their room, then spun on her heel and faced him again. "And you don't just shove a relationship into a safe house while you traipse who knows where to do whatever it is that you do so you can say you've done *enough*. You're trying to keep us under guard so that *you* won't get hurt. Forget whatever I feel about it.

"Relationship is a risk and being *here* is a risk and letting someone in is a risk." She patted her hand over her heart twice. "If you want me and if you want us then you're going to have to take that risk. You're going to have to quit being so selfish and have some trust. Otherwise I can't be responsible for what happens to us."

His heart hammered against his chest hard and fast. Protecting her was the one thing he had worked tirelessly for. Yet there was no denying the truth in what she'd said.

She placed a hand across her stomach and went inside the stateroom.

He walked to the doorway and watched her dismantle her hairstyle. Long chunks of pin-curled blond hair fell onto her pale skin. He knew its lavender scent without even being close enough to it to actually smell it. Quite suddenly he wanted to go to her and do just that—lift a section of her hair and inhale its old world fragrance.

He missed her.

She was right—he'd created a distance between them. He wanted to close that gap, though how that would happen he wasn't sure. The closer he got to her emotionally, the stronger his fear grew that he would lose her.

She paused with her hand to her stomach again and he knew the ship's movement was bothering her. More fresh air was what she needed. He could at least help her with that.

He glanced around the room. It had a private promenade, a sitting room, bedroom and private bath, the stateroom was one of the nicest on the ship. However, the windows did not open, and the doors to the private deck wouldn't stay open by themselves—which was a problem because he knew Addie needed a steady supply of fresh air. So he went to work. He needed to *do* something. Hopefully, in those few moments he would figure out how to respond to her and how to bring them closer together.

He produced several lengths of cord that he'd stuffed into his pocket earlier and proceeded to tie a black wooden chair between the two partially open doors that led to the deck. He caught sight of Addie who brushed her hair at the vanity and mumbled something to herself. He was certain he heard his name cursed somewhere among her utterances.

He wrapped the cord around one of the doorknobs. He kept his eyes on the work at hand and he drew in a deep breath and cleared his throat. He'd never told anyone what he was about to tell her. He knew now that she needed to know.

"When I was young, very young, Otto had left. I knew that he searched for us, and I used to have these...moments."

She lowered her brush and it clicked against the wooden vanity. "What kind of moments?"

"Ah, sort of paralyzing ones. I guess. I was six or seven. At first it was just a persistent fear that he would find us and that Carolena would be taken away. That I would be left to care for myself and my baby sister on my own. They got worse with time and they became more of a distraction." He jerked the rope tight and began tying the other side of the chair to the other door.

"Then at thirteen I had nightmares that became so intense Carolena took me to a psychologist, this reserved Frenchman with round, wire glasses. He told me that everyone had something they were afraid of. It was how we responded to those fears that helped us move beyond them.

"That was the moment I decided that I could account for every contingency and beat Otto at his own game. I vowed that Otto would no longer be a threat to the people I loved. I took control and I planned. The nightmares went away. When I was finally old enough, I started putting my plans into action."

He jostled the chair to make sure it was tied well and wedged tightly enough between the two doors to keep them open. When he was satisfied with his handiwork for a makeshift ventilation system, he poured himself a scotch and took a long swallow.

"Planning. Taking control. It's my responsible way of combatting the fears. It's how I take care of the people I love."

"I see." Her voice was calm. "So, all that fear you felt when you were a boy. You transformed it into action and it gave you a sense of power over a situation that must have felt was so...uncontrollable."

"Yes. Though it seems that fear or how I've dealt with it has interfered with our happiness. You're right. I've ignored you in favor of trying to control too much. For your safety, but still." They sat on the edge of the bed, side by side. "I'm sorry." He searched for more words to offer but couldn't find any.

"It's a little like your father. To control so much. To ignore how other people feel."

Adrenaline shot through him. Carolena had often made that comparison. "I'm not like him."

"I guess we all share a few characteristics with our parents. Not all are positive."

"Look, I wasn't making excuses by telling you about my history."

"I know. But it has to change. You have to change."

He felt a pang of guilt. He wasn't sure how much of himself he could change in the short term, especially since they were getting closer to Otto. He had to make sure she was safe, but he could work harder to put her first and to be more considerate. He could take better care of their relationship.

"Without trust, I don't know how much of our relationship will survive."

"Our relationship will always survive. We're meant to be together." The trust, he'd work on that, too.

"I need you to let me in, Blake." Her voice was hushed and subdued.

"I know." He caressed her soft cheek with his fingertips. She really was the most beautiful woman he'd ever known, in any lifetime. "My heart is your heart. What's mine is yours." He grinned in such a way that he knew she would smile in return.

She laughed a little and the heaviness in his chest subsided enough that he could take a full breath. She could do that. Just the sound of her voice, its exact tenor plucked a tender place deep in his heart. Her ability to do that scared the heck out of him on some days. Other times, her intangible reach healed him and brought him back to himself.

A knock sounded at the door.

"Ms. Greenwood?" a young-sounding male voice called from the other side of the door.

"Just a moment, Ms. Greenwood." Blake whispered alongside her neck. He had purchased their tickets under his name in part to keep her name hidden.

A fairly short man in a porter's uniform stood in the

elegant hallway. "I want to let her know that we'll dock in the morning by nine a.m. She'll want to have her bags ready for us by eight o'clock." The porter tried to lift his line of sight around Blake, probably because a fairly good breeze was now blowing through the stateroom and into the hallway.

Blake closed the door a little further and made sure his body blocked the porter's view. "She'll be ready." He closed the door.

He turned to find Addie sitting on the edge of the bed, one strap of pale satin halfway down her arm. Her eyes focused softly on something unseen, shifting left to right as though she read information off of a moving ticker tape. She held the pillow he'd laid on for a nap, a bit of his pillowcase between her finger and thumb.

Her gaze landed on him and he forced himself to keep his defenses down. It took strength to be seen so deeply. The pain in his chest relaxed another notch. Another deep breath, this one stretched his lungs wider than the last.

"What are you reading?" He nodded to the pillow and wondered what she'd seen.

"Your story."

"Anything good in there?"

She stood close. "You're a very complicated man. Too guarded."

"I think you knew this already." He ran his hands along her arms and tried to stay open. Protecting was so much easier.

She escaped from his grasp and backed against one of the four posts of the bed.

He picked up his glass of scotch from the table and lowered himself onto a chair within a foot of where she stood. He knew the emotional connection she wanted and why she wanted it. He calculated how long he could stay open in the way she wanted, with his walls completely down. Because she was right. Forever, in this way at least, wasn't something he could give her. Not yet.

He shook the ice in his glass and sipped the scotch.

"I'm wondering if I'll actually get the connection with you that we used to have."

He considered what he could do to meet the challenge. "All right," he finally answered.

He concentrated on all the love he had ever felt for her —this life and last. He stirred it together like a conjuring, spinning it together into a tornado.

He'd pushed people countless times—millions, probably. With a strong enough intent he could get them to feel whatever he wanted. It was a bending of their energetic boundaries and a building of emotional threads that were already there. This, however, would be different.

This time he took his genuine feelings for her, so real and exact they took on a life of their own—and he pushed them toward her.

She drew in a sharp inhale.

He pushed her energetically again, harder this time, mainlining his love for her into her body. He was supposed to be open with her, vulnerable, and offering her every access to the deepest part of him.

Instead, he owned her with his passion for her and he was certain he'd just found his newest addiction. He pushed her to feel a new wave of his love, everything he felt for her.

"How...did you do that?" Her laugh was low and dark.

He closed the distance between them with a few steps. "I'm not entirely sure—something new."

"You pushed me."

He pressed a line of kisses along her neck. "In a sense, yes I did."

"Something you promised you'd never do."

"Shall I apologize?"

"No." She pulled him closer to her. "But that's not what you were supposed to be doing."

"Then shall we try that again?"

He wrapped his arms around her.

He had missed her, even though the distance was his fault. Even though he'd told her he wouldn't do that again. Seeing her so close to another man made him realize how stupid he had been. The harder he worked to control the risks in this situation, the more out of control things felt with her.

He watched her face. Her hair spread loose, her eyes searching his. To be needed by her was everything he'd ever wanted and yet it was more than he thought he could handle. If anything ever happened to her—he'd never forgive himself.

The endless way that he loved her, the uncertainty of their future, and the danger they were in—he had no idea how to get control of any of it.

IN THE COOL quiet of Addie's floating stateroom, Blake knew had not done what she asked of him tonight. At least not entirely. She wanted unfettered connection between the two of them, and for him to want the same thing. She would bring that topic up again and they would have to work that out.

He would need to find a way to tend to the very real dangers that threatened them, without allowing that pursuit to destroy what they shared. Something had shifted between them tonight that brought them closer. She understood him better. He had opened a little more.

He knew he had to change. He had to keep himself from getting in the way of their happiness. Nonetheless, vulnerability was not his main concern right now. The ship's speed had slowed and their tomorrow was rapidly becoming their today. They would have to face Otto soon and that fact brought all of his fears front and center once again.

18

Blake knocked on the door to Addie's state room. She didn't answer. He used his key and brought his luggage inside. The door to the promenade deck was still tied open and the room was about fifty degrees. He peeked in the bedroom. Addie was still sleeping.

He checked his pocket watch. The ship would dock soon.

He woke her. Then he called for coffee.

His mind wandered to the night before when Philippe had been sitting with Addie. His brother wasn't that hard to figure. Philippe's happy-to-see-you expression that he couldn't hide when she was around, the way he searched for excuses to be near her.

It wasn't that he didn't trust Addie, he did. He had just been gone too much. Philippe was available and he wanted her. For those reasons and more, he reinforced his decision to be more present, more available, more giving.

His mind shifted to Paris and what they might encounter. He had agreed to let her come, but he was still going to fight to keep her out of harm's way. She would call that controlling. Carolena called that arrogance. He referred to it as something that wasn't going to change any time soon.

He would remind himself whenever he could to give Addie the open emotional connection that she wanted. Other than that, he didn't think he was going to compromise on the other items. Not until Otto was gone, anyway.

He dug through his suitcase. Suitcases in this time were hard-sided and bulky, and there wasn't enough room in them to accommodate everything he needed. Especially when traveling from New York to Paris took the better part of a week.

He found Sarah's silver cigarette case he'd picked up. He meant to show it to Addie several days ago, but it had slipped to the side and fallen out of sight. He opened it. Inside was the note Sarah had dropped.

The word *yes* was all that was written on it. He assumed that yes was a secret note that was being passed to him when he was Jack.

"Since when do you smoke?" Addie stood in the doorway to the bedroom and stretched long and lithe in her robe.

"I don't. I meant to give this to you after my last trip."

"I appreciate the gift. But here's a newsflash: I don't smoke, either."

He laughed at how similar she'd become to her past-life sharp-edged self. "It's all clear to me now just how you got your past-life nickname."

"And here I thought my sassiness was just a pre-coffee thing."

She kissed him.

"Don't you want to know where I got this case?"

She took the cigarette case. "Oh, my gosh!" She slid her

palm in slow motion across the case from right to left. "Where did you get it?"

She had obviously picked up Sarah's vibration, and quickly.

"I've never read anything of hers before. Not directly."

Blake smiled with the pride that always came with making Addie happy. He closed the door to the promenade deck to shut out the wind.

"You handed it to me. Or she did."

"I remember this." Her eyes were trance-like while she read some faraway memory.

She was a blend now between who she used to be and who she was today. Those past-life threads were never more visible than when she held something from her past.

"I can see myself flipping it open. I had a little pattern for it. I flipped the switch with my right thumb, then I kind of caught it—" The case flew open and she caught it just as she'd just described. She gasped and stared at the partial row of cigarettes inside the case.

Blake watched the live memory in action. He guessed it would be okay to tell her now. Gary was far away. He told her about the meeting and how he sought out her former life self—Sarah, once he knew she was in the area.

"You approached her?"

"We weren't getting anywhere with Gary. I thought she might know something and I was right.

"You didn't tell me."

"I—there wasn't time, and, honestly I just—I forgot about it."

She shot him a stern you-have-got-to-be-kidding-me look. "Honestly."

He decided to let her have the last word on that one. He

had forgotten. And that fact would be unbelievable to anyone who heard the story.

"Blake—"

He expected more questions about Sarah, did she really look like the portrait, were their personalities similar, what did they talk about, did he meet Jack. Instead, he saw her with her hand covering the case as if it were a Bible and she were being sworn in. The color in her cheeks had paled into a near-white color.

"Are you okay? Do you want me to open the door again?" He reached for the doorknob.

"No. It's different."

"The case is different?"

"No, my life. Our life. Our past life. It changed."

BLAKE OPENED the door for a breeze and Addie drank down huge gulps of sea air. Goose bumps covered her arms and he wrapped a blanket around her shoulders.

"When I read the portrait and saw Jack's house, that was in New York or somewhere near there."

"Right." That was the way he remembered Carolena telling him about it, too, when she read the portrait for him years ago.

"Gary shot Jack in New York. We were on our way out of town someplace. But Jack died in New York." She held the case with both hands. "I don't see that now."

His heart pounded against his rib cage. "Maybe that's just because I took the case. It may not have absorbed that memory."

"Oh." She laughed, the sound edged with caution. "I just

saw Jack and Sarah planning a trip. It felt so real to me, like they—we actually went to France."

Blake felt the skin on the back of her neck. It was cold and clammy. "Maybe you ought to read it again on dry land. We're going to dock soon." He pointed to the land that was in sight now. "Why don't you get dressed? I've ordered toast and coffee. It ought to be here soon."

"Yeah. That's a good idea."

He kissed her on the temple and noticed her skin was salty and sweaty. "That really upset you, didn't it?"

She lowered herself onto a wicker chair. "I'm hoping I just read that wrong."

Blake put on his jacket and took an outfit from the closet for her. He arranged the rest of her clothes into the suitcase so she wouldn't have to.

"Are the portrait chips in there?" She pointed in the direction of the suitcase. "They ought to be in my purse. There. I want to read those."

Blake searched her purse for the small chips of paint he'd taken from a portrait of Sarah. He'd commissioned this portrait of her in his last life and managed to find it again in his present day life. When Addie touched the painting, or even just a few chips, she could read the energy and the memories that it had captured. He found the plastic bag in her purse and took it to her.

She immediately reached into the bag and rubbed her index finger and thumb over a couple of the colored paint chips from the portrait.

"Are you sure you want to do that now?"

"Shhh. Yes...let me do this."

He stood stock-still, hands on hips, and tried not to make any sound when he breathed. It took almost ten minutes until she opened her eyes again. The color in her face hadn't yet returned.

"What's the matter?"

She tried to swallow with some difficulty. "It *has* changed. I wasn't wrong."

"Tell me what you saw." Blake squatted in front of her. "It's okay. It can't be any worse than what happened the last time. Wait—are you okay? Is Sarah okay?"

"I saw him." Her eyes watered with tears.

"Who him?"

She placed her free hand on one of his hands. "Our baby. We had a son."

Heat flushed to his cheeks and he sat fully on the floor. "A son."

"Yeah. He has your eyes."

He put his palm to his forehead. Then he dropped it again. "Wait. Who raised him? Gary?"

"No. You. And me. Somehow you lived. I don't know how but this portrait—" She held several paint chips at the end of her fingertips. "It hung in the living room—our living room and watched over our happy family."

"Where?"

"Not anywhere in America. Somewhere in France. We were all speaking French." She drew in a deep breath. "Something changed, Blake. We've changed the past. Is that okay?"

An acrid taste flooded his mouth. He swallowed to make it go away but it didn't. Not entirely. "I think so. Everything feels okay. Did I kill Gary instead? Hopefully?" He hoped he hadn't said anything to Sarah that messed things up for them.

"I didn't see that. I didn't see a death scene at all, in fact. Maybe we just got away. Clean." She shrugged.

Time hung thick in the air.

"I'm just thinking about how my father and grandfather are always saying that changing the past changes the future somehow."

"Yeah, I remember. I don't know what to say. Everything seems okay. What did you say to Jack when you saw him? Anything that might cause him to do things differently?"

She squeezed her hands together until her knuckles turned white. "I don't think so. He snuck up behind me. He kissed me. I couldn't find an easy way out so I had to convince him that I wasn't Sarah."

Blake's chest tightened with an all too familiar fear. This is why he didn't want her involved in this search. Mistakes were too easily made in this arena. One wrong word and he could lose her all over again. "All right. Just think. What did you say to him?"

"I told him I wasn't Sarah. It wasn't a long conversation." Her words were short and clipped by fear. "I didn't do anything wrong here."

"I'm not saying that you did. I'm just trying to help. You said our past lives have changed. I'm trying to figure out how that happened in case we need to—"

"In case we need to what?"

"In case we need to fix something."

"That's gone wrong." Her eyes narrowed, sharpened, and Blake wanted to check his chest for something that felt like fire.

"Let's just take a step back for a minute. We're a team. We'll solve this together. Okay?"

Her eyes strayed to the ocean view that was now backed up by land. "I think I may have told him to be careful. Something like that. From the look on his face when I said it, he might have taken me seriously."

Blake's nod was curt. If he had been with her he didn't think this would have happened. At the very least he could have fixed it if it had.

"You're mad."

"I just don't want anything to happen to you. Or us. All right?" Blake restrained himself from taking over the situation. At least from being obvious about it. "We'll just have to see how this plays out."

"Could you have said anything to Sarah that might have changed things?"

"I just asked her if she knew where Otto and Carolena were."

"But you interacted with her and that could have changed something."

He ran his hand through the longest part of his hair. "I suppose."

A loud knock at the door startled them both.

"We're docking shortly, sir," the porter said. "We're going to need your luggage."

"Thank you. We'll have it ready momentarily."

The ship's horn blasted into the cold morning air and signaled their arrival.

Blake waited a moment until he was certain that the porter had moved on to the next stateroom. A knock from down the hall told him that he effectively had.

"They're in France?"

Addie glanced at the painted chips. "Or Canada, I guess. They spoke French."

"If they are in France, we're going to have to be very careful not to run into them."

19

———

A t four a.m. Grace sipped hot coffee and packed a few last items for their trip to Paris. Appropriately the extra large cup she found in Addie's kitchen cabinet was an elongated scene of "The Japanese Foot-bridge" by Monet. The name and 1922 were scribbled onto the bottom of the cup by the manufacturer.

It would have been strange for most people if they drank from some pop culture rendering while the original was created near relatives almost a century earlier. Addie and John and the rest weren't that far from where Monet finished this piece. If they were to drop in on him today, they might even witness his final brushstrokes on the canvas. This wasn't odd to Grace at all.

She sipped from the cup and stared at the photo she'd taken of Blake, Addie, and Alexa when they first arrived in Savannah several years ago. She'd purchased a new silver frame at the gift shop a few blocks away for it since the other one fogged. Simple, elegant, good quality.

The too-hot coffee burned her throat on the way down,

though she didn't flinch. She was more concerned about something else. The glass on the new frame was fogged now, too.

Only in one broad spot—over Blake's and Addie's bodies.

20
___

It took a train and another boat to get them from Southampton to Calais and then yet another train from Calais to Paris. Addie commented that time travel through a Wentworth would have been easier.

Blake had to agree.

He understood why some guests chose to make the Hotel Ritz their residence. It was simply too hard to get back to get back home again.

They checked in to their suites, and though Addie promptly dropped into an armchair when they entered the room, Blake insisted they move to a new set of rooms. "We can't be on the first floor. It's too accessible from the outside."

The bellhop informed them that the hotel was fully obligated for the next few days.

"That's fine. We'll work with it." Addie asked for a toothbrush, a hot meal, and a glass of wine.

When the bellhop left, Blake stared out the window. Once again Paris was the city of distress for him. In New York the constant disappointment from fruitless searches was bad enough—he followed up on every possible lead only to discover that they led nowhere. Now, he was one step closer to doing whatever was required to save and protect the women he loved.

And he would.

How would he handle it, though, if he found Otto in the Louvre? Or dining in an outdoor cafe? Yes, he could follow them until he knew where they lived. At some point, though, there would be a confrontation, and odds were that he would have to kill Otto.

How would that go? A bullet through the forehead while he was about to take a sip of his morning cafè? Or maybe one through the back of the head while he ate dinner at night? He might need to apologize to Carolena for the blood and brain matter if it splattered on her. That would go over well.

Furthermore, how did he get away with something like this? He didn't know anything about getting away with murder. Not in the present day or the 1920s. He had no idea what the laws were in this era or this country. In the present day, France had a reputation for being particularly harsh on criminals, so he assumed that rule was the same for the twenties.

He felt an unfamiliar flutter in his chest. Not an ache or a pain, just a strange sensation. There was a tingling in his arm and in his hands as well. He wouldn't be surprised if this scenario was giving him a heart attack.

It would have been easy for him to kill Otto and his bodyguards that day in his office. They broke into his private property, pulled guns on him and Addie, and they tried to take her away from him.

He could have shot and killed them right then. Then he would have called the police, they would have questioned him, and removed the bodies. That chapter of his life would have been over and life would have gone on. He wouldn't have felt guilty about any of it because it would have been justified. Self-defense.

Here, was another story. The conditions were completely different. Many of them unknown to him, which made it hard to get on top of the situation.

The bottom line was that he saw himself as a protector, a defender. He didn't think he was a murderer. At least not in a premeditated way.

"When was the last time you slept?"

He shook his head, his eyes focused on the outer border of the Place' Vendome, and searched faces and figures that might look familiar. "I don't remember."

"Come. Lie down." She slipped off her light jacket.

She snuggled in next to him, and he closed his eyes. He expected her to drift off to sleep beside him, and he wished that he could as well. His body felt heavy but his mind moved in circles. He didn't think he could rest.

When he was sure she was asleep, he would investigate the lay of the hotel. He wanted to find the library.

He felt her get up, to take off her traveling shoes, he imagined. Barefoot was always her preference indoors.

When she laid next to him, he found he couldn't open his eyes. He was so tired that he couldn't remember which life they shared in this moment or how they got there. He could only feel her arms that held him close.

He'd always felt this with her, an eternity, a timeless space of simply being with her where he only truly felt himself.

His world was perfectly secure in his arms. His final thoughts before he fell asleep weren't new, but they had proven true time after time. Life with her was the only one he wanted to live.

It wasn't the soft amber light in the room that woke him. Though the gold table lamp reflected in the mirrored dressing table was the first thing he saw. It was more the subtle jostling beneath him that moved his body from left to right. Rough seas, he thought, to feel such movement in their stateroom. Or, no. They had left the ship, this must be the train. He was lying down, so it couldn't be the train.

He reached to his side to feel for Addie. The fabric next to him was cool, almost cold. A slight breeze blew across his face and he sat up with a gasp. The window was open.

"Addie!" He lunged toward the open window.

"I'm right here. Blake. Right here," she said.

"What—" He looked at the open window.

"I wanted some air. Are you okay?"

He searched the room—door closed, window open, but Addie was okay. "Yeah. Fine." The outside was dark except for the string of car headlights that rolled along the front of the hotel in an evening parade. "What time is it?"

She glanced at the gold mantel clock. "A little after ten."

He squinted at the white dial and found only a blur of fuzzy numbers. He rubbed his eyes and fought for a stronger hold on his consciousness. "I slept a long time."

"Eight hours is not that long to sleep."

He blinked his eyes and found the room much clearer. Addie sat on her feet next to the top of the bed. "What are you doing with the headboard?"

Her closed-lipped smile tipped only in one corner, a blended mix of compassion and humor. "Have some water first." She pointed to a bottle of mineral water and two small glasses on the dresser.

He did as he was told.

"I feel like the walking dead," he said.

"Too much travel and not enough sleep."

"What's going on?" He nodded to her position on the bed.

"Well, it hit me. This is the nicest suite in the hotel, right? And if Otto and Carolena had been here, then they would have stayed in the best room available."

"Right." He said the word like a question.

"So, while you were sleeping, I started feeling around. Searching."

"And you found traces of them?"

"No. I found something far more telling." She pressed against the tufted fabric on the headboard. "This."

He crossed the room and stared at the same gold and beige flower-on-repeat fabric that covered the walls, the bedspread, and the chairs. "What?"

She stared him squarely in the face. "A sealant."

21

"I spent two hours examining every inch of that sealant." Addie's voice was just above a whisper and everyone at the table leaned close to hear what she was saying. "There are no breaks or holes in it anywhere."

The restaurant at the Ritz was full of guests, indicative of springtime in Paris. The round white fabric-covered tables weren't that close to one another, but Blake appreciated her cautiousness, nonetheless.

"Addie, I can't hear you, dear. Sit over here." John put a piece of bread on the small plate, brushed away the crumbs, and patted the upholstered bench next to him.

Blake's back teeth ground against one another when her seat next to her grandfather also meant that she sat next to Philippe. When Philippe extended his arm behind her, Blake's hand clenched into a fist.

"She covered every inch of that room in sealant—the chairs, the headboard, the desk, the light switches. I even checked the bathroom countertop."

"She couldn't have covered everything." Philippe gestured with his glass. He crossed his legs and his body angled toward hers. "Surely there's some small space left uncovered."

"Well, I didn't check the toilet seat. But barring that, everything is covered."

John froze with a stare on Addie.

Her wine glass hit the table hard enough that red liquid sloshed over the rim and bled onto the white tablecloth. "I am *not* reading the toilet seat."

"It would have been cleaned," Campbell said.

"Oh, no. *No.*"

"He probably spent time sitting there thinking." Philippe stifled a laugh unsuccessfully.

Addie rubbed four fingertips up her forehead.

"I wasn't actually thinking of the toilet seat," John said. "Although, if we can't find anything else, that may not be a bad idea. I would, of course, get you a pair of gloves. At the Ritz I may only be able to find over-the-elbow evening gloves, but I would make sure that your hands were covered."

"Thank you." She sipped her wine and stared beyond the four of them as though she were on the edge of revolt.

"What were you thinking, John?" Blake asked.

"The bathtub."

"That's a good idea, Dad," Campbell said.

The waiter placed an order of Dover sole in front of each of person and the scent of warm butter filled the air.

Addie shrugged. "I could try it. I haven't yet. I was focused more on furniture, and any place they might have transferred an impression."

"Carpet is covered, I guess?" Philippe asked.

Addie nodded. "Completely sealed."

"Amazing," he said. "To think of the time it required to do that."

"Otto probably watched her from start to finish," Blake said.

Everyone feasted on their meal with hard-earned appetites. Blake ate more slowly, listening to conversation and ideas about Carolena and Otto and where they might have left a record of their movements.

John polished off the last bite of his fish and asparagus. He nudged the plate forward an inch. "Start with the bathtub. I remember that Carolena enjoyed baths."

"She does." Blake pointed to him with the blunt end of his fork. "How do you know that?"

"You and she, when you were just a little thing, stayed in the townhouse for a while."

Blake smiled to hide the cringe of being described as "a little thing". Though he knew he had been quite young when they stayed there.

"When y'all moved she left behind a menagerie of bath soaps and bubble concoctions. Anyway, it's possible she left a trace during a long bath. If not, we'll keep searching."

"She left a good sealant everywhere else, I can tell you that. I was in that suite for several hours and I never sensed energy from either of them."

Mary rounded the far corner of the dining room wearing an evening gown Blake suspected she'd just purchased that day—a sleeveless black silk dress that dissolved into soft layers at the lower third.

"I think you're in for an evening on the town." Addie waved to Mary, scooted out from the bench, and kissed John on the cheek. "I'll head on to the room and investigate the tub. Please give her my apologies for leaving."

"I will. We'll talk in the morning, sweet girl." He kissed her on the cheek and stood for Mary. "Knock on my door as early as six, if you're up."

"I'll go with you." Philippe placed his cloth napkin on the table.

Blake gathered together his glass of wine and white bowl of Dover sole that sloshed in a fair amount of butter. Even with the wine in his hand he managed to point at Philippe. "No, you won't."

I KNEELED at the side of the white bathtub and dragged my fingertips over the curved edge of the porcelain. Inch by inch, I listened for images, conversations, thoughts or feelings that might belong to Carolena. I steeled myself to hear the impressions from too many people who had soaked in this tub.

It all depended upon how long they were here, I supposed. If they only stayed a night or two, it might be hard to find anything that belonged to her. My fingertips sank into the energy imprints layered on the tub—there was no sealant.

I moved downward slowly, hoping I wouldn't pick up an overload of stories from people I didn't need to know. Doing so was a bit like walking through a crowd—you couldn't possibly listen to every conversation or have an empathetic response to every concern.

After having traveled through the Monet and the Wentworth, interestingly, I now had a stronger sense of direction when it came to reading things. I could still become overwhelmed when too much information ran through me. However, the different avenues I'd traveled in the paintings required me to have a life-or-death ability to choose what I would read and what I could let go.

The farther my hand traveled into the deeper areas of

the tub, the louder the chatter became. I listened to a little bit of everything I came across and quickly moved on when I knew it wasn't Carolena. Tired children fighting bedtime. Unappreciated wives who cherished their bath time alone. Men who smoked cigars and strategized how to increase their wealth. None of them wanted to leave the pleasure and the catered comfort of the Hotel Ritz.

Except for one. I backed my fingers over an area where the energy felt familiar, like an old friend. Carolena. I dove in, even though it felt creepy to spy on someone during their bath. I could only hope there were lots of bubbles to block my view.

She worried for Blake. Though like a mother, she didn't worry for herself. The guilt she wrestled for leaving him was only assuaged by her belief that she was protecting him. As long as she babysat Otto, kept him occupied and focused, her loved ones were safe. It was a sacrifice that appeared to take its toll.

She rested her head in her hand. Weariness and apathy battled each other for control of her heart and soul. There was nothing left to look forward to. The joy of family and freedom and the empowerment of choice was something of the past for her now.

For the rest of her life, she would be a pawn in Otto's never-ending game to amass wealth and exquisite art for power and control. She thought about the various artists they'd visited in Paris—too many to count. She had grown tired of his need to own so much—rare pieces from the great masters that he couldn't have any other way. Carolena drew her arms around her legs and rested her chin on her knees. It was a *trahison des clercs*, stealing these masterpieces from the future, from the general public who would never see them. Art was important to a society. It made people think. It made them feel.

There was a knock at the door.

"Come in," she said.

Otto peeked in.

"What is it, *mon amour?*"

"The painting was just delivered," he said.

"I'll be right there."

"I think you will love it." The tone of his voice was rich with pride and accomplishment. "To give you a clue, it involves a mother and child. One of his most recent pieces."

Carolena twisted her body and rested her hands on the edge of the tub. "*Exquis.*"

"It reminds me of you." Otto kept his sight fixed on the painting that had to have been propped just outside the bathroom door. "And our son."

He didn't know that their son was Blake. She had told him that their son died when he was young and that was the reason she couldn't come back to him. It was too painful to be around someone else who knew him as she did. She told him she felt guilty, as though she had failed as a mother.

"I think it's important that we celebrate what we once had. Or at least memorialize it. It was the best time of my life." From the impromptu sound of it, his sigh was unexpected and genuine.

He finally turned to her and she smiled with an understanding that rocked between them like a gentle wave. A rare unguarded moment with Otto. He was the only one who was witness to that time in her life. A fantastic time. Magical. When everything was entirely possible and only to them. Those were the moments she had remembered most when they were apart. The good times with him had been better than the good times with anyone else. Of course, the bad times with him were more terrifying than any other time in her life, too.

"We meet with the artist tomorrow."

"*Oui?*"

"*Oui. Trois heures de l'après-midi.*" He ran a finger beneath her chin. "If you are charming, we may get to buy another piece." He gestured to the canvas on his way out of the room. "Come. Enjoy. I can offer you a private showing."

The door clicked shut. Carolena hoped Otto hadn't selected any paintings that featured bright splashes of red. A shiver ran up her body. Even though a lifetime had passed, she still couldn't look at that particular shade of true red without remembering the sickly sweet smell and Otto's blood-covered hands.

"THEY MET WITH AN ARTIST." I burst out of Carolena's memory center, otherwise known as our bathroom, and found Blake lying on the bed. Not something I had ever seen him do except to sleep at night.

"An artist?" He pushed himself upright and appeared a little worse for wear. Pale. Slightly sweaty.

"*Oui*—I mean, yes. Do you feel okay?"

He ran his hand over his face and exhaled hard. "I haven't caught up on my sleep, I guess."

I felt his forehead. No fever.

He moved my hand away and kissed it. "I'm fine. Where?"

"I don't know."

"When?"

"3:30, but I don't know what day. I couldn't tell."

"What else?"

"Otto purchased at least one piece, which features a mother and a child." I turned around to search for the canvas and then I realized that the art was only in my vision. I wasn't entirely in the present moment yet. "They, um. They may also have purchased another by now. Somehow we have to figure out which paintings they have. That's where our next clue is."

"Good job."

"Thanks. Do you remember any stories about Otto hurting someone?"

"Physically?"

"Yeah. With blood. A lot of it." I held out open hands.

"Well, there was Frank—"

"This is something Carolena would have seen. I had the feeling you were young when this happened. I don't know that for sure. She didn't say. I just had the sense that she saw something he did—something that ended with a lot of blood—before she left. Maybe it was why she left. Or part of it."

He pushed himself to the edge of the bed. "Not that I know of. But as we both know, Carolena likes her secrets."

22

———————

The library was impossible to find. I figured they designed it that way. I'd woken up early. I used the time to cover the first floor of the hotel and find the library of first editions. I'd knocked on Blake's door, but he slept uncharacteristically soundly.

An early train must have just arrived because the front desk was swarmed with guests ready to check in. I finally caught someone's attention at the front desk and asked them where to find the library, the clerk directed me out of the hotel and several blocks away.

"*Bibliothèque.*" He enunciated all four syllables as though I were deaf, even though I'd spoken to him in French. Not English.

The thought occurred to me that maybe he really didn't know about the library of first edition books. A more terrifying thought occurred to me as well, that maybe it didn't exist at the moment. Or anymore, for that matter.

"Merci," I finally said with the most polite traveler's smile I could conjure.

He waved to the next guest in the crowd. *"Suivant s'il-vous-plaît."*

I checked my watch: six a.m. I gave up my search and made my way through the still-unpopulated hallways, up the stairs, and knocked on Grandpa's door as he had suggested. Since it was only 2 a.m. New York time, Mary slept soundly. We knocked on Dad's door together. The three of us left the hotel to talk and share croissants at a neighborhood bakery.

Along the wet and unpopulated early morning streets, and in the absence of too many cars, it was difficult to tell the difference between 1922 and our present day. At his height of six feet four inches, I could still look up to my grandfather as I'd done all of my life. I slipped my hand into his always larger one and ran my thumb over the top of it and turned it over. There were more age spots than there used to be. My heart ached with the not-so-subtle wish to protect him and Dad from the inevitable end that aging brought.

When I was a child, their presence in my life was as unchangeable and everlasting to me as the sun that rose every morning. Unreasonably, but unfailingly so, I wanted it to be that way again.

We arrived early enough at the bakery that we had to carry our own table and chairs to the outside. Their baked goods and coffee were prepared, but their setup for the public, not quite so. Grandpa convinced them to take our money and to serve us early. I said something to my father about how his dad could talk the brick off of the side of a building.

I spoke with the both of them about everything I'd found in the tub. Grandpa sat in the wicker and wooden chair with his legs crossed, index finger set beneath his bottom lip, and he listened intently.

"This is good news," he said with his usual air of confidence. No matter the level of uncertainty in the situation, he always managed to locate his sense of positive direction. "Unfortunate that Otto has some new art, a masterpiece, no doubt. But that is the next viable lead for us."

"A painting with a mother and a child could be a Cassatt or a Renoir," my dad said.

"Picasso or Gauguin. Bouguereau," Grandpa said.

"Good one." I pointed at him. "Morisot."

"Also good." Grandpa pointed at me this time. "We need to get to the first edition library and get a note to Grace. List each artist we've mentioned and their respective pieces. Ask her to take an inventory of these artists, and any others she might think of who have painted mother and child paintings. She needs to see if any of their major works are missing from museums or private collections."

My dad placed his coffee cup on his saucer. "Assuming she can still remember which of these pieces of art was in museums prior to Otto removing it in this newly changed past. If anything looks unfamiliar to her, just have her check against your list."

"We would know the difference because we were not yet in the present. Right?"

"Right," my father said. "We're the only ones. Anyone in the future is already forgetting the piece that Otto took, assuming he kept it hidden away between now and present day."

"If I sent Grace a picture, could she remember both realities? Meaning, the one where the museums have owned these pieces and the one where Otto owns them?"

"Grace understands how these new realities are created,

so yes. If you sent her a picture and made her aware of what was going on, she would be able to comprehend both realities at once. She would have to choose to. It's not easy to see one reality while everyone else embraces another."

"I know this," I said. That was my normal psychic life, seeing what other people couldn't.

"The general public would not have any memory of the original reality, though."

I made a mental note of every artist we mentioned and sipped espresso from a small white cup. There were more questions I needed answers to.

"So, if something changed in Blake's or my past, like with Jack or Sarah, would we know it?" I cast the question as gently as possible.

"What do you mean?"

"I mean, if something became different in our pasts that changed our lives, would we remember both realities or just the new one?"

"You think something may have changed your lives?"

"Our present lives, yes."

My grandfather sighed long and deep. He avoided prying. "I think it's possible to remember both. Just like Grace. I remember when I gave some earrings to Ellen years ago. Drop earrings. Silver with aquamarine. She admired a similar pair on a movie actress from this era. A Miss Edna Purviance. She did a lot of those Charlie Chaplin movies. A little thing." He measured her height to be about the size of a junior high school girl. "Anyway. We were on one of our many trips to New York in the twenties. I found the earrings, gave them to her. She was thrilled.

"We get back to the present day and low and behold, Ellen finds pictures of Miss Edna and she's not wearing her earrings. She should have been wearing them, in these particular pictures. Turns out I inadvertently found *the* aquamarine earrings that Miss Edna was to have owned. Not just a pair like them as I thought." He lifted his hand in the air and slapped his leg. "I made a mistake and changed a little bit of history. Not sure what the odds are on something like that but I ought to have had someone buy me a lottery ticket on that day."

"So, Ellen knew that Edna was missing her earrings?"

"Yes, sorry. That's my point. Ellen remembered both realities—one where Edna owned the earrings, the other where she owned them. For a while, anyway. I think because she was familiar with time travel and its consequences."

"You said, for a while."

"Well, she eventually forgot that the earrings had belonged to Edna Purviance. Sometime later, when I suggested that the actress was the original owner of the earrings, she laughed and said I was crazy."

"Oh." I leaned my forehead into my hand.

"Let's not get ahead of ourselves." My dad steadied me with his hand to my shoulder. "Tell us what's going on."

I shared the story about Sarah's cigarette case, reading the chips from the painting, and seeing the new past. "I'm terrified to ask this question. But you don't think Blake or I have messed something up, do you? I mean we're both still here."

My father stared at his coffee, and adjusted his cup in the saucer. When he lifted his gaze to me, the wrinkles to the sides of his eyes deepened with a calm smile that encouraged me not to worry. But I paid more attention to the panic that shot through his heart like rapid fire. "How much longer did Jack live in this new 1920s life?"

"I don't know. In the scenes I saw, our son was little. Jack lived to see him and beyond, I guess. Unlike before when he was killed long before our child was born." I dug my nails into my palms.

"Mmhmm." My dad shifted his glance to his father. I knew he was debating over what to say, and he wasn't about to let me know how worried he was.

"Any change to the past isn't ideal. But there was quite a bit of time between that life and this one. Blake is still here, as are you. Maybe everything is fine." My grandfather patted me on the hand and squeezed it. His smile was lovingly given, but it was pasted on like a mask. I knew he didn't know for sure if everyone was okay.

"I hope you're right." I squeezed his hand in return.

"I'm rarely wrong. Best first step for you and Blake this morning is to get to the library and see if you can get that note to Grace. Write it ahead of time. You probably already thought of that. Be quick about slipping it in and closing the book. Hopefully, the burning scent that the book makes when it transmits a message won't be too noticeable."

"I thought I might try to close the book just before getting it back on the shelf. Maybe the paper from the neighboring books would absorb the smell."

"Good idea."

"Okay, so I need a clue as to where to find the library."

He wiped his mouth with his napkin, folded it and laid it neatly on the table. "What do you mean?"

"I can't find it. I covered the ground floor this morning. I even asked at the front desk and they directed me to a public library several blocks away." My heart beat faster than usual and I inhaled a calming deep breath.

"Interesting," was all he said. Concern flashed in his eyes, for a quick moment. A corresponding shot of panic shot through my stomach. If he was worried, I felt more worried.

"Campbell?"

"I doubt it," my dad said to the unasked question about Otto. "He had no way of knowing."

"The library used to be down a narrow corridor in the lobby. Just to the far side of the front desk. They may have moved it. Or it may be gone."

I exhaled in a huff. "Gone?"

"With people like us moving in and out of time, the past can shift. Search again."

"I'm going to go with the idea that they might have moved it. Do you remember where *This Side of Paradise* is located, assuming we get to the library?"

He squinted toward the sky and ran his tongue over the right side of his top teeth, as though he summoned the vision from his memory. "Used to be the right shelf, about halfway up, as you walk in the door. There used to be a desk beyond that area. Sometimes Monsieur Bernard sat there, I remember he kept a gun in that desk. Have Blake stand to the left of you to block his view if he's there."

"Blake is asleep. He's been tired lately."

My grandfather studied my face, knowing what worries were behind my words. It was funny to me that when I was a young girl, I found that kind of know-you-so-well relation-ship to be confining. As I got older all I wanted was for someone to see the real me and to love me for what was there.

"Then get Philippe to go with you. It will take two to get past Monsieur Bernard and into the book." He spun his cup in his saucer. "Seems unlike Blake to sleep in. Is everything okay with the two of you?"

"Mmmm." I hummed on a higher note from my regular voice. Stress, I figured. I cleared my throat to get to my more regular, lower tone. "I think so. We talked. Several times.

There's a lot of uncertainty in the search, and he feels a good deal of pressure."

"Well, that's to be expected of a man like Blake. The vulnerability of his loved ones weighs on him, I would guess."

"His salvation is to take control of everything, try to make it right. But where Otto is concerned, that hasn't always worked—"

"The need to control causes its own problems."

"Yeah. It's strange how someone can control you so closely and create distance at the same time."

He patted my leg. "You'll work it out."

"I don't think he feels well."

"He could have picked up something," my father said. "I wouldn't worry. The viruses and such aren't too strong in this era. At least not compared to what Grace tells me we have in the present. Or just the time zone change and all the travel. Let him rest. Go get Philippe. I'll tell Blake it was my recommendation." Grandpa winked. "Everything will be fine. Let's keep moving ahead. Y'all head on to the hotel. We need that response from Grace so we can get a plan in place."

Grandpa cleared the table for us and took our coffee cups inside. It was the first moment my dad and I had had alone in some time. He took my hand and kissed it, tucked my arm close to him while we walked.

"After twenty some odd years without you, it's still amazing to me that you're here." His lips broadened into the same loving smile I'd known all my life.

"To me as well." I leaned in and rested my head on his shoulder.

His sigh rode too many emotions to count. He squeezed

my hand three times. "Don't worry about Blake. We'll keep an eye on him, okay?"

"Okay," I said. His voice was tied to the very idea of home for me, but the worry in his heart kept me from relaxing my concern. I decided on a subject change. "So, I have to ask, and if this is none of my business, just tell me. But, when I saw the two of you together, I had the feeling that Ruth was more than a friend."

His lips pressed together for several steps. It was as though he sifted through all his words, determining which ones to share and which ones to keep to himself.

"You don't have to say anything if you don't want to. We all have our private lives."

"She's a friend," he said, then winced with what looked like regret. "Actually, she's been more than a friend for some time now."

I had guessed the truth, certainly. Though my heart dropped when I heard it aloud. Twenty years, I reminded myself. That's too long to be alone. I wanted him to have love and companionship and happiness. I just had a hard time fitting Ruth into the memories of my father and my mother, Isabella, dancing with one another in the kitchen by candlelight. Their love never died for me. I didn't think it had for Isabella, either.

I thought, for the short time, that I knew them as a couple, that they loved one another beyond measure. He'd never left her, he was taken from her. They were unfinished in my mind.

"I guess that must be difficult for you to think of me with someone else."

"No. I understand." My heart tossed up another memory of my parents together, their hand-in-hand walks along the low tide of the evenings. Shift forward through the years, and Isabella took those walks on her own. Now it was my turn to wince. "Why didn't you tell me about her?"

Another long sigh. "I guess I should have. I'm sorry about that. I suppose I could say I didn't know how, and that would be partly true. Mostly I didn't want to hurt Isabella. And I didn't want to upset you."

"You still love Isabella."

"I will always love Isabella. But I've not had a way to be with her in twenty years."

I nodded. "Does she know?"

His brows rose and created several horizontal lines across his forehead. His mouth dropped open to say something but nothing came out. I remembered he wore that same helpless expression years ago when I asked him if there was really a Santa Claus.

"She and I don't discuss that side of our lives." On his next step forward he scuffed his shoe through a shallow puddle. "I think we would probably still be together if I hadn't fallen through the rabbit hole."

"That's probably best." Isabella wasn't cut from the same cloth as Grace. She was more sensitive, an artist. I didn't think she'd been without her relationships over the years. But I also knew she wouldn't want any details about Ruth and how much Dad cared about her.

"I can introduce you to her when we get back. If you'd like. If not, I understand."

I felt a heart-centered thread pull loose from my dream that my family would be reunited one day. I'd not figured a place for Ruth in our family tapestry.

"No, I'd like that." I forced a smile for his benefit.

"Twenty years is a long time, Addie."

"I understand. I do." And I did. Mentally. My heart had no clue, though. She was a selfish organ who oftentimes ran how I thought about things. If I'd found Blake with another woman after he and I had been parted for twenty years, my heart wouldn't be understanding then, either. I glanced at the front of the hotel and was grateful for the out. "I'd better go find Philippe. We need to locate the library."

FAR AWAY FROM the main thoroughfare of the hotel, Philippe and I stood completely lost among tiny hotel shops of jewelry and perfumeries. Fashion-forward women wearing low-waisted dresses, some with pleated skirts, eyed Philippe with interest and invitation.

I shook my head, laced my arm through his, and turned us in a different direction. "Did you ever resent the fact that Otto had an affair with Carolena?"

His tongue clicked against the roof of his mouth. "I suppose. Once I was old enough to understand it. Mom did a lot for us. It was unfair to her. But secretly, I always hoped he would run away with someone. Just...disappear."

I stared straight ahead, bothered unreasonably by the images my mind conjured of Ruth and my father. He was an adult, irreparably separated from his wife. Yet I saw her as the interloper, the thief who stole precious experiences from our family—time and moments and closeness that ought not to have been shared with her. My cheek warmed. From my peripheral vision I saw Philippe stare at my face.

"You're thinking of Ruth? Or Mary?"

"You knew about Ruth and my dad." I felt one eyebrow raise.

"I figured as much. The way he reacted when she and her son came into the gallery seemed...more than friendly."

"Isabella hasn't stopped loving him."

He ran his hand along the top of my arm that was still looped through his. "He probably loves her, too. But what's he supposed to do when they can't be together?"

"No, I know. I've just...always wanted my family to come back together. I don't think Isabella would want to set a place for Ruth at the dinner table."

"Probably not. I have to say, I feel for your dad. It's miserable to share a love with someone and not be able to be with them." He looked off in the distance like he searched the area. My hand rested on his and the realization of what he felt knocked me breathless. He'd been referring to me when he said that.

"He said the library was on the first floor?" Philippe said in a rescue attempt to change the subject.

"Yes." I'd always felt a special closeness to Philippe, and lately, that had become more intense. I assumed that was just a result of spending so much time together, and that it would dissipate when things got back to normal. Assuming we'd ever see normal again.

"Well, we've covered the first floor. Officially." He glanced around the area. There wasn't a corner we'd missed.

One of the sales clerks who wore a black below-the-knee, button-front dress emerged from the back room with an oval hat box. "I believe this was the one you saw in the window, madam." Her English was heavily accented. She removed a wide-brimmed, taupe-colored hat with orangeish berries sewed into the base and said to her customer, "Perfect for summer."

"What if the library didn't move... What if other rooms of the hotel moved around it? To keep it private for some reason?" I felt for the pins that held my long hair short.

Philippe followed my line of sight when another clerk wearing an identical long black dress went through the service door to a back room. "So, you think it's no longer a public room?"

"The hotel may have become too popular and it's possible that it became too difficult to protect all the precious books."

"So, they kept the room from view. That would explain why the employees up front didn't even know about it."

I pulled him in the opposite direction of the shops.

"Where are we going?"

"Back to where it's supposed to be."

We zigzagged our way along a mile of marble and royal blue-carpeted hallways. Young maids singsonged *"Bonjour"* at almost every corner. When we finally made it to the front desk we found that the crowd was only slightly less thick. Most of the clerks were occupied with one male guest who complained that they had given his room away.

"The ship was late! Almost an entire day late! Not my fault."

"Je suis désolé monsieur." All the clerks muttered their apologies at the same time. One hotel employee tried to offer accommodations at a neighboring hotel for the night.

We paced the outer rim of the circular lobby like two wolves looking for a meal. An older man, short, round, with well-coiffed gray hair and wire-rim glasses perched on the end of his nose opened a door behind the crowd of employees.

I grabbed Philippe's arm and we jerked to a stop. Just beyond the door was a small room that, from what I could see of it anyway, was only a small office. "I don't think that's it," I said. "From what I've heard it was a sizable library. Big enough for floor-to-ceiling bookshelves."

Philippe took me by the hand and we navigated our way through the noisy crowd and around to the far corner of the long, curved front desk. He squeezed my hand and pointed toward the outline of a door that was visible in the gold fleur-de-lis wall coverings.

I shrugged. "Let's try it."

We took slow and cautious steps, watching the employees' movements carefully in order to time our own. We kept a respectable distance from the front desk in an effort to stay unnoticed.

I slipped my hand into my outer dress pocket and felt the note I'd written to Grace ahead of time. Assuming we found the library we needed I may only have a few seconds to get the message sent. I also needed a few seconds to search for any messages that might have come through.

Employees darted back and forth; the lobby was a circus. Like dancing to a waltz without music, we moved in counterbalance to the clerks. When the guest without a room smashed his fist into the front desk and demanded his room, we abruptly changed direction and slipped through the hidden door. With such a commotion I was quite certain no one saw us.

I had no idea, though, how we would leave this tiny area without being noticed. Philippe gave the door a shove with his shoulder and it fit snugly against the wall. Not as a door would fit into a door jam, but as one piece of the wall would slide against another. Fresh chips of white paint flicked onto the green carpet that was as bright as a fresh lime. That's when I noticed it—there was no door knob to open the door when we needed to return to the outside.

"That's a new wall." I pointed to the paint chips and kept my voice quieter than a whisper. "How do we get out?"

Philippe shrugged.

The hallway was quite short and it angled to the left. Like a crooked runway that deadened into the side of a mountain, the green carpet ended into a flat, white wall. With no windows or doors carved into it, the wall seemed to have no purpose other than to stop our progress. Light cast onto the far end of the carpet from an unseen source, and we had no choice but to check it out.

With Philippe's hand pressed firmly into the lower part of my back, we took a collective step forward and I found myself wishing that Blake was with us. If we ran into someone who was none too happy to see us, his ability to push would have come in quite handy.

I leaned around the white double doorway entrance, my head felt too large and visible. It seemed to take forever for my eyes to reach the spot where I could see what was in the room. I wished for a tiny camera to do my spying for me. I envisioned someone or several someones watching the top of my head slide into their field of view and my heart jogged at twice its normal speed.

What would the Ritz do if they found us snooping in an area they'd deliberately secluded from the rest of the guests? In the present, they would just toss us out. I assumed they would do the same thing here. Which would be a problem, since I needed to be in this hotel to read spaces where Carolena might have left a trace.

Cooler air poured from the room that was twice the size in height that it was long. The same lime green from the hallway carried into this room, its color as fresh as spring grass. It covered round tufted pillows and ran beneath gold couches that appeared as though they were taken directly from Versailles. Gold chairs boasted cream-colored panels on the sides with hand-stitched bouquets of flowers and perfectly matched green leaves.

Glass encased bookcases started at hip height and stretched to the elevated ceiling. A rolling ladder perched in one corner of the room and anchored itself to a gold rail near the ceiling. An elaborate sixteen candle chandelier bathed the room in yellow-tinted softness and highlighted a fragile spiral staircase in the corner.

I remembered what Grandpa had said, that the Fitzgerald book was—in the original room, anyway—to the right of the door. I searched there first.

Some of the linen book jackets were quite robust in color. Others were faded and muted, their bound pages slipped crooked inside their covers. *Tender is the Night* was only a couple of years old by this point in history, so I searched among the newer-looking novels. Philippe checked the other cabinets.

"Find it?" His voice was a loud whisper.

"Not yet." My voice was probably too soft for him to hear. Though I was more concerned about being heard by someone outside the room than I was with anything else.

He moved to the far left corner of the room and climbed up the ladder to examine the upper shelves. I gave up on my grandfather's direction and searched the lower shelves in the same area.

When one-quarter of the shelves had been thoroughly gone over, I guided the ladder over the corner so that we could inspect the next wall of books. The abrupt rasp of a stuck door being opened caught us off-guard. My entire body jumped like I'd been shaken from the inside out.

"Thank you for taking the time to sign. We try to have all of our authors' autographs whenever poss—" A thick diminutive Frenchman in a dark double-breasted suit and heavily slicked black and gray hair paused just inside the room. His mouth remained open with words seemingly built up inside of it. His head cocked to the side.

"Were you invited?" His heavily pronounced D at the

end sent his territorial rage through me. He liked a controlled environment. Without moving his head, his stare searched the room: countertops, shelves, furniture, back to Philippe and me.

"Yes," Philippe and I answered at the same time. It was the only reasonable response.

"Monsieur Bernard?" Philippe asked when he stepped down the rungs of the ladder. "We were referred to you."

"By whom, may I ask?" Monsieur Bernard tilted his chin upward, his stare now gliding down his nose and toward us.

"My family collects first editions." I made up the story. Though I relied on an old childhood teaching from Ruby, my grandmother's housekeeper: *the truth shall set you free.* "My father and grandfather visited your library when it was more...accessible to the public. They said we simply must visit."

"Our extensive collection prohibits us from allowing the public—"

"Did I hear a familiar accent?" A blond, blue-eyed American appeared from just outside of the Ritz's private library. His face was immediately recognizable to me, though only from pictures. One, specifically, with my grandmother, Grace.

"Yes, Mr. Fitzgerald. What an esteemed honor, sir." I stepped forward with American confidence and a surety that I knew Monsieur Bernard wouldn't approve of, but that Fitzgerald would. Maybe even appreciate. We shook hands, palm to palm, a vigorous shake. His hair was uncharacteristically parted on the side. In photos, I had always seen it parted in the middle. He didn't wear much styling creme and as a result, there was a bit of fluff and lift to his hair.

He was baby face young, about twenty-five, I guessed. He

glowed with the approval of freshly minted success and the anticipation of a bright, problem-free future.

"Where do you hail from?" His broad smile engaged his entire face—eyes, cheek bones, and even his spirit lifted along with it.

"Savannah and New York, sir." I couldn't believe that I just said "sir." I hadn't said "sir" since I was a little girl. I didn't think, anyway. At least not seriously.

"I'm just from New York, myself. Sit." He gestured toward the gold furniture.

Monsieur Bernard's exhale dragged audibly.

"That is, if we may, ol' man." F. Scott Fitzgerald looked over his shoulder. I knew he meant that term in the colloquial sense and not as a reference to his age, but Monsieur Bernard's exhale ended on a facial twitch that implied offense.

"Yes, please." He reached for something from Fitzgerald but then offered him the seating area when the author stepped away. He retired to a small wooden desk in the corner, folded his fingers together, and rested his upper lip against them.

When Fitzgerald sat on the couch, I noticed he took a dark green book from his side and placed it on the couch cushion. The raised gilt lettering was bright and new, but too small for me to read at a distance. It had to be the book we needed—it just had to be.

"I was there on business. Originally, I'm from Illinois."

"Are you in Paris for long?" I kept my attention on the book, though I dared not look at it directly. I didn't want him to feel how intently I needed to get my hands on it.

"I just sailed in to handle this signing." He patted the book next to him. "A fellow author told me that if you can have your autographed book in here, you're guaranteed a lifetime of success. So, I believe I'm all set!" He leaned forward and laughed with the robust perfection of a Hollywood performer. "I'll go home in a few days. What about you?" He gestured to Philippe and sustained his actor-quality smile.

"Oh, we're together. We both came in from New York. Is this your novel that's staying here in the library?" Philippe pointed gently to the book that Fitzgerald appeared to keep well-guarded.

I pulled the folded note from my pocket and kept it hidden in my hand.

"Yes, *This Side of Paradise* is my first big seller." He patted the book again.

"May I see it? I don't know that I've ever held a first edition novel before. I'm a huge fan of your work." I couldn't believe I was going to have to do this with other people in the room, and watching me, no less.

"Oh. Well, as long as it doesn't leave the room, I guess. Wouldn't want to break the spell. There is something special about having one's book in here." He lowered his gaze to the novel and passed it to me with two hands, like he handled a new baby.

A tingling of electricity jetted through my arm and I knew we had the right book. I assumed he couldn't feel the same sensation—surely, he would have made mention of it if he could. I glanced at Monsieur Bernard, whose eyes missed nothing in the room.

"You are in quite good company in this room, Mr. Fitzgerald." Philippe jumped in with distraction like a pro. He stood smack in the middle of Monsieur's line of sight, and of course Fitzgerald's eyes tracked his movements. He rose as Philippe did and followed him when Philippe guided him to the bookshelves. Thankfully we were still in an era where polite behavior was not uncommon.

I didn't have time to see what could fall out of it. Just in case an old message had been lying dormant. Or maybe Grace had already arrived in Paris. Neither could I get away with shaking this book with present company in the room. However, I slid the note inside the front cover and turned the book over so it looked like I examined the back cover. I opened the front cover again—the note was gone.

My sigh of relief was quiet and unnoticeable. Still, Monsieur Bernard glared at me for the unwanted guest that I was. I gave him my sweetest southern smile and fanned myself with the book a few times to blow away the distant burned scent.

"How long have you worked here, Monsieur Bernard?" I asked.

He lifted his mouth just over his hand. "Since the Hotel Ritz opened."

"Oh, my. So, you assembled this magnificent library?" Compliments. Flirtation 101. Usually, it worked. This time, I didn't see any signs that it would.

Philippe and Fitzgerald returned from their off sides conversation and I handed the author his book with care.

"Thank you," I mouthed.

"Cesar Ritz assembled the original choices for the library. I am in charge of new additions." Monsieur Bernard crossed the room in a hurry and guided Fitzgerald to the right side of the room. He gestured in a right-this-way-movement, directly to the spot I had searched when we first entered the room.

"Your novel will always be here in our collection. You may visit it any time you like."

Fitzgerald slid the book into the opening on the bookshelf that Monsieur Bernard created for it.

"Voila," Fitzgerald said.

"Voila!" Philippe and I said together.

"Well." Fitzgerald clasped his hands together in front of him. "I hate to cut this short. But I have an engagement I must attend to."

"Such a pleasure to meet you." I shook his hand.

"Yes, a pleasure." Philippe shook his hand as well.

Monsieur Bernard cleared his throat from the corner of the room and gestured to a narrow hallway I hadn't noticed earlier. Each of us had to turn sideways to fit through it and it was only dimly lit with sconces along the right wall.

"Well, it's a good thing that none of us are too sizable. Isn't it?" Fitzgerald quipped with what I'd recently come to know as his upbeat sense of humor. I wished it could last him through the next few decades, though I knew it wouldn't. Life's difficulties would ultimately prove to be too much and he would lean heavily on alcohol to numb the hurt.

We exited the narrow passageway and found ourselves confronted with a gate. They looked more like bars, actually. Jail cell bars. Monsieur Bernard sorted through a jingling ring of keys until he found the one he wanted. Thankfully, he unlocked the swinging door and escorted Fitzgerald, Philippe, and me out into a nondescript rectangular room.

"I say, ol' man. What's with all the cloak and dagger for the comings and goings in this place?" Fitzgerald's exuberant smile left his mouth slightly parted.

"We had a theft several years ago. So, we closed off all access to the library."

"But you didn't shut down the library," I said.

"*Non*," he answered simply.

"Monsieur Fitzgerald, please return anytime." He handed Fitzgerald his personal card. "Call me for an appointment." He unlocked a heavy door that looked like a section of the wall had been carved for access.

"Why thank you ol' chap." Fitzgerald's demonstrative wave held in the air, rather like the effects of his smile. "Let's gather in the bar for a drink later on—Miss Montgomery. Mr. Albrecht. Shall we?"

"Yes, of course," I said, even though I was aware we had no way to get in touch with one another. He disappeared into the wide corridor next to the lobby.

"Madam, monsieur. Do not return here without an express invitation from me." Monsieur Bernard gestured toward the corridor when Fitzgerald had exited.

We stepped out and turned around just in time to find the dark section of heavy paneled wall shut in our faces.

23

Grace tapped her fingernails on the armrest in her first-class cabin. Before they left for Paris, Grace took the snapshot of the photograph of Blake, Addie, and Lexie that had fogged two frames. She snail mailed a copy home to Isabella and Lex for their input. Then she put the original in an envelope and tucked it into her carry-on bag to keep it close to her on the trip.

When her cousin Eva disappeared some years back after traveling through a Wentworth on her own, Grace often checked photos of her for any signs of change. She wondered if Eva died or altered something in the past, and if anything would change in the photos they had of her.

Grace slipped the photo of Addie, Blake, and Alexa from the envelope. Tiny dots of color appeared to have been transferred from the photo onto the white of the paper envelope.

Fowler stood next to her seat. "I'm guessing it wasn't exposed to any heat?"

She shook her head, firm and resolute. She couldn't

prove it, but she knew it. "Something is wrong. The past has changed."

24

"I'd give Grace a few more hours before she gets to the book. Assuming I ever get home, I do want to try this computer and inter net y'all have mentioned." John stumbled between the syllables of *inter* and *net* as though he wanted to make certain he had pronounced the unfamiliar word correctly.

It was moments like this that made Blake realize just how long John and Campbell had been away from the present day. They'd never seen a computer or worked on a laptop. They weren't familiar with the internet, websites, or email. The idea that everyone traveled around with untethered palm-sized phones in their hands that allowed video calls, texting, carried your library, and connected you anywhere in the world without an operator, was beyond their comprehension.

"It's all very Buck Rogers," John usually said. "And I've never much been into science fiction. I prefer the simple and sure ways that have been around for centuries."

"Addie does as well." A flutter of worry coursed through

Blake's system. It was concern for their past, concern for their future, and mostly, concern for her well-being. To him, Addie was all that was good in the world. She was beautiful, honest and kind, and completely devoid of any need to hurt or harm. As such, he couldn't shake his need to spirit her away someplace to keep her safe.

"Must be a family thing because, modern conveniences aside, I do. By far." She ran her fingers along the pins that held her hair in place.

They passed the front desk on their way outside and Addie and Philippe exchanged a glance. She elbowed Blake with a slight nod toward the new guard. He wore a red jacket and stood behind one end of the long front desk, just outside the nearly hidden door that led to the library of first editions.

"Monsieur Bernard didn't like finding us unannounced," she said.

"From the looks of it, I'm not sure that being announced would have made any difference." Blake growled. "There's no other way in?" He squeezed his hands into fists and worked to leash his frustration. People he cared about had their lives at stake and these hotel employees were delaying his ability to help.

"There was a room behind the main library, but we didn't see it. There was a spiral staircase that led to another room upstairs. We didn't see that one, either. The end of the one hallway moved forward at an angle, but we never saw where that went."

"There's probably a doorway in one of those back areas that leads out," Blake said.

"Has to be," Philippe said.

Blake side-glanced the guard and the secret doorway

when they passed through the lobby. He noticed that Philippe had done the exact same thing.

With some time to burn before Grace responded, they walked outside of the Hotel Ritz and gathered together in a makeshift huddle for a moment.

Paris was crisp with brand-new tulip blooms and green leaves on tree branches. The spring breeze carried a piquant floral scent into the outdoor carpeted alcove and blew small cherry blossoms at their feet. The entire scene belied the real urgency at stake—that Otto could leave with Carolena whenever he wanted. And the Wentworths would probably be hidden from them forever.

"Will Grace have to figure out access to a hidden library as well?" he asked.

"She tells me that security is tight with cameras and sensors. That gives the hotel enough of a sense of comfort to allow a few visitors at a time. She, of course, has developed a rapport with the manager of the library. So she is given the access she needs," John said.

"Of course she has." Addie's grin showed how proud she was of Grace's ability to break through barriers and make things happen. It *was* impressive.

"Let's have an early lunch." John offered. "Keep our minds off of things."

"I don't think I could eat," Blake said. "We're close on this. I can feel it." With his hands on his hips, he paced in a slow circle.

"I don't think I could sit still," Addie said.

"Let's go around the corner and see if there are any external doors that might lead to the library. Maybe we can find another way in." Blake started down the stairs. He didn't mind if the group stayed behind. He was better as a lone wolf anyway. Besides, he needed to do something with his time besides wait.

Mary arrived wearing a long and pale pink, fur-trimmed coat. "Well, I don't know why we need to waste time, but I had a very late breakfast. If no one else is hungry, I'm going to just take a walk. See the sights. Take in the street fashion."

"Capital idea, Mary." John offered her his arm and she took it and snuggled it as a child would cuddle a teddy bear. "Let's start in this direction." He gestured toward the path where Blake walked.

The outside of the building bent at an angle toward them so that the entire front sides of the hotel were visible. There weren't any exterior doors. Just long, full-story windows every few feet or so, some of them shadowed by awnings.

"What about from the second floor?" Addie asked. "Maybe some unmarked door opens into that area?"

"Good idea, sweetheart," John said. "If that doesn't work, you won't have a choice, Blake. You'll have to push your way in."

He thought about it. Pushing the guard in the public reception area meant others would see the guard let them in. They would ask questions. They may very well get caught that way. So he decided against it. "Let's just walk around the side and maybe some of the back of the building. We may find a few unmarked doors." Addie walked ahead. Blake followed.

His focus narrowed. Not just onto the task at hand of finding another entryway to the first edition library. With every step, he saw the world in front of him through Otto's eyes. What opportunities would his father take? What schemes would he put in place to make himself a wealthier, more important man?

What lengths would he go to in order to protect Carolena? Not for the benefit of her safety or happiness. No. She was just another possession for him. A love of his life, perhaps. But for a man who did not know how to truly love anyone, that didn't say much.

What concerned him most was that she was the possession who betrayed him. She left him, took his son away from him. She humiliated him and set him on a life-long journey of searching for her. One that didn't end until she wanted it to. Since he wasn't one to forgive, how did she get him to take her back?

And what of their son? What had she told him about that? Surely, he would ask and Blake had no idea what Carolena would have told him. Blake ran a hand across his forehead.

The group divided and rounded the outside corner to search the facade of the hotel for service doors as well as the lush gardens.

Blake watched Addie touch park benches, fountain edges, and even flowers in search of any trace Carolena might have left behind. He didn't think she'd find anything but he appreciated the tireless effort. What he didn't appreciate was Philippe shadowing her so closely. He reminded himself that he didn't have anything to worry about.

The search behind the building yielded a few locked and windowless doors that were painted in the secure color of gray. None of them were in the right position to line up with a hidden library.

Addie stood facing Place Vendome and scanned the stores and the buildings that lined the streets. Her eyes squinted slightly and took on that faraway expression, the one that said she was reading something.

"What do you see, Addie?" Blake ran his hand over her back.

"I'm not sure I see it, yet. But something is familiar in this area." Her hand glossed over everything the eye could take in. "I'd like to walk this way, I think."

Blake made arrangements for Philippe to accompany the rest of the group. He wanted as much distance between the two of them as possible. "Where are we headed?"

"I don't know. I'm just sort of feeling my way through this area. Seems like I've been here before."

After three blocks she stopped. "There." She pointed to a narrow corner store, its entryway jutting onto the curved sidewalk. Deep reds, blues, and greens colored a stained-glass window fitted into a rectangle over the wooden door. Oddly, the center icon was the image of an eye.

"I can't believe it. This is the exact jewelry store where I found this ring. Alexa and I came here on one of our trips." Her thumb spun her sapphire and diamond ring that had traveled with her through the better part of two lifetimes.

"Shall we go in?" he asked.

"I think finding this store is too much of a coincidence to ignore it."

They paused at the corner to let a noisy tramway pass, its large one-eyed light on the front unlit at this time of day. They crossed the street with a small hoard of other pedestrians.

There were two sets of doors. The first pair was ornate and stood heavy under the stained glass window. They pushed through the second pair, which had frosted glass inset with hand-painted flourishes around the perimeter.

"This is almost the same as it was when Lex and I were here." Addie's voice was low and quiet. "There are fewer glass cases and those cloth-covered tables weren't there."

They parted ways. Blake circled to the left, Addie to the right. Rings and necklaces were carefully displayed and monitored by a middle-aged woman with short dark hair and an older gentleman with carefully combed white hair. The owners, he suspected.

The couple eyed them strangely when they walked in. They looked at one another and then, he realized, they stared mostly at Addie.

Addie glanced at her outfit and smoothed at the front of it. He was sure she wondered if something was askew.

"*Bonjour.*" Blake tipped his hat when he removed it.

"*Bonjour*, monsieur. Madam." The gentleman's voice as smooth as a warm breeze.

Addie complimented them on their lovely shop and admired the yellow silk wall coverings. Blake commented on their exquisite art deco brooches and rings.

But even with Addie's casual and polite approach, both of the store workers stared at her with paralytic attention. If this had been their present day Blake would have assumed they'd walked in on a robbery. As it was, he didn't know what they had walked in on. Clearly, they'd interrupted something.

Addie charmed the gentleman behind the main counter when she admired a ring watch fashioned with diamonds and sapphires. He appeared to relish the opportunity to show off a special piece.

Blake was sure it was time to get back to the hotel and check the book. But the blush of unguarded happiness on Addie's face kept him from moving. It had been a while since he'd seen her with that carefree expression. A few more minutes wouldn't hurt. It might even help, overall. He wandered to the opposite corner of the store.

"Monsieur, may I show you something?" The saleswoman wore a long black dress with white lace cuffs. She waved her hand across several of the round tables covered in yellow linen, strategically placed tulips and jeweled rings.

He'd known for some time now that he wanted to buy Addie a ring. A special ring. One she would wear for the rest of her life. But their past two years together had not gone as planned and he hadn't found the right moment to give her one.

Addie modeled the ring watch on her right hand and tilted it gracefully in the light. Blake placed one finger across his lips when the salesman glanced in his direction. The man gave one nod of quiet understanding.

He'd always thought he'd have to spend weeks, maybe even months, to find a ring special enough for Addie. That was part of the delay, he rationalized. But today it was right in front of him.

The ring held three vertical sapphires, the largest in the middle, with three diamond-laden rectangles arranged beneath in splendid art deco elegance. He pointed to it without saying a word.

While the sales lady handed it to him, he reached into his pocket for his wallet.

"Do you want her to try it on?" she whispered.

He shook his head and handed her the money. There had never been a more perfect ring for Addie. Well. Actually, that wasn't true. There was one other one that was perfect. But she was already wearing that one.

Blake slipped the boxed ring into his pocket and strolled to where Addie still admired the ring watch. He peeked at the handwritten price tag and handed over another small stack of cash.

"It's beautiful." She kissed him. "Thank you."

"Maybe we ought to leave," Blake suggested in a secretive tone. They'd probably done enough changing of jewelry history as it was.

Halfway out the first set of doors, a man with a thickly accented voice entered the room, along with another couple. "We are so pleased that you returned to see us, monsieur. All the way from Chantilly, and with your lovely wife. This necklace is the perfect complement to her ring—"

Blake turned in time to see a young Frenchman bent at the waist, kissing the hand of a woman who resembled Addie. Markedly so.

Sarah, her past-life self, stood with Jack, his past-life incarnation. She wore the same sapphire ring that Addie did. Jack's baby blues were a near replica of Blake's, and he wrapped his arm securely around Sarah. Everyone else in the room stared at the two nearly identical women.

"Is this your twin? The two of you are sisters?" the Frenchman asked.

Jack and Addie exchanged a glance and Sarah spun toward him. "Is she the one you told me about?" She placed a hand protectively on her swollen belly.

Blake remembered Addie's past-life memory, how she sat in the bathtub after Jack had been killed. She said she couldn't have been more than three months pregnant, possibly less. Today, Sarah was much further along, five months he would have guessed. Large enough to wear a loose dress, anyway.

He pressed his hand into Addie's lower back. "I think we should leave." His voice lowered to an urgent and private whisper. "Hurry."

Addie didn't move, and he wasn't sure if she'd heard him.

Jack shook his head slowly. "If I weren't seeing it again, I wouldn't have believed it."

"And you—" Sarah pointed at Blake, her eyes wide and disbelieving.

"Excuse us." Blake popped his hat on his head and grabbed Addie by the arm. This time leaving wasn't a suggestion.

25

———

"That man said they were in from Chantilly." My engraved silver shoes pounded rote, breathless steps on the sidewalk scrolling beneath our feet. "That must be the location of our new past, where we started our family. I know when I read the painting the first time that he died somewhere in America. Everyone in that scene spoke English."

He nodded, staring at the sidewalk as well. When I stopped, he did.

"Blake. Do you feel any different? I mean, I know you've felt tired. Maybe that's a result of these giant shifts in your past life somehow. But I mean, otherwise? Your demeanor is different. Sometimes I barely recognize you." I expected him to argue with me.

He pushed the back of his thumb over his upper lip, a new movement I'd only seen him start recently. Then he sighed reluctantly, as though I'd exposed a secret he didn't want to be revealed. "I've noticed it." His stare took in the slice of elegant history that surrounded us. This included seemingly costumed pedestrians who were not quite rushing, but rather moving along according to an unseen schedule. "First time I felt it was when we were still in New York. After you and I interacted with Sarah and Jack."

"Do you think it's because something...has changed?"

"Maybe. I don't know. I'm still here. As are you. I think we'll be okay."

I stroked my new ring watch with my thumb and hoped that time wasn't working against us. Our walk toward the hotel began again, this time hand-in-hand. "Then, are you worried about what you have to do next, when you finally find Otto?"

"Not really. I'm going to do whatever I have to do." He caressed a long section of my hair that had fallen loose and his energetic veil dropped over his feelings. I knew immediately that he was lying. Not about doing whatever he had to do, but about being worried.

"Even if that destroys who you are?"

"Losing you would destroy who I am."

"I'm afraid that I'm going to lose you one way or another."

He held my hand and squeezed it. "We'll be okay."

I didn't nod in agreement and I wasn't sure that I believed him. But I did kiss him.

We entered the lobby and I nodded to a new guard who stood to the right of the door in the wall, hands folded in front of him. His chin tipped up, his head almost completely still, and his dark eyes actively scanned the area. If this had been the present time, a thin wire would have connected an earpiece to a small microphone on another device. He would have been in cahoots with their security center.

"I think our unexpected appearance in the first edition library has set the hotel's teeth on edge. We're not getting inside the way we did last time."

"You're right about that." Blake eyed the ceiling above the front desk, then gauged the distance from that area to the red-carpeted grand staircase. "I have another idea. If Monsieur Bernard is as pretentious as you say he is, he's going to want his own private entrance to the library."

We walked calmly but quickly up the grand staircase so as not to attract any attention to ourselves, and we took a left along the first hallway. Clear crystal sconces lit our path every foot or so. Blake began marking his strides in deliberate foot-long steps.

"You don't think he would want to come in every morning through the grand entryway? I should think someone like him needed to feel special like that."

"Oh, I definitely do. He's not going to be relegated to an employee entrance. But since this library is now too precious to leave it open to the public, they aren't going to have an entryway in public view. That would draw too much attention to an area they're trying to hide. It would also pose too much of a risk for theft. There." Blake stood still.

"Where?"

"Here. If I counted right, we ought to be right over the area where the library is."

"These are just guest rooms." I gestured to the white doors that lined the wide hallway.

"I'm guessing...that one of these doors actually serves at Monsieur's private entrance." He examined one door and then the next, figuring which one to select. "Of course, if I get the wrong one, someone will complain about us."

"Or just you. I'm out of here if you open the wrong door."

"Would you mind?" Blake pointed to the doorknob on the first door.

"Happy to." I nodded and accepted with a hint of cheer in my voice that I didn't expect.

I rested my fingertips on the brass doorknob and stared at the blank door, or just shy of it, while the movie of its history played in my head.

"No. Not this one." I wiped my hand against the fabric of my pants, as I often did post-read. "No scent of him."

"Okay then, this one." Blake walked across the hallway. He listened at the door, and peeked through the keyhole. He stood upright. "Go ahead."

I scanned the quiet hallway, then placed three fingers from my left hand on the doorknob. "Dang. Definitely him." I paused, my sight focused on the many moods of Monsieur Bernard. "You're right. This room is obviously used for hotel business."

Blake selected the gold skeleton key farthest from the left and next to the Ritz Carlton Charm. He slid the key into the lock slow and quiet, in case someone was sitting near the opposite side of the door,. He turned the key and I hoped no one would hear the metal on metal clicking.

He tried each key with the same level of quiet, and the process took almost more patience than I had. Out of the twelve keys on the ring, number seven unhinged the lock. I exhaled a breath I had forgotten I was holding. The doorknob turned without a squeak and the door brushed across the carpet in a near-silent *swoosh*. He closed the door behind us.

Carpet the color of spring moss illuminated the smallish room. Floor to ceiling bookshelves were stuffed end to end with rare and ancient books like Mary Shelley's *Frankenstein*, Oscar Wilde's *The Picture of Dorian Gray*, and Joseph Conrad's *Typhoon*.

I tiptoed in the direction of the spiral staircase that

burrowed through the floor to the lower level. After moving around the iron railing to see if I could see anyone downstairs, I waved Blake over.

Once there, he gave me the wait sign with his hand. He listened intently, as did I, for any kind of noise—an inhale, a shift in body position, a loud swallow—anything. After several minutes of stillness, he placed his right foot on the first metal stair. Then the next, until the both of us were fully on the first floor.

I knew exactly where the book was located and I ran on my toes to retrieve it. With no one around to scold me, I held the book on its end and gave it a good shake. A yellowed letter floated from the book and I quickly stuffed it into my pocket. I took a different letter from my other pocket and tucked it inside the front cover. I'd written it earlier. It simply said: *Got it.* I wanted Grace to have confirmation that her message had been delivered.

I replaced the book on the shelf, the burned scent drifted through the cool air. "Let's go." I gasped.

We both stared at the smallish, well-suited man whose arms crossed and whose glare hit Blake like a punch to the gut.

"Monsieur Bernard, thank you for inviting us into your exquisite library." Blake pushed hard, his psychic ability convincing Monsieur Bernard to agree with him.

"I—I invited you," he said.

"Yes, you invited the both of us. You were happy to do it, and we've had a wonderful time."

When he pushed someone energetically, Blake steered their thoughts and emotions in a particular direction. As a rail guides the train, his intent determined theirs and their resistance drifted away. They had no choice but to follow his lead.

Monsieur Bernard blinked his eyes several times.

Blake wrapped his arm around him and they walked toward the spiral staircase. "You remember. There were a few books you wanted us to see. We had an appointment, you showed us the books, and now we have to leave. You're hoping that we come back sometime. In fact, whenever you see us, you feel compelled to invite us or ask us into the library. You're looking forward to having us back inside."

"*Oui*, monsieur. I would very much like to have you back."

"You want us to return tomorrow, in fact." Blake shook his hand and glanced in my direction when I climbed the spiral staircase.

"*Oui*. Tomorrow. I shall look forward to it, indeed." Monsieur Bernard bowed slightly at the waist.

"The next time you see us, you will welcome us into this library."

"Welcome you as only the Ritz can."

"You realize we don't mean you any harm. And now you have to return to work."

"*Oui...oui*. I must. Very busy."

Blake gestured to the small desk and Monsieur Bernard sat. He shuffled and organized a few papers. "You want to stay there until we're gone," Blake assured him. He climbed the spiral staircase, stepped into the hallway, and locked the outer door behind him.

I glanced up, my grandmother's letter in one hand, the torn envelope in the other. "Picasso. Three of Picasso's "Mother and Child" paintings are gone."

26

Carolena sat on the rooftop balcony and sipped her wine.

Otto now had three new masterpieces in his collection. She had foolishly thought that would be more than enough for him. Now she realized its wasn't. He would never stop. He would want more. Many more.

The original plan was to purchase the one masterpiece. Maybe two new pieces for his collection. Then they would retire to the French countryside and have a quiet life. Otto would build a private room for his art. He could visit it whenever he liked.

It had been a little over two years since she gave up her life to protect Blake and Addie and Philippe. She'd do it again if she were called to.

However, all had not quite gone according to plan.

Otto was more difficult to manage now than he had been all those many years ago. She had betrayed him by leaving when Blake was young. Otto didn't trust her now. So he was harder to control.

It was a daily existence now of being tethered to him by

an unbearably short leash. Her medication to survive was to drink. Not just in the evenings. This was France.

If they didn't go out, Otto retired to his office to plan his next purchases. He kept a black notebook. He used index cards. He obsessed.

She was a strong woman, she always had been. Even though she knew she'd never see her children or her grandchild again, she thought she could handle it. Because she was doing what needed to be done to help everyone concerned. That should have been enough.

She sank deeper into the wicker chair, adjusted her scarf to guard against the wind and downed another long sip of wine.

She felt low on most days. There wasn't enough coffee to keep her moving. Something was wrong. Yes, she expected a painful emotional price to be paid for giving up her life. But this was different.

It was as if she were on the wrong train. Or maybe the right train, but it was heading the wrong direction.

No, that wasn't it.

She knew when she flew in to interrupt Otto's plans for Addie and Philippe that she was saving their lives. Probably Blake's too. Maybe even John's and Campbell's lives. Otto might very well have gone back in time and finished everyone off just because he had the idea to do it.

So, it wasn't that she made the wrong move. But maybe the personal sacrifice was too steep this time.

The second thing she did to stay emotionally afloat was to check in psychically on Blake every day.

Several times a day, usually. It was almost as good as a face-to-face visit, though without the two-way conversation. She could tell if he was healthy, happy, and safe. She knew first hand that if every mother had those three items checked off, they would sleep well at night.

Blake, or Tristan as she had named him at birth, would forever live in the heart of her soul. Knowing he was alive and healthy, even though he wasn't in his own time, was enough for her. If only she could escape his attention long enough to get him to give up on finding her. Move on.

Being with Otto was her choice. She went with him because Blake had an entire lifetime to live and she wanted him to have the freedom to live it with happiness. To live his life according to the beauty of his life path. She didn't want his life dictated by anything that Otto would or would not do. That was largely why she took Blake away from him in the first place.

Before she left with Otto two years ago, she'd written a letter to Addie and told her that no one should worry for her. Though she knew Blake would. And did.

"Are you ready, *mon amour*?"

Carolena drank the final sip of wine and glanced at Otto from her comfortable nest. She had kept the door closed behind her to protect the priceless art from the humidity and the elements. And though she usually sensed his presence when he approached her, today she felt nothing. Maybe it was the effects of too much wine. Or maybe it was just that she was starting to settle in to things. Life as it were. He was always around, never far away from her. Like a guard dog.

"Yes. What do you think?" She stood and showed off her short, black sleeveless dress. She held her empty wine glass in one hand and a gauzy, tapered train in the other.

"*Exquis.*" Otto's wolfish smile revealed his appetite.

"Where are we going?"

When she asked the question she felt him ready to push,

just in case she didn't like his answer. She reached out, touched his hand, and soothed his concern.

"It's a surprise."

"Ah, then at least tell me who we're meeting tonight?"

"You'll see." He took her wine glass, placed it on a nearby table, and led her through the smallish room that was packed with canvases. All of them unframed, and many of them leaning against one another.

With Otto's newfound connections with soon-to-be-famous artists and his ability to push, he would make new acquisitions tonight. He'd study the artists who gathered, review their works in his mind, and push them to make appointments.

He would make progress with his quest and more art would soon disappear. Tonight or tomorrow, and long afterward. That was the price that the world would have to pay for keeping her family and loved ones safe.

Once downstairs they took a cab to rue de La Boëtie. From nearly half a block away, raucous male laughter poured from the second floor windows of the building. Without even knowing the specific address, she knew where they were headed. They were going to join this party.

They stood in front of the closed door. Otto inhaled deeply, adjusted his jacket and tie. He glanced at Carolena, his eyes as electric with as much anticipation as a young child on his birthday morning. She tried to read the emotion on his face. Excitement, yes. Something else.

Nervousness, a little, perhaps. Not uncertainty. He knew what he was walking into. He knocked twice.

When the door opened they were greeted by a young version of a very familiar face. Brown hair, parted on the far right side and slicked over, obviously in expectation of an evening out. His wide brown eyes, proud with boasted success, reached out to her with the expectation of fascination. He clearly waited for the adoration that was so common by this time in his career.

"Otto!" The artist's voice boomed with confidence.

"Pablo!" Otto roared.

They shook hands and kissed cheeks.

Pablo Picasso's eyes cut toward Carolena.

Carolena finally figured out the emotional response she'd felt from Otto earlier—it was social acceptance. Approval. He was secretly giddy over the prospect of it.

Otto once told her long ago, that when he started out in life, he wanted to be an artist. He was fascinated by all types of art and artists, but he was particularly entranced by the old masters' paintings. Tirelessly, he studied the techniques of the masters, to the point where he even conquered their know-how and delivery.

But he was never as good as others when it came to creating his own masterpieces—he was only truly gifted when it came to mimicking. Forgeries. His father told him that wasn't a skill or a talent. It was cheating, stealing. That at the very least, it showed a lack of effort and a shortage of imagination.

Not content to produce legal lookalikes in some tourist town, he stayed in the New York art community. He and John Montgomery opened an art gallery, which kept his hand on the canvases of some of the most prestigious private art collections.

When the moment was right, when no one was looking or suspected, he leaned on his own talents again. He kept clients' original artwork for himself, while he returned personally forged copies of their precious collections.

"I'll show them how well they know art," he'd often said. The prize he kept, a part of it anyway, was the art, yes. But more so, it was the knowledge that he had fooled them. He'd shown them.

"So-called experts. What a bunch of morons."

He'd proven to them that he knew more about art than they did. He'd convinced experts in the field, appraisers, even Christie's that his forgeries authentic.

She understood now. He would beat these art critics at a different angle of their same game. He would own their precious works of art before the museums ever had a chance to.

Pablo Picasso kissed Carolena's hand and slipped a muscled arm around her waist. In doing so he'd artfully wedged himself between her and Otto and he guided her into his spacious, white-walled atelier.

"How is it that I have not seen someone as beautiful as you in Paris before?" Stacks of finished canvases leaned against one another around in a room that, even with the windows open, reeked of paint and dog. Squashed tubes of paint lay scattered around the hardwood floors which were stained with blotches of both bright and muted colors.

The other men in the room stood when Pablo presented her. "Man Ray—a photographer who took my photo earlier in the month. One that shall be featured in *Vanity Fair* soon." Pablo's chest barreled when he referenced his ever-increasing fame. A hesitancy in his vibe told her he wasn't entirely comfortable with the idea, yet. He knew how much his popularity was worth and he wore it like a medal. Far better than starving.

"He is American, like your Otto here. But we forgive him that."

Man Ray ignored Pablo with deliberate focus and kissed her hand. "I should like to shoot you some time, madam."

Carolena felt charmed at his touch. "I'm a big fan of your Rayographs, Mr. Ray."

"Oh, you are...how nice to have a fan in my midst. Perhaps we could begin tonight? I have my camera."

"And you will make Kiki very jealous." Pablo removed her hand from his and escorted her forward to the next artist. "A creator needs only one enthusiast to justify him, isn't that what you tell the rest of us?"

"You are using my own words against me." Man Ray's smile was confident and seductive.

"This is Fernand Leger."

"Madam." Fernand kissed her hand.

"He is not only a painter, but also a sculptor. We talk mostly of this new art form we are creating." Pablo waved toward a thick stack of finished canvases that were obviously from his cubist period. The bright shock of red in the middle of the scene sent a cold, lifeless chill through her chest.

"Do you like the piece that your husband selected for you?"

Carolena used all her willpower to tear her glance away from the red on the canvas of masked faces. She found it a relief to stare into Picasso's dark eyes and to feel his overwhelming confidence. "*Exquis. Parfait.*"

Picasso kissed her lightly on the lips.

Otto's jealousy jolted through her like a live wire.

"You would be interested to sell us a few other pieces, as well, wouldn't you?" Otto pushed and Carolena felt Picasso's hand slip from her waist.

Otto was in control of him now.

27

The trip to Picasso's area of town was dark and frightening.

The Ritz, by contrast, was posh and elegant. A well-lit haven, Blake thought. Of course, well-guarded with too many rules about where one could and couldn't go throughout the day and night. However, their utmost concern was to make certain that, as a paying guest, you were happy. Out in the less structured areas of Paris, and certainly the less touristy ones, no one cared if you were happy. Or safe for that matter.

The location of Picasso's atelier was not public information and their ongoing requests to know this location were often met with inquisitive responses as to why one would want this information. *Pourquoi? Pourquoi veux tu savoir?* By 1922 Picasso had already achieved a good amount of success and it appeared the locals had adopted him and become protective of his well-being.

Cars whizzed by at their top speeds, barely acknowledging pedestrians on the corners who waited to cross.

When they finally found the correct building, they had hoped to find him in residence, or at least at a nearby restaurant. But his studio was dark and quiet and he was not in any of the nearby restaurants or bars that they checked.

Addie was tired. Exhausted to the point of feeling ill, and they chose to call it a night. They weren't making any progress anyway, other than they had found Picasso's atelier.

Blake decided he would return the next day. And the next. And so on until he found Otto. In the cab on the way home, Addie fell asleep on his shoulder. He'd wedged himself into the middle of the backseat to keep Philippe at a distance from her. So now Philippe sat on his left.

"Do you remember Otto getting involved in anything… bloody in years past?"

"Bloody…what do you mean?" Philippe asked.

John and Campbell sat across from them and turned, the topic of conversation of apparent interest to them. Their figures jostled back and forth in the dim light as the cab bounced over bricked streets.

"Don't know. When Addie read the bathtub, she said Carolena thought about his bloodied hands and how that repulsed her. Did he get into a fight? Or, what could she be talking about?

"When was this?"

"She said it was before Carolena left him. We all would have been young then."

"When we were young, Otto was easy. With Carolena around it was magical. She cast a spell on us all with her love, but especially over him. It wasn't until we got older that he changed," Philippe said.

Blake noticed his hand had unconsciously rounded into a fist. He didn't like the idea that he had shared his mother with Otto's other sons. Otto had taken enough from his family—his father, his freedom, and, he felt, much of his mother's happiness.

"He changed when Carolena and I left, I guess?"

Philippe looked out the window and appeared to mentally calculate. "It was actually just before then. Something happened that split them apart."

"Had to be his forgeries. The Gardener theft. Must have gotten too dangerous for a young mother with a child."

Philippe's heavy sigh said he didn't quite agree. "Maybe. I think it probably started then. But something else changed him. I thought it could have been when he sent the two of you away." He nodded to John and Campbell.

John's eyes shifted to Blake. "I could tell you what it was."

The car held an unusual quiet. "You were there?"

John's nod was slow with reluctance. "In a sense. He told me what happened. After the fact."

"What did he do?" Philippe's words were slow and even.

"He killed a man." John said it matter of factly and stunned the car into complete silence. The cab pulled up to the front door of the Ritz. No one moved except for John, who paid the driver. The valet opened the door and John gestured for everyone to exit.

Blake guided Addie, who nearly sleepwalked to her suite. He unbuckled her low-heeled shoes and draped a blanket over her. She was asleep before her head hit the pillow.

His walk to the bar was dreamlike. Noises were only heard at an unintelligible distance and he didn't quite feel his footsteps against the thick carpet. He remembered Addie saying that she thought Carolena tried to protect him from killing Otto. He wondered if, when he did, he would be more like him than not.

They gathered in the hotel bar that would one day be known as Bar Hemmingway, though it wasn't yet. The lightly paneled walls and low lighting surrounded a crowd of hotel guests. All of whom were dressed to the nines and returning from a grand evening out in Paris.

Everyone drank martinis except for Blake, whose hand gripped a rocks glass of scotch. There was enough noise in the bar to cover the details of any conversation. Still, John leaned close to the group and kept his voice low and calm. "It was after the Gardner incident and there was a lot of attention in the media and whatnot. Some low-level rookie cop had the bright idea to visit all the galleries in town. He was interviewing everyone to find out if they had been approached by the thieves who wanted to sell the art.

"It was a moronic effort. No one was going to offer up information like that. Being a rookie, he obviously didn't know any better. His boss, whoever that was, probably told him to just get out there and find something.

"Otto had been in the vault sitting with the Gardner art. We hadn't had it that long and he was blown away by the fact that he could host a private audience of one with a Renoir and a Vermeer. It was after hours, when everyone had gone home. He had gone upstairs to open a bottle of wine, then he was going right back down to the art.

"When he went up, he found the officer standing at the front door. Knocking. Otto had to let him in. They spoke for a few minutes, the officer gave him his card, and left for the night. That was supposed to be it."

"Only it wasn't." Blake stared at John.

"The cop snuck back inside. Otto found him going to the vault area downstairs. Something had tipped him off. Otto said he didn't know what it was. I figured it had to have been nerves. Of course, the rookie was going to be a big shot busting the case wide open himself." John sucked down half of his martini.

"They fought," Campbell said. "Otto called us and Ellen. When we got there, the cop was lying on the floor, his head busted open, and he was dead. Otto said it was an accident. But I don't know."

"When did Carolena see him?" Blake asked.

"He called her. When she showed up he was sitting there in the hallway muttering to himself with blood all over his hands. Dad and Ellen and I cleaned up the mess. We thought if we didn't that when Otto got caught—and he would have—that he would out my dad on the art theft. Out of a sense of revenge. So we put the body in an alleyway and moved the art. Otto was never the same after that."

"He was darker, wasn't he?" Philippe asked.

"Changed him forever." John nodded slowly, and seemingly traveled through a haunted memory. "He started drinking too much. He couldn't sleep. Used to say that he'd wake up in the middle of the night and find the cop standing at the foot of his bed. Staring at him."

"I remember that time," Philippe said. "It was like his soul just died after that."

"Wasn't long after that he banished us into history," John said.

"Carolena and Blake left." Philippe rubbed the back of his neck. "He was hateful after that."

Blake shook the ice in his rocks glass. It was the first time he'd ever felt lucky that he and Carolena had a life on the run. Listening to Philippe's story, he knew his experience was better than what Philippe had endured.

He felt a strange kinship with Otto, the father he'd hated

most of his life. He could see himself falling to the same fate, too, if he killed someone. Addie was right—he wasn't a murderer, and killing his father would change him forever.

28

It was one of the two weeknights that the Louvre stayed open late for visitors. Because it had been well over a year since they'd last known Carolena—or at least someone fitting her description—to visit there and sketch, hopes were not high.

On schedule, they made their evening tour through the former palaces to search for her. Blake, Addie and Philippe traveled together in a group. They couldn't cover as much ground this way, but the Louvre was too large for them to split up. They didn't have the ability to text or otherwise get in touch with one another if one of them found her.

Blake eyed every person they passed. He eliminated those who didn't fit her description as quickly as possible. Wrong gender, wrong hair color, wrong age or height, and so on.

Once in a while, a woman would fit all of Carolena's characteristics. His heart would thump and nearly pound its way out of his chest until he saw her face. And realized it wasn't her.

Tonight was the same drill. He'd startled two women

already this evening in an attempt to see their faces straight on. He fully expected for one of them to file a complaint and for the museum to toss him out. The French had no patience.

The woman he stared at now had Carolena's shoulder-length dark hair. She wore a white silk shirt and a long knit skirt with a close-fitting white hat, which was similar to Carolena's style. She stood at the permissible edge of Napoleon III's formal living area, an exquisite room of painted ceilings, gold walls, red brocade and fiery chandeliers and crystal sconces. He and Carolena had visited this former palace several times with Anya when they were growing up. This particular residence had been one of her favorites.

This woman held her sketch pad—the end of it perched on her midsection, her left hand wrapped around the top of it to hold it in place. The object of her sketch was a piano, slightly undersized by today's standards, light brown and known to have had a unique history that involved Chopin.

He nodded to Philippe and Addie, who had also spotted the woman.

Addie stepped nonchalantly to the left of her and waited for a small group of tourists to pass so she could see the woman's face. Time crept until they finally did. Addie turned to Blake and he hardened his stomach against the usual disappointment.

Only this time Addie gave him one upward nod.

His heart seized and he instantly felt he was standing guard over the two women. He wanted to grab them both and run. But he didn't approach her. Knowing Otto as well as he did, he had to assume he was nearby. An ill-timed rescue attempt could result in Otto calling for security.

His goal to rescue her nearly realized, he felt his chest

rise and fall more quickly than normal. "Careful steps. Careful steps," he muttered under his breath. He hoped Addie and Philippe both remembered the procedures they'd discussed. He'd drilled them until he was reasonably certain they had the plan memorized. Surely they would.

On cue, Philippe stopped at the right of the wide entryway.

Blake walked along the roped off back area reserved for visitors and stopped at the entryway to the sitting area. Once both exits were secured, he gave Addie the sign.

She moved into position.

"IT's amazing to think of Chopin playing on this piano, in this very room. Isn't it?" Addie gazed at the piano and spoke as though she were talking to herself.

Carolena's posture deflated. She breathed in and out several times, as though she'd just received a disappointing blow. "How did you find me?"

"Like the Bonapartes, we are a determined group. Especially when it comes to family."

Carolena glanced over her shoulder where she found Philippe. Her lips lifted in a disappointed smile.

"Where is he?" Her voice was a mother's urgent whisper.

Addie directed her eyes toward Blake on the other side of the room.

Carolena followed Addie's direction. When she faced front again she closed her eyes for a deep breath. "You should have forgotten about me. You are all in a great deal of danger now."

They stood in a poorly lit dead end hallway just outside of Napoleon's residence. Louvre guards strolled past and stared at them suspiciously.

"Where is he?" Blake asked. He eyed unmarked doorways and wondered if they could be emergency exits that they might use.

"I don't know, *mon amour*. Why did you come?" Carolena placed her hand along the side of Blake's face. Then she held him in her arms and he knew she didn't want to let him go.

"Where is Otto?" Blake distanced her to arm's length.

She sighed, deep and heavy with worry. "He's wandering around nearby while I do this." She waved her sketch pad. "You have to leave." She hugged Blake quick and tight and took three fast steps in the opposite direction.

He caught her.

"You're leaving with us. Do you have the Wentworths?" Blake held her arm. He'd never been forceful with his mother before because she had always had an unbeatable strength. Today that would change.

"I can't. I have to keep him away from you."

"Do you have the Wentworths?"

"We have them. *Oui.* Or, I have them, he doesn't know. I had copies made. I'll get them to you." She held his face with both hands now. "Go back to New York. I know how to reach you. I'll get them to you as soon as I can."

"No." He had never been more resolute in his life. She was leaving with him if he had to carry her out of the museum.

She stared at him. "I won't—" She wrestled against his firm hold on her.

"Enough! I won't have you sacrificing your life for us any

further. Come with us. Together we'll figure out what to do with Otto."

The light was missing from her eyes, and she was thinner than he'd ever known her to be. Her skin had lost some of its color. She'd sacrificed too much for him this time and his heart ached.

Blake held his hand open in front of her and she stared at it. "Let me help *you* this time.

Addie placed her hand on Carolena's back. "Come on. Come with us. No one is more grateful than I am for everything you've done for us. But Blake's right. Enough is enough."

She stared at each one of them for a few seconds. Then she finally nodded. She lowered her head to Blake's chest.

He took her in his arms and held her close. She was never one to cry but he felt her body shake in quiet sobs.

"Come on." He squeezed her gently. "You're going home with us."

He made a point to stick to the more popular hallways where the crowds were thick, even at this late time of day. He steered them clear of the statue galleries, which were open and spacious, and couldn't offer them the camouflage that the crowds did.

Philippe walked in front, Carolena and Blake in the middle and Addie slightly behind. They walked at the leisure pace of tourists so as not to draw any attention to themselves. Blake wanted to move faster but he was limited to the pace that Philippe set for the group. It was what they had agreed upon ahead of time, but he privately cursed the fact that he had to work with the team. He would do better by Carolena if he could have worked this job on his own.

Blake had mapped their escape some time ago. Out the front doors of the museum and to the left, through the

Tuileries Gardens where the crowds tended to gather well into the evening.

He glanced at his pocket watch, frustrated that everything was moving slower than he liked. They needed to quickly make it to the entry of the gardens, then to Place de la Concorde, one of the busiest areas of the city, where they would blend into the crowds. From there they would catch a cab to the hotel and Carolena and Addie would disappear forever from Otto's life.

"Does he know we're here?" Blake kept his sights straight ahead, and tipped his hat to a passerby.

"No, not in Paris." Carolena shook her head. "Maybe you *should* let me go. If he figures out that you've done this he'll think nothing of killing you all."

She turned away and Blake grabbed her arm. In one fluid movement, he threaded it around his own arm and held tight to her hand. "The world doesn't need another martyr."

"I can handle him," she said. "I've done it before."

"From the looks of things, I'd say those days are long gone." Blake narrowed his eyes at her. His fury at Otto pushed beyond the confines of his skin and he held tight to his mother. "I appreciate all that you've done to help Addie, but I'm not going to sacrifice you. Understand?" He felt like the same young boy who had nightmares that his father would take his mother away from him one day. But he was old enough now, old enough to make sure that didn't happen, old enough to make sure she would stay safe.

"Do you know where he is?" Philippe asked.

"No." She glanced at her watch. "Probably heading toward the courtyard to meet me, I would imagine. The Louvre closes soon."

Blake picked up the pace. Place de la Concorde was,

curiously enough, the exact spot where the guillotine used to stand. Marie Antoinette's and Louis XVI's lives came to an end there. For his family, though, this would be where their new beginning took place.

"He's nearby." Carolena breathed quickly, her eyes scanned the area. "I can feel him."

"Does he know?" Blake asked.

"I don't think so. I'm not sure. I have too many nerves."

Addie and Blake exchanged a concerned look. Though neither one of them said it, their expressions said they both agreed that this was not the Carolena either one of them knew. She was deeply afraid and not in control.

"It's okay, Carolena. Just come with us." Philippe rubbed her back gently and Blake whispered to him, "We need to move faster."

The crowded roundabout at Place de la Concorde was filled with a rumble of cars, open bed delivery trucks, and horse-drawn carts. French policemen with short-billed hats and black capes were stationed at various points of the traffic circle on horseback, blowing their whistles and waving their arms to keep the chaos moving.

He checked over his shoulder for the first time since they'd left the museum. Carolena was on one side, Addie on the other. He reminded himself to be careful. Not to miss any cues to Otto's presence. Panic crept through his brain and made him doubt.

"Over here." Blake pointed to one of the side streets to the right, where traffic moved slower. "Let's try to catch a cab over there. If we can't find one, then we start walking in the direction of the hotel. Fast. We need to get out of this neighborhood."

"I think it's better if we go directly into the Place de la

Concorde the way we agreed," Addie said. "It feels safer to me."

Blake shook his head and regretted that Philippe and Addie had come on this particular trip to the Louvre. Teamwork and partnerships were better for other people. "Everyone follow me. New plan."

They dashed across the busy street where Blake led them halfway up a store-lined alley at a pedestrian cross street. A cab idled at the top of the hill. "There. See? Come on."

Carolena slowed to a near stop. She stared at Blake who was now several steps ahead of her.

"This isn't right." She took several steps backward. "I can feel him nearby. We should leave this area."

"Blake!" Addie and Philippe were already at the cab. "Get in!" Addie waved him toward the car at the top of the hill.

"*Non*. Blake. We can't walk toward the top of the hill. I can feel him nearby." She walked several more steps backward.

"Don't move." Blake said to Carolena.

He ran to the top of the hill and grabbed Addie. "Come with me!"

"No! This isn't right. We need to get out of here. This doesn't feel right, Blake."

He turned toward Carolena who continued to walk toward the main street. He didn't trust her at a distance, and wasn't sure what she would do or if she would run.

People appeared from the cross street that dead-ended where they had gathered half way to the cab. Blake startled every time someone rounded the corner, shopping bags in hand. The corner sign of an antique store swung and creaked over the street in the breeze.

"Carolena! Get in the cab and let's go!" Philippe yelled.

"Addie, come with me." Blake grabbed her by the arm.

"Addie, get in the cab," Philippe said.

"No!" Blake yelled.

"She's leaving—" Philippe pointed to Carolena. "Grab her!"

"Carolena, stop!" Blake tugged Addie halfway down the hill with him.

"This isn't right, I know this isn't right." She resisted. "Get Carolena and let's get in the cab!"

He stopped with her at the corner of the pedestrian cross street, half way between Philippe and Carolena. "Stay here. Do not get in that cab." Then he ran the rest of the way down the hill and grabbed Carolena by the arm. "We have to stay together. We need to get in that cab and get out of here." He tugged on her arm and she pulled in the opposite direction.

"We should go the other way. I don't know what he'll do if he finds us." Her eyes shifted just over his shoulder. Her inhale was sharp and short.

Blake spun around in time to see Otto grab Addie from behind.

"All of my favorite people are here in one place. What were the chances?" Otto's voice was syrupy smooth. He held Addie around the waist and pressed a small knife at her midsection.

Philippe ran toward her and Otto stiffened his grip.

"You're going to rescue your first love. Is that it?"

Philippe stopped. "Let her go." His voice was strong as steel.

Otto chuckled. "Get my wife for me, and I'll let Addie go free."

"Let me go," Carolena said to Blake. "I'm the one he wants."

Blake tightened his grip. "No." He swore on his soul that Otto would not leave with anyone on his arm. Not today. Not ever again.

"Let me go with him and he'll leave everyone else alone." She scream-whispered her words. Tears filled her eyes and he realized just how desperate she was to protect everyone she loved.

He pressed his face close to hers. Adrenaline shot through his veins, making his thoughts clearer than they had been in months. "I will not let him use you this way. Stay here. Don't move."

Carolena exhaled, her eyes pleading with Blake to be careful. Finally, she nodded.

The seconds dragged and spun thick in the space between where he was and where Otto held Addie at knifepoint. His steps were sharp and decisive. He lifted his hands in the air. "I'm not armed."

More shoppers emerged from the alleyway of stores and scurried by when they saw his hands up in surrender.

The cab sped away.

"Police will be here soon." Blake nodded toward the people who were now running away. "Do you want them to find you here like this? With a knife at a young woman's side?"

Addie held still. Her eyes pulled wide.

Addie in Otto's possession. Blake's nightmare come true.

"What do you want with my wife?" Otto nodded toward Carolena. "Is this your doing?" He glared at Philippe. "Carolena came with me willingly. Leave us alone."

Otto looked at everyone in the group. "Do you all want to go home? Is that what you want? I have the paintings. I can give you that. You all go home and leave us to live out the rest of our lives. We're not hurting anyone." Otto's tongue licked the corner of his open mouth.

No one answered. Everyone watched.

Blake noticed a round circle of blood spread on Addie's white dress where Otto held the knife. His heart seized. He did what he knew to do. He pushed.

"Let Addie go. You don't need her. You have your Gardner art."

"When my wife comes with me, I'll let go of Addie. Then the rest of you can go home. Got it?" Sweat dripped down the side of his face even though the weather wasn't hot.

"Fine," Blake said.

Philippe jerked his head toward Blake.

"Drop the knife first. No one needs to die today." Blake gestured to the weapon.

"I'll keep it. Thanks."

Otto stepped toward Carolena. Blake blocked his advance.

"I'm not sending some innocent woman off with you when you have a knife. Drop it." Blake pushed with every ounce of his energy to get Otto to drop the knife and leave. His hands flexed at his side. He would grab that blade with his bare hands if he had to.

Otto pushed back just as hard. As usual, they were evenly matched.

"Who are you to tell me who I can spend my time with? Carolena? Are you okay?" Otto called to her.

She nodded.

Blake flushed with fury at the sound of Otto addressing her. He rolled every ounce of his rage into his next push. "Drop the knife!" His words were slow and clear and backed with more emotion than he'd ever felt.

It was a brief advance. Like physically pushing too hard on a stuck door and then falling forward when it gave an inch.

Otto's eyes widened just before he steeled himself again. Blake could tell he'd felt it. He had pushed Otto into the margins of their fight. Only for a moment.

Blake redoubled his strength and pushed again. "Drop the knife and let her go." His world grew silent around him, and with his gift he searched inside Otto for the leverage he needed. Guilt would have been the most useful, but he couldn't find any. The man didn't have a soul. Let alone regret.

"You want to drop that knife, Otto. You want to—"

Otto breathed harsh and quick through an open mouth and appeared to summon more effort. "What I want is for you to get out of my life. Walk away, Blake."

He guarded himself against Otto's push. "Not happening, old man."

"Go back to the house, Carolena!" Otto yelled across the alleyway.

"Leave her out of this!" Blake's body shook when he yelled. He dove deeper into Otto's psyche for some sort of a toe hold. Brute force wasn't going to be enough to get Otto to let Addie go.

He needed something else. Like a soldier at war, he stole through his father's hidden emotions. They gathered in his mind like an overcrowded attic of unattended memories, smothered by will and ego like they could be overpowered. They rotted and festered as old wounds did, controlling him in ways he could no longer recognize.

Otto's anger surged and his own resistance weakened. The control he had over his own mind and his father's, wavered and almost bowed to his father's power. Otto had an undeniable strength when it came to making other people do what he wanted them to.

"Come on," he muttered under his breath while he searched. "Something *has* to be here." Stacks of Otto's emotional secrets involved rage, unresolved and blameful, none of which Blake could use. Last thing he wanted was for Otto to be more angry, and possibly stronger. He dug deeper.

Fear. Look for the fear beneath the anger.

With his goal at the top of his mind, he was guided to a giant morass that pulsed like a heartbeat. The fear was old yet immature; it was round, red and tender like a hot button. Given these exact circumstances it just might work like the kryptonite he needed it to be.

Otto's eyes quickly shifted to the side to look in Carolena's direction. From his stunned expression, Blake knew he'd called it right. "She doesn't love you. She hasn't for a very long time. Not since the beginning, and that was a lifetime ago. You know I'm right." Blake grabbed Otto's fears over Carolena's feelings for him and he spun them around his father's brain until he knew he wouldn't be able to think of anything else. "She left you once. Now she's left you again. You don't have anything to fight for. So, drop the knife. As soon as you do, the pain will be over."

"She's my wife." His resistance held strong and he pressed the knife even closer to Addie's stomach.

She startled with a gasp and Blake's heart pummeled his chest.

"You want to let it go. You've been afraid for too long. Just drop the knife and the pain will end. You'll be free." Blake was the whisper of doubt in Otto's mind, leading the way to the edge of the cliff, coaxing him so powerfully, so subtly that Otto didn't even ask how Blake knew their history.

"She loves me."

"She wasn't with you all those years. You know in your heart that she doesn't love you. Maybe she never did, right?" Blake took the fears he'd found in Otto's emotional annals and made them cover his brain like an army blanket. It would be a single point focus for him now, weakening him as fear did for everyone. "There's no one left to fight for. Drop the knife."

Blake's push burst through Otto's resistance like a blade finally puncturing its way through a leather hide. The knife clattered to the ground. Addie elbowed Otto hard in the gut and pulled away from him. Blake snatched the weapon and slashed it at Otto's chest, leaving a red line in its wake.

Otto's scream was choked and he bent at the waist in obvious pain.

"We can do this the easy way or I can take you out here and now. It's up to you."

Otto gasped for air, pressed his hand to his chest, and examined the red on his palm. "What would be the easy way?"

"You come back to the present with us, turn yourself in for the Gardner theft, and I'll let you live."

Sweat dripped from his brow. "And the hard way?"

"Everyone here gets to witness your final day."

Police whistles screamed in the distance.

"And you're the man who's going to make that happen?"

Blake adjusted the grip of the knife in his hand. "Did I stutter?"

Otto's mouth spread into a wicked smile, "If you could have taken my life you would have by now."

Blake lunged at Otto and slashed another bloody line across his chest. This one was more diagonal, a deeper, bloodier cut. Otto grunted. His heel caught on a raised brick in the street and he stumbled two steps, catching his balance at the last minute.

Blake shifted the knife to his left hand, balled his right hand into a fist, and struck him hard in the gut, twice and in rapid fire. Otto doubled and groaned, stunned such that he leaned on his own thigh to hold himself up.

Blake landed two more fierce blows, one right after the other, both across Otto's face, and blood spurted from Otto's mouth and nose. The last punch sent his head swiveling to the right and blood seemed to float in slow motion when it flew from his mouth. His eyes closed when he fell to the ground, and his head smashed hard against the curb.

Adrenaline shot hard through Blake's veins.

He'd done it.

He hovered over the man who had dominated and controlled so much of his life—this once unbeatable force who now lay broken and crumpled in his own blood.

Blake expected to feel a sense of victory, but the triumph he felt was hollow.

Carolena gasped, both of her hands covered her mouth.

A young policeman ran up the hill, his cape blowing behind him. He stopped cold when he saw Otto.

Blake hid the bloody knife into the back waistband of his pants and under his jacket.

The policeman stared at Otto and asked what happened. *"Qu'est-il arrivé?"*

Addie pointed to the blood on her dress and explained that he was a crazed man who attacked her.

"Est ce que tu vas bien?"

She shrugged. *"Oui, je suis d'accord. Ce n'est pas si mal."* Yes, she was okay, though she had been held at knifepoint, and typically she didn't wear her blood on the outside of her body.

Otto's eyes were closed and blood ran downhill from the back of his head.

The policeman leaned close to Otto's mouth. When he sat up he shook his head. "*Il est mort.*" He stood and searched the surroundings, seemingly uncertain as to what to do next now that he had pronounced Otto dead. "*Reste ici.*" He pressed both palms out toward the group and told them to wait where they were. "*Reste ici.*" Then he ran down the alleyway.

Blake glanced at Otto and broke into a jog down the hill to retrieve Carolena who came with him willingly.

They ran to the top of the hill and turned right through a busy thoroughfare. His primary focus was to get them out of the immediate area and away from police. When they could make it to the hotel unnoticed, they'd plan next steps.

"Cab!" Addie yelled. She held her stomach where Otto's knife had sliced her and flagged the cab to a halt. Everyone piled inside.

"Le Louvre," Blake said to the driver as calmly as possible.

29

Back in their hotel room, Blake scrubbed Otto's blood from his hands at the sink and stared at the red soapy liquid that swirled in the basin. He was stunned that Otto was dead, sick that he had been the one to kill him, and worried that he and Addie had to separate on the way back to the hotel. She needed medical attention for that knife wound.

Their group had divided into twos to take different, twisted paths home from the Louvre to avoid being traced. His and Carolena's path involved a series of tramway cars, cabs, and traveling by foot within mindless crowds. He wasn't sure how Addie and Philippe were getting through the city. There hadn't been time to discuss their plan, and now there was no sign of them. He rubbed at his red-tinged skin again. His father's blood. He figured that might always leave its own unique mark.

He was especially pissed that Philippe was once again playing his stand in. It was Blake's job to make sure Addie was okay and to keep her safe from harm. *Not Philippe's.*

The couple who flagged the police might be able to

describe them, or at least Blake. They definitely got a good look at him. He hoped the police were too busy or at least too inexperienced to conduct a search. All the same, if Philippe and Addie weren't home soon, he would search for them.

He elbowed the bathroom door open another foot to check on Carolena. She sat where he left her—curled up in a chair, drinking wine, and staring at the floor. He muttered about his father and questioned why the evil were allowed to live so long.

"Are you all right?" he asked.

"*Oui.*" She feigned a weak smile. "*Et toi?*"

"*Oui, Maman.*" He dried his hands and glanced toward the door.

"They'll be here," she said. "She'll be okay. Philippe isn't going to let her suffer." She patted the bed cushion. "I would bet they stopped at a doctor's office or hospital."

He sat on the edge of the bed and leaned forward on his knees. She was right. He could at least trust Philippe to make sure she wasn't suffering. He had examined the cut in the cab and it did look like she needed a couple of stitches.

"Sit. You look tired."

"If I didn't think it would earn me a slap on the back of the head, I might say you were the pot calling the kettle black."

Carolena scoffed and shifted her stare out the window.

"Well, he's gone now. It's over." He said it more casually than he felt. He'd never had anything to do with someone's death before. Though he wasn't sorry that Otto was gone, he did wish it could have happened another way.

"There was no hope for him. You realize."

"I know, *Maman.*" Blake paced and half expected to run

into Otto's ghost on a turn. The man would probably haunt him for the rest of his life.

"I understand that he killed a man when I was young."

Carolena's swallow was visible. "That was when you and I left."

"These last two years with him took something precious from you, I can see it in your eyes."

"I would do it again—give all of myself to help you and those you love. I think you've done the same."

Yes, they were alike in that way.

A key turned in the lock and he spun around. Philippe entered first. When Addie followed, Blake rushed to her and held her in his arms. "Are you okay? What took you so long?"

She brushed a loose piece of hair away from her face. "We took a wrong turn when we got off one of the tramcars. Then we stopped at the hospital. They cleaned me up and bandaged me." She tapped her torso.

"No stitches?"

She shook her head.

He kissed her, held her gently, and breathed in the flower-sweet scent of her skin.

He couldn't resist shoving a glare at Philippe and was surprised when the man didn't budge. "Are you sure no one followed you?"

"Yeah, I'm sure."

"We're all here now. We should get something to eat." Carolena crossed the room and hugged Addie.

"Blake, what is—?" Addie looked at her hand and then at Blake's lower back. "You have blood on your back."

He ran his hand against his skin and examined it. "It's Otto's, from the knife. I'll wash it off."

Carolena hugged Philippe. "Are you okay?" She kissed both of his cheeks. "This is all too fresh, I know."

"I've missed you, Carolena." He held her close. "I really have."

Addie waved briefly to Philippe and followed Blake into the bathroom.

❧

"How do you feel?" Carolena asked Philippe. She'd known him since he was a boy and cared for him as though he were her own.

"Honestly? I don't feel anything." He stared out the window.

"Because you can't believe it or—"

"Because I stopped feeling much of anything for him a long time ago." He ran a hand through his hair and sighed.

"Perfectly reasonable." She wrapped her arms around him again, and a surprisingly stronger wave of his emotion washed through her. When she pulled away she said, "You still love her." Carolena nodded toward the closed bathroom door where Addie had gone.

His lips held together tentatively. His chest rose up and down too quickly for him to pretend he was calm. At long last he shrugged. "How do I stop?"

Her eyes closed when his heartache rushed through her. "These things have a way of working out." She held her hand in his and hoped he could feel the comfort she sent. "There will be someone special for you. Hang in there."

❧

ADDIE RAN her hand along the bare skin of Blake's upper back.

Her soft touch settled him into his body and caused his worry to relax.

"You're okay?" He looked at her reflection in the mirror and her smile gave him his answer.

Without a word she went to work, erasing the visible signs of the struggle with Otto that were smeared along his back. She filled a washcloth with soap and warm water and rubbed it against his skin.

"What about you?" she asked.

He knew she wasn't asking physically. He and the rest of the group had openly discussed how he didn't want to have to kill Otto. Capture him, yes. See him punished, definitely. He didn't relish the fact he'd taken his father's life. "I did what I had to do."

She dried his back with a fresh towel. "I wish you hadn't had to do that."

"Doesn't matter now. It's over and you and Carolena are safe. That's all I care about." He examined the bandage on her stomach and leftover adrenaline shot through him. Her wound could have been so much worse. She could have been killed. Or kidnapped. "You're sure you're okay?"

She nodded "And you?"

"There wasn't any way around it."

"No. There wasn't. Just remember that in the weeks and months to come."

He nodded, this time in acknowledgment *and* agreement. She was right. Today's decisions didn't need to be revisited.

Addie ran her fingers over the knife that laid on the counter and he knew she was reading it.

"For the record," she said when she finally looked up. "He was prepared to kill the both of us."

A chill ran through his veins. He stifled the cold shiver that ran beneath his skin.

Tonight marked a new beginning. A life, finally, without Otto.

Addie and Carolena were free and a smile pulled at the corners of his mouth as Blake and his loved ones gathered in the future Bar Hemmingway. He rubbed his hand over Addie's back and she leaned into him.

Everyone felt the same thing—relief. It was done.

"How are you, son?" John asked.

Blake took a long drink from his beer and ran his hand over his face. "All right." He caught sight of his own knuckles, raw and red, and he flexed his hand.

John patted him twice on the back, then gave his shoulder a man's grip. "He didn't give you a choice, you know. We have to take care of those we love." He turned his upper body to the other side of the table. "How about you, Philippe? You okay?"

"Yeah." He nodded though his brows lifted slightly, as though it had all been too much. "Yeah. I'll be fine."

Carolena wrapped her hands around her glass. "Take your time."

"He was never going to stop coming for you, Blake. Or Carolena or Addie." Campbell patted his daughter on the leg. "It was the inevitable end. Regardless of how it happened. I'm just glad none of you were hurt."

The table was quiet for a few moments, no one sorry that Otto was gone. No one celebrated, either.

"There is an old Tibetan saying, 'With every meeting there is a parting.' I've often found that saying to be a good reminder to cherish the ones I love while we're together," Carolena said. "Because with every relationship, there is a beginning and an end. Sometimes the end is because of death or divorce, perhaps a shifting of someone's path. Today is all we have with one another. Tomorrow...is unknown." Carolena raised her glass of beer. "This ending is a new beginning for all of us."

"To the new beginning," Addie said.

"Here, here." John and Campbell raised their glasses, enthusiasm growing in their voices.

"To the new beginning," Philippe said quietly.

Everyone clinked their glasses together in a toast. A new breath of life wove its way through the group, a gathering whose one main connecting point used to be Otto. Now they would have new and far happier reasons for their relation-ship with one another. Blake leaned over to Addie and kissed her. "To the new beginning." He tapped his glass against hers in a toast that chimed like a clear bell.

"*Maman*, tomorrow morning, we'll go get the art and make arrangements to get it home. We also need to think about where we should place the Wentworths and how to protect them through time."

"Can you get the Gardner art back to the museum?" John asked.

"I have a contact with the FBI Art Crime Team, and I'll get it to him. We'll lay the blame for the theft with Otto. I'll just say that I recovered it from him, which is true."

John took a swallow from his beer, then nodded enthusi-astically. "Excellent. I've wanted to get that art back to them for a long time now. In terms of the Wentworths, I think they ought to come back to New York. I have a warehouse we might use for its storage. I'll have to ask Grace to look into what happens to that property over the years to make sure it's a good option for us."

"I'll return the Picassos to their creator tomorrow." Carolena sipped her wine. "That should return them to their rightful place in the future."

"I'd like to go with you on that trip." Addie's eyes were wide with a sense of adventure. "Once in a lifetime chance to meet Picasso and all that."

Carolena rested her hand on Addie's. "I welcome the company."

Blake downed the last of his beer. "Long day. I'm going up."

"I'll go, too," Addie said.

John pulled a letter from his pocket. "I know you're worn out after a day like today. But would you mind getting this message into the book on your way up?" He handed Blake the letter. "I want to let Grace know what's happened. She's waited a long time to hear this news."

With a nod, Blake slid the note into his jacket pocket. He kissed his mother goodnight. "Do you need a key to my room? I can sleep on the chaise. Or you could share Addie's room."

"Campbell has extra space in his room. I'm going to sleep there tonight—the hotel is still full. Maybe tomorrow I'll have my own room." She smiled and patted his hand and he was glad she wouldn't be alone for the night.

30

The only task left to sort was the Gardner and Wentworth art, so everyone slept late and enjoyed leisurely breakfasts at the hotel. When they finally stepped out into the late morning, Blake noted that Paris' glorious spring had become a more befitting celebration today than it had been the day before.

Up until now Blake wondered if any part of their lives would ever reach normal again. But today, on this crisp Parisian morning when tulips celebrated the season of new birth and new beginnings, everything in their close-knit group had become just that—normal. Aside from the fact that they were gathering together to recover nearly a billion dollars' worth of stolen art, and then to travel through time, that is.

They all managed to fit in one cab that was owned by the hotel. Mary, as usual, chose to visit shops and take in more Parisian fashion. So far she had sketched an entire notebook full of noteworthy trends. Addie commented to her grandfather that she would like to have Mary shop for her sometime. Blake could just see it—regular trips to the twenties for shopping trips and fun-filled weekends, as it had been done nearly three decades before.

The front door of Carolena and Otto's apartment opened to a marble hallway flanked by gracious palms. The furniture and patterned hall rug were more bohemian and less art deco than Blake expected, probably because of Carolena's influence. Throughout Otto's life, she was the only person to whom he had ever acquiesced.

Carolena led everyone through a narrow arched doorway and to a small reading room at the back of the house. "Campbell, if you would, please?" She motioned for him to push on one side of a bookcase. "I had one similar to this constructed at my home in the present. It's far more elegant than this one, but this one worked well. Even though it's a bit cliche, no one suspected it was here."

The bookcase slid across the carpet and revealed a darkened room. She reached into the dark and finally pulled on a long piece of string. With a click, a singular naked bulb gave shadowy light to a room as big as a walk-in closet. "Not much, but it did its job. I didn't have a lot of time or space to work with."

"This room wasn't here when you moved in?" Blake asked.

"*Non.* I had a carpenter work on it when Otto and I had our regular outings. The carpenter lives just down the street. He didn't much like Otto. He never asked why I wanted this room."

"Remind me to pay him extra before we leave." Blake helped her move several framed canvases out of the way to reveal the three Wentworths. He squatted in front of the paintings and sighed with relief. "And there they are. Our way home."

Addie placed her finger on the corner of one. Paint slid

up her finger and over her hand, and she laughed aloud. "Apparently, you can go home again."

"What about the Gardner art?" John asked.

Carolena led them through a maze of narrow hallways, then unlocked the door to a relatively small, dark, rectangular room. Internal wooden shutters were closed over the windows to keep out the light and curious uninvited guests. She clicked on a side lamp and gasped. "It's gone!"

A sick disappointment landed hard in the pit of Blake's stomach. He had been looking forward to returning them to William Condon, his former boss with the FBI, and to the Gardner museum. "What would he have done with them?"

"He must have moved them."

"Moved them, where?" he asked.

"I'm not sure." Carolena's fingers drifted over the wall where Blake assumed the paintings used to hang. "I would suspect he took them back to the present. I think he was planning to move all the art piece by piece. It wasn't that long ago—and before the Wentworth copies were complete —he disappeared for a couple of days, on what he called it a business trip. That must have been when it happened.

"I didn't come into this room all that often. Once in a while when he bought a new painting, other than that I mostly stayed away. It was just—too tragic."

"Where would he have left them in the present?" John asked.

"His son Nicholas is still there. Maybe he was overseeing the new collection."

"Nicholas has issues with the mob." Addie squatted in front of a Modigliani. "And he's an idiot. If he had them I doubt he kept them safe."

John clicked his tongue. "Exactly what I didn't want to

happen to those pieces." He stood in the middle of the room with the works from Picasso and Modigliani and the others and shook his head. "He was building an unmatched collection of masterpieces, Gardner art included, then taking them back to the present, where he would have become a wealthy, important figure in the art world."

Carolena gave a nod that accompanied a sigh of resignation. "That was his plan."

Blake shoved his hands into his pockets. Only the ghosts of Otto's demons were left now. They would clean them up by returning the art to its creators and hope that the pieces would travel a more normal trajectory through time now. One destined for museums, not private viewing rooms. An almost unfamiliar feeling whooshed through him. Relief.

His hand found the envelope he had stuffed into his jacket pocket late last night. John had asked him to send a message to Grace through the Fitzgerald book. When he opened the book to do so, there was already an envelope there with John's name on it. He'd forgotten he still had that envelope until this moment.

"Oh, John." Blake handed him an envelope, his name in small blue script on the outside. "This was in the book last night. For you. I just remembered."

"You got the letter off, I guess?" John ripped at the envelope and removed a photo.

"Yeah, no problem—"

John's face turned red, his voice stressed with panic and fury. "Dang it!"

"Is everyone okay?" Addie rushed to her grandfather's side.

"No, Addie. They aren't." He handed her the photo.

Addie's jaw dropped slack and the color drained from her face. "Oh. No."

"What is it?" Blake pried the picture from her shaking hands. It was a snapshot that Grace had taken when he, Addie, and Alexa first arrived at Grace's home in Savannah. The three of them stood on the front porch, smiling—a nice shot, a happy group. Except for the fact that Blake's image had faded to a transparent shadow that was less than half of its original vibrancy.

That's exactly how he had been feeling since they had arrived in Paris. Like half a man, if that.

"Something has changed the future," John said. "And not for the better."

31

The front door slammed, and two sets of footsteps ran fast down the hallway. Otto and some other man appeared in the doorway. Otto was silent, with only a gun. A gun he pointed straight at them.

Blake thought for a flash that he must be hallucinating. Otto was dead.

He grabbed Addie and pushed her behind him, each of his movements too slow and stiff, as though something outside of him forced him to move.

"Carolena!" He yelled and reached for her, dread harnessing every muscle in his chest. She was out of his reach and within the aim of Otto's gun.

"Don't move!" The blond bodyguard, his chest full and muscular, stood beside Otto, gun focused on Blake. His voice filled every corner of the room.

"Carolena. What's going on here?" By contrast Otto's voice was calm. Questioning but settled. As if he'd just come home from a long day of work and was surprised to find all these strange people in his house.

The normally fine angles of Otto's tanned face had

become distorted, bloated, and bruised. He had risen from the dead to come after them. Evil did that.

Blake worked to catch his breath. He felt just like he appeared in that photo. Powerless. Fading. His heart pounded a fast but irregular beat. Its cadence limped along to the living nightmare.

"Otto." Carolena pressed her hand to her chest. "Are you okay?" She said it flawlessly, as if she really cared about his well-being. Blake thought she must have practiced it time and again over the years, preparing for a moment when she might accidentally happen upon him.

"I'm fine." He waved his gun in a way that told everyone else to move to the back of the room. "Though I'd shoot every last one of you if the blood wouldn't ruin my art. Especially yours." He trained his gun on Blake.

"Otto. Look at me." Carolena inched close to him and held his newly fattened face in her hands. "I've been so worried about you."

Otto took one of her hands and guided her to stand at his side, like the ally he believed her to be. "Everyone stay still. Don't move." His voice was loud but not necessarily strong. There was a thinness to it that belied his armed strength.

The group stayed quiet, except for Carolena, who stroked Otto's arm and tried in vain to get him to focus on her. Blake had visions of Otto popping everyone off like a hunter shooting ducks on a pond. He would be first, he was certain. A sick feeling flooded his chest.

"I thought you were dead." Carolena stayed close to him. "Where were you?"

"The hospital assumed I was dead, too. When I woke up in the hallway outside the morgue, it was a big surprise for everyone. That's where I met Oscar, an orderly at the hospital." Otto slapped the overgrown boy on the shoulder. He likes money. As such, he was happy to help me get back home."

Blake eyed Oscar, who chewed on something now and then and swallowed. He rubbed his nose with the back of his hand.

"I've been thinking. It's not just the Wentworths you want, is it? You want to make my life as miserable as I made yours. All three of you." He waved the gun at them in one sweep. A pain clenched in Blake's chest when the aim of Otto's gun spanned across the group.

"Otto, you don't need to do this. Let's leave. We'll go right now." Carolena pleaded like an abused wife, like someone who had never known love without fear.

"No—" Blake said.

"What is it with you?" He removed his hat and wet bandages squished.

Carolena brought her fingertips to her lips. "We should get you back to the hospital, mon amour."

He waved her off. "I have something to take care of first. Oscar?"

The blond man tugged on Blake's arm and made him stand about four feet from his new boss, who held his gun like a one-man firing squad.

"No, Otto. *Non*." Carolena's tone was firm.

"Otto, you—" Addie said.

He raised the gun toward Blake's face and cocked it, ready to fire. Blake's heart took a free fall dive. He expected to feel the bullet rip a hole into his forehead. Despite the stampede of panicked emotions that tightened his chest, his heart only moved at a thudded pace.

Carolena screamed, "He's our son!"

"He's your son, Otto!" Addie yelled at nearly the same time.

Otto startled slightly, his eyes narrowed on Blake, seemingly searching for something familiar, questioning the truth in Carolena's and Addie's claim.

Carolena pushed the gun's aim away from Blake's body and she tried to pry it from his his fingers. Each one that she lifted from the shiny black weapon curled around the handle again and resumed its grip.

"Our son?" Otto's appeared oblivious to what Carolena tried to do, as though she were adjusting a cuff on his sleeve.

Blake's heartbeat sped forward now. Stumbling at first, out of step, its panicked lack of coordination drummed faster until it rolled its way into a full stampede. It was the first time Otto had known him as his son since he was about five years old.

"You're—you're—"

Blake tracked the movement of both guns in the room and watched for an opportunity to take one.

"He didn't die?" Otto asked Carolena.

"No," she said softly, gently.

"Then why did the two of you stay away?"

"Because your life had become too dangerous for a child."

Otto inhaled, his eyes locked and fixed on his son. "You're alive."

"Let's call it a truce, old friend," John said. "No one here wants to hurt you."

"I think my *son* here does. He tried to kill me."

"If I had tried to kill you, you would be dead. I just wanted Addie away from the point of your knife."

The muscles on the side of Otto's jaw flexed. His eyes

narrowed with enough hatred to shoot a hole through Blake's head. "So, you weren't taking Carolena away from me because you wanted a trip home through the Wentworths or because you wanted revenge. You took her because she's *your mother*."

No one said a word. Blake only distantly recognized the rapid thudding inside of his head as the effect of his own heartbeat.

Otto turned to Carolena. "You came with me to the twenties to save Blake's sweet gifted Addie? Is that why you came out of hiding?"

"No, Otto, *mon amour*, I came to be with you. I've been with you for two years!" Her eyes and hands darted over Otto's face, searching, Blake knew, for some pathway to convince him.

Otto's glance slid over and around the group like a snake looking for a meal. "I see. Then, Carolena. I think you have a choice to make. Me. Or him. Who is it going to be?"

"You, Otto. Of course it's you. Let our son go and you and we can spend the rest of our lives together."

"Otto, enough of this." Blake pushed Otto the way he had conquered him the day before, reaching inside his father's mind for leverage to weaken him and to get him to drop the gun. The world in front of him went black and dizzy and he wavered, physically. He was fading from this world, just as the photo had shown. Addie's hand flew to his side and held him up.

"Enough of what—*Blake*?" He stuttered over the name. A foul grin of ridicule spread across Otto's joker-esque face.

Blake tried to steady the image of Otto and Carolena in front of him. "She won't leave with you," he managed to say. He fought the velvet blackness that surrounded his vision.

Panic screamed in his head. He looked around the room —Campbell, Addie, Philippe, and John stood there as helpless as he was. Everything he had fought for, everything he had hard-won, was dissolving into nothingness and he was going with it.

"You're sure of that, are you? Have you made your choice, Carolena?" Neither man looked in her direction, rather, they met each other's stares.

"Of course, I'll go with you." Slowly, she sealed her hand to Otto's arm.

The blood left Blake's head in a dramatic *whoosh* and only adrenalinic horror managed to hold him upright.

Oscar used his gun to escort everyone out of the house. Everyone except Otto and Carolena.

Voices turned to overlapping echoes inside of Blake's head, their words no longer making sense to him. Even Oscar's face took on a psychedelic trail and Blake guessed as to which image belonged to the man. He reared back and swung hard, missing and stumbling forward.

"Blake!" Addie yelled.

"Dang it, Blake." John lifted him to his feet. "Campbell, help me. We need to get him back to the hotel."

Oscar's humiliating laugh reverberated through his head.

""He'll take her through one of the Wentworths." Blake turned toward the now closed front door of the house. Blackness closed in the rest of the way and took him under.

32

———

The hotel room at the Ritz was mostly quiet and still, except for muted traffic noises outside the closed window. Dark descended around Addie, Philippe, John, and Campbell. They stood in complete silence around the photo that Addie held in her hands. Blake slumped on the edge of the bed and stared at the chair where Carolena had sat the night before.

They had won. It had been over. Otto was dead. His mother and Addie had finally been free to live their lives. Now all of that disappeared.

He thought of writing new plans in his notebook, but he didn't have the strength to cross the room, much less the energy to start a new search.

John lowered himself into the chair across from Blake. "We'll find her, son. We found her once. We'll do it again."

Blake shook his head, his face pale, his eyes glazed. He felt sick and dead. "They've gone by now. He will have taken her through the Wentworth. Knowing Carolena, she'll set it up where I'll never find her."

John placed his hand on Blake's shoulder. "She didn't

have another option today, not from a mother's perspective. Stay with me, Blake. Right now we have something more pressing."

"There's nothing more pressing." Blake tried to stand, but the darkness that overtook him earlier in the day threatened to suck him under again. He returned to the bed and laid down this time, dark shadows framed his sight. He couldn't remember when he'd felt this weak.

"What does this mean? Daddy?" Addie's voice was thin and panicked and pitched high like a girl many years younger. She shoved the photo at her father and shook it, but took it away again before he could say anything. She stared at it, her head shaking back and forth in a tremor. "No. No, no, no, no, no."

Blake took the five by seven piece of paper.

"This is not happening." She paced in front of him twice with the photo clasped to her chest. Finally, she handed it to him.

He propped himself onto his elbow and held the photo toward the light of the nearby lamp. The news hit him like a baseball bat against his skull. He felt a cool sensation, like liquid draining over him, like his own blood leaving him.

"There's a letter as well." John read it aloud.

Dear Campbell and John,

I've been watching this for some time, trying to find a rational explanation for it. I had hoped it might be humidity or poor quality of photo paper, maybe even the effects of a cheap frame. But since Blake's image is the only one fading, a new past must be in place—or almost so. One that is eliminating his life in the present.

I don't know if you know what's caused this. If he is to be alive in the same way he is now in the present, you'll have to reverse whatever has been done. If possible. If you can't, then Blake will cease to exist.

Send a message through the book at the Ritz if I can help.

Godspeed.

Love,

Grace

"Events must have gotten confused—changed—after you met Jack," Campbell said.

"Or after you met Sarah," John said to Blake. He rubbed his finger beneath his lip, faster than normal. His eyes were wide and glassy.

"I thought everything was okay." Addie's voice was laced with panic, driving her pitch even higher.

Blake sat up, feeling worse than when he'd been shot. "They're here, in Paris. The timing is off."

Campbell turned to his daughter.

Tears spilled down her face. "We saw Jack and Sarah at a jewelry store. It's the same one Lexie and I found in the present, when I got...my ring." She held her hand in front of her. "We didn't really interact with them."

"I don't think, at this point anyway, it would matter if you had." He paced across the room.

"Because Jack was supposed to be dead by now." Addie was shaking, shuddering like she was freezing. She rubbed her hands over her arms.

Campbell nodded. "Because he didn't die when he was supposed to, that means that—" He pointed at Blake. "You didn't reincarnate when you were supposed to."

"Oh..." Addie lowered herself to the edge of the bed and held Blake in her arms.

"When was Jack supposed to die?" Philippe asked.

Addie looked at Blake, her mouth half open, her head shook back and forth like the tremor had started again. "Three months ago, maybe? I don't know exactly. When we saw Sarah the other day, she looked to be about five or maybe six months pregnant at the most. I don't think she could have been more than three months pregnant when Gary shot Jack."

Blake pulled away from her, held himself up at the windowsill and breathed deep. It had finally happened. He'd lost her. And Carolena, too. He'd done everything he could to keep them safe. In the end he'd lost. Himself. He felt himself dissolving into nothingness.

He now thought he ought to have kept Addie with him when he traveled. Or maybe he ought to have made sure that she was never alone. He wiped his upper lip with the back of his thumb.

It was back. The anger he'd noticed before they'd left New York. Only it was outside of his control now. It surged through him. He wanted to yell at Addie, scream for what she'd done and throw something just to hear it smash. He ran his fingers over his eyes.

It was a new life taking hold, one without her, and he was mad.

He pointed at her. They needed to find a solution to this, one where he and Addie would be together and one where Carolena would be safe. "We're not..." His breath was ragged and his head was dizzy. "We're not together anymore, Addie."

His words, which were nowhere close to the ones he wanted to say, hit her hard enough to knock the breath out of her.

"What? It's not my fault that I resemble Sarah. He

surprised me—he had me pinned. How do we know that your walking right up and chatting with Sarah didn't throw something off? You could be the one who screwed everything up!"

"None of this is her fault," Philippe said. "Jack—*you*—could have been superstitious. He could have taken the encounter with Addie as a sign that he needed to be more careful about how he and Sarah eloped. Or maybe Sarah did. Either one could have been enough to change it."

"You just stay out of this!" Blake yelled. He would have charged him if he'd had the strength. There wasn't anything he wanted to do more right now than punch someone. Philippe had had it coming to him for some time.

"It was a fluke that he found her. You can't blame her for that." Philippe's face turned red and fierce.

Blake didn't think he was afraid of anyone, but something about the particular tenor Philippe's voice hit. A familiar shot of adrenaline went straight to his heart.

That tone. Reminded him of someone, someone he hated.

Otto.

"She was careless. She shouldn't have said anything to him!" The words burst from his mouth like a bullet from a gun, and probably did as much damage. But he didn't stop there. "I'm gone. Dead. She and I are over. This has blown up in our faces. Again."

"Leave her alone, Blake." Philippe moved toward him.

"What would you know about it? What have you done to help in any of this besides play it safe and get close to Addie wherever she happens to be?"

"Oh, because your way of handling things is the only right way. Is that it?" Philippe shoved Blake backward.

Blake raised his fist in a ready shot. Philippe responded in kind.

"Enough!" John's word was fast and ferocious and he stepped between the two brothers.

The two of them glared at one another, each of them like pack leaders, neither one willing to give up.

"Knock it off." John stood between them until both of them lowered their fists.

"Where is Gary?" A trace of anger remained in Philippe's voice.

"New York, I would guess. Unless he's traveling," Campbell said.

John shrugged. "Impossible to say. I could send him a telegram. I know he'd be interested to find Sarah. Once he found them together he'd kill Jack without being asked."

Addie gasped.

"Gary *has* to kill Jack if Blake is going to live," Campbell said sternly. "And fast."

Blake lowered his head into his hands.

"Okay." She nodded. Seemingly trying to calm herself as she did. "But Jack is more careful now. He might kill Gary this time."

"We may not be able to get the timing back on track." Her grandfather paced. "We have to try, though. I'll send the telegram. Where are Jack and Sarah living?"

"Chantilly," Blake said with a deep exhale. "Better send him a phonetic description of how to say the name of the town. Otherwise he'll never find it."

"Do you know where they live?"

"We don't know," she said. "He'll just have to ask around. Someone in town will know them."

John, Campbell, and Philippe discussed how and where to send the telegram so that Gary would receive it.

Addie approached Blake. Cautiously. Her expression delicately set. She was either on the verge of tears or she was going to knock him unconscious.

He had calmed himself, his breathing was more even. But he didn't give her a chance to show him her response. Instead he swept her into his arms and held her close. "I'm leaving again, Addie. I can feel it."

Her arms clung tight to him and inch by inch she squeezed him closer.

"We'll fix this." She pulled away, abrupt and forceful enough that he relaxed his grip. "But you need to hold yourself together." She hugged him again and he sank into her. "We need to work together on this."

He stood there, paralyzed by everything that was happening. He saw the photo of his transparent self in his mind. He was almost gone. Soon he might be erased from her mind like an inconvenient detail. Should they ever meet again in another life she'd never give him a second look. This had been too hard, too much trouble, and all for naught. His surroundings felt unreal, like a staged set, ready to be wiped clean and reset with something different at a moment's notice.

"I'm sorry." Those two words, he was tired of saying them. But they covered the gambit. He was sorry he'd let her down, he was sorry he'd said what he did, and he was a sorry he'd failed.

"I'm sorry, too. I shouldn't have said—"

He placed a finger over her lips. "This probably happened because I approached Sarah. I just wanted to try to make things right. Make things better."

She shook her head. "We need to fix this."

He took her face in his hands and sighed. His whole world was right there in front of him and slipping through his fading fingers. He kissed her and his heart leaned toward her, diving in to the closeness they had always shared. But there was a distance between them, a flux, as though he were being carried out with the tide. "I love you, Addie. I do. I love you. And I'm so sorry."

~

JOHN, Campbell, and Addie left to compose and send the telegram to Gary. Philippe stayed behind to keep watch on Blake.

Blake lowered himself into the chair and rested his head in his hands.

"You alright?"

Blake lifted his head. He gave Philippe a look that told him that was a fantastically stupid question. "I'm half-dead. What's left of my life is draining out of me as we speak. How do you think I am?"

Philippe leaned into the armchair just a few feet from Blake. "You're so much like him."

"Who?"

"Our father."

"*What*?"

"With a few exceptions, you're just like him. You trust no one—not Carolena, not Addie, none of the rest of us. Never mind the fact that we have dedicated our lives to helping you to find your mother."

"I've told everyone how much I appreciated their hard work—"

"You've said it, but you don't walk your talk. You don't trust anyone beyond your ability to control what they do and when they do it. Because it all comes down to you, doesn't it? All any of us have done for the past two years is follow your orders. You're obsessed. You're so driven to get your father, that you've excluded all the people from your life who care about you most. It's all about you, isn't it, brother? Just like Otto."

Blake jammed his hands through his hair. "That's gratitude for all the work I've done. Coming from the guy who can't wait for me to knock off so you can have Addie all to yourself." He inched closer to Philippe's face. "You love her. It's all over your every move."

Philippe's expression shifted several times, like he tried to figure out how to deny it. Then his chin tipped up, completely resolute. "You're right. I do love her. I've loved her all my life and I'm an idiot for letting Otto dictate who I should spend my time with."

"I guess I know what you've been trying to do behind my back all this time."

"Think what you want. I've been a good friend to her and to you." Philippe headed toward the door, then he turned at the last minute. "Though if I wanted to take her away from you, it wouldn't have been hard.

"What are you talking about?"

He glanced out the window and shook his head with a laugh that said he had no respect for Blake. "You think you know everything and you don't know anything. With Addie you've had the whole world in your hands and I've watched you ignore her. *For years*. You want my opinion? You're no different than our dear ol' dad. He did this to Carolena years ago. He loved her. But he treated her like one of his precious pieces of art. One day she left.

"When you finally push Addie away—and you will because you're not even close to seeing how much you're like *him*—I will be there for her. In every way she needs for me to be."

33

———

Blake drifted into unconsciousness.

He wavered more quickly now—between the man I'd known and loved, and something dark, moody, and angry. Someone I didn't recognize. Someone I really didn't want to know.

I wondered if all along, at least since I had met Jack, if this was the change that had been taking place. A new reality where he and I weren't together.

I sat in the chair next to the bed and watched him. His breathing was sporadic. He exhaled fully then didn't take another breath for several seconds. It was as though his existence tilted between life and death, his soul not fully decided which course it would take.

I paced at the foot of the bed. The same thoughts found a groove in my mind. What if Gary didn't receive the telegram that Grandpa sent? What if he received it and didn't care? Some men walked away from women who left them. Maybe he had effectively washed his hands of Sarah. Maybe he had moved on.

Or, on the positive side of things, say he did want to reclaim Sarah.

But what if he wasn't able to kill Jack? Something could go wrong. Jack might win this time.

There was the bigger question in my mind: how long would it take Gary to get here and put the original version of fate back into action? It would take a week for him to travel here by ship. How much time before he left and how much more time would it take for him to find them once he got here? Two weeks, I estimated. I didn't think it could be done in any less time than that.

I watched Blake's chest deflate and I stopped. Waited. Nothing.

Another moment and I would start CPR.

I rushed to his side, hovered over him, hand over palm, an inch from his chest.

"Blake," I said.

With a slow pull of energy, he inhaled again.

There was no way he would last a week.

Much less two.

It wasn't a sure idea. Not one that guaranteed *anything*. Though there was nothing to lose for trying it. I fished through the side pocket in my purse and prayed that the paint chips from my portrait were still there. It was possible the paint chips could disappear altogether. Who knew what path the portrait traveled in this alternate reality?

I dug through my purse and sifted through its contents in search of the slick plastic bag. A metal container of lip stain, a compact mirror, and a two slender packs of papier poudre. Underneath it all, I finally located the small plastic bag of paint chips. I slid my finger and thumb over their smooth delicate painted surfaces. The painting would have captured whatever new past it had witnessed.

A final look at Blake.

I closed my eyes and sank into the life of the painting.

I wandered through a tumbling of its experiences, searching energetically for threads of the painting's earliest existence, the one that oversaw Jack and Sarah's stolen moments.

The day when Sassy sat for the painting...

She sees the finished product for the first time.

A slight fast forward...the party.

But...Gary never makes an appearance.

Jack's murder never happens.

The environment switched—a mostly glassed-in room that jutted from an almost white house—like the curved end of a horseshoe.

I looked down from the new perspective of the painting...Sarah naps on the yellow couch, her head rests on Jack's chest. Her belly full. She's pregnant to term.

Fast forward again.

Sarah is lying on her side on the floor while a blue-eyed baby boy dressed in a matching color kicks and laughs atop a blanket littered with toys.

Another baby.

This time a girl with blond curls.

Then another boy.

His feet rarely touch the ground in the early years since he is usually in someone else's arms.

The room is menagerie of games and giggles and happiness.

I dropped the slice of paint into the bag and stared at Blake. Still sleeping.

The new full life we finally shared in the twenties.

It was stealing our future.

34

Carolena sat in the sunroom at the back of the house, her arms drawn around her knees. A large glass of red wine in one hand.

Otto had hardly spoken to her since he'd interrupted her escape, and thrown Blake and Addie and John and Campbell out for good. She assumed they wouldn't come back now. Either because they knew Otto would kill her, or for some other reason.

For over two years she had him convinced that the only reason she'd stayed away from him was because their son had died. He'd readily accepted that rationale.

When Otto learned their son was alive and well, and dedicating his every effort to imprison him, that shone a different light on things. Now, as she'd said in a panicked moment to protect her son's life, the reason she'd left was because their life had become too dangerous. Because of him, because of the things he had done.

Betrayal. Abandonment. Those were the crimes that Otto accused her of now, and he controlled her every move to keep her from leaving him again. He kept her in rooms that were too high off the ground for her to jump out of a window. He kept a gun in his hand when he escorted her to a new room. He locked the door behind him.

She was his prisoner.

The Wentworths were tucked safely away behind her. Otto hadn't yet figured out that she had copies made or that she'd had a secret room crafted to store them. She could effectively disappear from his life forever, and it was unlikely that he'd ever find her again. He wasn't gifted enough to travel to new locales on his own.

There was only one problem.

Her memories were shifting.

She knew it wasn't her imagination.

One moment her past was as she'd always known it to be. The next, she remembered her life very differently.

With effort and concentration, she was able to remember both at the same time.

She fingered the sugarloaf cabochon ruby ring that Otto had given her when their son was born. She had always liked the fact that the ruby was the birthstone for July—Blake's birth month. Otto had cared enough to do his research, to make it a meaningful gift.

Today she watched the ring shift into a square-cut amethyst. Deep violet purple. Beautiful. But amethyst was the birthstone for February, not July.

When it changed to a ruby, she remembered the hot summer birthdays Blake enjoyed as a child—swimming, popsicles, boating on the lake. When the ring became an amethyst, his birthdays were celebrated with downhill skiing and building snowmen who wore birthday hats and held blue balloons.

She thought of Blake and knew that he was younger now, by how many years she couldn't be sure. When her ring was ruby, Addie was his life. But as an amethyst, Addie was nowhere to be found. In fact, there was no special woman. Instead there were a string of random someones, and that changed him. Without Addie's love, he was cold-hearted and formal, easily antagonized and passionless about anything except destroying his father and by any means necessary.

A new past was battling for life.

If it won, it would change everything.

And everyone.

35

The man slept more soundly than the dead.

I'd been trying to wake him up for several minutes. "Philippe." I ran my hand gently over his forearm.

"Addie?" Philippe squinted his eyes. He clicked on the table lamp and covered his eyes with his hand. "You are here. I thought I was having a dream."

"I'm sorry to wake you. I need your help."

"How did you get into my room?"

"My dad showed me how to pick a lock. It's not that hard with these older lock chambers."

"You broke into my room?" Philippe propped himself up on one arm and tried unsuccessfully to open one eye fully.

In the glow of the lamplight, still somewhat asleep and obviously not quite comprehending why I was at his bedside in the middle of the night, he said, "Not that I mind, but why are you here?"

I dug through his suitcase and threw a pair of his pants, a shirt, and a sweater on the end of the bed. "Because I can't do this alone."

He took a deep breath and sat all the way up. "I could have guessed that you were going to do this. I just didn't think I was the one who was going to go with you."

"You know?"

"I'm guessing." He pulled on the pants, stood and tucked the wide hems of his boxers into his pants.

Something about the sleepy look in his eye softened my heart. It was unexpected and I didn't have enough notice to guard against it. "What are you guessing?"

He ran his hands through his hair, which was perfect in that messy present-day style. "That you aren't content to wait for Gary to set things to right. That you're going to try to take care of this yourself." He raised an eyebrow at me.

He went to the bathroom, applied hair pomade to smooth and slick everything down. Even in the dead of night, the ladies and gentlemen of the Hotel Ritz were well groomed. He would be no different.

I carefully observed his reflection in the bathroom mirror. He was a gorgeous man. He was kind, intelligent, funny. He was moneyed, though I hoped whomever he chose as his partner wouldn't care about that. His only flaw was that Otto was his father.

Blake had the same genetic imperfection.

My heart had squeezed and ached with regret and panic when I'd first seen the photo. Oddly I felt less upset now than I did then. Exhaustion, I figured. Numb, perhaps. I rested my forehead in my palm and drifted off for a blissful second, a moment's rest I desperately needed.

I felt something cold and hard against my forehead.

I examined my hand. A thick platinum band laden with diamonds fit snugly around my left ring finger. It fit beneath a brilliant round diamond inside a square of smaller diamonds. I frowned at the rings—a wedding set.

"I'm ready, babe. Where did you say we were going again?" Philippe ran his hand along his jaw and laughed, lighthearted, not a care in the world. "I got completely dressed and now I can't remember." A thick, curved platinum wedding band was on his ring finger.

"When did we start wearing wedding rings?" I pointed toward the shiny metal that moved with his hand.

"When you said yes and made me the happiest man alive." He laid soft kisses along my neck. He pulled my body to his. "In fact, seeing as I can't remember where we were off to tonight, it couldn't have been that important. What do you say we just stay in?"

"Wait, Philippe—I was here to see you for a reason." Unknown but familiar memories of time spent with Philippe spooled through my mind like scenes from a movie. He was the only man I'd ever loved, the man I'd married, the man I wanted to spend the rest of my life with. And—oh, the father of our little girl, Maddie.

Something knocked at the back of my mind. Someone. That reason why I had come into this room. I couldn't remember what it was.

He continued to kiss me until I, too, had forgotten where we were supposed to be.

"You're just not used to taking a break from Maddie. You always think you're forgetting something when she's not underfoot."

"No, I—" The memory of our little girl's baby scent hung in my mind and stole my heart and my concentration.

Cherry muffins. Buttercream icing.

It made it impossible for me to think about anything or anyone else. "It was...it was something. What if we were supposed to meet someone?"

"They'll get over it." He lowered me to the bed and frustrated himself with the fact that there were no buttons among the beading on the front of my pink dress. He gently gathered the draped tulle that glittered with more bead design. "I never get enough time with you anymore. He Groucho Marxed his eyebrows at me.

I giggled.

He smiled wide and I loved him with all my heart.

"You're so good at giving me all of you."

"Why would I ever want to hold back from you?"

"I don't know. People like to be in control, I guess. Protect themselves."

"I'm rarely in control when I'm around you, I learned this a long time ago. Besides, close to you is my favorite spot." He kissed me.

"Well, you've completely succeeded. I can't remember where we were supposed to go. Must not have been too important." I twisted my fingers into his hair. "Oh, you don't think we were supposed to meet your father, do you?"

Philippe lifted his head. "Addie. My love. Kindly refrain from mentioning either of my parents when I'm kissing you."

His classic Hollywood smirk left me giggling once again. "It's just that he feels protective about us being in the past like this. Especially the twenties. It's his favorite era. He likes to show it off to us. And you know what a temper he has. I don't want to set him off. So if we were supposed to meet him, I'd rather just go."

He fought the tulle until it was justly pushed down. "He approved our vacation to this era, he knows we're here to enjoy time on our own. We're fine. Besides, I don't remember making any plans to meet with him tonight."

As quickly as my eyes closed again, the man who intercepted most of my dreams leaned seductively against the far wall of my consciousness. His silken blond hair, cream-colored suit, and film-worthy crystal blues caught my attention. No matter what I was in the middle of. I'd silently crushed on him since I was a young teenager and long hoped to meet him. Though I had to give up on that hope. You can't build a relationship, much less a life, on a dream.

He hung on. Watching me from the landscape of my nighttime world. Refusing to disappear, even in the light of Grace's gifted efforts, which could clear just about anything from anyone.

Philippe was busy. Intent. His soft-as-silk tongue traced my collarbone.

"Your favorite," he mumbled against my skin.

"Mmmm." I wrapped my arms around him with love and desire.

"My beautiful wife."

36

"Any other messages through the book?" Fowler handed Grace a glass of red wine. He sat down next to her on the couch.

She sighed, tucked her bare feet beneath her, and placed the photo of Blake and her two granddaughters on the gold mirrored coffee table in their suite at the Hotel Ritz. "Nothing else. At least not so far."

She and Fowler watched Blake's image fade to a lighter shade until it disappeared altogether. Alexa and Addie closed ranks, arms around each another. Philippe stood next to Addie with his arm around her and a blond baby girl on his hip.

Grace quickly scribbled on a notepad and wrote all the new memories that flooded her mind: Addie's wedding, married to Philippe, pictures of family—including Otto at the wedding—and granddaughter Maddie.

Fowler leaned forward. "Does this mean that Blake is gone?"

Grace nodded. "Yes."

When she admitted it, her heart tumbled into a complicated canyon, filled with the rocky edges of regrets and what ifs. Addie had waited her entire life for Blake, she'd dreamed about him for as long as she could remember. Once she found him, her life changed for the better.

Grace wasn't sure who Addie would be now that Blake was gone.

37

"You'll need a gun if you're going to do this," the man from my dreams said.

Jack was his name. He called me Sassy. I didn't know what that nickname meant or why he called me that. But he liked it.

"We'll need a gun," I said distractedly.

"A gun?" Philippe lifted his head. "I brought mine with me from New York." He pointed toward his suitcase that rested against the wall, then he let his hand fall.

"A gun?" I asked.

"I'm not even sure why I would have a gun. Why are we even up in the middle of the night?" Philippe stood. He dropped his dark gray cotton pants to the floor. His belt buckle jingled when it hit solid ground. He crawled toward me. I stretched long and lightsome, but tired from something...I couldn't remember what.

He lifted the silk tulle on my dress. "How do I get you out of this elegant mess?"

I rolled away from him. "The buttons are hidden. Just push the fabric back and you'll find a row of them."

"A-ha…"

I went to the bathroom and shimmied out of my dress. A pale pink wonder of silk and glass beads. I slipped into my robe and returned to the bedroom.

Philippe sat on the edge of the bed and cocked a sly grin. "I have something for you. Sit." He went into the bathroom. I heard him rummaging through his bag.

Instead of sitting, I stretched out on the bed and closed my eyes. I was still feeling tired from I didn't know what. I felt like I'd run a marathon. I drifted into a sleepy dream.

"Sassy?" Jack squatted in the front and center of my mind's eye. "If you want me, you're going to have to choose me. Wake up, sweetheart."

Vibrant colors swirled around him in this fantasy world that often came about when I slept.

"What are you talking about? Choose you? I don't know why you have stayed with me all these years if I can't have you."

"You can have me any time you want. Wake up sweetheart," Philippe said. "You're dreaming."

I pushed up to my elbows and found Philippe sitting on the edge of the bed, a ring box in his outstretched hand. I glanced around the room, half expecting to see Jack.

He'd seemed so real just then.

"I found this in a jewelry store down the street. Open it."

I lifted the lid and found a large round emerald ring surrounded by a circle of diamonds.

"Oh, Philippe. It's gorgeous!" I kissed his lips until his smile broke us apart. "Thank you."

"I know you like this sapphire ring, but I wanted you to have something special from our trip." He took the sapphire ring from my finger and put it on the bedside table.

"No!" I grabbed it. "I—I like this ring. I'll wear the emerald on another finger."

"You don't think that would be a bit much? Your wedding set, the sapphire, and the emerald?"

"I'll work it out." I slid the sapphire into its place on my finger, slipped the emerald halfway onto my middle finger, and placed my hands on his chest.

"I don't know why you're so attached to that ring. You're sure this is one you just bought for yourself?" Shades of vulnerability shone through his words. My heart cringed.

"I am. Can't explain it. I've loved it from the moment I saw it. You love me in spite of my quirks."

"More than you know."

I held his face in my hands and I felt as I always did with him. That I was the luckiest girl in the world.

"Oh, how I love you," he said.

"I love you, too."

"Sassy, do you want me?" Jack asked.

Jack, my nighttime visitor who courted me since I was a teenager. Those eyes, so handsome. It was like I had known him before. I *wish* I had known him.

There was some sort of pressure shift, a change that made Philippe draw back.

He and I stared at one another in awkward closeness.

"Addie, I—I'm not complaining but, I'm...confused."

Everything stilled between us. I had all the memories of our marriage, our love for one another, Maddie—our sweet baby girl. And Blake. And Jack. They were there, on the outside looking in through a fog. I assumed Philippe could see as I did.

"I—um. I don't know." I slipped off of the bed. "What's going on?"

"We're married, right?" Concern and worry painted

across his face in lines and angles, shadows and silent prayers.

"I—yeah. We are." I held his face in my hands and kissed him, our lips pressing against one another as I'd always known them to. But today I felt our life slipping through our fingers. I held out my hands. My wedding rings and the emerald and diamond ring on my other hand glowed with love and sparkled in the low light. "I'm wearing my wedding rings. The rings you gave me."

"Because you said yes. We're married." He held me close.

"Right. Yes." The words felt right but altogether wrong. Yes, we were married. But I also remembered breaking the lock on his door to ask him for help. To help Blake.

Wait.

Blake?

That guy I'd seen at Otto's firm?

Why would I do that? Philippe and I were married with a child.

"Then why am I thinking that you're also with Blake?" He grabbed both of my hands and we watched as my wedding set disappeared and reappeared. The new emerald ring did the same.

They disappeared for the second time. My heart broke at the loss of my marriage and our child. They were gone from my life, but not forgotten.

"Oh, Philippe." I curled into him. We held each other in the wake of the lifetime we shared.

Blake had been strong one minute and weak the next. I assumed that Philippe and I had dipped in and out of the reality that would have been, an alternate life that flickered and tried to find a steady heartbeat.

Our realities were shifting.

I had no idea which would win over the other.

38

―――――

I held the key steady at Blake's hotel room door. I glanced at Philippe one last time. My heart hovered at the middle of these two lives, and I nearly ripped in half when I threatened to move in one direction or the other.

I exhaled hard across pursed lips, and expected to find Blake asleep in bed, right where I had left him. What I found instead was an empty bed.

Gone.

He was gone.

I sat on the edge of the chair, my fingertips pressed against my lips.

Philippe stood at the foot of the bed, his eyes glazed and fixed on my face. He was caught somewhere between what had been and what might be.

As was I.

"Maybe he's just in the hotel somewhere. We should check with John and Campbell. He could have gone to see them."

I shook my head. I couldn't sense him anywhere. I

glanced at the tossed sheets on the bed. "He already feels like a faraway memory to me. Like a dream. I think he's disappeared altogether."

Philippe wrapped his arm around me and pressed his lips to my forehead. His kiss was slow. "Addie, I'm trying at this. To help you. But if we're going to do this, we should get going before it's too late. I don't know how much longer I'll remember."

I glanced around the room. Seemed like there was something I ought to take with me. Nothing stood out. The nagging feeling was probably just a leftover need to find my cell phone or car keys. Or Maddie. "I'm coming."

THE HOTEL RITZ had several cars available to its guests, though not this late at night. At least not until they woke up a driver. We had to wait about twenty minutes until both the car and driver were ready for us.

It also took some explaining for the driver to understand that yes, we were going to Chantilly. No, we didn't know exactly where, and no, we didn't have an address.

The driver muttered an extended tirade about being ripped out of bed in the middle of the night, forced to drive in the damp open air and directed by people who had no idea where they were going.

I slumped into the backseat and stared out the window at the night that flicked by in dark shapes. No one knew where Blake was. I was about to have to murder the man I'd loved for at least two lifetimes, the same man who loved me so much he kept a presence in my dreams to help make sure we would meet again.

Even after killing him, there was no guarantee that

would work to bring back the life that Blake and I shared. Too much time could have passed.

Philippe reached across the seat and held my hand. His thumb rubbed over my fingers and pushed against my diamond wedding rings that had returned. Our memories held two realities: one with, the other without one another.

Heartbreak.

Heart. Break.

I'd heard the word a million times and said it at least that many. But I didn't think anyone could fully understand what heartbreak was until they literally felt their heart ripping in two, each half reaching toward a great love. No matter which side won out, my heart would break. Irreparably so.

I kissed Philippe and traced his face with my fingers. The outline was so familiar and tender beneath my touch, I could have drawn it with my eyes closed.

"No matter what happens, I'll always love you." His kiss was soft, loving. A kiss I knew he hoped wasn't goodbye.

Once in Chantilly, we had the driver navigate slowly through the residential streets. Gas lamps lit only a few feet in each direction and I squinted at the shadowed houses. I tried to figure if any of them had been the one I'd seen in my vision. It was like swimming through murky waters. The passing of time was our greatest peril. A moment more and I might simply forget him altogether.

His face, remember it.

The defining details were foggy and I could only make out his eyes. Jack's eyes. I closed my own to see him. His broad confident smile never wavered in this strange intersection of time. I from the future, Jack from my past. Somehow I was aware of the constantly shifting sands beneath us all.

He reached to me with those eyes the way he always had. Reminding me of who we were together, never letting me drift too far. Until now.

"*Un moment s'il vous plait. Arrête s'il-te-plaît.*"

Last time I checked the paint chips from the portrait, there had been a solarium. Quite pronounced. Attached to an off-white house with a slanted roof. I saw the house to our left. It was nestled between two uneven walls of hazel, oak, and lime trees, the forgotten remnants of ancient Roman woodlands.

Philippe and I stepped into the night, silent except for the soft shuffling press of our shoes onto the dirt and grass. Yellowed lamplight highlighted Jack's form, which was hunched over papers at his carved desk, his white sleeves were rolled up to his elbows. I stopped, my stomach pitched. I could remember leaning behind him to kiss his neck while he worked. I remembered the warm spiced scent of him.

Philippe ran the back of his hand across my cheek, his caress anchoring me to the moment. When my eyes met the softness of his, the tears fell before I could stop them.

"This is up to you," he said.

"I know. It's just that I still remember all of it. Us. Every-thing. The years we dated, our wedding, the day Maddie was born. I remember every one of her birthdays. I remember how her hair smells like spun sugar." I rubbed the hurt in my chest and cried for our baby girl who, after this moment, I would never see again. "I can see the roses that you bring me on my birthdays and anniversaries and I see the silver fluted vase I put them in. I remember sleeping next to you every night and the way you touch me when we make love. I love you, Philippe."

"If I have to leave you, it might actually kill me." Tears gathered in his eyes and spilled onto his cheeks. He held me tight against him. He kissed me, and I struggled to remember why we stood in the dark outside of this house.

Jack lifted his head. He squinted into the dark, close to where Philippe and I stood. I saw his face in my mind's eye from his visit to me earlier in the night, as well as from his dreamtime visits throughout my life. "Come back to me," I could hear him say.

Philippe placed the gun in my open palm, his wedding band caught the glint of a moonbeam. "Are you sure you want to do this?"

"Honestly?" My voice broke at the end. "Don't ask me what I want right now. I just have to fix this."

"No, I—I know. I wouldn't ask you to give up my brother. I just mean...pulling the trigger. Would you rather I do it?"

All at once, I understood Carolena's situation. Just as she didn't want Blake to carry the burden to end Otto's life, I didn't want Philippe to have to kill Jack. I didn't want murder on his karma, his conscience, or in the energetic makeup of his relationship with the man who would be his future half-brother.

"I'll do it." I pushed his hand away from the gun and tried to remember how to shoot the weapon that would ruin and save lives all in one. Alexa had taken me to her shooting range in present-day New York several times. Of course, this gun was much older than the one I'd learned on. I assumed they were basically the same. Aim the gun, pull the trigger.

I took aim at Jack. He sat behind a desk that was positioned in the outermost part of the curve of windows. A desk that was supposed to move to a different room in the house once the children arrived.

Tears filled my eyes and though I tried to blink them away. They wouldn't leave. I lowered the gun and wiped them away.

Jack moved across the room. I walked to the right to see where he went. He kissed past-life me, who was curled up and sleeping on the couch, belly huge with our boy.

When he returned to his desk, he stretched, his palms pressed against his lower back, his chest arched and spread as a target for me. My hands shook and my aim wavered. I lowered the gun, again. Wiped my eyes.

"Addie. My wedding band hasn't left my hand for several hours and—" His words ended on a sigh.

I looked at the wedding set on my hand and covered it with my right hand. Partly to protect it, partly to keep it from my view. "Mine, either."

"If you're going to do this, you need to hurry. For Blake."

I nodded.

"Here, sweetheart." He stepped behind me and helped me aim the gun.

"No, I don't want you to do this. It's not right for this to be on your conscience."

"I'll let you do it. I'm just going to help you aim." He placed his cheek next to mine, his hands covered my own, and his arms wrapped securely around me. He didn't beg me to stop, he didn't remind me of everything we had together, or of the plans we'd made for our future. But I remembered them. All of them.

"I can't ask you to do this. I know how badly this is hurting."

"I would do anything for you, Addie. I'm doing this for you." He pushed a lock of hair away from my face and behind my ear, then pressed his cheek to mine. "Blake is going to be fine, right after you do this. Just focus on that."

I nodded. Even though we weren't certain.

"Now, deep breath."

I inhaled with him.

"On the exhale, squeeze the trigger."

I thought of all the times my father, grandfather, and Blake had said, "Leave no trace!" Here I was with a gun in my hands. I was sure going to leave a trace tonight.

"You're ready, Addie."

On the exhale I pulled the trigger and a deafening blast burst around us. The gun kicked in my hands. Jack fell, a red stain spread across the front of his white shirt.

"Come on!" Philippe grabbed the gun and my hand and we ran through the dark and the wet grass.

Sarah's screams trailed after us.

INSIDE THE BACK of the limo, I was made up of two warring halves. The first half celebrated what we had just done and hoped with everything possible that it had returned our lives' paths to their original course. The other part of me felt like a murderer, and not only because I had just shot a man. But because I had actively tried to destroy the life and family I shared with Philippe.

Philippe examined his wedding band. "It didn't work."

The cool night air seeped into the car and a chill covered my body. I stared at my own wedding rings, as well as the emerald ring on my right hand. He was right. "Jack must have lived."

Philippe's expression was drawn and conflicted. "I don't see how he could have."

"Should we go back?" I put my hand over my stomach to stifle the wave that rolled through it. Trying to kill Jack twice in one night was a horrifying thought.

"He's probably at the hospital by now. Maybe in surgery. There won't be a way to get to him."

We each seemed to have a tentative hold on both potential realities. But that didn't make it any easier. I loved Philippe and wanted my life with him. I loved Blake, too, and wanted my life with him.

I twirled my wedding rings around my finger and wondered what would happen next. If Blake ceased to exist in this life, would I forget him entirely? I had earlier in the evening.

I remembered what my grandfather said about Ellen's jewelry and Grace's knowledge of the Picassos. I remembered how, because we were still in this era, we could remember both realities if we worked really hard at it.

Would some part of me always remember Blake as I did right now? If Philippe and I were firmly on this path of man and wife, would he remember Blake and how much I loved him? Wouldn't that destroy us and our family?

I was reasonably certain that the dreamworld visits from Jack would stop, considering I had just shot him. If I saw him in my sleep now, it would be more of a haunting. I curled against Philippe's warm chest, and he tucked me closer to him.

There was nothing left to say.

And certainly, nothing left to do to save Blake.

39

Philippe and I returned to the hotel. "Because we're married," I said to my father and grandfather. We had woken them up and told them know what we had done.

"We have a little girl together. Maddie." The words tumbled from my mouth with quick enthusiasm. "And she's adorable. She smells like sweet cherry muffins and buttercream icing..." I placed my hand over my heart.

My sweet girl. My beautiful baby.

My father and grandfather stared at Philippe and me with their mouths agape. I showed the photo to them, the one that used to feature Alexa, Blake, and me. Now Alexa and I had closed ranks, arms around one another. Philippe stood with his arm around me and he held a blond baby girl on his hip.

"I may have killed a man, a good man and for no good reason." The part of me that desperately wanted Blake was only held upright by the other half of me who was pleased my efforts had failed. I had one foot in each reality. My brain was about to split into two.

"You know this life with Philippe and you also remember Blake?" my grandfather asked.

"Most of the time, though, the awareness kind of wavers in and out. Earlier tonight...everything shifted. I remembered going into Philippe's room to ask for his help. The next thing I knew I'd always been with Philippe, we were married, had a family. Then there was this fluctuation of energy and time changed back to the old course. Since then, if I really work at it, I can pretty well see both realities. It's getting harder. I feel this tremendous pull toward the life I have with Philippe." The muscles in my legs turned to noodles and I had to sit down.

"Where is Blake now?" My grandfather ran two fingers and a thumb along his forehead like he rubbed at a pounding headache.

"When I left him he was sleeping. His energy was so weak I didn't think he would wake up until the morning."

"You don't know where he went?" My father ran his hand along his jaw.

"He's not in his room. I don't even know if he still has a physical presence anymore." I gestured to the photo.

We all stared at the floor until my father sprang upright. "I have an idea."

ON MY GRANDFATHER'S ORDERS, the car stopped a half-block away from Otto and Carolena's house. Before we left the hotel, my father had asked one of the front desk clerks if anyone else had taken a hotel limo in the last twelve hours or so. He was told that just one had. A tall gentleman with dark hair, American, but spoke fluent French. We assumed that was Blake. We hired a driver of our own.

The main streets of Paris were not without their traffic. But the domestic neighborhoods held an eerie thickness. I felt like I was swimming through mud.

"I'll bet he's in there." My father nodded to the house.

A singular lamp glowed inside Otto and Carolena's front window. I stared hard at the dimly lit room and hoped to make out Blake's silhouette. My fingers traced the pronged edges of the central diamond in the engagement ring Philippe had given me. It hadn't left my hand since long before I'd killed Jack.

"He may not remember you," my father said.

I wondered if he could remember two realities as I could. I also wondered if he were married to someone else. A part of my heart folded in on itself.

"If he is alive, I can't imagine he has the strength to fight Otto." I searched the street for the other limo Blake might have taken but saw none.

"Let's go to the back side of the house. Stay away from the lights." My father gestured to the gas lamps that lined the avenue. Yards were gracious and offered plenty of shadows for our path. I eyed the area and planned my approach until Philippe leaned toward my ear.

"Do we really need to be here for this?" Philippe's voice was as soft as the kiss he pressed behind my ear. "This trip is supposed to be our second honeymoon. Which, so far, is not quite as active as our first honeymoon, and I'd like to remedy that." His lips grazed along the side of my neck.

"I'm sure we're here for a very important reason," I said to my father and grandfather with a giggle. "But I think we're going to head back now. We don't get much time alone when Maddie's around. I'm sure you understand."

"Addie. Stay with us, sweetheart. We have a job to do here. We need to find Blake and help him, he could be in danger." My father placed his hand on my knee. He always did this when I was a child and he wanted me to listen to him.

"My only job this week is to remember all the reasons why I married this amazing man." I ran my hand along the side of Philippe's face.

"I think we should tell them," Philippe said.

I shrugged. "Tell them what?"

He faced the two of them with a deep breath. "Addie and I have decided to move here. Permanently. It's a better era to raise Maddie and maybe a sibling or two."

Philippe gave me a side squeeze and a thrill dashed through me. I remembered that part of the reason for the second honeymoon was to work on our family's expansion. "Our plan is to buy a house while we're here."

"Addie. Come here." My grandfather took both of my hands in his. "Sweetheart. Listen to me."

My dad pushed in close.

"Did I do something wrong?"

The men glanced at each other.

"Do you remember Blake?" My grandfather's voice warbled, like it was underwater and his words took on an annoying echo.

"Blake...?" I had that feeling again, that I had forgotten something. I didn't think it was Maddie this time.

"I think he's inside and he might need our help."

"Well. I'm not sure what I'm supposed to do with that."

"Do you trust me, Addie?"

"Yes, I—"

"Then come with me. Just for a few minutes." He held my hand and guided me from the car. "If he's there, I want you to look at his face. Real close, alright? And tell me if you recognize him."

"Okay."

My father wrapped his arm around Philippe's shoulder and seemed to keep him from getting too close to my grandfather and me. Philippe broke away and took my hand.

We dashed into the shadows alongside the house and snuck quietly toward a large picturesque window on the back of the house. The room was lit by three lamps, one that I had seen from the front of the house. Otto held a gun on a man who was tied to a chair.

My grandfather made a fist to his side and shook it. "I knew it. Addie. Look closely at the man in the chair. Do you recognize him?"

40

Blake secretly wrestled against the ropes that bound his wrists together behind the back of the chair.

"You've got a lot of nerve breaking in here. What do you want, Blake? Do you need a way home?"

Blake stared hard at his father. "I want you to let her go."

"She's free to leave any time she'd like. She could walk out the front door right now if that's what she wanted to do. Carolena?" Otto turned toward the open doorway and called to her. "Sweetheart?"

With Otto distracted, Blake wriggled a small amount of freedom in the ropes. He watched when Otto stepped into the next room, a smaller area lined with canvases from famous artists five or six deep against the wall.

Oscar stood across from Blake and chewed on a piece of cinnamon-scented gum once, twice. He sniffed and rubbed his nose with the back of his hand while holding a gun loosely with the other. Blake timed it. Oscar would swallow then he would bite his nails on his left hand for a minute or so, then he would repeat the same pattern all over again.

Chew twice, sniff, rub his nose, swallow, look at his nails, bite a couple of them. Repeat.

Behind Oscar, and at the end of the room, was a wide rectangular window that overlooked the backyard. A head appeared in the lower left hand corner. A blond female peeked into the room just enough so as not to be seen. Adrenaline shot through Blake's heart.

"What are you looking at?" Oscar followed Blake's line of vision and turned toward the window. The woman ducked down.

Blake's hand wrestled the rope and his right hand broke free. He left his arms in position.

Otto brought Carolena into the room. "*Mon amour.* Our son thinks that I am holding you hostage in this era. You are free to leave any time you like. Right?"

"*Oui.* I can leave whenever I choose to."

Blake considered briefly that the angle of Oscar's gun meant that he might get shot. It was the only chance he had. The overstuffed makeshift bodyguard lowered his nail-bitten hand and chewed the gum twice. Blake took his only chance. He raised his eyebrows to Carolena with an upward nod, as if she'd said something to him. Otto followed Blake's line of sight and turned his head toward her.

Blake's knuckles crushed Oscar's nose in a right hook that Oscar never saw coming. Blood spurted. The gun went off before it fell from his hand, and fired a shot into the floor. Blake dove for it and rolled, then aimed the gun at Otto.

Father and son pointed guns at one another, both of them energetically pushing hard to get the other to back off.

"That won't work on me, Dad. I guess you know why now."

Oscar held his nose with both hands and cursed. He reached for Blake.

"Back off, Oscar," Blake said. "If I kill him you'll never see another dollar from him."

Oscar looked at Otto, who gave him the okay to step away.

"What do you want, Blake?"

Blake pushed hard. "I've told you. You're going to let my mother go, and then you're never going to bother us again."

Otto laughed.

Something caught Blake's eye, a movement toward the back of the house. They were no longer alone.

"Carolena *wants* to be with me."

"She was only with you to protect me. I'm putting a stop to that."

"You're just like me, son. I'm not sure why I didn't see it before. You love who I love, you have the same passion for art, you want all the same things I do. You want your freedom and you take control. I'm just a little better at being me than you are." Otto cocked his gun.

"I'm not you."

The two men paced in a circle.

"Oh?"

"There are differences between us. In fact, there is one thing I can do that you can't." Blake kept his peripheral vision on Carolena's and Oscar's location. His chest tightened. He and Otto were in a dead heat. It was too early to predict the winner.

Otto's soulless laughter echoed in the room. "If that were true you would have done it already."

"What little bit Carolena told me about your father, it's like he's standing in front of me. Cold, selfish, no respect for another human life. Not even when that life belongs to his own son. That proves my point. I am different from you. I'm more of a man than you could ever be."

"And yet you've chased me for years with nothing to show for it."

"No? If you kill me—which you won't—you should know that Carolena will have nothing to do with you. She would probably kill you herself and with only her hands as a weapon.

"You see, unlike you, who is never quite sure if anyone loves you, I know how much she loves me. I always have.

"If I kill you, her love for me won't stop. It won't flinch. After you're dead, she and I will move on with our lives. Just as we did when we left you the first time. You're a failure, Otto. No matter how many priceless pieces of art you collect, you'll never have anything because you don't know what's important in life. You had Carolena and me and all the love we could offer. You threw it away. That makes you the biggest loser of them all."

A dark shadow crossed Otto's face, one Blake had seen before. Both evil and childlike, a memory from something long ago. An axe still to grind, an intent to make someone pay.

Otto's nostrils flared and Blake felt his father's next move. Otto's eye squinted slightly, his lips pressed in determination. His father prepared for the recoil. The bullet was coming.

It hit Blake in the chest, the left side, no less. The bastard had good aim.

He felt himself falling.

He pulled the trigger.

He pulled it again.

41

———

Blake's chest hurt worse than any pain he could remember. Worse than when he was a kid and the neighbor boys shot him with a toy arrow in the face. Worse than when he had been shot in the arm. The place where the bullet hit was like a hot knife. Stabbed in the heart. Maybe the bullet had.

The impact hit him harder than he imagined it would. Molten lead had set him flat on his back and knocked the breath out of him. What a strange feeling when you knew you could die. The breath didn't come, your chest didn't rise, your body stopped. Life just came to an end. Like a wrong turn off the highway. The journey was just over.

Someone screamed his name. Someone pushed on his chest. Life jolted through him.

"Blake!"

The blond woman hovered over him, giving him CPR.

"One, two, three, four, five..."

Her lips pressed to his and she blew into his mouth. He coughed and wheezed, his lungs struggling. His chest ached like he'd gone ten rounds in a ring with someone twice his size.

She tried to push on his chest again, but he grabbed her hands.

Carolena stood on his other side. "Blake!"

He studied the blonde again.

He closed his eyes and rubbed his chest where it hurt. When he opened them again she was still there. His memories of her were convoluted. She was the one he longed for, the one he waited for, and the one he didn't think would ever show. But she was also the great love of his life, the one he did find, and the one he fought hard to protect. "Addie?"

She caressed his face. "You're alive."

"How?" Carolena asked.

Blake looked down at the two bullet holes in his shirt. He unbuttoned the top few buttons. He revealed a white vest beneath his shirt.

Carolena examined it closely. "A bulletproof vest? How? Where did you find it?"

"Monsieur Bernard," Campbell said, solving the mystery. "He was never without his."

Blake nodded. "He's without it now. I pushed him for it before I left the hotel tonight."

"Good show!" John laughed and clapped. "Well done!"

"Do you know me?" Addie asked.

He stroked her face, the one he thought he'd only ever have in a portrait. "Yes. Yes, of course. But, I can't remember how." He ran his hand over his forehead.

"I know what you mean," Philippe said in a low voice from the end of the room. He appeared stunned, like he'd just been hit by a car, like his life had taken an irreversible turn.

Addie unwrapped her hand from Blake's, took note of

the wedding set that was still there, brought it to her chest and held it tight.

"You're married...to him?" Blake pointed to Philippe.

A wheeze rattled from Otto. He was across the room.

"His gun," Blake said.

"I have it." Carolena held the handle with two fingers and a thumb.

"Where's Oscar?"

"He ran when the guns went off." Campbell closed the front door. "Someone was bound to have heard the gunfire. We need to get out of here."

"What are we going to do with him?" Addie pointed toward Otto.

Carolena hovered over him. "He's alive. Barely."

"If we leave him here, the police could come after you," John said to Carolena. "They'll think you had something to do with it. If you ever return to this era, that wouldn't bode well for you."

"We'll take him home. Through the Wentworths." Blake rubbed the sore places on his chest where the bullets had been stopped.

"There are some blank canvases..." Carolena ran to the next room. She reemerged dragging an oversized canvas. Campbell helped her lay it next to Otto's body. He struggled for breath.

Philippe stared at his father's face.

Blake placed his hand on his shoulder. "I'm sorry, Philippe. I didn't want it to end this way." He felt Philippe's muscles tense beneath his palm. His brother's next move quick and unexpected, a swift jerk that swatted Blake's arm and a fierce shove to his chest.

"I came here to get Carolena out, not to kill him."

"I don't think this is about that," Addie said from across

the room. She pressed her hand to her heart and closed her eyes briefly.

Philippe stared at her with a look Blake had just seen on their father's face—abandonment, betrayal.

Blake turned to Addie and said carefully, "I have two different realities in my head—one where you and I are together and one where you and he are together."

"We've all been straddling two lives." John guided Blake away.

Blake broke away from his grip.

Addie opened her mouth. She closed it again without saying anything.

"What's the last thing you remember? Before coming here tonight?" John shoved his hands into his pockets and tilted his chin toward Blake.

This felt like a pop quiz or a test he hadn't studied for. He thought for a moment and tried to sort out the answers that competed in his brain like hyperactive overachievers.

"How did you get to this era? The twenties, that is."

"I uh, I snuck into the painting behind Otto and Carolena, then I waited for the right moment to confront him—"

"No, that's—that's—not it," Addie said.

"There are two realities at play here, son," John said. "It's confusing, I know. But think of the other life. If that makes sense at all."

Blake sighed. *Two realities. One with Addie. One without.* He tried to remember his life with Addie. There were only flickering images.

"Just before you came here, you would have been at the hotel. The Hotel Ritz."

Otto's raspy breath rattled thick and liquidy in his lungs. John clinked the change in his pocket with his fingers. The casualness of John's habit while a man lay dying nearby made Blake cringe.

But Otto had worn everyone out over the years. There was no sympathy left to offer his father.

Blake saw an image of himself in his mind's eye. He was walking out of his hotel room and going into the library a back way. "I woke up. I decided I needed to make my move to rescue Carolena—"

John leaned close to Blake, his voice calm but his eyes wide and too focused. "I suspect that was you in an alternate life that has taken off." He went into detail about how everyone seemed to be shifting between these two realities and sometimes without notice. He told him how Addie had shot Jack in an effort to eliminate an alternate reality, but that there were signs—outward signs (he pointed to his ring finger)—that Jack may not have died.

Philippe pulled Addie away from the group.

"I've done the honorable thing every step of the way here." Philippe's voice wasn't as quiet as Blake thought he intended it to be. "And if you ask me to step aside because he's who you want, I'll do that. I'll do that for you because I love you. But on the chance that you want the life we have, our marriage, our daughter and the other children to come, I want you to know something.

"I love you. I've always loved you and I want you to choose me. Choose us. Choose what *we* have together. You haven't been happy with Blake in all the time you've been here. But I can promise you that our life together will always be the way it has been in your memories: *happy*. You'll have everything you've ever wanted. As well as someone who puts you *first*."

Distant sirens sang like a soundtrack to Blake's horror movie.

Addie didn't refuse Philippe. In fact, she kissed him. Hugged him. Held him close.

Blake exhaled hard like someone punched him in the gut, like a wave slammed him hard against a cliff, like he'd fallen hard to his death.

Campbell moved toward Otto. "I don't know if those sirens are headed toward us, but we'd better get a move on just in case."

"Get him on the canvas." Blake stifled the sick anger inside. He grabbed Otto's shoulders, Campbell and John each took a side. Carolena grabbed an end of the canvas.

"On three, everyone. One, two—" On the third count the men lifted Otto's body. Carolena slid the oversized canvas beneath him. She opened the bookcase and made space for the men to guide Otto in.

Car engines rumbled and roared through the darkness, louder now. Closer. Police cars. Four or five officers would have packed themselves into each car.

"The sirens are getting closer. Put him on the ground and come help me." Carolena dashed into the main room. "Philippe and Campbell, clean up that blood. There are towels and cleaner in the kitchen." She ran into the smaller room on the side of their house and lifted one of the canvases. "Blake, John, and Addie, grab the paintings and bring them into the secret room. We can't lose these."

Everyone took turns loading priceless canvases into the hidden room, and it didn't take long to realize that there wasn't going to be enough room for Otto, the art, and the rest of the group.

"Hurry, load him in." Blake lifted Otto onto the portrait.

Addie crossed into the Wentworth first. Though he had seen this before, it was still strange to watch her disappear into a piece of art.

Philippe followed to help tow Otto through to the other side. Blake didn't like that Addie and Philippe were together and out of sight. The men on the outside of the painting hoisted Otto up and into the painting. Philippe and Addie's arms shot through the painted scene to reach for Otto. She tugged on him and he groaned.

"Carolena!" Otto's voice was loud and strained and something gurgled in his throat.

The sirens stopped. Car doors slammed in rapid fire. Carolena continued to load paintings into the secret room.

The front door opened.

"Hallo!" a stranger's voice called into the house.

"Police!"

42

A hoard of footsteps thundered into the house.

Blake quickly shoved the top half of Otto's body in the painting to keep anyone from hearing him. "Close that door!" Blake whisper-shouted.

Campbell reached for the inside handle of the bookcase, Carolena pushed him aside. She grabbed another masterpiece from the hallway, this time a Modigliani, and brought it inside.

Blake and John shoved Otto the rest of the way into Wentworth's world. He finally disappeared, his polished black lace-up shoes the last part of him to go.

Police shoes pounded toward them through the hallway.

Blake's heartbeat kept rapid time with the beats.

Carolena rushed toward the remaining canvases. She struggled to get it into hiding. Blake pushed past her and grabbed the last three all at once, ignoring any damage he might inflict upon the art. He had lost patience with her care for these pieces. He only cared about her.

With his last step barely inside the hiding space, Carolena slid the bookcase shut behind him. Police were close by now, their voices muffled by the moveable barrier that kept their location a secret.

Blake stared where the inside of the bookcase met the wall. If it moved he would shoot whomever came in from the other side. No questions asked.

Quickly, silently, the men loaded the rest of the canvases into Addie and Philippe's ready hands.

"Carolena, go. We'll follow." Blake's voice was as quiet as a breath, and he gestured to the scene they were about to join.

She entered into the Wentworth, joined with the painted scenery, and allowed it to consume her as easily as a swimmer sinking into a pool of water. He watched as the avalanche of paint tumbled down her leg and over the red, squatty heel of her shoe.

"Go on, son." Campbell patted him on the back.

Blake quickly reached for his mother's shoe and followed her into a dimension that time and space couldn't reach.

Philippe and I stood in the clearing, holding one another's hands, our wedding rings still firmly in place, as were the memories of our life and family.

Blake glided into our side of Wentworth's painted reality on his mother's heel. His clear blue-eyed gaze touched a tender place within me that knew and loved him. Just as it had when we first met.

Time was a fickle tide that carried me in one direction, only to shift without notice, and with equal commitment into a different life.

My father and grandfather entered behind Blake. At

least my history with them remained comfortingly familiar. "We should get going."

They shared a look with one another, one I'd seen between them several times over the past couple of years. One that guarded secrets. My grandfather shoved his hands into his pockets, clinked change together, and stared at the dirt floor that was made of brown paint and Wentworth's emotion.

My father took my hand to his chest. "My princess. Seeing you again was an answered prayer."

I pulled him toward the path. "Me, too. Let's go home."

He waited several beats and let go of my hand. His thin smile offered sympathy and gave me more reasons for concern than comfort. "I'm not going, precious girl."

I moved toward him. "What do you mean you're not going? You're not staying *here*."

"I'm going back to New York. I'm staying in 1922."

Something left me. The thing I'd pushed for, prayed for, and driven for more than half my life. My life-long dream of my family together once again settled, unfulfilled. Blake wrapped his arm around me, I thought in part to give comfort, in part to lend strength.

"Why?"

My father held both of my hands in his. "Addie—I've been gone a long time, with no way to get home."

"We have a way now—"

"Just..." He squeezed my hands. His pained expression told me what came next would hurt. "The boy that you met at the gallery. Sweetheart. He's mine. Ruth's and my boy."

"You—you have a son?"

"His name is Cameron. We call him Cam."

If he let go of my hands I thought I might just float away. "But we're your family."

"You are, sweetheart. You are. I didn't plan to fall in love with Ruth; I wasn't looking for it. We didn't plan to bring Cam into the world. For twenty years I've known that I didn't have a way home, so I've had to make a life here for myself." He cleared his throat. A small noise, but it was like a thundering energy shift when he did it. As though a root shot through the ground.

He'd made his decision. He wasn't moving forward with me. "I can't leave Ruth and Cam behind. He's young. I can't very well bring them with me back to the present, either. Isabella and I... I'll always cherish what we shared. I don't know what we'd have today if we lived in the same home. We're different people now. You and Lexie are grown."

I wanted to be mature and to say that I understood. I was an adult, and he had his own life to live. But tears filled my eyes. I felt all of four feet high, ten years old. A little girl who couldn't bear the idea of being without her father. "No! I—No."

He held me close. My fingertips found the gold rope chain I'd always known him to wear. "I want you to come home."

My grandfather rubbed my back. "We are home. At least in this era."

"You, too?" I sniffed.

"Oh, Addie-belle." His smile was broad, all-knowing, ever-comforting. "I've been here for a long time. I don't know how to live in your world with this inter net and phones that go in your pocket and books without pages. Grace moved on without me a long time ago. Your dad is right—you and Lexie are grown. No one needs me where you are. My business is here. My life is here."

"I need you. And what about Ellen and Nathan?" As soon as the words left my mouth I knew what he was going to say. The same thing my father had said. That they had been gone so long, those relationships had moved on.

He kissed my cheek. I held their hands, memorized the feel of them and the love that ran through them.

"Do Grace and Isabella know...about Ruth and Cam?"

My dad shook his head. "No."

"I guess you want me to keep this information to myself?"

"I'm not going to ask you to keep secrets from your family. I'll write to them and I'll tell them. Isabella first, of course."

I had that strange feeling I did when I was a child. The one that gripped me when I was told that my father and grandfather were dead, that I would never see them again. "So, this is good-bye."

"Just for a while. Do whatever y'all are going to do with Otto." My grandfather waved toward his former business partner, and for the first time, without any apprehension. "Go visit your mother, Grace, and Lex. I know they're worried about you. Then, after you've had a little rest, y'all come back and stay with us for a bit. Bring Lexie."

I swiped tears from my cheeks. I breathed deep with hope for future visits. "Okay."

"Good. Because Mary will never forgive me if you don't come back and soon. She's taken quite a liking to you." He squeezed my arms in a most grandfatherly way and I knew I would agree to anything he asked me to do. I circled my arms around his neck. He hugged me tight. The scent of his skin brought back precious memories of being curled up on his lap on Christmas Eve while he read *The Night Before Christmas.*

"Come back to see us." My father squeezed my hand in a way that told me he didn't want to let go, either. I nodded, both in agreement to the trip and in acceptance of the new "us" he referred to.

"Will you return these pieces to the artists before you go home?" Carolena dug into her pants pocket with one hand and placed her hand on my back with the other. "Here are the keys to the house. It's paid for. Stay here whenever you like, but find someone to maintain it for me, please."

"We'll take care of it." My grandfather hugged and kissed Carolena, then my father took a turn.

My father accepted the keys and gave Philippe a hearty slap-type-pat on the back. "You're always welcome, you know. Just send us a note. Let us know you're coming."

"We'll take you up on that." Philippe's usual effortless smile was missing.

Blake shook hands with my father and grandfather.

"Philippe—" I touched his arm. There was a deep vacancy in his eyes. It scattered through me like debris trapped in a fierce wind. Bitter chaos.

His heart was caught between the two lifetimes we'd shared.

With no way to fully reclaim one or the other.

43

———

Addie stood solemnly.

Blake watched her stare at her father and grandfather.

They stood alone in Carolena's hidden room, discussing how and when to return the art.

Blake took one side of the canvas that held their father. His half-brother Philippe lifted the other. Otto's feet dragged a trail in the painted dirt behind them. It seemed only fitting that this job fell to his sons. Had this been a proper funeral for their dying father, they would have been his pallbearers.

Like a procession, they carried him along the path and over the bridge. Otto's breaths were timed by his loud and infrequent and rattled inhales.

Otto coughed drops of blood that splattered onto Blake's suit. Blake stared at the dark red dots that marked the end of his father's life. For as much as he had hated his father over the years, for as many times as he wished his father dead, in this moment the hatred didn't come.

The croquet scene appeared on the horizon. Everyone paused. They were almost home.

"I need to put him down." Philippe breathed fairly hard. Otto was not a light load. They propped him seated and upright against the trunk of a tall oak tree. His body lacked sufficient energy to even lift his hands, and each of them laid palm up in the dirt.

He inhaled through the thick liquid in his lungs until he gagged and coughed a fountain of blood from his mouth.

When he was finally able to, he said to Blake, "You must hate me." His eyes lolled to Philippe, pleading in his final moments for some consideration.

Blake studied Philippe's expression over the dying body of their father. The corners of his brother's lips pursed and firmly closed in disgust.

He lowered himself next to Otto. He wanted to remember him like this, eyes wide and full of the hurt and craziness that had driven him throughout his life. It was easier to see his father's innermost qualities in order to do what he needed to do next.

It was the life he could remember without Addie that taught him something—how a life-long obsession of hating someone could ruin your life. "I have hated you for a long time. For taking away the father I loved—the one who played baseball, who taught me about art. The man who loved me and my mother. I hated you for destroying the life I could have had." In his peripheral vision, he saw Philippe look at him and he knew he wasn't alone in these feelings. "I hated you for controlling everything and everyone to make up for what you didn't get from your own father.

"You've ruined a lot of lives, Otto. Wouldn't have been hard to go on for the rest of my life trying to punish you," Blake said, referring to the life he remembered without Addie. "It wasn't until recently that I realized this was how you became who you did. You didn't learn from your father's poor example. You emulated it."

He held his father's limp hand. "I'm not going to do that. So, I forgive you. For everything."

A small gasp escaped from Carolena.

Philippe knelt and held Otto's other hand. "I hope that in your next life you can find some peace. I really do."

It was a slow movement. So slow that Blake had to look down at their joined hands to see what he was doing. Otto's hand curled around his and he squeezed.

Blake nodded in understanding. He returned the gesture.

Otto's grasp released, his eyes lost focus. His head drooped to the side. Slow. Fading.

Philippe and Blake exchanged a look mixed with sadness and relief.

The crickets and the birds slowed their chirps, their silence unexpected and eerily quiet. Blake placed Otto's hand across the upper part of his stomach. Philippe did the same.

Addie placed two fingers on Otto's wrist and searched for a heartbeat. "I want to make sure he's really dead." She adjusted her fingers and held them on the pulse point for another minute.

Blake understood. No one tried to dissuade her. In fact, each member of the group took turns to make sure that the man was indeed dead and not coming back. After three minutes, everyone stood around him in agreement. He was gone.

Addie shrugged. "Do we still take him home?"

Blake shook his head. "I don't see how we can. Not without being implicated in his death."

"We can't carry around his dead body," Carolena said.

"We can't even bury it. Especially after the court case between the two of you." She waved her finger between her son and former husband. "It would be too suspicious. Blake, you would be blamed for his death. And you probably still wear the proof...on your hands."

Blake examined his open palms. If Otto's blood weren't enough, the proof would be there in gun powder residue. He curled them shut.

"We have to bury him here," Philippe said.

"No!" Addie said. "There's canvas just beneath the grass. I've seen it. You can't dig. Who knows where we'd end up."

Philippe's eyebrows climbed. "Right. No digging."

Everyone stared at Otto. He lay slumped against the tree, vulnerable and defeated. His slightly open mouth no longer served any purpose and revealed teeth stained in bright red.

"What a waste of talent," Philippe said.

"And brilliance." Carolena covered her mouth with her fingertips.

A loud crackling pierced the relative quiet. Like kudzu growing around a pole, streams of paint pushed upward in spirals and over his body. The colors swallowed him, absorbed him into its fractal pattern until his energy ceased to exist. The Otto they knew could no longer be sensed. His body became a collaboration of colored brushstrokes that played upon light and depth. He was no longer himself, but rather a representation thereof.

He had finally become a memorable part of the art world.

BLAKE WAITED WITH CAROLENA. She took one final look at Otto's still, painted body. The varying shades of red splotches on his brown suit were only slightly darker than the red berries painted on a nearby bush.

"With every meeting, there is a parting," she said with a turn and a sigh. She took Blake's hand and pushed forward.

"Sometimes not soon enough." He felt the metal of the engagement ring Otto had given her and turned her hand to see it. It was amethyst. He could also remember a life, a far happier life, where this ring was a ruby with diamonds.

Across a soft green meadow, just shy of a croquet game, Addie and Philippe faced one another, hands joined together. It looked like they stood at an altar, in front of a minister, in a ceremony. Though he couldn't hear what she said to him, they were long sentences, slow, and she pressed her hand to her chest now and again. Philippe smiled. He scooped Addie into his arms and buried his face in her neck.

Sick fury burned and twisted in Blake's stomach.

He pushed himself to remember one life, then the other, but no matter which one he checked, he had lost the woman he loved. He released Carolena's hand and ran toward Addie. He wasn't going down without a fight.

The croquet gathering followed their game to the other end of the court, and Addie knelt and ran her hand through the blades of painted grass.

"Addie!" Blake yelled. He thought he could feel Wentworth's ingrained despair pull at him through the images of the painting, but he pushed it away. Right now, Addie was his only concern.

"We came in right through here somewhere, a few feet this side of the center wicket." She searched with both hands. "It's just a tiny access point."

"Do you want me to help?" Carolena asked breathlessly, arriving a few steps behind her son.

"Addie—" Blake reached for her, but his grasp missed

when her arm sank into the ground as though she'd struck quicksand.

"Found it. Hang on, everyone."

Philippe grabbed Addie's shoulder and Blake jerked it away. "Behind me," he said coldly.

The Wentworth was propped against the library wall with two guardian foo dogs on either side to hold it upright. Once out of the painting, he army-crawled his way across the fine carpet and farther into his current day penthouse apartment. He fought the usual dizziness and nausea that always happened when he transferred from the world of Wentworth to the regular world.

Addie rolled onto her back, and held her head with both hands to stifle the same type of symptoms he experienced, he guessed. He glanced at the portrait of Sassy, which still hung on the wall.

He could remember two lives with her when he was Jack. One a long life with her—full of love, children, and happiness, as well as another life cut short that left him without her. Strange, he thought, that they couldn't have two full lives with one another—a life with her bookended to a life without her. "Addie."

She turned her head toward him.

"Do you know who I am?"

She stared at him for a moment.

44

———

"It helps with the recovery." Blake handed Addie a scoop of chocolate gelato purchased from the neighborhood stand. He couldn't remember if this flavor was her favorite or Sassy's.

She accepted the golden yellow plastic cup he offered.

Their fingers grazed against one another, and he noticed.

Her wedding rings were gone.

His gaze lifted to her eyes. Her slight smile kept a distance between them in a way he hadn't known since they'd first met. He didn't bring up the missing rings, he didn't know if she'd seen. His heart thumped with optimism.

She asked to sit while they ate, needing time, he thought, to adjust to this era. Or maybe she was trying to process all the changes.

Afterward, they strolled along Fifth Avenue. The warm summer breezes were a comfort in the damp night air. The city barely retained any trace of the excitement that had been so prevalent in the 1920s. Though the imprints were there, still influencing, unbeknownst to those who were affected.

Blake didn't know why she agreed to take this walk with him. Now that she knew love with Philippe, maybe she was about to tell him good-bye. Maybe she was about to say that after sharing so much with Philippe, too much had changed. That nothing could be the same between them again.

Either way he would fight for her. To the end, to the death. He would never give up.

They entered into Central Park's Conservatory Garden through the magnificent Vanderbilt Gate. It was the tall iron one that graced the front of the Fifth Avenue Vanderbilt mansion when they were in 1922. "Can you remember the life we began together...in this time?"

She stared at the pink and white blooms of the crabapple trees that lined the prominent green lawn. "Right now I remember both of my lifetimes. One with you, one without."

"I can, too. I know which life I'd choose if I had the choice."

Addie nodded, her lips pressed together in a way that held her response from him.

He wasn't sure he wanted to know what her life was like without him, especially since she hadn't been alone. But he asked. She told him about being married to Philippe, and how they shared a daughter.

"I won't be angry if something happened between the two of you while we were living different lives." If she confirmed that they had, though, Blake thought he might punch something. He stopped walking and let go of her hand. The feeling that he'd lost her to someone else consumed him.

"I don't know that I have a right to ask. But I need to know. *Did* anything happen between the two of you?"

She seemed to stare at the jet fountain in the distance. Blake stood as still as a block of cement. He couldn't breathe.

"We were more affectionate with one another than if you and I had been together. We didn't sleep together, if that's what you're asking."

Blake breathed in what felt like the first time since they'd left Paris in 1922. "Yeah, I guess that was part of what I was asking." Though he had a bigger question in his mind. "Do you still love him?"

She met him eye to eye. He fully hoped for a solid *of course not.*

"Yes. In a way," she said too honestly for his comfort. "He was a good husband, a good man. He loved us. It was a good life." She frowned like she tried to make sense of it. "A strange memory, I guess."

They walked s in silence and he knew what she meant. He could easily remember the life without her and the numerous, meaningless encounters he'd had with other women, each one more disappointing than the last. So it stood to reason that she could remember her feelings for Philippe from this other life.

"Addie, I know what we've been through is incredibly odd and I guess it's going to take some time to readjust. In the meantime, I don't know how you feel about Philippe. But if you have any leftover feelings for him, I should let you know that I will put up a world class fight for you. He won't stand a chance." He thought it might actually kill him on the spot if she said that it wouldn't do any good.

She lowered her gaze and rubbed her ring finger.

"I see that your wedding rings are gone." He said it

calmly. Like he mentioned she was wearing a new pair of shoes. "That must mean that Jack died and I reincarnated in time for this life."

If she hadn't noticed the missing rings before, she did now. She had to know they could be together again. He wrapped his arms around her in a tight grip, but it was like hugging a stuffed doll. Three-dimensional and unresponsive.

"What's the matter?" The familiar out-of-control-feeling pumped through his veins again. His stomach hollowed.

He needed a plan. He needed control.

He guided her to a park bench.

"The rings disappeared while we were in the painting, toward the end of our trip through the Wentworth. Jack must have died right about then." She was pale.

He placed his hand over hers. "I know that killing him must have been hard—"

"You have no idea."

He nodded. She was right—he didn't know. "But this is *good* news. We can move ahead now. Our future is safe." He heard the doubt in his voice. "This is *us*, Addie. We're meant to be together."

There was more silence.

Blake thought he might burst from his skin.

She drew in a deep breath and his out-of-control-feelings grew stronger. Like he'd just been jerked back for the long trip to the top of the roller coaster.

"I remember what it was like when we were Sassy and Jack. I know what it's like to be loved by you. Back then." She closed her eyes and inhaled something specific. A memory, perhaps. Or a feeling. "It was like that when I met you in this life. But I haven't felt that with you in years."

He thought he felt himself falling backward, like he'd

been punched hard enough to lose his balance. "It was the search. It was Otto. I know I was over the top at times. We're home now. We can start fresh, I'll make it up to you. We can get back to being who we were." He said the last words softly, to comfort and persuade.

It had to be the effects from the trip through the Wentworth, or the dip into an alternate reality. She hadn't yet recovered. She would. He just had to be patient.

She shook her head like he had missed the point. "The first time I met Carolena she told me she was worried that you were too much like your father. I think she's right. That distrust and the obsession, the controlling. For different reasons than his, maybe. Ultimately they're the same. These are distancing behaviors, fear-based behaviors that have no place in a healthy relationship."

He cringed at Philippe's words coming back at him. "So, you're an expert in psychology, now?"

"No, definitely not. Though I am an expert when it comes to you and our relationship."

They stared at one another for a long motionless second.

Addie looked away with a weighted sigh. "Look, you should be whomever you want to be. I know who I am. I know what I need in order to be happy. I've seen how I behave in this relationship when you are driven by fear—"

"I wasn't *driven* by my fears. I did what had to be done." He knew he had been all the things she'd said. Maybe he was the one who hadn't yet recovered from the trip through the Wentworth or the alternate reality.

She nodded. Too quietly. Too resigned. "That's fine, Blake. But here's the thing. I saw how I functioned in this relationship. I spent all my time either making excuses for your behavior or fussing at you to change or trying to smooth things over when you didn't. As much as I love you

—and I do love you—I can't spend the rest of my life doing that." She sighed heavier this time, as if she'd just walked across hot fire coals and made it to the other side. "I know me. I will. And I'll be miserable if I keep doing that."

"Addie, we're home now. You're my only focus." He held her hands at his chest. "All of this craziness with Otto is behind us. We can be together without his threats hanging over our heads. We finally have the chance to love one another the way we want to. None of the stuff from the last couple of years will happen again."

"The past two years didn't mean nothing. They were real and we lost something. Something precious that won't just come back because we've changed addresses, or because Otto's dead. There will be some other challenge that we face, there always is, and you'll take over in the same way that you do and I'll end up on the sidelines somewhere."

He felt the roller coaster tip over the peak and free fall its way to the bottom curve. "Addie, please don't do this."

"My head is telling me to stay with you because we're home and I'd like to think it could all be different now. My heart—" Her voice choked. "My heart wants what we used to have. I know me. I won't be happy with anything less."

"Is this about Philippe and what the two of you had together?"

She stared at her nails, clicking them together now and then. "I'm not leaving you to be with him. If that's what you're asking."

Leaving you.

"Though I would be lying if I said my relationship with him didn't influence my decision. He gave all of himself to me. To us. He trusted me. He trusted himself when he was with me. Otto was in his life, but Philippe had a strong sense of direction around that. He was his own man. And there weren't any hurdles or land mines to dodge in order for us to connect. He wanted to be with me. I'm sure he was afraid of losing me, the same that anyone would be concerned about losing a loved one. But he didn't let that get in the way of our happiness."

The roller coaster turned on the curve and flipped him upside down, sending his heart on a similar path. His head spun and he leaned into his hands, and the dizziness continued. "Think about what you're doing, Addie."

"I've thought of nothing else for the past two years but you and us and how we can be fixed. I've done everything I know to do to help us."

"I—I—" His mouth was held open by an unholy mess of competing defenses and self-vindications. Every justification he came up with, he quickly shot down. He tried reasonable explanations but he shot those down, too. Because they were all empty and without any merit. He had no choice, no answers, no winning card to play. She had asked him to change and he hadn't. He hadn't looked past his own needs enough to take care of hers.

"You can be so intuitive, Blake. I've seen you read people and situations so perfectly, it couldn't have been done better by anyone else. Over the last two years, I've seen you leave that beautiful gift behind in favor of trying to control everyone and everything in your path.

"You don't trust me, anymore. Not to make a good decision or to be faithful or to handle myself capably in the world. You don't even trust my judgment on how to handle an emergency or where to stand in the road."

He knew she was referring to how he'd insisted she not take the cab in Paris and to stand half way down the hill after they'd left the Louvre. Had she followed her own guidance she would have been fine. But when he moved her,

Otto kidnapped her and held her at gunpoint. She could have died. Otto could have taken her. His heart thumped heavy and hard with guilt and panic.

"I think the real issue here is that you don't trust yourself anymore. You've lost touch with that pulse, that connection to yourself and your guidance. For the last two years you've acted like you can outsmart the world and arm wrestle it and everyone else into doing things your way.

"I've tried so hard to get you to relax that fear. To settle into yourself. To come back to me, to us. But you wouldn't. I wish you had been willing to change, Blake. I really do."

"Addie—"

"No. I'm not going to be one of those women who becomes bitter and angry because she spent her life catering to someone else's need to control. I'm not going to ignore what I really want in life. First and foremost I am intuitive. I may not have always been at peace with that, but I am now. I trust it. Control and trust are at opposite ends of the continuum. Your need to control so much—it just— It sucks the soul right out of my body. It swallows me. It doesn't leave any room for me in my own life. It doesn't leave any room for me—in us."

"I'm sorry, Addie. You're right. You're right. We can do this differently from now on." He reached for her.

She pulled away.

"You're always sorry, when you're not feeling utterly terrified that you'll lose me. When you do, that fear blocks out the sun, and you can't see anything else when you're in it. Did you ever stop to think that fear has more to do with something *you* need to learn?"

She had tried to stay calm in the beginning, but her voice was scolding now. Almost berating. He'd expected too much of her. He saw that now and it was too late. She was done.

She drew in a breath and calmed herself. "Maybe you need to stop blaming yourself for how insane Otto was. Maybe you just need to accept that he was the way he was. I don't know.

"For me, I know that if I spend the next however many years tolerating how much you control, or arguing about it or trying to change that, I'll regret it. I'll hate my life and I'll come to hate you.

"So, I'm leaving, before that happens. I'll always love you, Blake. I will. What we've shared has changed me and my life forever. Because of that, I'm not going to deny what my heart wants."

She stared straight ahead and nodded once, as if to confirm she'd said all she needed to say. She didn't kiss him goodbye, she didn't say anything else, and she didn't look at him one last time.

She walked out of the gardens and out of his life.

45

___

My townhouse was neat and clean and a little too cold, thanks to Grace's good care while I was gone. I threw out the dying flowers she'd left in a vase on the island and tried not to make analogies to them in terms of how I felt. I threw out the vase as well. I didn't feel like cleaning it and I knew I'd probably never use it again anyway.

An odd numbness coated my brain and body and I was grateful for it. Some sort of safety switch must have been flipped to keep me from feeling too much or from going into overwhelm. Or maybe this was overwhelm. Could have been shock, I guessed. Either way, I was glad for the break from feeling too much.

I glanced around the kitchen I'd stood in a couple of weeks ago, and yet it was a lifetime ago. The coloring of the kitchen was much the same as it was in 1922. Of course, the flooring and the cabinetry and the countertops had been upgraded several times. And I was pretty grateful for little things like a dishwasher, ice maker, and a disposal.

I half-expected Blake to round the corner with his notebook in his hand, throw on his 1920s suit and vest, and dash out the door. My exhale filled the empty room. He'd changed so much since we'd first met. He used to be a near replica of Jack. Now he bore too close of a resemblance to Otto.

I plopped into one of the kitchen chairs and stared at the Wentworth I'd brought with me. Carolena hadn't said a word when I returned to Blake's apartment alone, picked up the painting, and carried it out with me.

It was *my* father and grandfather who remained in 1922. My family. I needed to have this painting as a bridge to them for whenever it suited us. We had been without those means for too long.

Without ceremony and without delay I took it on a walk around my home, trying to find a suitable spot for it. I finally chose the small bonus room upstairs since I decided it needed to be out of sight, and it wouldn't be difficult to install a lock on the door.

I hammered a nail into the wall of the even smaller closet inside this underused room and hung the Wentworth. Then I rummaged around and found and an old blue towel that I draped over the front of the painting. This was partly to protect it and partly because it seemed to me that portals shouldn't be openly displayed, even in private rooms.

On the way downstairs I heard a key slide into the chambers of my door lock and someone opened the door. I jumped out of habit, even though I reminded myself that it couldn't have been Otto. It was probably Blake. I'd have to tell him to give it some time. I wasn't ready to talk again so soon.

Ellen's expression was a blend of surprise and worry. "Oh! I didn't know you were home!"

Ellen had shed her French twist. She brushed it back

now and her thick blond hair fell in loose chunky curls around her shoulders. She had also traded in her severe dye job for more selective high and lowlights. "I was coming in to check the book for messages, to make sure that everything was safe. Anya and Grace and I took turns. Is this okay?"

Her face was thinner, as was her figure, and it appeared that being away from Otto and the firm agreed with her. She gently fingered the strand of pearls around her neck and I quickly realized how similar they were to the necklace my grandfather had given to me years ago. He must have given those to her as well. He probably bought them both at the same time.

I made espresso for the both of us and told her briefly about the trip, that Carolena was home and that Otto was dead. She drew in a deep sigh that I thought had probably been several decades in the making.

"Are you certain?"

"I am."

She closed her eyes briefly and she nodded once. Then two more times. It would be a long time before she rested in that truth, I knew.

"Where's Blake?" She glanced around the townhouse as if expecting him to come in from the other room.

"I think he's still at his place." I didn't go into any detail.

"Lots to organize after being gone so long. I well remember."

"Ellen, do you know anything about the Gardner art or where it might be? Did Otto say anything to you about it?"

She shook her head. "No. But I did get a panicked call from Nicholas a while back. He wanted to know if I knew how to get in touch with Otto. He was out of his mind scared, he said that someone from the family—I'm guessing he meant the Pulizzi family—saw him leaving the ware-house where they put the art. He said that he wanted Otto to tell him where to move it. I haven't heard from him since."

"They probably took the art and Nicholas."

"I doubt they had much use for him. He's probably just off the highway upstate somewhere in a shallow grave. Or at the bottom of the Hudson. Otto sold to that family for years and they're ruthless."

"It's all too bad." I referred to the loss of the art. It felt inappropriate to talk about that when we both thought Nicholas was gone. To be honest, I didn't feel anything for the loss of Nicholas. He was Otto's right hand and if I didn't have to worry about him anymore, I was fine with that. It had been a long, hard road.

It occurred to me that I hadn't checked for mail since I'd come home. "I'm just going to look inside the book, if you don't mind. I haven't had a chance, yet."

"Please." Ellen raised her arm in a lead-the-way gesture and followed me to the library.

Again, I thought it strange to be in an updated version of the room Blake and I had spent so much time in in 1922. I slid the F. Scott Fitzgerald book from the bookshelf and found an envelope that had my name on the outside.

"John isn't coming home, is he?" The tone in her voice told me she was confirming her suspicion. That really, she already knew the truth.

"No. I'm sorry. He's not."

Her lightly pinked lips pressed together and I could only imagine the waterfall of words they held back. "There's someone else, isn't there?" She nodded short and quick, the movement clipped to stifle the hurt.

She knew. After twenty years apart, she would of course, suspect that there was someone else.

"I think he feels that he can't be successful here anymore. Not in this time."

She shook her head.

"He doesn't know how to use a computer or send an email. He wouldn't even know how to use a cell phone."

"Well, you don't actually need a degree to do that. Do you...?" Her face twisted with sarcasm and old hurt.

"I'm not making excuses. I wanted him to come home, too. This is not how I saw my family's' happy ending."

"Mine, either. It's a good thing I didn't tell our son that he might have come home. Nathan would have been very disappointed. You'd think after twenty some odd years that I would have given up on him. Moved on. Any reasonable woman would have. Maybe now that Otto is gone and the firm has shut down, I will. Being with John is a dream that has run its course."

My heart stuttered. That had been *my* reality with Blake. In fact, I'd almost used those exact words—run its course. I thought of Mary and her first husband. "You know, I met someone in the twenties. She had lost her husband in the war, the first war. When she started her next relationship she said it only worked because he didn't ask her to give up that love. She says her first husband will always have a place in her heart—not in her relationships, but in a sacred place in her heart.

"Perhaps, with a love like the one you and my grandfather have shared, I think you have to take that love with you so you can move forward." My heart caught when I said it, and I knew I'd have to follow the same advice. Mary must have known that on some level.

Tears filled Ellen's eyes and she held my hand. She gave it a squeeze and a pat and nodded.

"I would like to meet Nathan sometime. He wouldn't need to know who I was, if you didn't want him to."

She pulled a tissue from her purse and wiped her nose and sniffed. "I'd love for the two of you to meet."

"He's my...what—cousin? No, uncle. Half-uncle. Of the younger sort, I guess."

Ellen's deep laugh came from a genuine place within. She wiped the tears from her cheeks and sniffed again and clasped the balled up tissue in her fist. "There's no pressure."

"Of course not. I want to know him, though. I'm sure Alexa will as well."

"As long as it doesn't cause a rift in your family. Especially with Grace."

"I don't think it would. A lot of time has passed. Grace has a different life now."

"Well." She pressed her fingertips to my knee. "Then I would love for you and Alexa to meet him. He shares a lot of John's qualities, and I think you'll enjoy getting to know him."

Another family member. My heart fluttered with excitement at the thought of it. Someone else to love, someone else to cherish, someone who would be like the brother I'd never had.

"Addie, there's some money you need to know about."

"What money?" Grandpa had probably done something in the past to provide for Ellen and their son. Maybe she had questions around what happened.

"It's cash from Otto's forgery business. I transferred the cash from the transactions to the safe deposit box. Technically, it ought to go to Otto's wife, Marilyn, or Nicholas, Philippe, or Blake—"

"Ellen, whatever is there, keep it. Marilyn has Otto's life

insurance payout, plus all the money he left behind. Philippe has enough, and only God knows where Nicholas is. Put it in a trust for Nathan or take a trip around the world. Enjoy a happier retirement. After all the work you did for Otto and the firm, you've more than earned it."

"Well, there's just one thing. Some of this money dates back to when he and your grandfather were partners. Quite a bit of that money is his. I've saved it for him all this time, and I was going to give it to him when he returned. But now, I guess it should go to Grace or you and Alexa."

"Grace has more than she could spend in ten lifetimes. Alexa and I have been well-provided for." I thought of the Egyptian art that was collecting dust in the attic and the antique jewelry I'd sent home. "Keep it."

She sighed. More deeply this time. I thought she might almost feel a tad relaxed. "Very well. I'll do that." She walked several steps toward the door. "Are you sure, Addie?"

"Yes, take it."

"No, I mean—yes, and thank you. But I need to ask again. Are you sure that he's dead? You're certain that Otto is dead?"

"I'm certain."

"You saw him die?"

"I did, actually."

"It's just that, if he wasn't dead, if there were even a small chance that he might come back—I would need to know."

"We made sure his heart was no longer beating before we left his body." I went into patient detail about how we each took his pulse for several minutes before we were certain we could leave. Even Otto couldn't hold his breath for several minutes, especially after he'd been shot. He was dead, dead, and dead.

IN SPITE of the fact that I had assured Ellen, and gave her all the reasons why and how he couldn't possibly be alive, I decided to check again for myself. I took a pair of white gloves and a magnifying glass with me.

I went to the small room. I rubbed the corner of the worn towel between my finger and thumb. I didn't want to see Otto again, not even a small painted representation of something that used to be him. On the count of three I flipped the covering away and a shot of adrenaline pumped through my heart. I half expected to see him standing and staring straight at me.

Everything was as we had left it. The croquet player with the red mallet took aim to knock his ball through the wicket while the other players watched. One woman with a white parasol whispered to another who wore a straw hat. In the distance was Otto, his body propped against the tree on the edge of the painting where we left him.

Still not completely satisfied, I held the magnifying glass and examined the reclining figure in the small patch of trees near the path.

I thought I saw his tiny eyes blink. I poked the figure with a gloved finger. My heart whammed against the inside of my chest with enough force to take my breath. I could have sworn I heard the distant echo of his mocking laughter, soft at first and then growing.

I dropped the towel over the scene.

In my mind's eye, as my visions often appeared, I could see Otto stand and stretch and take in his new abode. I heard the croquet players arguing about a particular shot and Otto asking if he could join their game.

I wondered what would happen if I lifted the towel

again, what I might see this time. Perhaps Otto with the red croquet mallet, taking his shot and waving to me from his new world.

I sidestepped out of the small room. I shut two doors between me and him. I took in a small breath of relief. "That didn't happen," I said.

Once downstairs, I opened the letter that had been addressed to me. My heart still wasn't sure which way to turn when I thought of my father and grandfather and how they wouldn't be coming home again. For a moment I thought about going back for an extended visit.

Jack was dead, and there was no chance I would run into him. Sarah was either tucked away in France or Gary had reclaimed her. Either way, I doubted our paths would cross again.

MORNIN' Addie-belle,

We made it home safely. Police left after an hour. You know, they don't yet have the forensics that they will.

The gallery and the townhouse are terribly empty without you and Blake around. It's late. Sun is setting over the buildings. Mary and I are heading out for dinner and wine. Wish you could come along.

Come see us again soon.

Miss and love you with all my heart,

Grandpa

MAYBE I COULD GET Grandpa to meet me halfway through the painting. With Otto, or some representation thereof, still in the Wentworth scene, I didn't want to go in alone. Or maybe Philippe would go with me. He would. I knew he would. And not just because of his feelings for me. I knew he'd rather live in the twenties than in any other era of time.

I made the call and invited him. It didn't take any persuading to convince him, he readily accepted my invitation. The next call I made was to Grace. I needed to go home for a while.

46

———

Blake laid on the chaise near his still-covered pool, a glass of scotch dangling from his hand. The near-empty crystal decanter was next to him on the paved ground. He'd lived in his penthouse for several years before he met Addie. She'd not even spent that much time here. But her imprints were everywhere and her memories held too strong for him to be inside right now.

"What are you doing out here, love? Where's Addie?" Carolena sat next to him on the opposing chaise and sipped a glass of red wine. "You look terrible."

"Thank you, *Maman*."

He didn't look at her. He half hoped she would pat him on the shoulder and walk away. Traffic honked and roared below in typical unrelenting New York City style. The fear that had consumed him over the past couple of years was mostly gone now. Otto was dead. Addie and Carolena were safe. They'd managed to recover most of the art he'd stolen. But he'd still managed to lose Addie. Again. So that fear was now replaced with something darker. Something he'd only tasted when he had to live in that brief alternate reality in the absence of her.

"Did something happen?"

He nodded.

"She left?"

He kept nodding. She touched his hand, probably to read him, he guessed. But the stream of comfort that came from her softened him. He was strangely grateful that she asked.

"Did she say why?"

He gave her the rundown on Addie's side of the story. Brief and to the point.

Now it was Carolena who nodded. "When Otto and I first fell in love, he was a different person then. Very present, emotionally available, so giving of himself. He trusted me. He believed in me. That combination was intoxicating." She shrugged, sipped her wine.

"When he lost his ability to trust and he became so paranoid, we were over then." She slid both hands around her glass and stared at the deep red liquid. "I often wondered, when he reached the point where he didn't trust anyone, if that wasn't a projection of some kind. You know, at the root of it all. Maybe he was the one he didn't trust, but he just couldn't admit that. At least not to himself."

Still reeling from his conversation with Addie, his mother's words sent him into a ceaseless free fall. He closed his eyes in an attempt to stem the emotional tide. Addie had said almost the same thing earlier today.

"I guess it doesn't really matter now that he's dead." He shot the rest of his scotch and reached for the decanter to pour another glass.

"I read an article years ago that highlighted several case studies of children who never knew their parents. They followed them over the years and found that they exhibited many of the same personality characteristics of their parents. Even though they'd never met. Fascinating, isn't it?"

"I'm hardly paranoid, if that's your point. Unlike Otto, I don't think everyone is out to get me."

"Who do you trust, *mon amour*?"

His free hand clamped into a fist full of frustration. "I did what I had to do to get you and her home safely. Yes, I was pretty much a one man show for the past two years, but that's how I work best. And it worked out, didn't it? I wasn't going to sit back and wait for the group to reach a consensus on how best to move ahead. It scared the heck out of me to see you in Otto's grasp and Addie within his reach. I wasn't going to trust the safety of the most important people in my life to anyone else!"

He crossed the open deck, his heart so full of fear and hate he thought it would burst into a fit of red venom.

"No, of course not. I appreciate your hard work and every one of your efforts, I do. I'm far better off here than I would have been with him." Carolena paused while a jet plane roared overhead, the noise from its engines too loud. "But I do wonder if you are afraid for you more so than you are afraid for anyone else."

He didn't turn around. His mind was busy with his mental game—outmaneuvering, outarguing, and outgaming every move or comment Carolena, Addie, or anyone else might throw at him.

She crossed in front of him and his eyes followed her.

"You need to come to grips with what you're really afraid of. Right now you don't want to admit to it because it feels like a weakness to you. I taught you better than this, Blake. Don't reach for control. Reach for understanding, insight— reach for what is true and real about this situation. And accept it. Accept all of it. The past. Otto. What you did. What you didn't do."

"And that will bring Addie back?" Sarcasm flavored his words and he wiped his upper lip with the back of his thumb. He'd started that odd habit before they left for Paris, just after Addie encountered Jack. It wasn't his habit. This was a habit from his desperate, angry life that almost was.

Carolena raised a wicked don't-you-dare eyebrow at him. He raised his hands in surrender.

"You have work to do. Think about what I've said. If you are interested to find the answers, you will. Then maybe you will be the kind of person who can bring her back."

He watched her until she reached the covered walkway, expecting her to disappear without another word the way Addie had left his life. But she turned around at the last second.

"I wouldn't wait too long if I were you. Philippe loves her, and she has very fond memories of their life together."

47

Alexa, Grace, Isabella, and I sat around the polished mahogany dining table in Grace's Savannah family home. The table was lovingly littered with half-full wine bottles, a plate of biscuit crumbs that Alexa kept picking at, and separate plates of sliced sugar-cured ham and cheese remnants. There were also small crystal jars of mustard and mayo, because Grace wouldn't tolerate condiment bottles on the table.

Isabella had built a fire in the fireplace and the patio doors were open such that the cool ocean breeze meandered around the heat from the flames. It was my favorite kind of arrangement—the warmth of hearth and home, seasoned generously with fresh ocean breezes.

I was cocooned in my family's care and concern, swaddled in their endless love. It was the perfect place for me to be right now. Even in spite of all the questions. They asked *lots* of questions.

Grace returned from Paris with Dad's letter about Ruth and how he and Grandpa weren't coming home. Grace was neither surprised nor bothered by the news. She and

Grandpa had parted ways years ago. Though legally they remained married, she didn't have any expectations of a relationship with him. She was just glad they were healthy, happy, and safe and that they had the Wentworth as an option available to them. If they needed to come home.

Isabella was more disappointed, but very understanding. I secretly thought she held on to dreams of her and my dad reuniting, and that she didn't want to admit to them.

Philippe texted occasionally to see how I was doing. He was in New York and organizing his life so that he could return to the twenties with me. He knew the breakup with Blake was hard. He also knew what I'd had to do to Jack was weighing on me. And would for a while.

"I think it's too soon for you to run off with Philippe." Isabella had a mother's tongue that while elegant with speech, was rarely held.

My eyeballs rolled before I could stop them. It was a well-patterned habit left over from my teenaged relationship with her. "I'm not running off with anyone. I'm just escaping reality for a little while. There's nothing romantic between us."

"But there *was*." She whispered her words as though this truth were a secret or a morsel of illicit information. "It's too soon to start something like that again. Especially with him. That would be too confusing."

"I'm not—"

"I have to agree." Grace nodded in either judgment or agreement, or both. I wasn't sure.

"Look, I don't think it's a good idea to go through the painting alone. And Philippe loves the twenties—"

"You, too, probably," Isabella said. "I doubt he's over all that's happened."

"Why don't you just do Greece like all other young

women who are trying to get over a difficult breakup?" Grace asked.

"Because I'd like some stress-free time with Dad and Grandad. Jack is...gone, so there's no danger of running into him." I ran my hand over my forehead and fought the flashback of the night I had killed him. Philippe and I stood outside of Jack's house, the gunshot sounded loud in my head as though it hit me in the chest.

Grace patted my other hand with a triple pat. "It's over and done with now, sugar. You did what needed to be done." She rubbed my hand and gave me the blessing of her triple pat again.

I love you.

It was enough to prompt a cleansing breath and I continued on.

"Sarah has probably been reclaimed by Gary. If not she's in hiding somewhere. It would just be fun. For a change. I need that before I figure out what this next chapter of my life is going to look like."

"You two were so perfect for one another." Alexa reached over the corner of the table and held my hand. "I can't believe this is happening. Are you sure?"

I smiled a half-smile, which was all I could manage. "The only thing I'm sure about is that I can't share the rest of my life with someone who continually pushes me away. He's so afraid of losing me, he can't even let me in anymore." I'd thought we were the together forever deal, and now I was explaining why I'd left him. I still couldn't believe it.

"It's his past-life imprints. He lost you once because he couldn't protect you and there's a deep part of him that can't forget that. He holds himself responsible for the fact that you ended up back in Otto's control. It's a theme that keeps reappearing in his life."

"Then it stands to reason that he doesn't trust himself when it comes to me. It runs deep. He becomes so obsessed. He says he's doing it all for me, but I don't even think he notices me when he's in that space."

"No. I don't guess he would.

"He puts so much pressure on himself." I rested my forehead in my hands, tired from too much emotion.

"He puts the whole world on his shoulders," Grace said.

"Exactly." I drew in a deep breath at hearing the truth.

"It's a lonely, burdensome place." Isabella gathered the plates from the table and kissed my head when she walked by.

Alexa tugged me from my chair. "Come on. You need to walk."

"I don't feel much like walking, Lex."

She handed my glass to me and offered a smile that only sisters could share. "Then bring your wine."

We made it just to the point where the grass met the firm, wet sand and Alexa unleashed a question I figured she'd been holding onto since I'd told her about the alternate reality with Philippe. "Did you break up with Blake so you could be with Philippe?"

I squished my toes into the sand and chuckled. "Why? You're going after Blake, now?"

She smacked my arm. "Because I'm your sister and you have to tell me."

"Then, no. I didn't." My mind flashed to the memory of Philippe and me when we were a family, and parents of Maddie. For a moment in time we had been each other's everything, and yet Blake, in the form of Jack, was still there, haunting the back of my mind.

She looped her arm through mine. "Philippe had something to do with the breakup. Am I right?"

"Okay. In a weird sort of way, yes. He did."

"So, spill. Tell me."

The waves crashed a few yards from where we walked and the cold water washed over our feet.

"You know when you're in a relationship with someone, a long-term relationship, and maybe something isn't going right?"

"Mm-hmm."

"My approach, I guess, was to be patient. Too patient, I think. We talked about it. I yelled about it. I just kept thinking that if he loved me he would change. He would give me that emotional intimacy I needed if he really cared. Because that emotional closeness is a real life need in a relationship, it's the glue that holds it together. I thought he knew that. Unfortunately he just kept distancing himself from me."

"Then Philippe came along?"

"Well, that was rather sudden and obviously unexpected. In the blink of an eye, we had this relationship that spanned decades and we had a family, and—"

"And?"

"He wasn't afraid to connect with me the way that Blake was. There was no holding back. He wanted that connection with me as badly as I had ever wanted it— He trusted himself. He trusted me."

"Ohh." Alexa pressed her wine glass to her chest.

"After our realities shifted to their original track, that stayed with me. You know, how freely Philippe had given himself. By comparison, I realized how much Blake hadn't and, how he wasn't motivated to change. He could have made us more of a priority if he'd wanted to. He put his fears first. Always first. Very loyal to his paranoia. After Philippe, I guess my patience with Blake seemed stupid."

"Well. I think you're being very brave and very smart about all of this. You know what a healthy relationship is, you know what makes you happy, and you're not willing to be taken for granted."

Lexie's bottle-green eyes were soft and glistening and they offered the show of support I needed.

"I feel like I'm walking around with broken glass in my chest."

"I'm sure. Give it time. I think the trip to the twenties is a good idea. It will give you time to think things through. You're really going with Philippe?"

I sighed and felt as though I'd just passed through an emotional threshold of some kind. Talking things out with someone close could do that. "Yeah. He wanted to live there when we first went back. He loves it there."

"And you really don't have any feelings for him?"

"Our life together is more like a past-life memory now. It added a dimension to our friendship, for sure. But, I think we're still just friends."

"Hmmm." Lex cast a wary eye that said she wasn't quite convinced. "Well, maybe you should take me along just to be safe. I can chaperone."

"Oh my gosh."

"What?"

"You in the twenties. You know there are rules that you have to abide by. Otherwise, trust me, things can get really fouled up."

48

We all sat around the fireplace, every woman wearing pajamas and varying colors of fuzzy socks. The patio doors were closed and locked now. The fire warmed the room just enough to make me fight to stay awake.

"When do you leave?" Isabella asked. I thought I noted a tinge of jealousy in her voice.

"I don't know. In a day or two, maybe."

"She's taking me with her." Alexa nodded with supreme confidence.

"I never said that."

"You nodded."

"No, that was a head tremor. I was having a panic attack when you suggested it."

"It's not a vacation destination, Alexa," Grace scolded.

"Well, you used to think that it was."

Grace's evil eye was a little sleepy but just as threatening.

"Sorry, I just want to experience it."

"All right. Well, we'll talk about it tomorrow. Addie, you coming up?"

"Mm-hmmm." I'd snuggled against a couple of the couch pillows and was having a hard time getting up. I felt someone drape a blanket over me and kiss my head.

"I'm glad you're home, sweetheart," Grace whispered.

"Good night, my love." Isabella kissed and touched my head with a mother's pat.

Alexa scratched my back when she passed by.

The lamps were turned out and I was left with the warmth and the glow of the fire that flickered in the fireplace. Somehow couches were more consoling than a bed after a breakup. Beds could be lonely. Couches never were. I figured I'd still be on this particular couch when Grace started breakfast in the morning. Which was fine with me. Family was giving me a much-needed respite from having to deal with my heartache. Soon enough, I'd have to return to reality and begin living the rest of my life without Blake.

The wine and the warmth drifted me right into a deep sleep and dream where rain and sleet pelted against the windshield of a car. I was driving along a dark street searching for Blake. Bits of ice tapped against the windshield, loud and sharp while I called his name. "Blake!"

I knew this street. Narrow road, gas lamps. It was Jack and Sarah's street, in Chantilly, where they thought they would be safe from harm. I drove slowly by their house and saw Philippe and me standing in the side yard, his hand on my back while I fired a gun into the solarium.

The gun went off and I screamed, "No!"

There was near silence while Philippe grabbed my hand and we ran. Only the tapping of ice against the windshield remained. I turned slowly toward the driver's side window, to a man who had approached.

"Jack—"

He stood there with a hole in his chest, and his white shirt filling with blood. "Why?"

I startled awake, and sat upright. Sweat covered my upper back and guilt swam through my insides. I sat on the edge of the couch and calmed myself, breath by breath. Grace's words about past-life imprints rang through me like an alarm. Maybe Blake and I had fallen apart because I had killed Jack.

The tapping started again and goosebumps shot across my skin in a race with one another. When I saw the man at the glass patio door my heart attacked the inside of my chest —*bang-bang-bang*!

He raised his hands in surrender and tapped again. He waved. It was Blake. I blew out a breath.

His face shone clear in the light on the back porch. And those eyes. Those crazy blue eyes that softened my heart on sight. I took the key that Grace hung on the wall and opened the door.

"What are you doing here?" I whispered. At this hour of the night my heart was too innocent, unguarded, and completely unprepared to see him. It needed time and more cushiony layers around it before we saw one another again. And it needed to stop reacting to those eyes.

"I'm here to see you."

"How did you know I was here?"

"A friend of yours told me."

"What friend? No one knew I was here except—Alexa?"

Blake pressed his lips together and shook his head. "Philippe."

"*What?*"

"He called me. Told me where you were in case I wanted to find you."

I stepped inside and ran my hands through my hair.

"He loves you, Addie. He wants you to be happy."

"Well." I ran my hand across my forehead. "This is ah—y'all need to get out of my business."

"You're right. I'm sorry."

His quick agreement and yet another apology rubbed me the wrong way. I gestured to the door.

"Give me five minutes and if you still want me to leave, I will."

I exhaled and thought I saw our future if we had stayed together—my endless talks about how he shut me out and how lonely I was. Then, his defensive comebacks because in the end he just wasn't interested to change.

"Blake, I can't do this. I just can't."

"Five minutes, Addie. That's it. Then I'll leave if you want me to. You'll be free to go back to the twenties with Philippe if that's what you want to do."

I spun on my heel. "Philippe told you about that, too?"

"He did. He also said that if he thought for a moment that you loved him a hair's breadth more than you loved me that he'd take you back to the twenties and I'd never see you again. As it was he thought we should talk one more time."

I stood there, struck dumb. I started to say that I didn't have any romantic intentions with Philippe but then I noticed something. Blake wasn't unreadable. He wasn't his usual energetic block of cement that kept me on the outside. He was open.

Soft.

Vulnerable.

Scared.

"All right. Five minutes," I said softly. I pointed to the inside and we sat together on the couch where I'd been sleeping just minutes before.

He rested his elbows on his knees and met me eye to eye.

"I'm not here to make excuses or to offer more apologies. Though I am sorry." His voice cracked and quivered and a faint pallor fell over his face. "Since that very first day I saw you working in Otto's firm, I've been terrified that—one way or another—he would take you away from me. I let that drive me. Which, wasn't all bad, I know. He was an enemy that needed to be fought.

"But I think what handicapped me—with us, anyway—was the fear that I wouldn't be able to do enough to stop him. Past-life hangover, I guess. When someone has killed you once that's apparently a hard thing to overcome. That fear made me feel about an inch tall and it became a wedge between us." He measured an inch with his finger and thumb. I found it hard to believe that someone as strong and powerful as he was could ever feel that diminished.

"I let that happen. I didn't catch on to it soon enough, and maybe it was easier to blame—Otto, you, whatever. All I can say is—that that has been my lesson to learn. As well as accepting what I can and can't change. You were right. I shouldn't have blamed myself so much for what Otto did— in the last life or this life.

I ought to have accepted all of it—the past, Otto, who he was, who he wasn't. When it came to you I should have grown up and taken responsibility for what I did want in life, instead of running from what I didn't want. I think this fear that something would happen to you, that I could never do enough to protect you had become a type of mistress in our relationship. If that makes any sense."

"It does," I said. "She certainly belonged to you."

"You're right," he said without any intensity. "I spent more time doting on that self-obsessed need than I did actu- ally taking care of you and our relationship, at least over the last couple of years. Not that I didn't have seeds of this obsession brewing since my last lifetime, but I guess being back in that era brought it all up for me. I didn't handle it well."

"Hmm." I said.

"Carolena and Anya, and maybe even you might have called this arrogance. And maybe it was. I'm going to call it something else. I've been lazy. I've been a fool. I've taken you for granted. I took *us* for granted. I thought since we were meant to be together, I kept assuring myself in the face of all this fear that we would always be together. No matter what, come what may. Relationships don't work that way, even with soul mates. I should have been more sensitive to what your needs were. And I ought to have taken more responsibility for being the person I wanted to be. I ought to have realized that I couldn't control my way out of it. And you were right. I've trusted my fears more than I trusted myself, more than I've trusted you. That was wrong."

I felt the burn of tears building behind my eyes.

He reached into the back waistband of his pants and pulled out his black notebook. It was stuffed to overfull with index cards and bookmarks and plans for finding Carolena. "I'm giving this to you to do with as you like."

I stared at the notebook for a moment. "You have a new one?"

"No. I'm going more with my gut these days. Trusting myself. Trusting you. Hopefully, we can still be a team."

I swallowed hard. The memory of being pushed aside was still front and center in my mind. I picked up the notebook and threw it into the fireplace. Sparks flew and the flames engulfed the pages, turning them into black ash that floated in pieces up the chimney.

"I have to admit that felt pretty good to do that." I laughed until my concern choked it to a halt.

"I know I've hurt you."

"You don't know what it's like to be kept on the outside by the person you love most in the world. You don't know what it's like when you can't reach that person because they're so...self-obsessed."

It was that realization that seemed to bring tears to his eyes. "You're right. I don't." He took my hand and ran his thumb over the top of it, like he held something precious, as if he hadn't seen it in a very long time. "But I do know what it's like to live without you. While you were raising a family with Philippe in that alternate life, I lived alone. I knew I'd never have you."

The grandfather clock in the hallway struck twice. He drew in a deep and silent breath and for a moment I wasn't sure what he was doing. Until one by one, I felt the walls he'd always held strong, crash and fall around us. He was open and giving and his love rushed forth as though the floodgates had busted wide open.

"You're letting me in." I heard the gasp escape my lips. I half expected him to close up shop and to shove his more tender emotions into dark, dusty corners that I couldn't quite see. But he didn't. He was wide open for the looking. And look I did. I placed my fingertips and read everything I could.

"I lost you. More than once. I don't want to lose you again. I'll change however I need to to make sure you're happy and we're together."

His fear of loss was still there, withering and slowly being conquered. I knew it would take some time before they were completely gone. Real change took time. But those past-life patterns were under the realm of his responsibility now, I could see that. He owned them. No longer would they be cast about in an effort to find a new owner.

He was frightened. Scared to death to lose me. More than that he loved me and he meant it when he said he would do anything to make me happy and to make sure we were together. There was a space in his heart that he'd long ago dedicated just to me. It was a room that had always been our own but I hadn't been able to reach it with him in some time. Here that space was open. Waiting. Loving.

In brilliant colors, his energy wrapped itself around me and tangled with my own in a mix of love and tenderness I had only known with him.

"That connection with you is like a drug." I pressed my fingers to my chest and inhaled several times, slow and deep and long. Connecting with him like this was an extraordinary experience. It made life worthwhile.

His fingertips traced along the outside of my face, seemingly to study everything he saw. "I still remember a great deal from the other life I had to live without you. It was meaningless and empty, no matter what I did I couldn't fix it. Because you weren't there."

I glanced at my hand in his and remembered how even in my life with Philippe, Blake as Jack was still a presence. He was there in my mind, in my dreams, holding tight to what we had.

"Oh, Addie. Our lives are so fragile, so transient. I want to live every moment I have left in this life, with you. I mean really live it, the very best I can. I don't want to waste time worrying that I might get hurt. And I don't want to misuse the time we have left, worrying that I might fail.

"Whatever echo our love might send forward into time, I want our song to be brave and brilliant. I want it to have the clear ring of true love that I've always felt for you. Because if I ever have to endure a life without you again, it will be the memory of that love that will get me through it."

Devotion spun outward from this place in his heart that he made for me, and it wrapped around us, protecting us far better than any cautionary fear. He pressed a kiss to my lips. A new imprint was taking place. A reverberation of love, yes, but also one of trust and a wise and hard-won recognition that the most precious things in life can disappear in an instant.

49

———

The warmth of the sunrise bathed the backside of my grandmother's house in wide streams of yellow gold. The sweet smell of the grass tangled with the salty scent of the ocean and reminded me of the long summer days of my childhood.

"Sun's barely up. What are you doing?" Blake's voice was gravelly from recent sleep. His eyes were not fully open and his thick hair wild and reaching in several sexy different directions at once.

His bare feet shuffled through the soft grass, his jeans dragging behind his heels. He sat behind me, one leg on either side of my hips. I leaned against his shirtless chest and enjoyed the even rise and the fall of it. I breathed in the pleasantness of his morning warmth and his ever-familiar vineyard scent.

"Sunrise." I closed my eyes and faced the sun. "Used to do this every morning when I was little—soak the sun into my body and soul. It's a privilege to be here for the birth of a new day. My father used to always say that." I tipped my chin to see Blake's expression and found him with his eyes closed to the sun as well.

He opened one eye in a wink and kissed me through a groggy smile. His heart was wide and open and loving me with all he had. It was a moment of simple perfection. It was the stuff of pure happiness.

Our bodies fit against one another easily now. There wasn't any wedge or off-limit boundary, no fence or distraction that pulled us away from one another. My heart could feel the attentiveness of his and the cadence we set was once again uniquely our own.

A whiff of strong coffee and over-crisp toast drifted by, Grace's telltale sign of an early breakfast. I peeked at the closed drapes on the second-story window where Alexa was still asleep. And then to the upper balcony where Isabella would paint at some time today.

I was certain my father was eating breakfast with Cam and maybe teaching him the same lesson he taught me— about how witnessing the birth of a new day is a privilege. Ruth probably packed her son's tin lunchbox for school. My grandfather would be sipping coffee and staring out the window while Mary slept in.

The memories of my life with Philippe had faded beyond a distant horizon. They were still there, still visible because I had worked to remember them, though they were fuzzy around the edges. Like most past lives, that reality was far away and inaccessible to me.

I turned to the southwest end of our property, where the water met the grass. This was the backdrop to the nightmare that had haunted me for so many years. This time, the water-bound meadow laid empty before me. Otto would never show up there again, in my dreams or otherwise.

My family was safe. Though not under one roof, or even

in neighboring cities, and certainly not reunited as I'd so wanted for everyone to be. They were still safe. I would have to be happy with that.

"When I was young, I always wanted more of my family. More time to play with Alexa, more time to swim with my dad, more fishing with Grandpa. When the sun went down I would pout and drag my feet when it was time to go inside. Isabella would say that we could finish our game or swim more or fish more tomorrow. "There will be plenty of time tomorrow," she always said.

"But then one day that time is just gone. For the rest of your life, those moments become more precious than air, because they're all you'll ever have of them."

"Time with our loved ones is very precious." He laid his cheek against my head, slow and tender with a rush of love and gratitude.

"Promise me we'll always be together." My throat closed tight with an unbearable ache.

He ran his hand along the frame of my face and looked at me in that timeless way that only he could do.

BLAKE HELD ADDIE CLOSE. The water sloshed against the grassy bank in a lazy Southern rhythm that lulled him into a state of peace. He understood how she felt. A life with her was the only one he had ever wanted. Even though that want gave birth to a fear of being without her, a fear that scared the heck out of him on most days. He had to lean into their life together with everything he was.

"With every meeting, there is a parting," he could hear Carolena say. It was true for everyone. When and how no one could know.

He spun upward and guided her to sit on the flat board swing that hung from one of the majestic water oak trees. Sweet laughter burst through her smile like the angelic notes of champagne bubbles, though when he took a knee in front of her, she gasped.

"Blake—"

"Addie, no amount of time with you will ever be enough. I understand that now. And I know that our moments together are so precious because even in the long expanse of however many lifetimes we'll share, our time is always without the guarantee of a tomorrow.

"From this day forward, I promise you that I will cherish the right now that you and I share like it is a lifetime in and of itself. And I will give to you, all that I am in the here and now.

"I promise that I will always love you. No matter the lifetime, I will always be yours."

He pulled the platinum ring from his pocket, the one he'd purchased in 1922, right under her nose and without her knowing. It was an authentic art deco design with three round sapphires arranged vertically, the largest in the middle, and set in three layers of diamond-encrusted rectangles.

"Oh, Blake." She glanced at the ring and laughed through fresh tears.

"Marry me, Sassy."

He slipped the ring on her finger and breathed a little easier when he saw that it was a perfect fit and stunning on her slender hand. "There are three sapphires this time. One for our past, the biggest for our present, and the third for our future together."

She lifted her gaze to his, and in her eyes he saw the

same woman he'd loved in the 1920s, the one who even a lifetime later, he loved on simple sight.

"Yes," she said. "Always. Yes."

He counted his blessings, most of them right there in his arms, and he wished for a few more. A son, maybe. And a daughter, like the children they shared when she was Sarah and he was Jack, in the past life that almost was.

ALSO BY ALYSSA RICHARDS

THE FINE ART OF DECEPTION SERIES

THE FINE ART OF DECEPTION, UNDOING TIME

SOMEWHERE IN TIME

LOST IN TIME

THE FINE ART OF DECEPTION, BOXED SET

THE ALCOTT MANOR SERIES

THE HAUNTING AT ALCOTT MANOR

A MURDER AT ALCOTT MANOR

A STRANGER AT ALCOTT MANOR

THE CHASING SECRETS SERIES

CHASING SECRETS

FORCED PERSPECTIVE

Be the first to know about Alyssa Richards' next novel, sign up here: www.AlyssaRichards.com

and follow her on Amazon or BookBub to receive a new release alert!

ABOUT THE AUTHOR

ALYSSA RICHARDS is the USA TODAY BESTSELLING AUTHOR of romantic suspense and mystery thriller novels. She loves living in the South with her husband and two children. She also loves good espresso, her rescue dogs, magnolias and gardenias, and, of course, reading a great book. She grew up running barefoot in the Blue Ridge Mountains of North Carolina, where her favorite weekly adventure was a trip to the library with her mom.

Sign up for Alyssa's newsletter at www.alyssarichards.com to receive special offers, and news about her latest releases.

For More information
www.AlyssaRichards.com
Contact Alyssa at:
authoralyssarichards@protonmail.com

instagram.com/alyssaauthor

amazon.com/Alyssa-Richards/e/B00S1IGJ9O

bookbub.com/authors/alyssa-richards

goodreads.com/alyssarichards

ACKNOWLEDGMENTS

My heartfelt gratitude...

...to my husband and my two boys for cheering me on with such heartfelt love and support. Clearly I did something right in a past life to be able to share this life with the three of you.

...to Libby Murphy, for being so gracious with her enthusiasm, her encouragement and her friendship, and for sharing her considerable editing talent with me. Girl, you are the bee's knees, the cat's whiskers and the eel's ankle all rolled into one.

...to all the readers and reviewers everywhere who wanted more Blake and Addie, what a joy it has been to hear from so many of you. Thank you for your comments, your reviews, your posts and your emails, you make all the hard work worthwhile.

www.ingramcontent.com/pod-product-compliance
Lightning Source LLC
Chambersburg PA
CBHW072010110726
47910CB00005B/1707